"A speech, gentlemen. Listen closely now. This is important. I'm the big boar grizzly from the top of the mountain. I'm the old he-cougar from the head of the creek. When I raise my voice the avalanche warnings go up all along the Rockies from the Sangre de Cristos north. When I pound my chest the San Andreas Fault gets very nervous. And any sonofabitching creep who interferes with me in the line of duty—my duty—or waves a gun at me from now on will wind up in the hospital or the morgue and I don't care what kind of fancy badges or ID's the bastard carries. . . ."

Matt Helm

THE
INFILTRATORS

THE
INFILTRATORS

Donald
Hamilton

FAWCETT GOLD MEDAL • NEW YORK

A Fawcett Gold Medal Book
Published by Ballantine Books

Library of Congress Catalog Card Number: 84-90885

ISBN 0-449-12517-3

Manufactured in the United States of America

First Ballantine Books Edition: June 1984

BOOK ONE

BOOK ONE

and find transportation from there. But let's talk as we ride, if you don't mind."

She hesitated; then she said bleakly, "I stopped minding anything eight years ago when they put me in here."

"You'd better put your coat on," I said. "It's a bit wintery outside."

She looked rather startled when I took the garment from her and held it for her, and picked up the suitcase she'd put down. That was a painful thing, as painful as seeing the brutal physical changes prison had wrought in her. The lovely and self-confident girl I'd known very briefly all those years ago had taken for granted that doors would be opened for her, and cigarettes lighted for her, and bags carried for her, and coats held.

I'd met her at the trial of a second-rate professional killer named Willy Chavez. I'd attended hoping for a line on a first-rate professional killer with whom he'd been associated, in whom we were interested at the time. Although very young, not long out of law school, her bar examination just behind her, she'd been assisting with the defense; and I'd realized that she was the one to approach for help, not the rather remote and formidable senior partner with whom she was working, Mr. Waldemar Baron.

Before going up against her, I'd done a little research and learned that she was the kind of youthful female prodigy all firms, including law firms, were looking for in those days—maybe they still are—hungry and handsome and super-bright, the kind who could be groomed for important positions and trotted out when needed to prove that sexual discrimination had never reared its ugly head around *that* shop, no siree. At the time there had seemed to be no doubt in anybody's mind that unless something inconceivable happened, Madeleine Rustin, as she was then, would eventually become the first woman partner in that eminent legal firm.

She'd received me in her small office and we'd discussed my problem. This had involved my identifying myself and letting her check the identification with Washington. I'd been impressed by her quick intelligence, her clear grasp of the facts and their implications, her ambition, and of course her striking good looks.

I'd asked her out, as she'd just said, and over dinner we'd argued the obvious things. She'd asked if I enjoyed tracking down human beings as if they were wild animals, and I'd asked if she enjoyed turning wild animals loose on society as if they were human beings. We never came to an agreement there, nobody ever does, but she argued well and I liked the assured and good-humored way she handled herself without being too cocky about her brains and looks. At least she didn't try to kid herself self-righteously, or me, that the client was necessarily innocent simply because she and a senior member of her firm were working hard on his behalf. Her point was the quite valid one that even a guilty man is entitled, under law, to the best legal defense possible—not that she was admitting the client's guilt for a minute, of course.

That was all. Afterwards I delivered her to her apartment, shook the firm young hand she offered me outside the door, thanked her for arranging a jail interview for me in the morning, and never saw her again until this moment—but of course I did see her picture in the newspapers a few years later when the inconceivable happened, and the prestigious legal partnership vanished into the rosy mists of might-have-been, and the prison gates closed behind Madeleine Rustin Ellershaw, as she'd become, for an eight-year term, which she'd now served in full. But it was hard to recognize in this colorless ex-convict the bright flame of a girl I remembered, so confident and eager and ambitious, with the world at her feet.

That was the thing I found so shocking: how completely prison had destroyed her. Some change had been inevitable, of course. It was a dozen years since I'd seen her, and personal disgrace and professional ruin would

6

inevitably have marked her, not to mention the daily indignities and degradations of prison life; but I hadn't anticipated that the disaster would be so total. Confinement had softened and thickened the firm slender body I remembered. The fine bright face had become coarse and dull, like the once shining brown hair. There was nothing but apathy in the stony gray eyes, which had lost the golden glow of youth and anticipation that I recalled very clearly.

Seeing her like that, I found it difficult to recall her true age, although the lack of gray in her hair was a cruel reminder. I suppose I didn't really want to accept the fact that in the normal course of events Mrs. Madeleine Ellershaw would by now have become a slender, well-groomed, very striking and handsome society lady, as well as a very successful professional woman, probably looking considerably younger than her thirty-four years, instead of this plain, sagging, badly dressed female who looked as if she'd soon be crowding fifty. She'd paid a high price for what she had done, if she had really done it. Actually, according to the record, she'd maintained her innocence to the last, even when a confession, and a little cooperation with the authorities, might have earned her a considerably reduced sentence.

"That's right, Mr. Helm," her voice said, totally without expression. "Not much left of Madeleine Rustin, that smart young career girl, hey? Makes you uncomfortable, don't it? I didn't want to meet nobody who'd recognize me, at least not right away. That's why I maybe looked kinda startled when I saw you. But it don't matter all that much. You might as well all get a good look at what you done to me."

The slovenly grammar and the flat convict tone she'd used shocked me again. The carefully reared and expensively educated young lady I remembered could never have spoken like that. Then I saw a faint gleam of malice in the slaty eyes, and I realized that she was playing a savage joke on both of us, getting some kind of masochistic satisfaction out of appearing even more coarsened and tarnished by her prison years than she really was. But the bitter amusement she'd found in my reaction was quickly replaced by apprehension.

"You're not . . . I mean, you can't be taking me back to answer new charges! God, they haven't dreamed up something else to try me for after all these years, have they? I can't . . . can't be locked up again, it would kill me!" She stopped herself and grimaced bitterly. "Not that *that* would be such a fucking loss! What's left to lose?"

"Having you get killed is exactly what we're trying to avoid," I said. I expected some response to this, some sign of fear or curiosity, but there was none, so I went on: "No, you have nothing further to fear from me or the authorities, Mrs. Ellershaw, I assure you."

Then we were outside. It didn't seem to mean much to her. She took no deep breaths of the fresh air of freedom; she gave no sign of appreciating the sunshine unobstructed by prison bars and walls. The shutters had come down again, and her face was expressionless. The car towards which I guided her was a rather flashy little Mazda RX-7 sports job, silver-gray, but she accepted it without comment as a perfectly normal vehicle to find outside the penitentiary gates—but again there was that faint, rather pitiful double take when I opened the door for her, reminding me again how long it had been since she'd last received such small courtesies, or any courtesy at all.

As she entered the low-slung vehicle a bit awkwardly—it takes practice, and her last sports-car ride had to be almost a decade behind her—I couldn't help noting that there was, after all, something left of the strikingly attractive young woman I remembered. Her ruinous experiences had failed to affect the lovely shape of her legs, unspoiled even by her dull stockings and cheap shoes.

CHAPTER 2

"YOU don't have to know that," Mac had said when I asked what the hell it was all about. "We don't need to know that, so we have not been told."

His voice was dry. We often get limited instructions like that; and almost invariably it turns out that the information that was withheld was exactly the information the agent involved should have had to keep him from stepping on the wrong toes or digging up the wrong dead bodies or shooting the wrong live bodies and making them dead. Or getting shot himself. But they do keep sending us out blindfolded and with earmuffs on. Security, they call it.

It was a rather shabby second-floor office with a window that looked out on a rather run-down part of Washington, D.C. The light from the window made it difficult to see the face of the man behind the desk, but it didn't matter. I knew what he looked like, having worked for him—or with him—longer than I cared to remember.

It was always hard for me to realize, seeing him, that I was looking at one of the most dangerous men in the world. With his neat gray hair and striking black eyebrows, in his neat gray suit, he could have been a banker or broker, a little worn by worrying about interest rates or investments or the gross national product. However, I knew that his real worries, now and always, concerned life and death, mostly death. The polite word for our function—well, our primary function—is counter-assassination. When some government agency, any government agency, comes up against a hostile operative too tough for them to handle safely and legally, an expert killer, they send for us to deal with him unsafely and illegally. Sometimes they ask us to handle other kinds of risky problems as well. Sensibly, they prefer to lose one of us rather than one of them.

"Good old need-to-know," I said. "One day we'll wake up and find the commissars running the country, and we'll have no idea how it happened because somebody'd decided that we didn't need to know."

Mac said, "It's interesting to know that you're thinking along those lines, because the person you're to pick up at the federal penitentiary for women at Fort Ames, Missouri, was convicted of spying for the Russians—or rather, of helping her husband spy for the Russians. The husband disappeared, along with another female who was involved, a known Communist. The wife got eight years. She's being released in a few days."

I frowned. "Fort Ames? What the hell is that? I thought the maximum-security federal ladies' pen was at Alderson, West Virginia."

"Officially it is," Mac said. "Unofficially, there's an old state prison at Fort Ames that has been rebuilt and restaffed to meet the requirements of certain government organizations like, for instance, the Central Intelligence Agency and the Office of Federal Security for female inmates whose preservation is considered essential to the nation's safety. The trouble with Alderson is that even though it's designed for women guilty of the most serious federal crimes, it's pretty much an open prison. Apparently it has been determined that women are, for some reason, much less likely to escape than men, and even the worst female offenders don't require the strict security measures necessary in a male institution. I've heard Alderson referred to as a ladies' seminary and a country club. Yet the system seems to work; there are very few escapes."

"So why wasn't this particular prisoner sent there? It seems like the logical place for her." I watched him carefully. "If we're thinking of the same girl, she didn't look very dangerous to me the one time I met her. Not in that way. I shouldn't think she'd require the manacles and leg irons. In fact I'd expect that the big problem with a girl like that, when she found herself behind bars with a lot of common criminals, would be to keep her from dying of shame and humiliation." I glanced at him. "You do have in mind the young woman I knew as Madeleine Rustin, don't you, sir?"

He nodded. "Yes. I hoped you'd remember her."

"I remember her. But regardless of what she did, if she actually did it, I can't quite see the need for throwing her into an escape-proof dungeon. She was hardly the type to dig her way out of prison with a teaspoon or shoot her way out with a homemade zip gun."

"Apparently there were other considerations. Her accomplices had got away, and it was claimed that they or the people they worked for had considerable resources. The Office of Federal Security, which handled the case, persuaded the judge that there was considerable danger that they would organize an attempt to free her, or to silence her, not altogether impossible at Alderson. Hence Ames." He paused, and glanced at some paper on his desk, and looked up again. "As a matter of fact we have reason to believe that somebody still wants to silence her, now that she's free—well, will shortly be free."

I sighed. "I see. It's a bodyguard job, then."

"In part, yes. We most certainly want her kept alive. But also we want to know why somebody wants her dead, and we want to know the identity of that somebody. We also want to know everything she knows, and hasn't told, about the disappearance of her husband—Dr. Ellershaw, you'll remember, was a brilliant young physicist employed at the Center for Advanced Defense Research at Los Alamos."

I said, "She wasn't married when I met her, so all I

11

know about the husband is what I read in the papers at the time of her trial. And the facility to which you're referring is a more or less independent installation, up a side canyon," I said. "Conejo Canyon. Rabbit Canyon, if you want the translation."

"The information doesn't seem particularly significant, Eric, but thank you," he said, using my code name to emphasize that this was business, and irrelevant linguistic digressions were inappropriate. "But that's one of the reasons you were selected for this assignment. You're familiar with the Santa Fe–Los Alamos area, having lived there. And you're at least slightly acquainted with the female subject."

I said thoughtfully, "After the time that has passed since Dr. Ellershaw disappeared and his wife was arrested, you'd think any scientific information involved would be pretty damn obsolete. Why this belated interest in an eight-year-old espionage case?"

"Nine-year-old, to be exact. The young woman didn't go to prison until a year after her husband's activities were uncovered, what with the trial and the appeals." He shook his head. "And why she's still of interest is precisely what we have to find out. Who's afraid of Mrs. Ellershaw at this late date, afraid enough to still want her silenced? And why are they afraid?"

I frowned. "How about the possibility that she may be innocent, sir? That she may have been framed, and that the people who framed her are scared that, having had eight long years to work on it in her cell, she may have figured out how it was done to her and who did it?"

He glanced at me sharply. "You keep sounding as if you had some doubts about her guilt, Eric."

I said, "One year from arrest to prison! Considering the present state of our judicial system, that's some kind of a record, isn't it, sir? My God, I know of considerably less important cases that have been in the courts for five years and more. Doesn't it look as if somebody with a lot

12

of influence worked damned hard to get this girl tucked away behind bars in a great big hurry?"

Mac shrugged. "Maybe. And maybe her guilt was self-evident and her lawyer incompetent so it took less time than usual."

"I believe she had the top brains of her law firm defending her," I said. "Anyway, the whole thing's out of character. Her character. I only saw her that one day, but she had everything going for her. Why would she risk it all like that? She was an ambitious kid eager to get ahead in her profession and not particularly idealistic—hell, when I met her, she was helping to defend a fairly unpleasant murderer even though she knew damn well he'd done the killing. I can't see anybody selling her the glorious revolution of the proletariat. And she had doting parents wealthy enough to finance a top education for her and, probably, help her out generously if she needed it afterwards. Anyway, she was making a pretty good salary with promises of great things to come. So it seems unlikely she'd do it for money." I grimaced. "I know, sir, it's exactly that kind of privileged kids who wind up robbing banks and blowing up things for the Weather Underground or whatever the currently fashionable protest organization may be. But I wouldn't have expected it of this kid."

"Hardly a kid now, after eight years in Fort Ames," Mac said dryly. "If she was convicted wrongly, it's unfortunate, but I want you to bear in mind that her innocence, or guilt, is of interest only to her, except as it affects whatever problems we face out there in New Mexico. Curb your chivalrous impulses, please. We are not in the business of righting wrongs or correcting injustices. What we are interested in is finding out just what is going on in that Rabbit Canyon of yours. What has been going on there for nine years, or perhaps even longer, that Dr. Roy Ellershaw was mixed up in guiltily or stumbled upon innocently? Who considered him enough of a threat that he helped the young man to disappear voluntarily or caused him to disappear involuntarily? Who arranged for the young wife to be arrested and sent to the penitentiary, justly or unjustly, to get her out of the way also? Who, now that she's being set free, feels threatened enough by her continued existence to arrange for her murder?" Max shook his head. "At least that's one series of possibilities; there are others. I think the lady is the key. Well, her husband is the real key, I suspect, and if you can persuade her to lead you to him—assuming that she can—so much the better. Otherwise you'll have to use Mrs. Ellershaw herself; and in order to employ her usefully you must of course prevent her from getting killed. You can have Jackson to assist you. The two of you worked pretty well together on that recent Chicago operation, didn't you?"

"Jackson's fine," I said. "But he'll need help if he's going to cover us with any efficiency."

"He'll have help, all he requires," Mac said.

I looked at him for a moment. Unlike that glamorous outfit that operates out of Virginia, we don't have unlimited manpower at our disposal; but he seemed to be giving Jackson and me pretty much a free hand with such reserves as we did have.

"So it's a big deal," I said.

"It could be very big. But we don't need to know exactly why. Or so we have been informed."

"I see." I made a wry face. "Just give it everything we've got and don't ask questions. The fate of the nation rests upon the shoulders of one lousy lady ex-con. Well, soon-to-be ex-con, and I'll bet it can't be soon enough for her."

Hardly a kid now, after eight years in Fort Ames. Mac's rather callous remark returned to me as I guided the little sports car out of the parking lot, with the drab penitentiary graduate I'd once known as a very smart and attractive young professional woman sitting silent

14

beside me, holding her imitation-leather purse on her lap.

It was time for somebody to say something, and I said, "I had a big four-wheel-drive unit for a good many years. Used it for camping and hunting whenever I got the chance; but it started to wear out at last and at eight miles to the gallon I couldn't afford to feed it any longer, anyway. Brace yourself, you'll find current gas prices a real shock. So I thought I'd try something different for a change. It's the rotary Wankel engine, which seems to be a smooth and reliable piece of machinery; and it handles very well. Of course it's really too damn comfortable for a true sports car. A real sports car is supposed to sound like a boiler factory and ride like a rock and drip water down your neck when it rains."

She gave no indication of hearing any of this nonsense. She just sat in the bucket seat beside me, unmoving, until at last she turned her head to look behind. I knew what she was watching: the prison was just disappearing from sight back there. When it was gone she settled herself looking forward once more.

"Did you ever catch up with that man?" she asked abruptly.

"What man?"

"The one you were after. When you came to see me that time and I arranged for you to talk with our client, Willy Chavez." She hesitated, and said with a hint of reminiscent pride, "We got him off, you know."

"I didn't know," I said. "But I thought you would, all that high-powered legal talent."

She said, rather grimly, "I had exactly the same kind of high-powered talent, Mr. Helm, and you can see how much good it did me. It's not always a matter of who can bring the biggest legal guns to bear. But you haven't answered my question."

I said, "I caught up with him, in a manner of speaking. I got to look at him in the morgue after somebody else had shot him."

"Was that a satisfactory ending to your mission?"

I shook my head. "Not really. The man's name, the inoffensive name he was going under, was Horace Bixby. He had others. He got off a shot before he was killed. I was too far behind in spite of what I'd learned from your client, Chavez; a day behind. If Bixby hadn't thrown his first shot a bit, hurrying, or if his victim's body-guard had been slow and let him fire again, my mission would have been a total failure. As it was, I could kid myself that Bixby rushed into the job under unfavorable conditions because he sensed I was closing in on him. However, an important man took a nasty little wound and spent unnecessary time in the hospital, something I was supposed to see didn't happen, since we knew what was planned even if we didn't know whom it was planned for." I turned my head to look at her. "It was exactly the opposite situation to the one you're in, Mrs. Ellershaw."

She frowned. "I don't understand. What . . . ?"

"I told you, we're trying to avoid having you get killed, remember? In your case we've learned the person it's going to be done to, but we don't yet know who's been sent to do it."

She focused the expressionless gray eyes on me. "Don't con me, man! Why the fuck are you trying to scare me? I mean, it just don't make no sense!" She heard herself employing the ugly speech with which she'd lived for the past eight years and winced. "I mean, why in the world would anybody want to kill me now, Mr. Helm, after all the time I've been locked up in . . . in that p-place?"

I said, "Presumably because you could do no harm in there, but you're out of there now."

"Are you certain it's me they're after? How can you be sure? How can you even know that such a thing is being planned?"

"Look, Mrs. E.," I said, "we deal with all kinds of people, mostly nasty people. In fact it's been said that

16

we're pretty nasty ourselves. But there's a certain amount of give and take. Occasionally somebody gives somebody a break and it's kind of expected that eventually, if the opportunity arises, something will be done in return. In this case, a certain agent let somebody go free maybe he shouldn't have—apparently the basic assignment was finished and he was avoiding unnecessary complications—and the guy who was let go was grateful enough to get in touch about a week ago with what he considered a good tip."

"What tip?"

I watched the road ahead as I drove, reproducing the words from memory. "It went something like this, a voice on the phone saying: *Somebody calling himself by a name you've been asking about is shopping for talent to hit the dame in the Ellershaw case when she gets out of that federal slammer, and don't expect any more favors, see, this squares us.*"

After a little, Madeleine Ellershaw shivered abruptly. "What did he mean by a name you'd been asking about?"

"Did you ever hear of anybody named Tolliver?"

I hoped I made the question sound casual enough. The security freaks who'd saddled us with this assignment had thought the name important enough to give us. We might kind of listen for it if we had nothing better to do, they'd said; and if we heard it we should report the circumstances immediately with all relevant details. No, we didn't need to know why.

"Tolliver?" My passenger's voice indicated no recognition. "No. It's sometimes spelled Taliaferro, isn't it?"

I said, "We don't know the spelling; we've only heard it over the phone."

"I'm sorry. I know it as a name, of course, but I can't think of anybody . . . Is it important?"

I shrugged, and dismissed the subject, a little pompously: "Who knows what is or isn't important these days, Mrs. Ellershaw?"

She turned her head to study me for a moment, and

17

asked, "To what do I really owe your presence, Mr. Helm?"

I liked the elaborately formal question, which she would have phrased quite differently back in the grim building we'd just left. The woman was digging inside herself for grammar and vocabulary that had been unused for years and trying it out on me; it was a hopeful sign.

"I told you—"

"Yes, you're supposed to protect me." She glanced at me sharply. "But why *you*? Why were *you* selected to be nice to the convicted spy and disbarred female attorney when she stumbled out of the joint in her cheap new clothes?" Her voice was flat and expressionless. "Just because we'd met once in the past and you'd bought me a dinner?"

"That was part of it," I said. "Also, I know a bit about Santa Fe, where you live."

"Live!" she murmured. "Where do I really *live* now, Mr. Helm? Last permanent residence, Fort Ames, Missouri! I had to sell the house and both the cars and my jewelry. . . . Roy and I lived very nicely, but we didn't have all that much, really. Two young people with good incomes, we'd assumed a lot of debt for the kind of life we wanted together. We could have handled it easily if everything had gone as we expected, but it didn't go that way. When Roy disappeared and I was indicted it was like a pretty soap bubble, *pop!* I fought to keep the house, it seemed important to maintain appearances and stay living as I had, but it was more important to keep my freedom—going to jail seemed inconceivably degrading then." She drew a long ragged breath. "That meant money for the bail. And the legal costs, even though the firm—Mr. Baron—was very generous about conducting my defense. But in the end it all went, the creditors got their share, and my court expenses took care of what was left. I wound up borrowing, too much, from my parents."

She was silent for a little, watching the blacktop road

rushing towards her. I didn't speak. She drew another long breath and went on.

"They're dead now, both of them," she said. "My parents. I was their only child. They'd been very proud of me, of my . . . my professional success. My happy marriage. This killed them." After a little, she said, "But I suppose I have to go back there first even though I don't really want to. I'll be bound to meet people I know—knew—and I don't expect to enjoy their reactions when they see what's become of the clever, clever girl who was going to set the world on fire. I was a bit self-satisfied in those days, I'm afraid. So it's not something I'm looking forward to, but Dad's lawyer, old Mr. Birnbaum—I call him Uncle Joe—wrote that he wanted to see me as soon as I got out. Some things still to be done about the estate. There wasn't much left for me, I understand, just a few thousand, perhaps as much as ten or fifteen, but I guess that won't go very far these inflated days judging by the little TV I got to watch in there. They gave me everything they could spare while . . . while it was going on. But it's better than nothing; it'll keep me for a little, while I'm figuring out some way of earning a living as . . . as a rehabilitated criminal who's paid her debt to society. But God only knows what way."

I said, "The record shows that while your prison behavior was exemplary in most other respects, you took no advantage of any of the educational or vocational—"

"Educational!" Her voice was suddenly fierce. "After . . . after all the academic honors, *real* honors, I'd earned, was I supposed to let a bunch of semi-illiterate stumblebums give me a degree in finger painting? Call it being stuck-up, they did, but I couldn't bring myself to that. And as for vocational, can't you see that I couldn't do that? After all the years and all the effort and all the money that had been spent to make me an educated person and a good lawyer, a real professional woman, how could I? Standing in that ghastly shop learning how to set women's hair! Or even learning how to work a simple computer like a good little office girl! That would have been admitting that . . . that there was no hope for me at all. That there was no real life left for me, the kind of life I'd been brought up to and educated for. Nothing but a gray tawdry hand-to-mouth existence stretching endlessly off into the dismal future. . . . Of course I was kidding myself. That *is* all that's left now, isn't there?"

She was a contradictory mixture of elitist arrogance and hopeless despair. But I was glad to see the arrogance; I'd been afraid that all pride had been knocked out of her. I changed the subject deliberately.

"Did your husband have any distinguishing marks or scars in intimate places, Mrs. Ellershaw?"

She frowned at the sudden switch. "Why do you ask?"

"He disappeared and left you holding the bag, didn't he? And now somebody wants you dead. Maybe Dr. Ellershaw has surfaced somewhere else with a new identity and a new appearance—plastic surgery, contact lenses, dyed hair—only there's something he can't change, something only a wife would know about. And he's still a wanted man. Maybe he's afraid that now you're out you'll come looking for him, one of the few people in the world who really know what to look for. Did he have any sexual peculiarities that might identify him?"

She shook her head. "I don't quite know what you mean by that. Physically, well, his penis was perfectly normal, judging by my rather limited experience with penises, if that's what interests you. Circumcised, if it matters, although he wasn't Jewish. He had two testicles like half the human race. He liked the mouthy stuff sometimes. A blow job really turned him on." Her voice kept switching disconcertingly between university refinement and prison vulgarity. "At the time we were married I thought it was . . . well, quite disgusting. I was terribly shocked when he first suggested it. I was sexually rather innocent and fastidious back in those days. I just liked

20

having my husband on top of me doing it the nice old-fashioned way. The missionary position, I believe it's called. Warm and cozy. But I loved him very much and I forced myself to do it the way he wanted when I realized it meant a lot to him. I enjoyed being able to please him so much, even though I still found the act itself rather revolting." She glanced at me coolly. "You see, they have me well trained, Mr. Helm. No matter what intimate and personal and prying questions you ask, Ellershaw will speak right up like a good little felon who's forfeited all rights to privacy." After a moment, when I didn't react to this, she went on: "Several million other men like oral sex, so it doesn't give you much to go on, does it? Anyway, it's a bum scenario you're writing there, man. You're way off the beam. Roy is dead."

I drove on through the sunny countryside for a while before speaking. "Yes, I know that's what you said before the trial, but you never offered any proof, any evidence. And no body has ever been found."

She laughed shortly. "It's probably just as well. The way they were acting, they would have tried me for his murder, too. In fact, they thought I was confessing to it when I first told them he was dead. They wanted me to take them straight to where I'd hidden the corpus delictus. Then they decided that I was just engaging in a deliberate campaign of misdirection to cover my own guilt. I don't think they ever really looked for a dead body, just for a live Roy, the principal in the crime to which I was an accomplice."

"But you think he was murdered?"

She said, "I know it."

"How?"

"He never came back, did he? He wouldn't have done that to me, left me 'holding the bag,' as you called it, if he were alive. It would have been strictly impossible for him to do it, just as impossible as for him to hire somebody to kill me, as you just suggested."

I studied her face for a moment, and returned my attention to the road. "You mean," I said, "he couldn't have done it because he loved you?"

She gave me her slow flat glance once more. "That's exactly what I mean. Don't sneer at it."

"I wasn't sneering, but it's hardly evidence."

"It's evidence to me," she said firmly. "But of course I always knew, after that first night they had me in jail, that he wasn't coming back. He died some time after two in the morning—I could have told you more exactly, but they'd taken away my watch, along with my purse and jewelry, when they put me into that cell after questioning me. That was about one-thirty in the morning. I'd never been locked up before in my life. I fell on the cot completely drained and exhausted, too tired even to take my shoes off, but I was too outraged by the way I was being treated, too shocked and angry and frightened, to really sleep. I just kind of half dozed; and suddenly I sat up with a gasp knowing that Roy was dead. He screamed before he died. I heard him." She threw me a contemptuous glance. "You don't believe any of this, do you? Nobody believes it. They all think it's some kind of a trick. They're all puzzled by what that smart Phi Beta Kappa girl with all those university degrees magna cum laude hopes to achieve by telling such a stupid and implausible story."

I said without expression, "Last year I was down in Latin America, at some ruins in the jungle. They had an old native high priest there. As a matter of fact, his name was Cortez, just like that restaurant we ate in. One night he called to me to come help him. He was way underground in a cave being beaten by some men, never mind the details, and I was sleeping in a hotel almost a mile away, but I awoke knowing that he'd called me and I had to go. And a lady archaeologist who knew the cave, whom I needed to show me the way, was coming up the path fully dressed when I started for her cabin to wake her. She'd got the same message. Somehow. Don't tell me what I believe or disbelieve, Mrs. Ellershaw."

She licked her lips. "All right. Sorry. You're the first one who hasn't laughed."

I said, "You woke up on the cot knowing that you'd heard . . . felt him scream and die. Go on."

She swallowed. "It wasn't *exactly* like that. I might have dismissed it as imagination, something triggered by all the ugly unfamiliar sounds disturbing me in that strange and awful place—at least it was strange to me then. I got to know places like that very well, later." She gave a sharp, rueful little laugh. "I hadn't realized how different a jail looks when you're in there for real, not just as a lawyer visiting a client. But there was something else that made me know what had happened."

"What?"

"The light had gone out," she said.

I frowned. "In your cell?"

She shook her head, annoyed at my stupidity. "I thought you'd understand, after what you just said about that high priest calling you. When . . . when you love somebody, and they love you, there's kind of a glow in the world, isn't there? Call it the light of love if you want to be very corny, but it's there, you must know it's there, if you've ever truly loved anybody and had your love returned. Even when he . . . when the other person is away from you, it's like a reassuring little night-light burning steadily in a private chamber in your mind, just knowing that he's out there somewhere and you'll have him back soon. Or maybe not so soon, but he'll surely come back to you. But that night the light went out. There was nothing left in the world—my world—but darkness. So I knew he was dead and it was his scream I'd heard and he was never coming back." Abruptly she shook her head in an angry way, glaring at me. "Hey, you're good, aren't you, you crummy confidence man! How the hell did you get me talking all this mystic bull-shit, anyway? Forget it! It's all a lot of stinking crap and we both know it!"

I looked at her sitting beside me, now staring straight ahead through the windshield; and despite the prison-ravaged flesh of her face I could see the sensitive profile of the girl I'd known for a day so many years ago—years that should have brought her success and happiness and instead had crushed and demolished her. Or had they?

It occurred to me that a woman who, after years of harsh imprisonment, could still speak earnestly of love lighting up the world might not be as badly damaged as she looked.

CHAPTER 3

In that open, rolling, midwestern terrain we could see the big interstate ahead a couple of miles before we came to it. I drove through the underpass, made my turn, and accelerated hard up the sweeping on-ramp, liking the smooth thrust of the rotary engine and the way the low little car clung to the curve. We hit the four-lane highway above at a good clip and I took us up to seventy, since I'd learned on my way here from where I'd picked up my car—the R-and-R establishment in Arizona we call the Ranch, which is also our training center—that nobody took the limit too seriously in this part of the world. After a little I became aware of the tenseness of the woman beside me.

"Something wrong?" I asked.

"It's very silly," she said, "but the limit is still fifty-five, isn't it? I do like driving fast after not having been in a car for so long, but . . ."

I was ashamed of my lack of consideration. "But

you're not in the mood to associate with policemen on your first day of freedom, right? Sorry, I'll hold it down. I wasn't thinking."

"Thank you." After a little, she asked, "Where are you taking me?"

"Santa Fe, New Mexico," I said. "You said you wanted to see your folks' lawyer, didn't you? And there are other reasons for going there—I told you we needed your help. But we can talk about that later."

She was startled. "But that's hundreds of miles!"

"Actually, something over a thousand," I said. "We should get there the day after tomorrow, even taking it easy." I glanced at her. "You still don't really believe me, do you? If you did, you wouldn't be expecting me to dump you at the nearest bus station and wave goodbye as you ride off into the sunset trailing a cloud of diesel smoke and a covey of hired killers behind you."

"It's still rather hard to grasp, although after everything else that's happened to me I suppose I shouldn't be too surprised." She hesitated. "Please tell me the truth, Mr. Helm. You're being very nice, and I have no complaints about my treatment, but . . . am I under arrest or aren't I?"

I looked at her, shocked. "Oh, Jesus, I'm doing this all wrong, aren't I?"

"Well, you do have a badge of sorts; you showed it to me once, remember? You don't seem to wave it around as much as some, but it's there and, well, my experiences with men with badges haven't been reassuring. Or women with badges, ugh!" She studied my face gravely and seemed to find her answer there. "Then . . . then I am free, really free?"

"Yes," I said, "and when we get out of the car I'll ask you to kick me for not making it absolutely clear. You've served your time, all of it, without parole, as your sentence stipulated, and nobody's got any strings on you— not I, not anybody else. If you want to tell me to go to hell, you can. But I'm offering you a free ride to Santa

Fe; and there is a contract out on you, as we hoodlums say. I can't guarantee you'll be safe if you stick with me. Nobody can. But at least I can make the guy very nervous while he's murdering you."

A little crooked smile, the first real smile I'd seen, touched her lips. "Well, you're honest, if not reassuring. Are we being followed right now?"

"I haven't been able to spot anybody, but there's been quite a bit of traffic." I was surprised that the lie came so hard; after years in the business you'd think I'd be a fairly accomplished prevaricator, but for some reason I found myself reluctant to be less than honest with the broken woman beside me. I glanced at the rearview mirror, at the little blue sedan that had been our shadow since we'd left Fort Ames, and said smoothly, "Anyway, I don't think they'll try any trick accidents. We've got too fast and agile a car, and it's never surefire anyway, unless you can run the victim off a mountain road into a thousand-foot canyon. And this midwestern landscape is kind of short of mountains and canyons." Well, at least that much was true. I glanced at her. "I await your instructions, ma'am. Santa Fe, New Mexico, or the nearest bus station or airport? Tell me which."

"Would you really let me go and get killed?"

"I'd let you go. I have no right to stop you. And I'm sure you've had enough people telling you what to do for the past eight years without me getting into the act now that you're free." I grinned. "Anyway, if I try to get tough with you, you'll just get mad at me, and as I told you, we need your cooperation. An angry dame is no use to us. Might as well let her go and get shot."

Her smile was stronger this time. "More honesty. It's very refreshing, Mr. Helm." She was making me feel like a louse, and I wished she'd stop. "Would you sneak along behind me and try to protect me in spite of myself?"

I nodded. "At least until I could check with Washington and get new instructions. But they might decide to scrub Operation Ellershaw if the lady simply won't play."

This was largely bluff of course; but with a big unfamiliar world staring her in the face she was very vulnerable, and I didn't think I was taking much of a chance.

"Oh, I'll play." Her voice was rueful. "I can't afford not to, can I? Bus tickets cost money, and it's a nice little car. And I don't really know if I'm up to facing a bus or plane ride yet, after all these years, with all those free and cheerful people who've never seen the inside of a penitentiary." Suddenly she was blinking her eyelids and turning away to hide the shiny wetness of her eyes. "Oh, God, there must be so many changes, so much to learn all over again, like Rip van Winkle! I'm a coward, Mr. Helm. If you really want to play nursemaid and . . . and lead the frightened lady gently back into the strange outside world, she's happy to accept the offer."

I nodded again. "The rules are very simple. First of all, here's a telephone number." I fished a piece of paper out of my coat pocket and gave it to her. "Memorize. If we should get separated, or I should be put out of action, or you should decide to go off on your own after all, and there's any hint of trouble, try to get to a phone and call that number. Somebody'll tell you what to do, and send help, although it may take a little time to get a man to you."

She studied it; I saw her lips move as she imprinted the number on her mind. "It's a Washington phone, isn't it? Unless they've changed the area code."

"Yes. Call collect and use my name. Next, instant obedience in any matter relating to your safety."

Her voice held sudden bitterness: "For obedience, you've come to the right girl, mister. I've just spent eight years in obedience school, remember?"

"I won't take advantage, I hope," I said. "I won't boss you around unnecessarily, but if I yell *down*, you flop, even if it's in the middle of a mud puddle. If I yell *run*, you run like hell. If I tell you to scream, you call in all the

27

cows from here to the Rockies. If I tell you to be quiet, you're a mouse. Okay?"

She said wryly, "Oh, dear. If I'm going to have to take all those orders, I might as well have stayed in . . . in p-prison, hadn't I?"

I could see that she'd had to make a big effort to joke about it—I'd already noticed that even the word, prison, was hard for her to speak—but she managed a smile as she said it that was a considerable improvement over her first two smiles of the day. With a little more practice she might learn to be quite good at it.

The mileage markers warned me when we got close; then I saw the signs for the rest area ahead. I slowed the little bomb, already rolling at a fairly sedate pace in deference to my passenger's wishes, and turned in. There were tables and johns, and a couple of big eighteen-wheelers parked in the truck area; but at this time of year there were no tourist vehicles in the passenger-car area. I parked and reached into the open luggage space behind the seats for the paper bag I'd prepared earlier.

"Coffee break," I said, and went around to let her out, taking her hand to help her up from the low seat. "I don't think you'll want your coat. The sun's getting almost hot. There's the rest room if you need it."

She gave me a real grin. "I thought you'd never ask."

"We'll use that table over by the trees."

I went over there and got out the thermos and cups and doughnuts. Straightening up, I saw her coming from the john. She'd shed not only her coat but her suit jacket, too, and run a comb through her hair. Watching her walk towards me, I decided that she was not really bad-looking if you thought of her as a woman in her forties who hadn't taken very good care of herself. It was the memory of what a slender, shining rapier of a girl she'd been that had made her present appearance such a shock when I'd first been exposed to it.

But I was getting used to it now, and realizing that she

28

still had some possibilities. She wasn't really fat, just a bit heavy and obviously in poor physical condition. A better-tailored and better-fitting skirt and perhaps a girdle, and enough confidence to hold herself erect, would have made a lot of difference, as would some careful makeup and a reasonable hairdo. The short-sleeved pink sweater, although hardly cashmere, was all right; but it did reveal the soft, pasty-white arms and the oddly bent wrist.

When she came up, I asked, "Do you have to do that? May I look?"

She started to protest, shrugged, and let me take her hand and turn it over to see the scars of the hesitation marks and of the final deep desperate cut that had done the real damage. I found it painful to think of her being driven to do this to herself. I had to remind myself firmly that her innocence was just a shaky theory of mine. It was quite possible that, with the help of her missing husband and his subversive female companion in exile, wherever that exile might be, she'd brought all these disasters on herself.

"Dumb," I said.

Resentment showed in her eyes, as I hoped it would; the woman was coming back to life. Well, that was fine. Traitor or patriot, she was no use to me as a zombie.

"Is it dumb to want to die when there's nothing left to live for?"

I shook my head. "As far as I'm concerned, copping out is anybody's privilege. Overpopulation is our big problem. If you want to give up your place on earth to somebody else, be my guest. But that wrist routine is stupid, stupid, stupid, as any doctor will tell you. Oh, people have managed it, but mostly they just make a mess of themselves and keep right on living with crippled arms, which can hardly be considered an improvement over the previous state of affairs, no matter how lousy that may have been." I bent the hand back and forth.

"They did a good repair job on you, but you didn't do your remedial exercises to stretch the damaged tendons, did you?"

"What was the point?" Her voice was sullen now.

I felt a strong need to shake her out of her defeatist attitude. I reached into my pocket and brought out a small penknife and opened the larger of the two blades.

"If that's the way you really feel, you'd better have this, it's good and sharp. But no more wrists." I pointed the blade at the front of her skirt. "Down there. . . . Here, I'll show you on my own leg. The inside of the thigh, up here. Ram it in and dig around a bit and you'll get the prettiest pumping red fountain you ever saw, the femoral artery, no lousy little bloody trickle like you probably managed. It won't take more than a couple of minutes before you're all bled out and as dead as you could wish. I'll put it in your purse in case you get in the mood. There."

She gave me that flat gray prison stare. "That's pretty cruel, isn't it?"

"Cruel?" I asked harshly. "I'll tell you what would be cruel, or at least damned inconsiderate, and that is for me to work my ass off, and maybe risk my life, to keep you safe, and then have you crawl into a dark corner and start hacking stupid holes in yourself again. If you're going to do it, please do it now. I'll take a little walk if you're shy about having a man see you bleeding all over your panty hose."

We faced each other for a long moment. Then she did an odd thing. Tentatively, almost shyly, she reached out and touched my arm.

"Tough, aren't you?" she murmured. "May I have that coffee before I open my veins and arteries, Mr. Helm?" Deliberately dismissing the subject, she turned to the picnic table. After a moment she said, pleased, "How did you know I loved glazed doughnuts, *pink* glazed doughnuts?"

"Sheer genius," I said. "They had several kinds in the

little bakery and I got two of each. They're both yours. I'm a cinnamon man myself."

The awkwardness between us faded gradually as we sat there eating our doughnuts and sipping our coffee. I saw it happening to her now, what I'd expected to see at the penitentiary gate. Relaxing on the wooden bench, she breathed deeply as she looked about the pleasant rest area with its trees, undoubtedly prettier in the summer with green leaves and grass, but obviously beautiful to her as she savored her freedom at last, forgetting for the moment the prison ugliness that lay behind her and the bleak ex-convict existence that probably lay ahead.

I could see the girl I'd known like a blurred image viewed through wavering layers of unclear water, and I was aware of an angry sense of waste. Something valuable had been wantonly destroyed here. The question was whether she'd wrecked her life, and herself, through her own criminal folly, or whether she had been the victim of vicious plotting by others. It was all very well for Mac to say that the problem of her innocence or guilt was academic, but I wouldn't know how to deal with her until it was solved.

"I want to apologize," she said abruptly, turning to look at me at last.

"What the hell for?" I asked, surprised.

"A little while ago I said I didn't believe anybody could be trying to kill me. I as good as called you a liar. But I'd promised myself that when I got out I'd never ever do that to anybody else after the way they treated me." She drew a long breath. "Maybe it sounds childish, but it was the horrible *rudeness* that shocked me so, the total lack of consideration, as if I had no feelings that mattered to anybody; and I guess I didn't. Men contradicting me flatly, men calling me a liar to my face, men telling me what a dumb broad I was to expect them to be taken in by . . . I mean, after the verdict, all right. I suppose all right. I was legally guilty then, legally a felon, with no further right to polite and respectful treatment.

31

But that was a year later. Before, damn it, when I was first arrested and questioned, I was Madeleine Rustin Ellershaw, Attorney at Law. I was Mrs. Roy Ellershaw. I had a very good position with a very good law firm. I was the wife of a respected research scientist. I had a lovely house in the best section of town. I was accustomed to a little . . . a little courtesy." She shook her head irritably. "Oh, I'm making it sound so petty, aren't I? But when you've been brought up, well, gently, tenderly, always treated as an important human being, you can't quite cope with people suddenly acting as if you were . . . dirt."

I said, watching her, "Don't talk about it if you don't want to."

She licked her colorless lips. "I have to talk about it," she said quietly. "I've been living it over and over for eight years, nine since they marched into my beautiful home like storm troopers and showed me the warrant and mouthed *Miranda* at me and dragged me away all dressed up in my new and very smart and expensive black crepe with the rather good diamonds Roy had given me for my birthday. And sheer black stockings and pretty high-heeled pumps and my hair up because he always said he found the back of my neck very sexy. Oh, God, I still remember every detail of that awful night. I keep thinking of all the things I should have done to protect myself—you'd have thought I had no legal training at all, the things I let them get away with! But the whole thing was so totally unexpected, so completely incredible. . . . I think I was actually in shock. I kept telling myself it was all a ridiculous mistake, it just had to be, and the best thing to do was just ride along with it, and in a minute somebody would come in and say, sorry, we got the wrong Ellershaw, and they'd take me home with abject apologies and Roy would be there waiting for me, wondering where I'd got to."

She stopped. I remained silent, letting her find her own way. I just divided the remains of the coffee between her cup and mine and shoved the box of doughnuts closer to her. She hesitated, glanced down at herself, shrugged, and took one.

"I really shouldn't, of course, I'm much too big already; but I didn't eat either breakfast or lunch today, I couldn't." She drew a long breath. "It had been a very busy time for me at the office, Mr. Helm," she said. "I knew something was bothering Roy, but I had so many business problems of my own to think about that I never took time to ... I know now that he must have wanted to talk about it, but I was full of my own important affairs. I thought I was doing quite enough when I ran some stupid little bank errands for him."

She stopped, and discovered the doughnut in her hand, and took a bite, watching the flickering colors of the freeway traffic through the sheltering, leafless trees. At last she breathed deeply once more and went on.

"In fact, I was rather annoyed that he'd bother me when he knew how busy I was. And then I got a nice bonus, big enough to let me know they really had their eyes on me and were making wonderful plans for my future with the firm. We had to celebrate, of course, and Roy made the dinner reservations, and we got dressed up for the occasion; but as he was tying his tie the phone rang. It was a very short conversation. He only said that, yes, this was Dr. Ellershaw. He listened a bit and hung up. He reached for his coat and told me he had to step out for just a minute. I . . . I was annoyed at the delay and reminded him that our reservation was for seven-thirty. He kissed me gently on the cheek so as not to smear my fresh lipstick; and he said that it really wouldn't take a minute, he'd be right back. . . . But he wasn't. Ever."

She was silent for a moment, watching a pair of crows flying over the trees, talking raucously to each other. They settled in the woods behind us. Madeleine went on as if there had been no pause.

"I waited and waited, getting madder and madder of

33

course. He was spoiling that wonderful bonus glow I'd had. The doorbell rang. When I opened, they shoved their way in with their warrant and a couple of them grabbed me and . . . and suddenly I was standing there staring incredulously at the handcuffs on my wrists! Handcuffs! They took me away like that in full view of the neighbors—that popular young Mrs. Ellershaw being roughly marched away between two big men, stumbling down the front walk of her fine house in her high-heeled party pumps with those . . . those *things* shining on my wrists! And then making my phone call downtown and trying to explain the mad things that were happening and not being able to get hold of anybody but Walter."

"Walter?"

"Walter Maxon. A young attorney who'd just joined the firm. Well, actually he was a year older than I was, but he acted very young. I will say he came right away; but he might as well not have. He was a shy boy and he'd had no experience at all with criminal cases; he'd never had to deal with anything like that before. They bullied him mercilessly; he was no use at all."

She paused again, and sipped her coffee, staring into space, into the past, but at last her voice continued:

"Hours and hours of questioning! Where was my husband? Where did he say he was going when he left? Who helped him slip away so neatly right from under their noses? Who'd tipped him off that the warrants had been issued? Where was I going to meet him? When was I going to meet him? Liar, liar, liar, don't try to pull that innocent line on us, we know you're in it up to your pretty neck, where did he go? And was this my signature on this safe-deposit form or wasn't it? Come on, baby, forget that stuck-up lady-of-the-manor crap. It's no good, we've got you cold and you know it, so why don't you come clean and make it easy for all of us, the court will take your attitude into consideration and maybe you'll only have to serve four-five years, think about it, the Rosenbergs got the chair, remember?" She drew a long, ragged breath. "And Walter trying to protest, trying to remember his law, and I sitting there stupidly trying to explain that I didn't know what in the world they were talking about—my God, they were threatening me with imprisonment and execution and I didn't know *anything*! And knowing I was the more experienced attorney there, I should take charge and put a stop to it. Knowing they were way out of line, legally, and Walter was being no help at all so it was up to me, but I . . . I was just so shocked by it all, and so worried about Roy, that I couldn't seem to pull myself together. . . . And being shoved into that cell at last with my eyes aching from the lights, my head aching, crying helplessly as I fell on the cot, like a dumb ingenue instead of a competent professional woman. And then the dream, if it was a dream."

I saw her hand reach out for still another doughnut; but she glanced down at her fairly substantial figure and drew it back empty. We sat for a little in silence, listening to the cars and trucks roaring by beyond the trees.

"And then it was morning," she said. "I'd finally gone to sleep, exhausted; and they came and told me that Walter had arranged for immediate arraignment, and I hardly recognized the awful creature in the mirror. My elaborate hairdo was a crazy bird's nest, my face was a streaky mess of tears and makeup, and my lovely new cocktail dress was a wrinkled and slept-in ruin with a big smear of mustard on the front from a hamburger they'd given me in the middle of the night—I'd never got to dinner, remember? And my sexy black hose had runs in them. They made me look like a cheap whore after a hard night on the streets, so I peeled them off and threw them away; and I managed to clean myself up a bit, tidy myself up, but I still wasn't exactly the well-groomed lady attorney when I came up before Judge Hillman, stringy-haired and bare-legged in my crumpled black dress. I thought I'd die of humiliation. And two hundred

35

thousand dollars bail, my God! And then having to face the newsmen and their cameras like that . . . !" She shook her head abruptly. "Not that it really mattered. Nothing mattered anymore, because Roy was dead."

She drew a long ragged breath, and I saw that her eyes were wet. After all the years, she could still cry for her lost husband. Or, I reminded myself sternly, pretend to cry for him, for my benefit.

"I was right about that," she continued. "It didn't matter a bit in the long run. There was much worse to come. But even then, when I forced myself to go to the office the next day, the chill in the air told me where I stood. The crown princess had slipped on a banana peel and got egg on her face, to scramble a few metaphors. She'd suddenly become a liability to the firm instead of an asset. But they were nice about it. They gave me leave of absence and continued my salary clear up to the verdict. And Mr. Baron himself handled my defense. But I knew that even if he got me off, my special favored place with the firm, that I'd worked so hard to achieve, was gone forever, and nothing in my life would ever be the way I'd hoped."

There was a sudden flutter of black wings over the trees as the two crows, disturbed by something, rose and flapped away into the distance. A crow isn't normally the most graceful flier in the world, although he can soar like an eagle if he feels like it, but he gets the job done in a professional and businesslike manner.

Madeleine licked her lips. "Strangely, those are the only things I remember clearly, the early things: the pleasant married business of getting all dressed up for a celebration dinner with my husband, the terrible shock of seeing those handcuffs on me, the ghastly trapped-animal feeling of being locked up in a cell for the first time in my life, and the dreadful indignity of having to face the court and the newsmen looking like that. Of course, that was only the beginning, but the rest . . . I guess I was kind of numb through all the rest. I didn't really *feel* anything through all the months of legal maneuvering, even the verdict and the sentencing and the appeals. Denied. And then being shipped across the country, passed from one federal marshal who happened to be going the right way to another, mostly in handcuffs with everybody staring at the depraved female criminal on her way to the pen; and those dreadful little jails where they parked me along the way; and arriving all bedraggled again, like that first morning in court, but by then I didn't even care how awful I looked in my grimy slacks and soiled blouse after all that traveling. I . . . I'd even picked up some bugs, you know, in one of those horrible little cells into which I'd been stuck between the various stages of the journey. It wasn't until later that I realized it was all deliberate."

"Deliberate?" I asked.

She didn't look at me. She went on, staring at the busy highway, "Yes. To break me down. They couldn't kill me, like Roy; to have us both disappearing and dying under suspicious circumstances would have been too much. So I had to be framed into prison, and not only framed, but broken, smashed, demolished as a thinking, potentially dangerous human being. It wasn't hard, considering my sheltered upbringing. The self-confident and self-satisfied young lady was very vulnerable. Drag her rudely out of her lovely home in handcuffs, throw some terrible charges at her, take advantage of her initial shock to expose her to scorn and ridicule at her very first court appearance on the . . . the wrong side of the law, continue to humiliate her at every turn, convict her of a dreadful crime against her country, sentence her to the most brutal penal institution available, and soften her up for it by shuttling her from one unspeakable little jail to another for a couple of weeks, presenting her at the penitentiary at last all filthy and lousy, stinking of the disgusting cells in which she'd been held, quite unrecognizable, even to herself, as the proud young professional woman she'd been." Madeleine drew a long, shuddering breath. "After that, of course, the prison routine took over. They stripped me and inspected me like a cow, every hole in my body from ears to anus, and scrubbed and deloused me, and stuck me into an ugly uniform that didn't fit, and herded me from place to place; but by that time I wasn't really there anymore. It was all happening to somebody else. Being brutally arrested and subjected to a shameful public trial like that had been degradation enough; but *this* simply couldn't be happening to me, not to wonderful, beautiful, intelligent, very superior me."

I heard the warning whistle in the woods near where the crows had taken flight. I grabbed my companion and swept her from the seat to the ground. A shotgun boomed from the brush at the edge of the trees, and buckshot ripped the dead winter grass nearby and splashed against the concrete uprights of the heavy picnic table that protected us. I slapped Madeleine on the rump and she worked her way obediently under the table. I had my own gun in my hand—a short-barreled Smith and Wesson .38 Special, if it matters—and I saw her look at it with interest. There was, I noticed, absolutely no fear in her expression. In fact her face was flushed and rather pretty with the excitement of the moment.

The shotgun boomed again, but the charge did not come near us; the heavy report was answered by a burst of fire from a lighter weapon. Silence followed.

"Oh, shit!" I said. "Stay here. . . . No, you'd better come along. There might be another one. You're all right?"

"Yes, I think so."

I raised my voice. "Coming out," I shouted.

A man's voice answered from the trees: "All clear here."

I backed out of our hidey-hole and she followed me and sat up, a little embarrassed because her skirt and slip had ridden up about her waist as she extricated herself.

38

She pulled them down, and examined the torn knee of one stocking.

"I'm surprised," she said calmly. "I didn't think you could damage these armor-plated hose they bought me with anything short of an axe."

I helped her up, and we walked together towards the woods, where two men now stood looking at something on the ground.

I said, "If you've got some objection to dead men, you'd better wait here. I think it's safe enough now."

She said, speaking in cold, even tones, "No dead man ever hurt me. It's the live ones I worry about."

The sudden hostility in her voice made me look at her in surprise. I saw that her exhilaration had vanished, and that she was regarding me with none of the friendliness she'd begun to show earlier; but I didn't have time for her at the moment. I moved forward and looked at the man on the ground, of medium height, dressed in windbreaker, jeans, and scuffed work shoes. And a lot of blood; he'd been pretty well riddled by pistol bullets, 9mm at a guess. I didn't know him. A heavy 12-gauge automatic shotgun lay beside him. Remington Model 1100, if it matters. I looked at the lined farmer-face of the older of the two men standing over him. Jackson was a wiry man with pale blue eyes. He was holding an automatic pistol; and I'd guessed the caliber correctly.

"You plan to use a Ouija board to interrogate him, I suppose," I said softly. "The word was he was to be taken alive, amigo."

"I don't play games with shotguns," Jackson said stiffly. "He was about to cut down Marty with his next load of buck; I had to ice him."

I looked at the younger man for a moment, husky and dark-haired. Unlike Jackson, who was in city clothes, he was in jeans, like the dead man. Well, I guess denim goes just about everywhere these days, although sometimes I wish it wouldn't. I nodded at the boy, reminding myself that Marty and I had worked together before and he'd done all right. Okay. It happens. Bringing them back alive isn't all that easy. Back to the old drawing board.

I said, "Well, find out who the hell he is and see if you can learn who's been talking to him recently. If you can. I won't hold my breath. Come on, Mrs. E. Let's put it on the road."

But she avoided the hand with which I tried to lead her away and stood looking down at the dead man for a moment longer, her face impassive. I sensed that she was testing herself. Once she'd been a civilized young lady living in a kindly and protective environment, and the sight of a bloody corpse would have left her shattered for days; but since then she'd spent eight years in Fort Ames. Now her world was a dreadful, cruel, primitive place without light or hope, and the bullet-torn body on the ground was just another indication of how far she'd come from what she'd been. She wanted to learn how this new creature, this destroyed woman who had once been Madeleine Rustin Ellershaw, could cope with the sights she could expect to see in this living hell to which she'd been condemned.

She turned without expression and walked beside me to the Mazda. She opened the door before I could do it for her and took out her brown flannel jacket, put it on, and buttoned it meticulously and unfashionably, top to bottom, before getting into the car. She didn't speak another word to me the rest of the afternoon.

CHAPTER 4

AFTER a silent and unsociable drive, with darkness falling, I spotted a chain motel that looked adequate. At this chilly time of year, accommodations were no problem, and I got us adjoining rooms, both doubles but to hell with it, Uncle Sam was footing the bill. I wasn't going to have her on the far side of the building from me; on the other hand I wasn't going to spoil her first night of freedom and privacy in eight years by forcing her to share a room, even platonically, with a strange man to whom she'd taken a dislike, for whatever reason.

"Dinner in half an hour?" I said, carrying her little suitcase inside for her.

"Whatever you say, Mr. Helm." There was no warmth in her voice.

"I have a bottle, if you'd care for a drink beforehand. I seem to recall that you used to like a cocktail before dinner. The motel restaurant doesn't serve booze, and that bar up the road looks like a real dive." When she didn't speak at once, I went on: "If it's just that you prefer not to associate with me unnecessarily, I'll pass it through the connecting door. Give me a minute or two to scrounge up some ice."

She shook her head quickly. "No, we might as well be civilized about this. I'll come as soon as I've changed out of these laddered panty hose and cleaned up a bit." But when she knocked on the door between our rooms a few minutes later—actually two doors, for soundproofing, and so either party could lock the other out—I could see that she regretted her sociable impulse. When I moved a chair into a better position for her, and brought her drink to her before sitting down myself, she said irritably, "Why do you keep it up, that solicitous-gentleman act? Now we both know what I am, and we both know what you are. Whom are you trying to impress?"

I liked that super-correct, grammatical "whom"; she'd never have used that in prison. I said, "Why don't you come out with it, Mrs. Ellershaw? What turned you off all of a sudden? Was it the fact that we set a trap for that hit man and killed him? I realize it wasn't pretty, and I won't claim we're great humanitarians, but in this partic-

41

ular case his death was the last thing we wanted. We wanted to catch him alive so he could tell us who wants you dead. And, if possible, why."

She shook her head quickly. "Once I'd have been terribly shocked and revolted by seeing a man shot to death for any reason, but I guess they knocked a lot of tenderhearted humanitarianism out of me in that p-place. No, it was not the shooting, Mr. Helm."

"Then what?"

"Are you really so insensitive? Can't you really understand how I feel about the way you . . . used me to bait your trap?"

I regarded her with some surprise. "You're a bright lady. I didn't think I had to spell it out for you. I told you you were in danger. I told you we wanted your cooperation. What else could you do for us but act as bait?"

"You lied to me. You said we weren't being followed."

I nodded. "Yes. And that was the only lie I told you. I didn't think you were a good enough actress to keep from looking over your shoulder and tipping him off to the fact that we knew he was there. As it turns out, I probably underestimated you. Sorry about that. But I don't feel I deceived you in any other way, Mrs. Ellershaw. And you might consider the fact that if it hadn't been for us you'd probably, right now, be lying in a morgue somewhere full of buckshot—wherever he got a crack at you along the route of the bus you would have taken."

She said coldly, "Yes. I should be grateful, shouldn't I? But my life doesn't really mean that much to me any longer, Mr. Helm. Maybe . . . maybe I'm even a little sorry that you interfered. It would have been one solution, and I wouldn't have to look at that slob-woman in the mirror any longer and wonder what kind of a slob-life . . ." She shook her head irritably. "Sorry, please ignore the self-pity. But you really are pretty obtuse, aren't you? You don't understand at all. It wasn't the fact that you used me, it was *how* you used me."

42

I looked at her for a moment, frowning. "All right, I'm stupid. You're going to have to explain it to me."

She sipped her drink, and looked into her glass, avoiding my gaze. "Can't you see how . . . how foolish you made me feel, how naive and trusting? I thought . . . I thought after eight years in Ames I was pretty tough. I thought I knew how to keep my guard up and my mouth shut. And then, after all those years of being a nothing, an animal in a cage, I'm free again and I meet a kindly gentleman who helps me with my coat and carries my bag and holds the car door for me, treating the unattractive female ex-convict in her bargain-basement suit as if she were a lovely lady in mink. Slowing down the car so considerately at her stupid whim. And those damn pink doughnuts. . . . And all my defenses crumbling before the first courtesy, the first kindness I've met in so many years! You must feel very proud of yourself. It was really a beautiful con job, even if the subject was fairly vulnerable. You are one slick operator, Matthew Helm!"

I tried to protest: "It wasn't like that—"

"It was exactly like that!" she said harshly. "The way you got it all pouring out of me, all the things I'd kept to myself all these years, all the misery and shame of the arrest and trial, and the ghastly journey to the prison that, with the reception I got there, completed my total degradation. . . . My God, I was even telling you how innocent I was, how cruelly I'd been framed. Jesus! There are two hundred and seventy-seven inmates in Ames—well, two hundred and seventy-six now—and every damn one of them is innocent, every damn one of them was framed, and it's a crying shame. I learned very early in there not to bore anybody with my lousy innocence; there wasn't a guilty woman in the joint, to hear them talk. But you had me babbling tearfully about how I'd been the victim of a sinister conspiracy to destroy . . . God, how did you keep from laughing in my face? But you listened so sympathetically, you were so kind and understanding. No wonder they picked you to deal with the poor beaten dame who'd served her time; you are very, very good. You had me"—she swallowed hard—"you had me feeling . . . almost like a real person again, after all the years of being a number. And all the time you were just encouraging me to prattle on and on so I'd make a nice harmless-seeming target for the man sneaking up on me you were trying to trap! All that lovely sympathy and understanding that I fell for so completely was merely a psych routine to keep me playing my part convincingly!" She drained her glass abruptly, and shook her head when I tried to speak. "No, please don't play any more smoothie games with me. I don't want to hear any sincere explanations; I'm sure you've got a million of them. Just take the dumb sucker bitch out and feed her. You want a nice plump target for the next marksman, don't you?"

There was nothing to say. Perhaps I had laid on the politeness more heavily than I otherwise might; but I'd thought I was doing it mainly to conceal my shock at what prison had done to her. And perhaps I had led her on to talk, deliberately; but I'd wanted to hear her story so I could make up my mind about her. But there was no doubt that I'd been conscious of the necessity for putting on a convincing act for the man sneaking up on us with a gun. In any case, in the conflict between the trusting girl she'd been and the wary ex-convict she'd become, the prison paranoia was once more ascendant; and I made no attempt to overcome it as I escorted her to the restaurant on the far side of the motel parking lot.

An hour later, she gave her empty plate a little push away from her and sat back with a satisfied sigh. "My God, real food instead of that institutional grease and cardboard!"

The meal hadn't been all that great, as far as I was concerned, but then I hadn't spent eight years being fed by the numbers in a penitentiary mess hall.

"Coffee? Dessert?"

She nodded. The pleasant experience of eating again

in moderately civilized surroundings—even just a run-of-the-mill motel restaurant—seemed to have diminished her hostility.

"Might as well be fat," she said with a wry little grin. "What the hell difference does it make now, anyway? It's too late for me to influence the jury with my sexy figure and dazzling smile, and I was found guilty even when I had them, wasn't I?" Then her assurance faltered, and her eyes grew shiny. "Oh, God, look what they've made of me, Helm! I really was . . . kind of good-looking once, remember?" Before I could respond, she said sharply, "Christ, the broad is getting maudlin on one little Scotch!"

I signaled the waitress, who brought coffee and took our dessert orders. When the woman had gone, I said in a challenging way, "If you really *were* innocent, Madeleine—"

"No!" she said sharply. When I looked at her, startled, she went on: "Call me Mrs. E, or Mrs. Ellershaw. Call me ex-inmate number 210934, Fort Ames. Or Elly, as the other women did in there. But not Madeleine. I haven't been Madeleine to anybody for a very long time, and I don't think I want to start again with you." For a moment dislike was naked in her eyes once more; then she looked away and said, "Sorry. I didn't mean to overreact like that. What the hell difference does it make what you call me? But really, all you have to do is just blow the whistle. Number 210934 will come running like a good little felon. What was that about my being innocent?"

"*If* you were innocent," I said, with deliberate lack of conviction, "then somebody certainly must have worked hard to make you look guilty. I've studied your history and read up on your trial, and the evidence against you was pretty damning. I think you'll admit that."

She sighed. "Here we go again! I keep telling you, you don't have to pretend to all this sympathy and interest. You don't have to pretend you find me attractive and fascinating. I know what I look like now, what I am now." She moved her shoulders in an ugly shrug. "But all right, if you want another installment in the sad, sad Ellershaw story, why the hell not? What else have we got to talk about? What do you want to know? About the trial? Have you read the transcript?"

I nodded. "Well, not all of it. It was pretty long. But somebody boiled it down for us."

"Then you know they had only four pieces of evidence, if you want to call them that. First, the fact that Roy had disappeared on the day the warrants were issued for our arrest, apparently because he'd been tipped off by a mysterious telephone call. They tried to use his flight, as they called it, as evidence of his guilt and, by implication, of mine as his accomplice. Second, the fact that we were both acquainted with a woman named Bella Kravecki who disappeared at the same time. Actually, we'd only had her to the house a few times on the strength of a letter of introduction she'd brought from a former colleague of Roy's in the East. But it was proved that she had definite Communist connections, and they claimed she was a courier waiting to take delivery when the . . . the shipment was complete. Roy was supposed to've been collecting the stuff for her, and I was supposed to've been holding it in my bank box as it accumulated. . . ." She stopped.

"Yes," I said. "That was the kicker, wasn't it? Actually, as far as I'm concerned, the Kravecki woman is a mark in your favor. I find it a bit hard to believe in a Commie courier who associates openly with the spies from whom she's supposed to pick up the stolen secret formulas. But that's kind of beside the point, isn't it? The cold fact is that super-classified materials *were* stolen from your husband's lab, presumably by him, since very few others had access. They were recovered from a safe-deposit box rented by you. You never denied renting it. You never denied putting the stuff into it. You did deny knowing

46

what it was, but that denial didn't carry much weight—"

"It was true!" she protested.

"You couldn't convince the jurors of that. They felt that if you'd really been an innocent uninvolved young wife tricked by a sneaky spy husband into hiding stolen national secrets unknowingly, which was what you were saying, you'd just naturally have been mad as hell at him—why, the creep had even slipped away to safety that last night without warning you that the cops were on their way! How could you help hating a treacherous louse like that, running off with another attractive woman and leaving you, the scapegoat, to stand trial for his crimes?"

"That's ridiculous!" she protested. "Bella wasn't particularly attractive, and Roy detested her. He'd never in the world have—"

"There you are," I said. "I hand you your defense on a platter and you kick it across the room. As you did at your trial. You refused to admit on the stand that there could have been anything between your husband and this Communist mystery woman. You refused to put on a convincing act of hating the deceitful louse; in fact you tried to stand up for him. For a while you even tried to present him as a totally innocent victim who'd been murdered by unspecified villains, which you'd learned through extrasensory perception. Pretty farfetched, wouldn't you say, the wild defense of a guilty woman struggling against the net of evidence in which she was caught? And let's consider the fourth item of evidence you mentioned."

She licked her lips. "That was the *real* frame-up. I did rent one bank box; and I did use it for some rather fat envelopes Roy gave me. But I knew nothing whatsoever about a second box—"

"A second box under your name in a different bank in a different town," I said. "Las Vegas, New Mexico, to be exact. A second box that contained fifty-five thousand dollars in used bills that you couldn't explain away and that hadn't been declared on the joint income tax return of the Ellershaw family."

She said stiffly, "As I said in court, I didn't rent that box and I had no idea where that money came from. Anybody can rent a safe-deposit box under any name, Helm."

"Two bank employees in Las Vegas identified the renter as you. And in those days you weren't a girl it was easy to mistake for anybody else, Mrs. E."

Then I was sorry I'd said it, in view of her present appearance. After a moment, she said in a subdued voice, "Those tellers were lying. I don't know why they were, but they were!"

"And then there's clue number five," I went on ruthlessly, "which you've neglected even to mention. The fact that your financial situation wasn't quite as happy as you've tried to make me think. You glossed over all your debts, and your husband's, very smoothly when you were talking earlier, but it wasn't quite such a cheerful picture, was it? You'd gone on a spending spree like a couple of kids when you got married, and the payments on the cars and that fancy house and its fancy furnishings were bleeding you dry. You *needed* that fifty-five grand—"

"We weren't that much behind!" she protested. "If things got really critical I was going to ask my folks for help whether Roy liked it or not—he didn't—but that bonus I got would have gone a long way towards satisfying our creditors." She grimaced. "That's why we had to celebrate! We were off the hook at last, and it was such a wonderful relief!"

"But you didn't know such a big bonus was coming until you got it," I said. I shook my head. "No, Mrs. E, it was a pretty convincing case. As far as I could make out, the only thing that saved you from a much longer sentence was that you were obviously only a minor character in the spy drama concocted by your husband and this Kravecki woman. They'd used you and discarded you.

So in the end the jury recommended a certain degree of clemency, whatever the legal terminology is, and you got off with eight years."

She said angrily, "You make professional ruin and being buried in a dungeon for most of a decade sound like a slap on the wrist! Where the hell is that dessert? Fuck it, I don't want it, I'm all out of the mood. I'm going back to my room."

"Not alone," I said. "Wait until I've signed the check, please."

Walking her back, I took her as far as the outside door to her unit, and stopped. I said, "Make sure this door is locked when you get inside. Do you have everything you need? What about something to read?"

"Don't *do* that!" The anger burst out of her stormily; she'd apparently spent the short walk reviewing her wrongs. "That phony considerateness is going to drive me right up into the rafters! You need me and I'm stuck with you unless . . . unless I want to be killed, and I guess I really don't; but you don't give a damn about my comfort, any more than they did in . . . in Fort Ames, so for God's sake forget that greasy solicitous act. Just tell me which way you want me to jump and stand aside. I'm well trained; I'll jump. Yes, Mr. Helm, I will lock my fucking door. No, Mr. Helm, I don't need *The Decline and Fall of the Roman Empire* to entertain me." She hesitated, and started to speak further, and checked herself.

"What?" I asked.

"All right, since you asked, if you've got a sleeping pill. . . . It's going to be a bit strange, in a real bed with a big room all to myself."

I said, "Well, I do have some sedatives, but why don't you try without, first? If you really can't sleep, knock on the connecting door and I'll dig one out for you."

She said contemptuously, "Nobody's going to catch you dispensing drugs without a license, huh? I'm sorry I asked. Good night."

49

"Leave the connecting door on your side unlocked, please."

She turned to look at me with cold and hopeless eyes. "God, do you think I dare risk it, a lovely desirable slim young thing like me? Good night again!"

CHAPTER 5

I read for a while, a hunting-and-fishing magazine I'd brought along, and wondered idly how the duck hunting had been down along the Rio Grande that fall. I'd been busy and hadn't been able to get away during the season. I don't go after big game much anymore after all the years of tracking the biggest—or at least the most dangerous—game in the world, but there's still something special about wing shooting. I listened to the shower running next door, and the john flushing, as the woman who'd been put into my care prepared to retire to the soft bed that was probably well over twice the size of the hard prison cot or bunk to which she was accustomed.

I remembered the happy, confident girl she'd been, and I reviewed in my mind the disturbingly erratic behavior of the hopeless, suspicious woman she'd become. Well, after long confinement it couldn't be easy to cope with liberty, particularly a liberty that held out very little promise. I was tempted to look in on her before going to bed, but I told myself she'd had eight years of bed checks; she deserved to be left alone on this, her first night of freedom. But I was uneasily aware that I'd leaned on her pretty hard at dinner, needing her com-

50

plete story to confirm the judgment I'd formed of her much earlier. I couldn't help remembering the ugly scars on her wrist. Even after I'd turned out my own light, a bright line showed under the connecting doors; and after a while I found myself getting up again, putting on dressing gown and slippers, and extracting a small plastic vial from my toilet kit.

There was no answer when I knocked on the door. A sudden panic moved inside me, and I pushed my way into the room beyond. She was sitting on the side of the nearest big bed, in the big, brightly lighted double room, looking bleakly at nothing. After a little, she turned her head, acknowledging my presence. Then she smiled very faintly, and opened the hand that was clenched in her lap, displaying the little knife I had given her, closed.

"It's all right," she said. "I wasn't going to. Do you want it back?"

"Not if you weren't going to," I said.

"I had to know," she said. "It *would* be an answer, wouldn't it? To everything. But sitting here I decided it was the wrong answer. Hell, I survived Fort Ames after a fashion; maybe I can even survive being out of Fort Ames. May I have that sleeping pill now?"

"Yes, of course."

I went into her bathroom for a glass of water. Returning, I gave her a capsule and the glass. The knife was lying on the bedside table. I left it there and helped her to rise and prepared the bed for her. When I looked at her again, standing there, she was smiling that faint strange smile of hers once more.

"Service," she murmured. "Do you tuck in all your clients, Mr. Helm?"

"We aim to please, ma'am."

I saw that she was wearing a nightgown that was very different from her cheap and unbecoming daytime clothes. Obviously expensive, it had two thin satin shoulder straps, some fine lace at the breasts, and a loose cascade of peach-colored satiny material to the floor,

51

with more lace around the hem. It made her look almost pretty. For all its richness, it had a soft and comfortable appearance, indicating that it wasn't new. She saw my surprise and laughed wryly.

"The only garment out of my past that still fits me, because it's cut like a tent," she said. "Walter sent it to me when I let him know I was getting out at last. Along with some other clothes I'd stored that I couldn't possibly get into now. The skirts were all the wrong length, anyway."

"Walter Maxon, the kid lawyer from your office? He's kept in touch with you?"

She nodded. "Well, as my attorney of record, Mr. Baron has too, or tried to. After a while I stopped writing back. But Walter seems to feel . . . very responsible for me, in a way. I guess he realizes he should have done better by me the night I was arrested, when I was too . . . too shattered to look after myself. Not that it made any difference in the long run, but I think he still blames himself a little. He must be a better lawyer now; he wouldn't still be with the firm, and doing pretty well with them, if he weren't. I let him take care of some things for me when I . . . went away. He even came to see me once in Fort Ames. I think the poor boy had fallen a bit in love with me in a perverse and guilty sort of way: the glamorous office colleague whom he'd failed in her hour of need. Even seeing me in that drab p-place looking just like all the other gray-faced female convicts in my baggy uniform didn't seem to disillusion him. He asked for permission a couple of times later, but that was after"— she glanced at her scarred wrist—"after I couldn't bear to have visitors gawking at me anymore. They made me feel like a mangy, scrawny female mountain lion I'd once seen pacing her stinking little cage in a roadside zoo, obviously dreaming of the sleek, glossy creature she'd once been and the wild, free, glorious life she'd led before the trap closed on her." She hesitated. "There was a note with the clothes Walter sent. Apparently he even got his

52

partnership recently. Perhaps the one I would have had if . . ." She stopped, and swallowed hard. "God, such a tragic figure! Don't I just make the tears pop into your eyes? Thanks for the sedative. I'll be all right now."

In the morning I made a phone call from my room, reporting to Mac, whose official day would already have begun, considering the one-hour time differential. When he answered, the sound of his voice let me visualize him at the desk in front of the bright window, apparently indestructible, no grayer now than when I'd first gone to work for him. Sometimes I wondered uneasily what would happen to the organization when time finally caught up with him. Mac said it was too bad we hadn't been able to take the shotgun specialist alive, and he'd been identified as an independent operator named Victor, George Victor, born Georgio Victoroff, from New York City; and while the woman he lived with off and on had known he was away on a job that promised to be quite remunerative, she had no idea who his employer had been, except that the name Tolliver had been mentioned, but she'd thought that was merely the contact man who'd arranged the contract. No, she didn't know how the fuck it was spelled. Taliaferro? If it was spelled Taliaferro, wouldn't they *say* Taliaferro, for Christ's sake? Mac said for me to stay with the subject; it seemed more than likely there'd be another attempt on her life. I said I could hardly wait, and hung up.

I shaved and put on a clean shirt and looked at my shapeless slacks, but to hell with them. Cross-country travelers are supposed to have sloppy pants. I was running a comb through my hair and reflecting that if the face in the dresser mirror had picked me up at the prison gates I'd have thought a long time before trusting it, when there was a knock on the connecting door.

"Come in," I said.

I made a final pass with the comb, which didn't achieve any sudden miracles of rehabilitation or rejuvenation. I gave up and put the comb away and turned to look at her. She was waiting in the doorway. She was back in yesterday's drab traveling costume, but there were small but important changes. The brown hair was still unbecomingly cut, but it had been brushed very smooth and seemed to have picked up a little healthy gloss. The shoulders seemed to be a bit more square than they had been, and the back more straight. And the bitter mouth seemed to have softened slightly, and had even been treated to a touch of lipstick. She was still no young glamor girl; but then I could hardly be called a young glamor boy, either. She colored a little, self-consciously, under my regard.

Then she said firmly, "Mr. Helm, could we start over, please? I was totally impossible yesterday, just a manic-depressive bitch. It was . . . it was the first day, and I simply didn't know how to behave after years of being told how to behave. We need each other, apparently, and there's no reason we shouldn't get along." She held out her hand, with a wry little smile. "I'm even going to allow you the tremendous privilege of calling me Madeleine, if you care to do so."

I took the hand and bowed over it. "Sir Matthew at your service, Lady Madeleine. Matt for short."

"I know. We went through all that twelve years ago, so I was being pretty silly yesterday, wasn't I, getting on my high horse like that?" She drew a long breath. "Now that we've got *that* out of the way, you can take it out and feed it, Matt."

In the motel coffee shop, waiting for our breakfasts, we studied each other warily across the table, almost as if we were getting acquainted for the first time.

"Well, let's get this operation organized," I said after a moment, and I took an envelope from my inside jacket pocket and pushed it across the table. "Some credit cards; any reasonable charge will be covered. Five hundred dollars in fifties; better break a couple of them as soon as you can and be sure you always have telephone change on you. You'll find you can make a credit-card or collect call from most pay phones these days without a coin—I don't think it was that way at the time of your involuntary withdrawal from society—but there are still a few that have to be fed."

She laughed softly. "'Involuntary withdrawal from society.' I'll have to remember that. It sounds much better than being thrown into the can."

"Spare key for the Mazda," I said. "A note stating that you have the owner's permission to drive it, just in case you meet a busybody cop who decides that, with your record, you must have stolen it. And a current New Mexico driver's license."

She reached for the envelope and hesitated. "Matt, I don't understand."

I said, "We still don't know how it will break. We could get separated, as I said before, or I could be disabled or killed. I want you to be able to jump into the little heap and blast out of there and take care of yourself alone until you've made that phone call and somebody comes to look after you. You can manage a stick shift; you had a sporty little Fiat or something, didn't you? Watch out for that rotary mill, it'll rev up to its seven-thousand red line before you know it. You can't double-clutch it, there doesn't seem to be enough flywheel to keep it spinning; they recommend the heel-and-toe technique if you want to get fancy."

She shook her head ruefully. "You're way beyond me. I don't know those racing tricks. I don't even know if I remember how to shift gears normally."

"You'll remember," I said. "And if you do get in a bind, keep in mind that it's a real sports car in spite of the air conditioning and the plushy seats. It'll out-corner practically anything that comes after you. Slam it into a curve wide open and watch them go off into the bushes trying to stay with you. But we hope you won't have to."

She drew a long breath and nodded. She picked up the envelope and tucked it into her purse, saying, "You could have given me this yesterday."

I said carefully, "I didn't know you yesterday."

She looked at me for a long moment. "I see," she said a bit coldly. "You had all the bases covered. Or to put it differently, this is Program A. If . . . if after studying my reactions so carefully—I wondered why you kept prodding me to talk so much about myself—if you'd come to another conclusion about me, you'd have had another approach."

I said, "Actually, this is Program B. You went and loused up our favorite Program A by . . . well, we'll get to that in a moment. Here comes the food; to hell with idle chatter."

We tackled our breakfasts in silence. At last she sat back with a little sigh. "God, I keep making a pig of myself; but it just tastes so damn *good* after what they fed me in . . . in there." She glanced at me almost shyly. "Matt, do you mind if I do a little theorizing aloud, just so you'll know what I'm thinking?"

"No, of course not."

"Well," she said, choosing her words carefully, "well, there's an obvious point that comes to mind. You must have been working on something important involving . . . well, involving CADRE, before you ever got that mysterious phone call saying I was to be killed."

I frowned. "CADRE? Oh, the Center for Advanced Defense Research, where your husband was working. Okay, go on."

She said, "It doesn't seem likely that a specialized government agency like yours would have concerned itself with a contract being put out on just any stray female being released from just any old federal penitentiary, or that your informant would have thought he was doing you a great big favor by telling you about it. My . . . my proposed murder had to be connected with something in which you were already interested, already involved. Otherwise you'd have dismissed it as mere nuisance information and passed it along to the proper authorities, wherever they might be."

I looked at her with respect. "That's pretty good theorizing. It happens to be slightly wrong, but that's my fault. I let you think the phone call saying you were to be killed came directly to us. It didn't. It was the kind of gratitude deal I described, all right, but I can't tell you what agency was involved because I simply don't know. We were merely given the information, told how it had been obtained, and ordered to do something about it without asking any nosy questions about things we didn't need to know about. That's how our great government works, if you want to call it working."

"I see. But the organization that did receive the tip was presumably interested in CADRE, since otherwise why would they care whether I lived or died? The only thing about me that could possibly concern anybody in the U.S. government is the fact that I'd been—still am, officially, since he's never been declared dead—married to Roy, who was employed there. And that I was supposed to have helped him carry out his nefarious espionage scheme. They must have thought I knew something important after all, that I'd kept to myself all these years. Or was in a position to learn it, now that I was being set free."

I said, "Obviously, somebody else thought so, too—thinks so, too—or they wouldn't be trying to kill you." I frowned. "You haven't any idea what it might be?"

She said rather stiffly, "I don't expect you to believe me, but I really don't."

I grinned. "You may be surprised at what I'll believe. But let's skip it for now. Maybe it will come to you, whatever it is, or we'll be able to figure it out as we go along."

After a moment, she relaxed and gave me a reluctant little smile. "And in the meantime I'm a docile decoy, trying not to scream every time somebody slams a car door hard. Now get me some more coffee, please, and a little more jam for my toast, and tell me all about Program A, the favorite one I've managed to ruin for you somehow."

I passed her requests along to the waitress and said, "Program A was based upon the assumption that there was an evil lady serving a well-earned prison sentence, let's call her Mrs. Mata Hari Ellershaw. This reprehensible female had conspired with her husband and another woman to steal documents that compromised the security of the United States of America in a very dangerous way. However, the plot went sour and she found herself deserted by her accomplices and left behind to take the rap. She spent her prison term kicking herself for being such a sucker, but fear of eventual retaliation kept her silent about certain important things she'd learned. Also the fact that, disbarred and discredited and penniless, she was going to need help when she got out. But her wicked associates considered her too dangerous to be allowed to go free at the end of her sentence, or maybe they simply didn't want a sullen, resentful ex-convict lady around to embarrass them. They laid plans to deal with her permanently upon her release from the penitentiary. My chief decided that somebody—like me—should be there when our Mattie, as we'll call her, realized the further double-cross to which she was being subjected. When she discovered that her husband, not satisfied with having thrown her to the wolves, so to speak, nine years ago, was now actually conspiring to have her killed, she might well get angry enough to break her self-imposed silence and supply us with valuable information, maybe even some hint of where to find him."

Having already creamed and sugared her coffee liberally, Madeleine was spreading large quantities of red jam over an already generously buttered slice of toast. Well, her figure was really none of my business.

She spoke without looking up: "But the evil female didn't react properly?"

I said evenly, "It turned out that we'd made a mistake, a rather grave error, in fact a real booboo. When the guns started firing, the lady in question obviously hadn't

58

the slightest idea of who was shooting at her. She showed none of the anger of a woman subjected to a terrible betrayal, none of the shock and disillusionment of a woman learning that the associates she'd counted on to help her rebuild her broken life had turned against her. In fact, she just looked kind of pleasantly excited. It was very disappointing, after all the careful planning we'd done. There we were, stuck with a sadly misjudged and mistreated lady who didn't know any more than we did about why she was scheduled to be killed. A lady who, it appeared, was probably quite innocent of everything she'd been accused of." I drew a long breath. "Of course, being careful professionals, we'd allowed for the possibility, remote though it had seemed. There were other ways of utilizing this victimized dame. Scratch Program A. Institute Program B."

She was watching me steadily. "So that's why you were so anxious to keep me talking, yesterday, to confirm—"

I nodded. "Having already studied your file pretty thoroughly, I wanted to hear your side of the story. Actually I never did really buy the case against you, persuasive though it seemed. As I said yesterday, that Kravecki woman was very unconvincing as a secret courier. And as for the money in a bank box under your name, hell, somebody set up exactly that frame for me once, so I know how easy it is. As far as the rest is concerned, well, damn it, I've stayed alive longer than some because I don't often go too far wrong about people. My chief was going by the evidence, and I had to play along with him up to a point. But I'd met you and he hadn't. There are lots of crimes you could commit, Madeleine, but spying for the nasty Red Russkies, particularly for money, isn't among them."

The gray eyes were very wide and a little shiny, staring at me out of the prison-pale face. I don't know what I expected—a little pleasure perhaps, a little gratitude for my faith in her innocence. I didn't get it. There was a lengthy silence. When she spoke at last, it was in a low, savage, shocking voice.

"Damn you!" she whispered. "Oh, damn you, damn you, damn you! The one man in the world who believes I didn't do it, and he comes to me eight years late, after it's all over, after it's all been done to me, after my life's been totally smashed and there's nothing left to salvage!" She drew a deep shuddering breath. "Where the hell were you when I needed you, Matthew Helm? Where, where, where?"

She jumped up, snatched up her purse, and ran out of the restaurant. I sat there for a moment rather stunned by the outburst. Then I reminded myself sharply that I had a job to do, and that the big emotional crises were times of distraction when things often happened that shouldn't have been allowed to happen. I rose and moved to where I could watch through the windows and make certain she got safely across the parking lot to her room.

I saw two men close in on her as she reached the door, and accompany her inside.

CHAPTER 6

I drew a long breath, walking back to the table to pick up the check the waitress had left there. The trouble was, I knew the men I'd seen—although I couldn't remember the name of one of them—and they were not the kind of men I'd expected to have to deal with on this mission. It was a complication I hadn't been warned about and didn't need.

I paused briefly to drain the last of my coffee. I moved quite naturally, I hoped, in case somebody was watching, to the cashier's desk. We'd slept late enough that the scattering of winter tourists had mostly all breakfasted and blasted off along the highway, east and west. The place was almost empty, and the money lady had retired to the kitchen. I'd already checked us out at the motel desk, so I couldn't put the meal on the bill. I rang a little plink-plink bell, and presently the woman came out to work the credit-card machine. Having rung up the sale, she went right back out again. So far, so good.

And where was the takeout crew? They wouldn't grab Madeleine without making provisions for neutralizing her escort. Most likely they were waiting to catch me outside, as they had her.

I located the lighted RESTROOMS sign, and walked quickly that way. It was a dark, blind hallway with a pay-phone cubicle just inside on the left, followed by the two doors. One of the discriminatory sanitation arrangements, I noted. Any kind of MEN, gentlemen or bums, could use the male facilities, but only superior-type LADIES were permitted in the female establishment. Women of lower social status were presumably sent outside to squat in the bushes. With a quick, guilty look around, I slipped into the LADIES' chamber, the first beyond the phone.

Waiting, hoping that none of the female help or remaining female customers would need to go, I extracted from a hidden inside pocket of my jacket the little drug kit we usually carry on duty, a new model this year. The old-fashioned hypos they used to give us had been pretty slow to load, and the needles had tended to snap off under stress before the full dose had been transmitted to the patient, unless he was first tranquilized with a gun butt. The new gadget was cartridge-loading

61

and spring-fired. I selected one of the green capsules—the red and orange ones kill—and charged the little squirt-machine and cocked it and waited, gun and hypo-gun ready in left and right hands respectively.

They held out for only about ten minutes, counting from the time Madeleine had run out of there. Then they got nervous about me and came in after me. Two of them. Holding the restroom door slightly ajar, I heard them enter the restaurant and make a quick check of both public rooms, the little coffee shop where we'd break-fasted, and the larger dining room, now unoccupied, where we'd had dinner the night before. I let the john door sigh shut automatically. It seemed unlikely that they'd be dumb enough to charge into the kitchen leaving the men's room uninspected behind them. They weren't.

I heard them hurry past my door—excuse me, the ladies' door—and I heard a whispered consultation in the little hallway. Then I heard the men's door being opened cautiously. In those cramped quarters, I guessed, only one man would actually go in; the other would wait out in the corridor as backup. I gave them a slow three-count and elbowed my door aside and stepped out there.

A handsome and neatly dressed young fellow with a revolver in his hand turned belatedly to meet the threat, but he was right-handed and his gun was on the far side of his body. There was no chance in the world of his swinging himself around far enough to bring it to bear in time.

"Federal government," I said. "You're under arrest. Drop the gun, *now*!"

Shock showed on his good-looking face, as I'd known it would. He was federal government also, whatever that might mean. He arrested people; nobody arrested him. But the .38 in my left hand spoke a convincing language of its own, and I heard his firearm drop to the carpeted floor. While he was still in a state of confusion, opening

62

his mouth to protest against this dreadful reversal of the normal and decent order of things, I stepped forward and slammed the little automatic hypo into his rump, which was still half turned toward me. The mechanism fired itself with a springy, clicking sound. Real KGB stuff.

He'd half raised his hands out of respect for my weapon. Now he reached down and back instinctively to investigate the stinging pain of the injection. His eyes got a vague and puzzled look and his mouth went slack.

"What the hell's going on out here?"

The door to the men's room opened to reveal Number Two, practically a replica of Number One except for an inch or two more height, ten or fifteen pounds more weight, and a bushy blond mustache. His face changed as he saw the revolver in my left hand, aimed directly at him. I can shoot lefty if I have to, pretty accurately. Either he'd read that in my dossier or he was not a gambling man. He made no effort to raise the weapon at his side.

"Drop it!" I said. "You're under arrest for interfering with a federal officer in the performance of his duties."

There was a distraction, as the first one suddenly slumped to the floor with a little sigh. His partner started forward, and checked himself.

I said to him, "You have less than three seconds left to live, amigo. If you're still holding that sidearm when I stop talking . . . Ah, that's better. Now grab your friend and haul him inside and set him on the john. He's all right. He'll sleep four hours and wake up frisky as a lamb. Oh, just one little detail. If either of you is packing an ankle gun or neck knife or other backup weapon and you feel compelled to use it, be my guest. Just remember, it's been tried before and I'm still here. Now get him in there."

I stepped back to let him get at the inert body and gathered up the fallen firearms as I followed him into the tiled room. I locked the door behind us while he was setting his friend on the toilet. He emerged and faced me truculently.

"I don't know what the hell you think you're doing," he said, "but I can tell you—"

"Don't tell me," I said. "I know. You're an important agent of the Office of Federal Security and I can't do this to you. Well, I'm an important agent of the Federal . . . well, never mind the exact title, and you can't do this to me. Which makes us even, and I'm holding the gun. Who's the guy with Bennett? I ought to remember his name but it's slipped my mind."

"You go straight to hell!"

I shook my head sadly. "You try my patience, boy. That *was* Bennett, wasn't it, who just grabbed Mrs. Ellershaw so rudely and hustled her into her room? The OFS top man, your boss. I had some dealings with him a few years back, in the Bahamas and Florida, and I couldn't forget that Roman-emperor profile and clipped hair. What the hell are you stupid bastards trying to pull, anyway, muscling in on me like this with guns waving? The lady is under my protection."

"Lady, hell!" There was an ugly sneer in the blond man's voice. "You call *that* a lady? Shit, maybe once she had a bit of class, but anybody can see that eight years in the joint have knocked it all out of her, the smart-ass bitch. She's just another cheap jailbird now. Serves her right, too, all the fine airs she put on when she was first arrested. Hell, she was even kind of a good-looking wench back then, but you wouldn't know it now, huh?"

It always amazes me, the pleasure some people take in seeing other people humbled, particularly people better than they are. Looking hard at my captive, I realized that he wasn't as young as his partner or as young as he looked; those handsome blond hunks of beef are deceptive. He could have encountered Madeleine Rustin Ellershaw at the time of her arrest and trial. He could have a personal reason for the vicious satisfaction he obviously

64

felt at seeing what the prison years had made of the proud and lovely young woman he'd known.

I asked softly, "What's your name?"

He hesitated, and said, "Dellenbach. Jim Dellenbach."

"Well, I'm very glad you said all that, Jim Dellenbach," I said. "You can't imagine how glad I am. Here I was kind of hoping I wouldn't have to hurt you, a nice young fellow government employee like you. But now I'm just wishing you'd give me an excuse, and it won't have to be much of an excuse. I'll ask you again: the name of the heavyset dark man with Bennett?"

He closed his lips stubbornly and stared at me, silent. I sighed and looked down at the arsenal I was holding. I'd already pocketed the trick hypo. Now I stuck my own weapon back into its waistband-holster. I dropped the unconscious agent's revolver into my jacket pocket. That left me holding Dellenbach's gun, a rather foolish firearm: a hefty .357 Magnum with a two-inch barrel. Since the .357 cartridge requires a reasonable barrel length in which to develop its impressive power—two inches isn't nearly enough to burn all that powder efficiently—the guy was putting up with the ferocious recoil and muzzle blast to get little better than ordinary .38 Special ballistics. Well, maybe he was one of those who get a charge out of creating a lot of noise and confusion regardless of results. I shook my head mournfully, and looked at him for a moment longer, and slammed his weapon backhand across his face, raking him with the front sight from ear to nose. He reeled back against the washbowl, clapping both hands to the injury.

I said gently, "The question was: What is the name of the man with Mr. Bennett?"

Dellenbach hesitated, his eyes wide and shocked above his bloody fingers. I raised the weapon to strike again. He flinched away and shook his head quickly, defensively.

"Burdette." His voice was muffled. "Phil Burdette."

65

"That's right, Burdette, how could I forget?" I drew a long breath, watching him. "Well, we seem to be establishing a useful relationship, Mr. Dellenbach, but wasn't that a foolish way to earn yourself a lifetime scar? I hope it's clear to you that I'm perfectly happy to chop you to bloody ribbons, regardless of what exquisitely important government organization you happen to work for. You see, the government organization I work for thinks it's pretty important, too, and it doesn't appreciate interference by other agencies. Do you remember one of your people named Lawson?"

"Lawson was murdered by a bunch of terrorists in Miami a couple of years ago—"

I said, "And then there was the one about Little Red Riding Hood and the wolf; and I'm sure you believe that one, too. Ask Burdette how Lawson really died. He was there; he knows. Lawson made the mistake of trying to kill me; never mind why. I'm trying to keep you from making the same mistake. Remember, you and your friends came charging after me with drawn guns; I didn't start this. Now grab some of those paper towels and mop yourself off and try to check the bleeding a bit. Then we'll go out of here and visit the *lady's* room, and you'll say whatever needs to be said to get the door open. I'll be holding your own weapon aimed at your back with the hammer cocked. . . ."

"For God's sake, man!" he blurted. "That single-action trigger pull is only two pounds!"

"Then you'll have to be very careful not to startle me, won't you, Mr. Dellenbach?" I said. "Now grab a wad of clean towels and hold it to your face and let's go."

A middle-aged couple in the coffee shop stared at us curiously as we went out, but I had the gun hidden from them and they decided it was just an unfortunate accident of some kind and went back to their corn flakes and coffee. We crossed the parking area, where the little Mazda now stood almost alone, and paused on the covered porch of the motel at the door with the right number.

"If there are any special signals, give them," I said softly.

"No signals, I swear it!"

"Then just knock and say you and your partner have me all sewed up, no problem."

He hesitated, and knocked. A voice from inside, which I recognized, asked a question. He said, "It's Dellenbach, Mr. Bennett. We got him, no sweat."

"Well, bring him in," the voice said, and the doorknob turned.

Dellenbach had to try it, of course. It was inevitable. He was big, strong, and a few years younger than I. He couldn't just let himself be marched in there Trojan-horse fashion, a docile prisoner, with his face a humiliating, bloody mess. I touched him lightly with the gun barrel, his gun barrel, to give him his cue. I'd already let the hammer down silently so there'd be no accidental discharge. He didn't know that, but it didn't matter. He had to go for it if he died for it; and he did the routine pivot, the left arm slashing back to knock the gun aside and maybe grab it as he swung around to chop me down with the right. But I'd already raised the .357 out of easy reach and stepped well back. He was off balance and wide open. I just kicked him hard in the crotch as he came around to face me, shoving him backwards with my foot, hurling him against his chief, Bennett, so they both went down in the doorway.

Then I was over them, past them, in the room, whirling right, gun ready, because Burdette was a pro and would be located where he could cover not only the outside door of Madeleine's room but the connecting door to my room as well. I was vaguely aware of Madeleine herself, sitting on a chair to my left, but I had no time for her at the moment. Burdette was there, all right, but he was leaning calmly against the wall, hands in plain sight, empty. There was a tolerant smile on his heavy-featured face. He looked like a grown man watching the boys at play.

"Burdette, shoot him, damn you!"

"Easy, Mr. Bennett. Don't pull a gun unless you want a goddamn massacre. That's what *he* wants. That's what he always wants." Burdette sighed and looked at me. "Old Wild Matt Helm himself! It's a wonder you keep on living. What did you do to that boy's face?"

I said, "I just pistol-whipped the loudmouthed creep a little when he wouldn't answer a civil question. Hi, Burdette. We're a long way from that muddy canal in Miami. What the hell do you morons think you're doing here, anyway? This is my assignment and Mrs. Ellershaw is my responsibility. I thought you learned hands off the last time we met. If not, I'll be happy to repeat the lesson."

There was a little silence while Bennett picked himself up and brushed himself off. Dellenbach was curled up on the carpet, hugging himself and groaning. I looked at Madeleine at last, realizing that she had not moved during all the commotion. Rage went through me as I saw that in the brief time they'd had her they'd sent her all the way back to where she'd been yesterday morning: she was the dull, stony-faced, stony-eyed prison inmate once more. She'd even been slapped a bit. There were red marks on her face and a little trickle of blood had run from her left nostril to her upper lip and was drying there. I knew she'd sit there unmoving until she was told to move elsewhere because, as she'd told me, she'd learned obedience well in that p-place where they'd had her.

I swallowed hard. I'd felt a little guilt for the way I'd marked Dellenbach, although it had been necessary: if I hadn't impressed him with my utter ruthlessness I'd probably have had to shoot him. Even as it was he'd wound up making his try, but only after he'd served my purpose. But now I wished I'd raked him a couple more times while I had the chance. And maybe kicked in a couple of his partner's ribs just for the hell of it.

I looked at Burdette, who showed some discomfort. I said, "Mrs. Ellershaw has paid her debt to society, whether a just or unjust debt we won't go into here. What the hell gives you thugs the right to grab her and knock her around like this?"

"She's a convicted traitor to her country!" This was Bennett, coming forward. He was a lean, handsome man with that big bold nose; and I don't suppose cutting your hair too short is any worse than growing it too long. It wasn't his coiffure I had against him. There was a fanatic gleam in his eyes as he went on: "If it hadn't been for the mushy sentimentality of all those women on the jury she'd have got the punishment she deserved: life imprisonment or the chair!"

There was nothing in that worth discussing. I said, "We can call it off right now, if you like. You slapped my girl; I slapped your boy. The honors—if you want to call them that—are even. But the next one who raises a hand against the lady is going to lose it at the wrist. A promise. In fact she's not to be harassed further in any way, for any reason. I may go as high as the elbow if you make me real mad." I looked bleakly at Bennett. "Damn it, we went through all this when you tried to muscle in on my agency's business once before! You got way out of line then, and you wound up losing a man and making me a formal apology. If you want to argue this one, call Washington; you know the number. But I warn you, he never pulls us off a job because of a little political pressure, and I might not come off it now even if he told me to."

I walked over to where Burdette stood and laid the .357 on the chair beside him. I took out the .38 I'd liberated from Dellenbach's partner, still nameless, and put that neatly beside it. I looked at the heavyset dark-haired man for a moment, noting that he was showing a little gray here and there. Well, who wasn't? We were the only truly experienced working pros in the room and we understood each other very well; and one day we might have to settle a few things between us, but because we respected each other we'd regret it however it turned out. I wheeled and walked over to Madeleine's chair and put a hand on her shoulder.

I said, "A speech, gentlemen. Listen closely now, this is important. I'm the big boar grizzly from the top of the mountain. I'm the old he-cougar from the head of the creek. When I raise my voice the avalanche warnings go up all along the Rockies from the Sangre de Cristos north. When I pound my chest the San Andreas Fault gets very nervous. And any sonofabitching creep who interferes with me in the line of duty—my duty, which at the moment involves protecting Mrs. Ellershaw from everybody, including jerks like you—or waves a gun at me from now on, will wind up in the hospital or the morgue, and I don't care what kind of fancy badges or IDs the bastard carries. One of your boys is bleeding on the motel carpet over there, Bennett. Another is cluttering up the restaurant john. Burdette has their guns. Now pick them up and haul them to hell out of here and don't let me fall over any of you again. Goodbye!"

CHAPTER 7

WE'D driven about five miles when I heard the odd sound beside me. I'd tried to be helpful after we had her motel room to ourselves, but Madeleine had said very quietly that she was perfectly capable of wiping her own bloody nose, thank you, and could even manage to pack all by herself; she'd be ready as soon as I was. And just let's get out of here, please—all this in her low, dead voice without ever looking at me directly.

We'd hit the freeway again, and the little rotary power plant was spinning at 2,500 rpm in its smooth and almost soundless way, propelling us across the sunny winter Midwest at the modest speed she preferred, when I heard her make the choked, disturbing little sound. I turned to look at her with concern.

"All you all right?" I asked. "I'm sorry, I know it was a lousy experience—"

"You!" she breathed. The sound came again, an unmistakable chortle of amusement. I realized that her eyes were bright, not with tears, but with suppressed laughter. "You! Standing there spouting all that nonsense! The big bad bear from the top of the hill! The fierce catamount from the head of the river! With a perfectly straight face!" She reached out and touched my hand on the steering wheel, lightly. "I'm not making fun of you, Matt, not really. It was a lovely speech. The first time somebody's stood up for me since . . ." She swallowed, hard. "I loved it, every word of it. But wasn't it just a *little* gaudy?"

They'd had her down, but she'd bounced back fast, and her growing resiliency pleased me. However, I was a little disappointed in her on other grounds. I'd thought her prison experience would have given her a stronger armor of suspicion than she seemed to be wearing, taking the scene just past at face value.

I said, unsmiling, "I don't think you understand. Consider it carefully. Suppose you weren't personally involved. Suppose you just heard me declaiming like that, what would be your opinion of me?" When she hesitated, I said, "Go on. You won't hurt my feelings."

Her laughter died. She frowned thoughtfully. "Why, I suppose I'd think you were a very arrogant and overbearing person."

I nodded. "And not really very bright, to beat my

chest and make with the war cry of the great apes like that. Me Tarzan, *AhhhyeeeAhhhyeeee*! Just a big, meat-headed blowhard, right?"

She said quickly, "That's not what I thought at all! I told you—"

"I wasn't talking about what *you* thought, sweetheart. I wasn't putting on my act for you."

She frowned at me. "Matt, what are you trying to say?"

"What did Bennett want of you? What was he asking you, when he had you in that chair?"

She started to ask a question, and checked herself. She licked her lips. When she spoke, her voice came out flat and harsh, mimicking: "'Listen, you cheap disbarred female shyster, we know you're heading for a sentimental reunion with your traitor husband, but where? *Slap!* I'm talking to you, jailbird! Where is he? *Slap-slap!*'" She drew a ragged breath. "Matt, I used to have a little pride once. Am I going to have to spend the rest of my life as an unperson who can be shouted at and slapped around by . . . by shits like that?" Then she shook her head quickly. "Don't answer that question. They don't really let you out of prison when they let you out of prison, do they? Just tell me what you're driving at."

I said carefully, "If Bennett were serious about wanting to catch your husband, and really believed you were heading for a meeting, wouldn't he simply have you shadowed hoping you'd lead him there?"

She licked her lips. "I still don't understand what you're trying to say."

"I think you're being very naive. Did you ever hear of the *ley de fuga*?"

"Of course. The law of flight, but it's not really a law, just an excuse to . . . Matt!" Her eyes held a sudden look of shock. "Matt, you can't be serious!"

"Sure I can," I said. "It's a fine old Latin custom. You've got a prisoner you want to dispose of perma-nently. You harass him . . . well, in this case, her. You insult her, torment her verbally, abuse her physically, until she can't take it any more and makes a break. . . . *Gosh, judge, we're just as sorry as we can be, but the woman was escaping custody and the officer fired a warning shot that was meant to go over her head but he stumbled and the bullet went low and we wouldn't have had it happen for the world!* But, after all, she was just a lousy ex-con just out of stir so who really cares?"

The car was silent for a while, except for the purring of the rotary power plant and the whistle of the wind and the whine of the tires. At last Madeleine licked her lips again.

"But . . . but the Office of Federal Security is a respectable government agency! Are you saying that even the U.S. government wants me dead? That's insane!"

"The OFS is a Johnny-come-lately outfit. It's got very big very fast, and nobody seems to know how or why; but a lot of people wouldn't call it so very damned respectable. And the U.S. government is a lot of people wanting a lot of different things. What my chief wants, and those who gave him the instructions he passed down to me, isn't necessarily what some other people want, the people from whom Bennett takes his orders. I may be getting paranoid, myself, but I think we'd better operate on the assumption that we've just witnessed, and forestalled, another attempt on your life; let's just hope that my chest-beating reaction fools them into thinking we're dumb enough not to realize it. We'd also better assume that this thing is bigger than I was told—not that I was told very much—and that we have more to worry about than just an occasional hired shotgunner or rifleman or pistoleer hiding in the roadside brush. I made a call before we left, back there, and arranged a meeting with the commanding officer of the support troops, a guy named Jackson—well, you saw him at that picnic area yesterday. We'll see what he has to say. In the meantime, I need all the information from you I can get. Like, for instance, what's Dellenbach got against you?"

She looked startled. "Was that the blond man—"

"Jim Dellenbach. He says you used to be a classy broad but you gave yourself too many airs."

She winced. "God, it's been eight years! I thought he looked familiar, but the mustache, and all that blood, and he's put on some weight. . . . Not that I'm in a position to criticize!" She hesitated. "He was the gofer, Matt. You know. Every time Mr. Bennett wanted to ask me more questions, Jim Dellenbach was the man who'd go for me—come for me—take me downtown, and bring me back home afterwards, as long as I had a home. After I found a buyer for the house, and I practically had to give it away"—her voice was bitter—"after I lost my own home I moved in with my folks. It didn't seem worthwhile trying to find an apartment when . . . when I didn't know how long I'd be . . . around to use it. Or how I'd pay for it. God, after all the years of driving so hard for . . . for success, day and night, I felt totally lost and meaningless with nothing to do and no plans to make that meant anything until . . . Just waiting for my damn case to come to trial! Anyway, they kept finding new evidence, new reasons to interrogate me, or making them up. I told you I thought it was a systematic break-the-dame-down campaign, but Mr. Baron said that, legally, we were obliged to cooperate. I told you I'd had to get rid of the cars, too. I couldn't afford the payments. I was trying desperately to save enough out of the awful financial shambles to stay out of jail and pay for my defense, and I didn't like to borrow the folks' beloved old Cadillac too often and leave them stranded. So Dellenbach was the man who ferried me back and forth. And sympathized with me. Oh, he was so friendly and sympathetic; he thought it was a terrible shame the way I was being harassed, a nice lady like me. And of course he gave me advice. He said *he* believed I was telling the truth, but I should be practical. The evidence was really too strong against me. But if I pleaded guilty and said I'd been under the spell of my evil husband and really couldn't

74

conceive of how I'd come to do such dreadful things against my country and was terribly ashamed of them, if I confessed and threw myself upon the mercy of the court, they'd probably—hush, he wasn't supposed to tell me this, but he'd heard them talking—they'd probably let me off with a slap on the wrist and a suspended sentence."

She was silent for a little as we drove, remembering. Her face showed that none of the memories were pleasant. She drew a shaky breath.

"Sometimes it seemed to me that the whole world was waiting irritably for the stupid, stubborn, half-dazed bitch to confess and get the whole thing over with, even Mr. Baron, who was supposed to be defending me. He told me frankly that he didn't think his chances of getting me off were very good, and a little plea bargaining might be in my best interest. The prosecution had indicated its willingness to be reasonable. But I was damned if I was going to confess! That would have killed my last hope of ever vindicating myself: a humble confession and an abject plea for mercy! How would I ever be able to convince anyone of my innocence after that?" She swallowed hard. "But as a lawyer I have to admit that making a deal would probably have been the smart thing to do. And maybe I would have agreed if I'd really believed in my heart that I—innocent me—could be convicted; and if I'd known what a destroying thing prison would be for someone of my background, particularly that secret federal maximum-security institution I'd never even heard of, with its old-fashioned dehumanized penal system of ugly uniforms and brutal regimentation. Even in my worst nightmares I'd never seen myself doing more than a few dreadfully demeaning but otherwise fairly easy years in Alderson. . . . Yes, I think I might have weakened and gone along with them if I'd known I was risking Fort Ames, and eight whole years without hope of parole; and how I'd come out of there with nothing left, not even . . . not even myself. The other way I'd have given up any hope of ever proving my innocence, but I might have managed to salvage a few tattered little scraps of . . . of me."

She waited while I jockeyed the little car through a clot of slow traffic; then she went on, more steadily now: "Anyway, Jim Dellenbach was right in there pitching for that confession. And for me, I realized. That was what he was there for, of course, to gain my confidence. And after a while he began to think he'd really made a conquest. He started by treating me to sympathetic pats and shoulder squeezes when things had been particularly rough, and went on to protective little hugs and soothing caresses; soon he just couldn't keep his big meaty hands off me. I stood it as long as I could, but that was back in the days when I still allowed myself . . . when I was still a human being with the right to lose my temper. Finally I blew up and told him that the only thing I needed less than his slimy solicitude was his greasy, groping fingers all over me. Only I didn't say it so briefly, if you know what I mean. I suppose it was a tactical error. Of course the place was wired for sound so everybody got an earful of me telling him off—I think they played the tape for each other just for kicks. He was pulled off that duty and he hated me ever after. He even made a point of being right there out in the hall, gloating at my downfall, when I was led away from the courtroom in handcuffs after being sentenced."

I frowned. "Let me get this straight. It was Bennett and his men who marched into your house that night and arrested you, and who questioned you and conducted the whole investigation afterwards?"

She said, "Well, not the *whole* investigation. Everybody seemed to get into the act, including the local police. After all, Roy was missing, and the word 'murder' had been spoken. But Bennett was certainly the one with whom I had most dealings, and Jim Dellenbach was one of his younger assistants at the time."

I said, "I didn't know Bennett had had any previous connection with your case. The condensed material I was given to study didn't mention the name of the investigating officer, which could be significant in itself. A cover-up of some kind involving the government's own files?" I shrugged. "Well, we don't know enough yet to do any useful theorizing, so let's leave it for the moment. Right now you have an important decision to make. . . . But first I want you to take it for a little. Get used to it."

"Take it? Oh." She hesitated as I pulled the Mazda off onto the shoulder and stopped the motor. "I don't really know after all these years. . . . Can't I try it first on a little empty road somewhere?"

"Easier here," I said. "You'll discover that little empty roads are kind of hard to come by these days, Miss van Winkle. Here they're only coming at you from one direction." After we'd switched seats, I said, "There's a manual choke over there to the left, but you only need it the first thing in the morning. Gearshift, neutral. Okay, start her up with the key, good. Hand brake, off. It's a five-speed shift, but don't worry about fifth right now, it's a kind of overdrive. All clear astern, go for it."

It was a pleasure to see how fast confidence returned to her as she swung the car back onto the highway and worked her way through the gears, taking it up to speed. After some experimental jockeying and lane-changing, she found fifth gear—with a defiant little glance in the direction of the bossy guy who'd told her not to worry about it—and settled back in her seat, relaxing behind the wheel.

Her face was alive with the excitement of remembering the long-disused techniques of driving. More clearly than before, under the prison-worn flesh of the woman she was, I could see the ghost of the strikingly lovely girl she'd been. I found myself speculating about how she might look even now if she lost a few pounds—well, quite a few pounds—and tightened up the slack, neglected muscles with systematic exercise, and got a little sun on the tired, dead-white skin. . . . The Helm Ex-Convict Rehabilitation Service, I thought sourly, reminding myself that this woman was supposed to be neither a friend nor a patient, but merely a useful decoy and source of information.

She spoke at last: "Now what was that tremendous decision I had to make, Matt?"

"Your hair," I said.

"My *hair*?"

I said, "Because of this council of war coming up, we'll be stopping early in a place called Stockville up ahead. They have two establishments to choose from, Madelon's La Mode and Blanche's Beauty Boutique. If we were superstitious we'd send you to Madelon because of the similarity in the names; but my spies inform me that Blanche is supposed to be the superior operator. But you'd better be ready to tell her how you want it done—"

Madeleine said stiffly, "What is this, a project to bolster the poor convict-lady's morale? My hair is perfectly fine the way it is, thank you!"

I said, "Actually, it's lousy the way it is, and you don't really like it that way yourself, do you? And afterwards you'll visit Milady's Fashions and Offenberg's Department Store, and use those credit cards in your purse. That suit is okay for driving, but I think a simple little dress for dinners along the way, don't you? And a pair of good-looking slacks, maybe, and some jeans for really rugged going, and shoes and shirts and socks and what they used to call unmentionables—underwear to you—to go with everything. If you want to give your lecherous traveling companion a treat, you might even pick up a few pairs of nice sheer nylons and throw away those cast-iron hose you're wearing; you've got very nice legs for an unperson. Sorry we can't make it New York or Paris, but do the best you can with Stockville. A new suitcase will probably be needed to handle the overflow. Have fun. Don't look over your shoulder. Act like a dame on a mad shopping spree after eight years in pokey, a dame who doesn't really believe her life is in much danger. Questions?"

She was silent for a moment. "I see. You'll be watching?"

"Somebody'll be watching. We want to know if Bennett has pulled his people off, at least temporarily, and we want to see if anybody else is interested."

She shivered a little. "And if you won't be watching—I suppose having you trailing along behind me trying to look invisible, all six feet plus of you, would give the show away—what will you be doing?"

I sighed. "I'm sorry you asked that question. Because, to be perfectly honest, I'll be visiting a porno shop and looking at all the pictures of nekkid ladies lying on their backs with their knees apart."

I was wrong. They weren't just lying on their backs. Some of the positions were really rather remarkable and, I would think, uncomfortable. And mostly total nudity was not displayed; filmy stockings and sexy little garter belts seemed to be the uniform of the day. Or night. Waiting, I worked my way along the wall racks full of fascinating literature—at least it must have been fascinating to somebody, considering the substantial prices asked. Personally, I'm a sucker for a pretty face, a pretty breast, a slim waist, a neat buttock, a slender leg, or a trim ankle; but I can't help feeling that when you've seen one vulva you've seen them all. Which undoubtedly reflects my inhibited youth; probably I'm just too embarrassed by such an intimate display to appreciate what I'm viewing.

There were a couple of other men in the place who paid no attention to each other or to me. Jackson came in at last and proceeded into the section devoted to cubicles in which, for a quarter a throw, you could watch feelthy movies. After a little I followed him to the specified booth. When I entered, he was engrossed in the fuzzy images being thrown onto a moderately large screen by some kind of a projection device. They depicted one naked man and two naked women doing odd things to each other in ring-around-the-rosy fashion.

I studied Jackson's face for a moment in the flickering illumination bounced off the screen. I knew that he'd got himself badly chopped up on a mission some time ago, but not badly enough to warrant his retirement; he was now relegated to backup duty helping out front-line heroes like me. I'd found him conscientious and efficient in the past.

"What went wrong?" I asked.

He looked surprised. "Hell, I was going to ask you! All of a sudden you're taking on the whole damn OFS single-handed. We closed in, of course, in case you needed help; but you seemed to have things under control so we stayed out of sight. Next time, if you decide to tackle the U.S. Army, or Navy, tip us off ahead of time, will you, so we know who the bad guys are."

I nodded. "Fair enough, but unfortunately I can't tell you who the bad guys are. So in the future let's just go by the good guys, and that's us. Only us. Anybody else, *anybody* else, assume he's wearing a black hat and take it from there. I don't care if J. Edgar Hoover and Wild Bill Donovan come back from whatever paradise, or otherwise, they're inhabiting now, and claim Mrs. Ellershaw jointly for the FBI and the good old OSS, I don't care if the CIA gets into the act, or the United Federation of Christian Churches if there is such a thing, or the cop on the corner or the crossing guard at the local elementary school—they don't get anywhere near the lady, and I want to know they're coming so I can keep them from getting anywhere near her."

Jackson said, a bit stiffly, "Sorry. Maybe I've just heard too many lectures about interdepartmental cooperation. I saw them arrive, of course, but who can miss the beak on that Bennett character? I figured, if the head of the Office of Federal Security wanted to talk to you, or the woman, it wasn't my place to interfere."

"Next time, don't be so modest. Interfere."

"I said I was sorry."

I grinned. "Don't get mad, amigo. It's a loused-up mess, and I don't blame you for being confused. I'm kind of mixed up myself. Any repercussions eastwards?"

Jackson laughed, dismissing his momentary resentment. "Are you kidding? Bennett has blown every microwave relay between here and Washington. A strong protest, to put it mildly. A poor little OFS agent disfigured for life. A personal assault on a top OFS official—*the* top OFS official. But the word from our side is I'm to congratulate you on your forbearance in not shooting that man Dellenbach, since apparently he had a gun in his hand when he was taken, as did his associate. Counter-protest: armed OFS agents threatening our poor little overworked operatives just doing their poor little overworked jobs. It's been made clear to the Director of the Office of Federal Security that our people are not, repeat not, required to tolerate interference by his pistol-waving goons and he'd better keep them out of our hair if he doesn't want to lose them. I'm to instruct you, however, in the interest of intragovernment amity, to maintain your commendable restraint—unless the risk becomes unacceptable, in which case you can count on full support from the head office."

I laughed. "Hey, it sounds as if he got mad for a change."

Jackson smiled thinly. "The picture I get is Bennett tried to threaten him with political reprisals, and you know how he loves *that*. Now you're to determine whether Mr. Bennett has a special motive for meddling in our business or whether he's simply hunting publicity in his usual greedy fashion by horning in on the Great CADRE Spy Scandal eight years late."

I said, "I think I've already got an answer to that. Back eight-nine years ago, Bennett was the federal investigating officer on the case."

Jackson whistled softly. "Interesting! How come we didn't know that?"

"Very interesting," I said. "I figure the files in the computer must have been doctored somehow, at least enough to keep his name from being turned up by routine inquiries like ours. I think the matter should be checked out, to learn how it happened and who was behind it, don't you?"

"I'll pass your suggestion along."

I hesitated. "Indications are that, contrary to official expectations, we've got an innocent woman on our hands. If there's trouble, and I'm not available, see that she's treated accordingly, will you?"

Jackson looked at me curiously; then he shrugged. "You deal it, we'll play it."

The blurry figures on the screen were now imitating a three-layer cake, not all layers oriented in the same direction.

"What do you need?" Jackson asked after studying the new arrangement of images thoughtfully.

"Ask him for everything on the OFS he can get. In his present mood he should be happy to go along." I grimaced in the wavering dusk of the porno booth. "Hell, I can remember when they were nothing but a bunch of glorified night watchmen responsible for the security of federal installations. Then apparently something happened around Santa Fe and Los Alamos, and a bright young scientific genius disappeared along with a mystery woman with Red associations, and the guy's pretty wife was railroaded into prison. Assuming that we're right about her innocence, or I am. And less than a decade later these time-clock-punching stumblebums are one of the nation's top law-enforcement agencies, run by the very guy who conducted the investigation into the alleged crimes of the Ellershaws and their alleged female accomplice. A guy we know from experience—at least I've met him before, if you haven't—would screw his own grandmother and then smother the old lady with a pillow to keep her from telling."

"I don't know what you're trying to say," Jackson said.

"That makes two of us," I said ruefully. "But I want all the dirt on that outfit that's to be got, and a complete rundown on Bennett himself. Maybe it's a lead, maybe it's a big waste of time, but since we don't know what the hell we're looking for, we might as well look for it at the OFS. While you're checking out Bennett, or somebody is, have his boy Dellenbach investigated as well. Jim Dellenbach. And the guy who was with him, whose name I never got."

"Roger Nolan."

"Thanks. Apparently he's on Bennett's first team, too, along with an older agent named Philip Burdette, who could just be a cynical old warhorse sticking with a crooked outfit out of misplaced loyalty or simple inertia. But let's find out about all of them. And see if there's anything new on the Center for Advanced Defense Research; and what the hell defenses do they research up that hidden canyon, anyway? I'd also like a complete rundown on the Santa Fe law firm of Baron and Walsh. Who's Baron? Who's Walsh? Who else is important there? What about a fairly recent partner named Walter Maxon? And then there's a mystery woman named Bella Kravecki involved somehow; check her out, please. Considering the amount of background material I waded through before meeting our subject at the jailhouse gate, I don't seem to know a damn thing, which is kind of suspicious in itself."

"That all?" Jackson asked dryly when I stopped for breath.

"It'll do for now." I frowned. "But if you need more manpower to cover us, for God's sake get it. All this interest in Mrs. Ellershaw, people shooting at her with shotguns, people slapping her around after she's spent eight years locked up . . . You wouldn't think she could be a threat to anybody at this late date, but having her at liberty seems to be making some folks awfully nervous, and I'd like to know why. So let's do our best to keep the lady alive and free."

I threw a final glance at the screen as I left. They were doing it standing up now, but I couldn't figure out exactly what. Well, there seemed to be a lot of things I couldn't figure out.

CHAPTER 8

MADELEINE was late getting back to the motel, late enough to worry me. I'd walked back from town, a two-mile hike, leaving her the car; I thought she'd get used to handling it in traffic more easily without having me breathing down her neck. It had been a pleasant walk after all the driving, and I'd been glad to be relieved of the responsibility of watching over her for a little. Besides, it was a certain strain being in the constant company of that prison-battered ego. But when twilight came without her, even though it was an early winter twilight, I started worrying. Finally, I stepped outside to see if she was in sight yet.

It was another motel in the same chain with the same liquorless restaurant—only a coffee shop here, as a matter of fact—and the same low sprawling buildings, again built within sight of the transcontinental freeway that here ran a quarter of a mile away on a raised ramp that lifted it up to the cloverleaf overpass to the west. I'd walked under that, coming from town, passing on the way a reasonable-looking restaurant that did advertise cocktails, which I'd earmarked for our evening meal. However, at the moment food was far from my mind, although a drink would have been welcome.

Then I saw the little silver arrowhead of a car approaching from town, headlights on in the growing dusk; and I was surprised at the relief I felt, surprised and disturbed. I mean, this defeated penitentiary graduate with her incipient middle-aged spread was nothing to me but a job. Wasn't she? But I had to admit I was very relieved to see her.

She must have spotted me standing there awaiting her; she blinked the lights twice as she turned into the motel driveway. I knew from this that she must be feeling pretty good. She wasn't just greeting me; that was only the excuse. She was having childish fun seeing the little sports car's tricky retracting headlights go up and down. When she pulled up in front, I walked clear around the car before opening the door for her, noting that she was beginning to take such courtesies for granted.

"All four fenders intact," I said without expression. "A miracle."

She made a face at me, getting out of the car. "You didn't tell me about those crazy lights. When did they start putting those funny stalks on the steering column? I had to look in the instruction manual. And the push-button trunk release on the dashboard! There I was, going clear around back every time to use the key."

"Things are tough all over," I said. "Let me give you a hand with the loot."

"Matt."

Her face was only a pale blur in the growing twilight, partially obscured by the dark silk scarf she was wearing about her head to protect her newly done hair. Even so, I could see the grim lines of surrender and despair had softened considerably.

"Yes?" I said.

"Please inform the treasurer of your organization that I had a lovely time spending his money. Thank you. And now I need to shower and change; and then I think the lady would permit the gentleman to take her out to dinner if he felt so inclined."

But she took her time about getting ready. After showering and putting on, among other things, some more respectable trousers, I sat down to read my outdoors magazine while I waited; but the long silence next door began to worry me. At last I tossed the magazine aside and marched to the connecting door, hesitated, and knocked.

"Madeleine?"

To my relief, her voice answered immediately: "Come in, Matt."

She was sitting in front of the dresser mirror, doing nothing that I could see, just sitting there. After a moment, she rose and turned to face me, smoothing down her dress. There was an odd little note of defiance in her voice when she spoke to me..

"Do I look all right?"

The transformation wasn't quite overwhelming, of course. She wasn't going to stop traffic on Times Square or even Main Street. Still, there was enough of a change to make my breath catch sharply. The beauty shop had put life back into her hair and cut and shaped it skillfully and arranged it becomingly about her face. Careful makeup emphasized the fine eyes and the strong, sensitive mouth. The simple, long-sleeved, zip-up-the-front beige dress she'd selected, while obviously not expensive, had good tailored lines that made her too-heavy figure look, if not exactly girlish, at least quite trim and pleasant. It was helped by the new sheer nylons and the new high-heeled pumps that flattered her always lovely legs and ankles.

"Hey," I said, "I'm glad I put on a pair of pants with creases in them."

"Don't overwhelm the lady with your fulsome praise."

She grinned briefly and was serious again, a little shame-faced. "Do you know what took me so long, Matt? I've just been sitting here trying to muster the courage. . . . I've suddenly discovered that I'm shy, damn it. The first time I've dressed up for a man in over eight years! You won't believe it, but I've been sitting here all dithery and self-conscious and afraid to knock on the door because I was afraid my goddamn sinister bodyguard wouldn't approve of my appearance! How utterly ridiculous can you get?"

I said, "You look beautiful."

"Let's not overdo it," she said dryly. "Just tell the timid wench she's not completely revolting for a change, and take her out and feed her, please."

On the way out to the car, she had to take my arm to steady herself; and I felt a frightening surge of sympathy and affection for this woman who, having once had everything, was now having to learn how to live all over again, even how to walk in high heels. The restaurant beyond the underpass was a rustic place with a big fireplace boasting a genuine fire, and copper cooking utensils hanging from the ceiling. The dark wooden tabletops were two inches thick, and the waitresses wore gray Puritan-type dresses with little bonnets to match. Unsurprisingly, the place was called the Pilgrim Inn. We ordered drinks, and did our menu research while waiting for them to arrive.

When they did, and we'd given our dinner orders, Madeleine said, sipping her martini, "You're going to have to watch me. I'm not used to this stuff yet." She regarded me across the table. "You look like a man with more questions on his mind. You might as well start asking."

I hesitated. "I hate to spoil a pleasant evening with a lovely lady with a lot of grim business."

She shook her head gently. "Please, Matt. I'm not a lovely lady, I'm a barely presentable ex-convict who's trying to learn who Madeleine Rustin Ellershaw really is

87

after everything that's happened to her. And a lot of glib, phony compliments don't help me at all."

I said, "Sorry. I'll consider my wrist slapped. Okay, we've decided that you're not the Mata Hari type, right? But I still don't have a clear picture of your husband. What about Dr. Roy Ellershaw? How does he stack up as a mastermind of espionage?" She started to speak quickly, angrily, and I held up my hand. "Whoa, there! Don't jump down my throat. He was your husband and you loved him. Or he is your husband and you love him. Depending on his present state of existence. But dead or alive he was or is a man, not an immaculate, infallible saint. Or to put it differently: even assuming he was or is a great guy, isn't it possible that he could have done what he's supposed to have done for very pure, idealistic motives?" She didn't answer immediately, and I went on: "CADRE. The Center for Advanced Defense Research. When they say defense research they generally mean attack research, these double-talk days. Could your husband have found himself working on an offensive weapon so terrible that he felt obliged to expose it in the hope of preventing its further development? Or distribute its plans worldwide to keep one nation—even his own nation, our nation—from having this fearful advantage and, quite possibly, using it?"

She shook her head quickly. "No, Matt. Roy was a true scientist. He believed that anything that could be known, should be known, and inevitably would be known sooner or later. Society would just have to figure out ways of coping with it. No, I can't see Roy trying to stop, or betray, any scientific research, no matter where it might lead. And if he had felt driven to do it, which he wouldn't, he most certainly wouldn't have involved me deliberately in his act of conscience, the way he did by giving me those papers for safekeeping. In fact he'd have tried very hard to shield me from the consequences."

We waited in silence while our rather pretty young Pilgrim lady put our dinners before us and walked away, her long skirts whispering. The restaurant was about half full. The customers were mostly quiet talkers and eaters, but a three-kid family at a round table in the corner made itself heard occasionally, reminding me, for some reason, that I had offspring of my own somewhere, although they were hardly kids any longer. I couldn't see anybody who looked like a dangerous assassin, but they mostly don't. Anyway, he wouldn't come where I could get a look at his face if he could avoid it.

I asked, "Have you ever tried to figure out just what really happened, Madeleine?"

"Of course I have!" She was indignant. "When the roof falls on you and squashes you flat you try to understand what went wrong, don't you? I've practically gone mad trying to figure it out!"

I shook my head. "I don't think you've really tried, not using your trained brains the way they should be used. I don't think you ever tackled it systematically and, let's say, suspiciously. Did you ever analyze your harrowing experiences thoroughly, working on the assumption that everything you believed was true was true, and everything you'd been told was true was probably untrue, no matter who told it to you?"

She looked at me for a moment across the little table, frowning. "I didn't quite follow all that. Run it past me again, please."

I said, "I think you never stopped taking certain things for granted. I think you always assumed that certain things were facts that weren't. I think you believed that certain people had to be telling the truth when they were really lying like hell. And I don't think you had enough faith in your own feelings and instincts; I don't think you ever followed your beliefs to their logical conclusions."

I saw dawning interest in her eyes. "Go on, Matt."

"Well, let's start with your husband," I said. "You don't for a moment believe he was a traitor-spy, right? You feel he's dead, probably killed to keep him quiet about something very disturbing he'd discovered—you

89

said he'd had things on his mind those last few weeks—but also to give an impression of guilty flight that automatically condemned him as a criminal and, by association, you as well. Have I got it pretty straight?"

She licked her lips. "Yes. Yes, that's what I thought—still think—but I could never get anybody to take the idea seriously."

"Now you've got me, you lucky girl," I said. "So we take that for one of our basic facts: Roy Ellershaw, murdered. You learned it in a dream, nobody's come up with a body, but so what? Nobody's come up with a live Roy Ellershaw, either, and they've been looking hard. We're assuming that what we believe is true is true, so let's see where this takes us. Your Roy hurried out of the house after receiving a mysterious phone call—"

"They claimed it was a warning that he was about to be arrested."

"I know, you told me; but we pay no attention to their claims. We know they're all pathological prevaricators, right? We assume that somebody decoyed him out of the house with that call so he could be grabbed and spirited away and killed, perhaps along with the subversive Bella. . . . Where and when was she last seen?"

"Bella Kravecki's movements on that night don't seem to have been clearly established," Madeleine said. "All that ever came out was that when they went to her motel to arrest her she was gone. Well, the man at the desk remembered that she'd stopped by to check for mail and messages a little earlier in the evening. She was wearing jeans as usual, and a purple silk blouse and a big concha belt and a squash-blossom necklace; she'd picked up some Indian jewelry since she'd come to Santa Fe, and she liked to display it. It made her look like a dressed-up horse. All right, I didn't like her. Neither did Roy. A big, dark, overbearing woman in her early thirties; I guess you could call her handsome. She got a phone call too, they remembered. That's all anybody knows. When they came for her, her clothes and luggage were still in her room, her rental car was still in its slot in front of her unit, but no Bella."

"Well, to hell with Bella," I said. "We don't know enough about her to theorize about her—except that your husband did *not* run off with her for amorous purposes, right?"

"Roy wouldn't have touched . . . !" Madeleine checked herself, and spoke in a subdued voice. "Right."

I said, "So we assume that your Roy was lured out of his house, your house, so that he could be taken captive. We assume that he was then killed—killed that very night around two in the morning, if we accept your dream, so it probably didn't happen too far from Santa Fe. Correct?"

Her face was pale. She nodded. "Yes. That's what I think, what I've always thought."

"How did he die?"

She moistened her lips again. "I don't know that. How could I know it?"

I said, "I told you you weren't using those good brains of yours. You heard him scream as he died, didn't you? If you want to call it hearing. What kind of a scream was it? A scream of pain as they tortured him to death? A last wild cry of protest as somebody put a gun to his head and pulled the trigger?"

She swallowed hard. She closed her eyes for several seconds, recalling that shocking night nine years ago when her successful, beautiful life had, for all practical purposes, come to an end in a dingy cell in the city jail. She opened them again, wide and dark in her pale face.

"It was a . . . a falling scream, Matt." Her voice was almost inaudible. "He was falling, falling, screaming, screaming; and then the scream was cut off short. . . . Oh, God!"

After a little, I reached across the table to take her hand. "I'm sorry. I didn't mean for it to get so rough. Do you want to stop?"

She squeezed my fingers lightly and freed herself. "No,

I'm all right. Let's go on with . . . with your game. Can we figure out where . . . it was done?"

I said, "You tell me."

"High?" she said in a tentative way. "A cliff? An airplane? No, if they'd shoved him off, or out of, anything like that, the . . . the body would have been found eventually, wouldn't it? Low, then. A well? But they're mostly drilled wells out there, and nobody could fall down one of those narrow pipes. There are very few dug wells, these days. So, a mine shaft."

She looked at me for confirmation. I nodded approvingly. "Now you're getting the idea. It seems likely, doesn't it? There are dozens of old mines within easy driving distance of Santa Fe. Gold, silver, coal, you name it. Used to be you could wander around that open country at will and you'd find old holes everywhere. Fences were just for cows in those days. If you really wanted to be dog-in-the-manger and keep people off your property you were supposed to use signs, but very few landowners bothered with POSTED or NO TRESPASSING signs. The good old days of the West. Nowadays the place is crawling with pompous characters with eastern ideas of property who think there's something sacred about a few lousy strands of barbed wire. And many of the old mines have been bought up, and fenced and locked up, by speculators gambling that they can revive them profitably once the price of whatever-it-is gets up a bit higher. That was true even nine years ago. So you can no longer count on finding a nice accessible deserted mine shaft any time you've got a corpse on your hands."

Madeleine was looking at me curiously. "You sound as if you'd lived in New Mexico a long time. I didn't realize that."

"I thought I told you. That was one reason I was picked for this operation." I shrugged. "Hell, I was brought up in the state; I even lived in Santa Fe for several years, later, back when I was married." I saw the question in her eyes and went on: "It was nice while it lasted, but she found out a little too much about the nasty character she'd picked to father her children, so she took off with the kids. A very gentle and nonviolent girl. That was back in the days I thought for a while I could turn gentle and nonviolent myself, but somehow it never seemed to work out." I grimaced. "That was a long time ago. Skip it."

Madeleine was silent for a little, watching me; then she said, "And later you met your cave girl?"

"My what?"

"The archaeologist lady who knew all about caves, the one who got the same telepathic message from that old high priest you told me about. Your voice changed when you mentioned her. Is she still your ... your girl, Matt?"

I shook my head. "She was for a little, whatever you want to call it, but she went back to her career and her pompous prick of a husband. A very nice, very conscientious lady with a strong sense of duty. Shall we catalogue my love life some other time when we have a month or two to spare?"

Madeleine laughed softly. "I'm sorry, it's really none of my business. Just a nosy bitch."

I said, "Locating the mine will be your first order of business when we get to Santa Fe. Well, after you've settled your private affairs with your dad's lawyer. Assuming that you're still willing to work along with us on this, of course."

She said, "What else would I be doing, getting a job scrubbing floors somewhere?" The old bitterness was back in her voice as she went on harshly: "'Expert scrubwoman seeks new position. University graduate and former member of the bar. Eight years of experience. Concrete prison floors our specialty. Last place of employment will supply glowing references.'" She shook her head abruptly. "Sorry. It keeps sneaking up on me. Yes, Mr. Helm, I will be happy to cooperate with your organization. All you have to do is keep me alive, although sometimes I wonder if I'm worth the trouble to you. Or to me."

I grinned at her. "Let's make a deal, Mrs. Ellershaw. I'll skip the phony compliments if you skip the phony despair. You don't have to work so hard for my sympathy. I'm a most sympathetic fellow."

There was a little silence. Then she smiled reluctantly. "Ouch! I'll consider myself spanked. I guess things really aren't all that desperate, are they? I've still got four limbs and a head, and a nice man to drive me around and buy me clothes and feed me, at least for the time being. . . . All right. I'll make a thorough search of the records."

"It's more in your line than mine; I wouldn't know where to start looking," I said. "Every mining property within fifty miles of Santa Fe, and the name of the current owner—correction, the owner as of nine years ago. These are careful people; they wouldn't have left it to chance. They had it all figured out how they were going to keep that bright and inquisitive young lady attorney, Mrs. Ellershaw, from nosing around afterwards; and they must have laid their plans for disposing of her scientific-genius husband with equal care. They'd have had a suitable place to take him, a good deep shaft where he'd never be found, and where they wouldn't be spotted driving in and out."

Madeleine swallowed. "I think it's safe to assume that the property was actually owned by one of . . . of them, don't you? I mean, you'd hardly go up to a friend or acquaintance and ask for the key to Starlight Number Three, or whatever, because you'd like to drop a dead body down it next Wednesday. But I also think we can assume that the man who had the property then probably has it now. He wouldn't have sold it complete with an incriminating"—she stopped, and swallowed again, and forced herself to go on—"an incriminating s-skeleton for the new owner to find. So I'll concentrate on the properties that have been in the same hands for that many years."

It was kind of exciting to see the fine lawyer-mind beginning to function again in the once fine woman-body she'd also begun to take some pride in again after the years of neglect.

I said, "Then we'll check your list against the names of everybody we turn up even remotely connected with the case. If the same name turns up on both lists, bingo."

"Matt."

I glanced at her. "Problem?"

She spoke wryly: "If I'd ever got up in court with a line of deduction as shaky as this—based on the dream of an exhausted and frightened girl, for heaven's sake!—I'd have been laughed out of my profession."

I said, "Lady, when you got up in court with plausible evidence and sensible logic you were drummed out of your profession and thrown into the can for a good many years, remember?"

She winced. "Well, it's a point, I guess. What other wild flights of fancy do you want us to follow?"

"We haven't finished with your husband," I told her. "We've agreed to operate on the assumption that Roy Ellershaw was murdered, but his death doesn't necessarily prove . . . I mean, thieves have fallen out before. He could have been silenced because he was involved with our mysterious villains in something big and dangerous, rather than because he wasn't. We're working from your instincts, so let's have your instinctive verdict. Roy Ellershaw, guilty or innocent?"

"I've told you! Innocent!"

"But innocent of what? From what you've said, I gather that there actually was a bank box stuffed full of fat, mysterious envelopes full of mysterious papers. Put there by you. Given to you by him. Your husband. In a disturbed state of mind, you said. So just how innocent was he?" When she didn't answer immediately, I said,

"Think hard. Would the Roy Ellershaw you loved and married have stolen important classified scientific documents entrusted to his care, for any reason? Is there *any* way he could have rationalized such an act to himself, being the man he was?"

She hesitated. "But the papers *were* there, Matt! We've got to face—"

"We don't got to face nothing, baby. If we don't believe it, if we find it inconceivable, it just ain't so. Give me an answer."

"The answer is no!" she said with sudden vehemence. "No, no, no!"

"And having stolen them, whether for idealistic or mercenary purposes, could this man who loved you possibly have given them to you to hide for him, putting you into terrible danger—actually sending you to prison and ruining your career and life as it turned out? You've already answered that, I think, but say it again."

"No!" she breathed. "Oh, God, no! That's the incomprehensible thing, the horrible thing! It happened—it must have happened—but it couldn't have happened. It didn't make any sense at all. It wasn't Roy at all, he just *couldn't* have done it, any of it! But—"

I said harshly, "You just won't play the goddamned game, Ellershaw. Never mind the lousy buts. He couldn't have done it so he didn't do it. We go on from there: he didn't do what he was accused of. He didn't do what you thought he'd done even though it almost killed you to think so. So just what the hell *did* Dr. Roy Ellershaw do during that time you sensed he was seriously troubled about something? Let's take it in two pieces. First, what did he do? Second, why did he leave you, his beloved wife, stuck with it?"

"But if he didn't steal anything—"

I shook my head irritably. "Who says he didn't steal anything? Nobody said anything like that, lawyer girl. Keep your eye on the ball. What was it we really said? It

96

wasn't that at all. Sure he could have grabbed something if he thought it really needed grabbing. We merely agreed that he was incapable of stealing secret scientific documents for which he was responsible. So obviously what he stole, and had you put away for him, wasn't scientific documents and he wasn't responsible for them."

There was a little silence. Madeleine shook her head in a bewildered way and said, "But several CADRE scientists testified at my trial. . . ." She stopped, watching my face carefully. "Matt, are you trying to say that what Roy gave me to put in the bank, and what I did put there, wasn't the material that figured in court? But that's crazy!"

I shrugged. "Crazy or not, that's where our logic leads us. And it explains a great many things, doesn't it? Did you identify the stuff yourself? Could you identify it?"

She shook her head again. "As I said on the witness stand, I never really examined the materials Roy gave me. The envelopes looked the same. I had to admit that. But they were sealed, and I never looked inside. I told them that, too, but of course they didn't believe me." She licked her lips. "You mean . . . you mean I went to p-prison for helping to steal something I never really touched, something Roy never touched? You mean somebody took away the innocent papers Roy gave me to store for him and substituted the incriminating material on the strength of which I was convicted and sentenced? My God, that possibility never occurred to us!"

I said, "I told you you'd taken too much for granted. Of course, it's just a theory so far, but it fits pretty well, doesn't it? And of course we don't really know how innocent the original box contents were. Clearly they were dangerous to somebody, or that somebody wouldn't have gone to all this trouble to get them back and kill or discredit anyone connected with taking them. That's why you were pressed so hard to confess, of course. As long as you remained a respected and respectable member of the community you were a threat, but once you'd admitted to being a lousy sneaking spy, they didn't really care whether you were locked up or walking around on parole or probation or whatever. Your word would have been worthless, just the shrill self-serving yapping of a confessed criminal." I frowned. "The stuff that was used against you, I suppose it was properly identified."

"Yes." She hesitated. "Well, within the limits imposed by security. Only the envelopes were displayed in court, but the contents were described in general terms, by CADRE scientists having the proper impressive clearance, as coming from Roy's laboratory. It was all research data referring to the new LS-system that was being developed at the time. We were told that LS stood for Laser Shield. When perfected, the system was supposed to make us all safe from enemy missiles, very sci-fi. I didn't understand it, and I doubt that the jury did. All we understood was that it was terribly important to the safety of the country, and that anybody who'd let the Russians have it, and perhaps learn how to penetrate it, was a wicked traitor to America." She shook her head quickly. "Legally speaking, I shouldn't use the word traitor, although of course that's what everybody was thinking. But in law treason is a very specific crime that's very hard to prove. It requires two witnesses, among other things. They never tried to pin it on me, officially; they were satisfied with the lesser charges. But of course the implication was always there."

I nodded. "But the invention involved was definitely a defensive weapon? It wasn't anything that could possibly have tortured your husband's conscience, as I suggested earlier?"

"That's right."

I said, "So there must have been a switch. Dr. Ellershaw got something and gave it to you for safekeeping, we still don't know what or why. And something altogether different turned up in the hands of the prosecution to convict you."

"But how could—"

98

"For heaven's sake, Ellershaw!" I said irritably. "You've got a mind, why won't you use it? What investigating officer probably opened that safe-deposit box and what do we know about him? The likeliest candidate is your friend Bennett, the fastest slap in the West, isn't it? One of the finest specimens of negative integrity around. Either he got those envelopes in the normal course of his investigation and looked inside and saw how he could cash in on them if he could only arrange a convincing substitution, or he'd been bought in advance and told what to look for and what to do about it if he found it. Probably the latter; the people we're dealing with obviously don't leave things to chance. But it's no wonder Bennett's nervous about having you loose again, knowing how he framed you. He'd sleep much better now if he could have tormented you into running yesterday, and put an 'accidental' bullet into the back of your head."

Madeleine shivered a little. "But what was in the box originally, Matt?"

I shook my head and said, "We can't even guess, yet, what it was your husband stumbled on. All we know is that it made him some extremely dangerous enemies. Ask yourself how a dim bulb like Bennett ever got the job of Director of the Office of Federal Security, not to mention the political backing to make that outfit as big as it has become. Obviously, Bennett took his payoff in prestige and power—but of course whoever's behind him probably had very good reasons for setting up a powerful law-enforcement agency run by an ambitious but not very bright man who'd jump obediently at the crack of the whip. And if they were that strong, whoever they are, providing Bennett with the top-secret pieces of paper he needed to destroy you wasn't very difficult for them."

Madeleine licked her lips. "It's . . . kind of scary, isn't it? People powerful enough to buy an agent of the OFS with promises and keep those promises. People ruthless enough to commit murder, and clever and influential enough to get away with it. People influential enough to rush a criminal case to trial and get somebody railroaded into the worst federal pen in the country on . . . on less than convincing evidence. And finally, people with access to secret materials in a high-security installation. . . . It seems to have been, well, quite a can of worms that Roy opened up, somehow. So they kidnaped him—"

I interrupted: "My guess is that Bennett himself called your husband out of the house, claiming official OFS business of some kind, perhaps connected with the stuff in your bank box, the original material we still don't know about. It seems very probable that Dr. Ellershaw had actually got in touch with Bennett quietly, knowing him through his security duties and wanting to report those dangerous discoveries, whatever they were, to somebody official as soon as possible. Your ivory-tower husband would probably have been naive enough to take for granted that, since Bennett was a government man, he could be trusted. Just as he apparently took for granted that if something was locked up in a safe-deposit box, it was safe. And it's very likely that Bennett learned from your husband that he hadn't confided in you at all; that you didn't know what was in those sealed envelopes you'd put away for him in the box you'd hired for him."

Madeleine nodded. "You're probably right. That must be why they didn't feel compelled to have me killed, too. As I said before, both of us dying or disappearing at once would have attracted too much attention, anyway. They were probably very happy to know I wasn't much of a threat. I could just be got out of the way with a phony espionage charge to keep me from making a nuisance of myself. That also made Roy's disappearance seem logical—it gave him a motive for vanishing, along with Bella, his Communist contact." She hesitated. "Do you think Bella was, well, planted on us deliberately?"

"It seems likely," I said. "That's another thing we'll have to work on. I've already asked for a thorough check on the woman. But all this doesn't answer the final question: Why did Roy Ellershaw put this dangerous material into the care of the wife he loved? He must have known she could be badly hurt by having it. As she was."

There was a little silence. At last Madeleine said quietly, "Maybe he gave it to me because it was so terribly important, Matt. Because he was doing something of which he knew I'd approve, and he knew he was in danger and might be killed. He trusted me to carry on after his death, not anticipating that . . . that I'd be put out of circulation, too. I'd like to think that. I'd like to think he had that much faith in me even though . . . even though I was so damned preoccupied with my own important affairs that I never gave him a chance to tell me about it." There was harsh self-contempt in her voice.

"It sounds plausible up to a point," I said. "Well, we'll know more when we find out what kind of a deadly secret it was he'd stumbled on. The question is, *did* he try to tell you about it somehow? Posthumously, so to speak."

She swallowed hard. "You mean . . . a letter from the grave? 'Dear Madeleine: I can't seem to catch you long enough to talk to you in this life so I'm writing you from the next to explain why I have put this terrible responsibility on your . . . on your shoulders.'" She couldn't go on.

"Don't be so hard on yourself," I said. "It's quite possible that Roy Ellershaw felt you were safer knowing as little as possible, as long as he was alive. But unless the papers, documents, photographs, diagrams, formulas, or whatever he left you were completely self-explanatory, he'd want to let you know how he'd got them and, presumably, how he wanted you to use them. Maybe it was all in that safe-deposit box; but then again, being a careful scientist type, maybe he arranged for a backup message somehow." I hesitated. "And knowing you wouldn't be using the material he'd given you unless he was dead, he'd also want to say goodbye, wouldn't he? That's item two on your agenda: to figure out where your husband could possibly have hidden a final message to you—"

But she wasn't listening. She spoke in a flat and expressionless voice: "Yes, of course. He'd want to say goodbye, although it's hard to see why he'd bother. I wasn't much use as a wife, so busy with my own career, when it came to a real crisis involving my husband's very life, was I? I don't . . . seem to be much real use for anything; I couldn't even do a lousy little stint in prison without falling completely apart and trying to kill myself." Her face twisted in self-contempt. "Look at me now; look what I've let myself become! God, look at the pasty-faced middle-aged female slob trying to turn the clock back, trying to imitate the fashionable and attractive young professional woman she used to be, in a cheap new dress and bargain-basement shoes and a small-town hairdo! Matt, take me back to the motel, please."

As I escorted her out to the car I wondered why, instead of being impatient with her manic-depressive behavior, I was feeling rather pleased with her. Then I realized that I'd just witnessed an important breakthrough. It was the first time she'd admitted that, while she'd certainly been the victim of monstrous injustices, she hadn't endured quite as well as she might have.

CHAPTER 9

IN the morning, at breakfast, she was surprisingly cheerful and wryly apologetic: "I don't know how you put up with me. It's just that I've started getting these attacks of total self-disgust, when I realize what I've let them do to me, make of me. So they put me in prison; it wasn't the end of the world. Gutless Ellershaw! No damn courage at all!"

She'd come a long way from the bitter woman at the penitentiary gates obviously blaming the whole world for her tragic condition. I told myself that I was letting myself get too involved with watching her fight her way back out of the gray limbo into which they'd thrown her, perhaps because at the beginning I'd really thought she was lost for good. But it was no business of mine. I should be concerned only with making sure she didn't slit her throat until she'd served our purposes, and that nobody did it for her.

I said, "Don't be too sure of that. With the help of your wealthy and loving parents, you'd got along on determination and hard work and a lot of brains. What occasion had you ever had to use your courage, in that sheltered lovely young life of yours? Like letting a gun lie rusting unloaded in a locked drawer. When you suddenly hear a burglar downstairs in the middle of the night, it's too late to get it out and load it even if you can find the key and the cartridges. And the action's probably too gummed up to fire after the years of neglect. And without any practice you'd probably miss your target anyway."

"You mean, it takes practice to be brave?" She smiled at me. "Well, maybe I'll be a real lioness by the time this dangerous expedition is over, but I'm not counting on it. Matt?"

"What?"

"May I drive today? We should get to Santa Fe this evening, shouldn't we? And I've got to do something to keep from thinking about the people I'm going to meet there, people I used to know who'll remember what I was, and . . . and how they'll act when they see what I am now after serving my sentence, a shabby, flabby alumna of Fort Ames U." She grinned. "Oh, God, there's the self-pity girl again. Please, Matt?"

It was wide-open country now, the real plains, treeless and desolate except along the infrequent watercourses. Even the occasional irrigated areas were bleak and bare

103

at this time of year. It was the kind of country that used to drive eastern women mad with loneliness when their land-hungry eastern men dragged them out here to settle; sometimes it drove the men mad, too. I guess if you get hooked on trees and grass at an early age you can develop quite an addiction and the withdrawal symptoms can be bad. Hell, even now when they move out to New Mexico—and lots of them do—they insist on using our scarce water to grow the damned little green lawns they can't seem to live without. But even though I no longer live out there on a permanent basis, whenever I leave the dull, safe, fertile Midwest behind, and enter this endless arid landscape with its fine hint of menace, I still feel I'm coming home.

"I forget, when do we see the mountains on this road?"

I glanced at Madeleine behind the wheel—she'd been driving steadily since morning with pauses only for gas and lunch—and I saw that in spite of the ordeal that awaited her, she shared my feeling of homecoming.

I said, "Not until we pick up the backs of the Sandias ahead, and maybe the Sangre de Cristos off to the north."

"There should be snow on the peaks," she said.

"The ski runs were hurting last year," I said. "I don't know if they've had any good snowfalls this year. But the higher peaks should be white, yes."

She said, "Matt, I don't like the smell of it."

Still a western girl no matter where she'd spent the past eight years, she'd noted it too: the oppressive stillness of the air, the sinister darkening of the sky.

I said, "I'd better have a look at the road map." I spread it out and frowned at it. "Nothing for forty miles except one little town called Riker's, and that's just a speck on the paper. . . . Oh, Jesus, there it comes!"

We'd topped a slight rise, and there was the storm ahead—a sooty black band across the horizon topped by boiling masses of dirty-gray clouds. I saw some little dots of buildings off to the right of the road about two-thirds of the way to the threatening cloud wall that blotted out everything behind it.

"That must be the town, such as it is," I said, pointing. I reached over and hit the trip odometer, setting it back to zero. "I figure about ten miles across the valley. Go for it, Mrs. Leadfoot. Let's see how close we can get while we can still see the pavement."

"Don't you want to—"

"Don't waste time talking, goose it!" As the car accelerated obediently, setting me back in my seat, I said, "I'll take it if we have to fight our way through the deep stuff. You probably haven't played around much in heavy snow lately. But we should make it before it starts piling up too high."

For a change, her laughter was pleasantly lacking in bitterness. "No, darling, I really haven't had many opportunities for practicing my skiing and snow driving lately. . . . What does that sign say?"

"RIKER'S 8 MILES." I hit the odometer again, relieved to have a more accurate zero to work from if things got so murky we had trouble spotting the exit signs. At least now we'd know when to start looking. I said, "And they have a motel, thank God. There's a billboard: MOTEL, CAFE, GAS, SOUVENIRS. We've got it made; all we have to do is make it."

"Does it hurt the speedometer to go over the top?"

I glanced at her. She was concentrating hard on her driving, urging the little car right along; but there was color in her cheeks and her eyes were brighter than I'd seen them—well, since the time we were being shot at. An intriguing and rather disturbing lady.

I said, "Hell, no, that's just one of the government's fool ideas. Since your time, so to speak. They have the odd notion you won't drive over eighty-five if that's all that shows on the dial. Take it as high as you can hold it. You can trust the tires; they're brand-new like the car, just barely broken in."

The RX-7 was howling happily now, driven the way it

should be driven, and I watched the miles click by—but we'd already lost the race. Riker's had disappeared into the menacing black front that was bearing down on us, and the first snowflakes were drifting down from the murky sky. I switched the heater to defrost, turned the fan full on, and switched on the rear-window heating element.

"Windshield wiper on the stalk to the left of the wheel," I said. "Just twist the knob counterclockwise."

"Thanks." Reluctantly, she was letting the car slow down now, as the visibility worsened rapidly. A few shadowy cars and trucks went by going east, on the other side of the wide median, but we could see nothing ahead or astern in our westbound lane. "I'd better turn on the lights, hadn't I?" Madeleine said.

"Watch out, here it comes!"

Then we were in the thick of it, in the wild twilight of the storm, with the car jolted by heavy gusts of wind, and a full-scale blizzard attacking the windshield with dense formations of swirling white flakes.

"RIKER'S 1 MILE." I read the passing sign that was almost invisible through the blowing snow. "Are you all right?"

"Fine, but I wouldn't want to buck this clear to Santa Fe."

I said, "Hell, you know you just conjured up this minor disturbance to put off the evil day."

"Maybe you think you're joking, haha," she said. "Minor disturbance, hell, I can hardly see the front of the car. . . . Ah, there's the exit sign!"

The snow was already beginning to stick, and the pavement was disappearing from sight as we pulled up in the shelter afforded by a two-story frame building, the motel, and an older one-story adobe structure that was decorated with lovely neon signs—at least they seemed lovely to us under the circumstances—reading RIKER'S CAFE–COORS BEER, and MOTEL OFFICE–VACANCY. It was a small oasis of safety in the screaming white hell of the storm.

"A little adventure for the dull jailbird lady," Madeleine said. The bitterness was back.

"You're a real little psycho, aren't you?" I said. "Up one minute, down the next. Why not just relax and take it as it comes?"

"I'm sorry. I must be a real drag to travel with."

"And don't give me that phony-meek bit, either!" I snapped.

She laughed abruptly. "Why are we fighting? Because we were scared? Of a little snow?"

I looked at her and grinned. "I think we need a drink. Luckily I bought a new bottle in Stockville. Come in with me while I register, please."

"But I'll get my shoes all . . ." She stopped, looked at me for a moment, and said in a questioning way, "Matt?"

I said, "The guy might get lucky, if there is a guy. The boys didn't spot anybody behind you during your shopping spree yesterday, but that could just mean he's smart and cautious. Right now our protection is out there on the freeway somewhere, counting snowflakes or sliding into a ditch or getting squashed by a skidding semi. And maybe our homicidal friend is out there, too, if there is a homicidal friend. But as I say, maybe he got lucky and, rolling a few miles ahead of us perhaps, ducked into the nearest haven when the storm hit, just as we did. And he happens to see a familiar little car drive up with a familiar female face at the window, and he goes boom once or twice and disappears into the blizzard never to be seen again. Two balls and one strike; but in this business all it takes is strike one and you're out. It's the kind of night—well, afternoon, although you'd never know it—when things happen, and I don't want them to happen to you."

"All right, Matt."

I started to open the car door, and stopped, and

looked at her again. "For the same reason, and because accommodations are going to be very tight around here tonight with everybody taking shelter from the storm, I'm going to put us into the same room if you think you can stand it. The Mister-and-Missis routine." I glanced at her, but her prison-trained face told me nothing. I went on: "I have a feeling something's closing in on us. Why should you have all the telepathy in the party? I got nervous about you last night—"

Her voice was gentle. "I know, I heard you come in and look at me. It made me feel . . . protected." She grimaced, and continued, briefly bitter again: "No objections, Matt. What the hell difference does it make? It's not as if that hardened felon, Mrs. Ellershaw, had any reputation left to worry about."

We signed in for a double room, Mr. and Mrs. Matthew Helm, and made our way to our assigned ground-floor unit, and hauled our luggage inside and shed our white-shouldered coats and stamped the snow off our shoes. It was really howling out there now, shaking the frame building; but once I'd figured out the control console of the all-in-one window unit—air conditioner in summer and heater in winter—we started thawing out pleasantly. It was a good big room, well worn but comfortable, and all the plumbing worked in the bathroom, although the original bathtub drain-closing mechanism had given up the ghost and been replaced by a rubber stopper.

I'd had sense enough to pick up some ice while I still had my coat on—I'd also, since there were no room phones in this desert hostelry, made a call from a chilly outside booth to report our situation—and I set out drink materials on the low round table by the curtained window. Madeleine emerged from the bathroom with her windblown hair tidy once more, but she paused to examine herself in the dresser mirror.

"I seem to have caught up with you, Matt, did you notice?" she said wryly. "I remember that one of the things that made me wary of you when we first met was that you were an older man with more experience."

"Thanks," I said dryly. "Nothing makes a man feel great like being called a senile Casanova."

She was not to be distracted. "But the woman in the office obviously thought we were a nice, well-matched couple just about the same age." Madeleine made a face at her mirror image. "Well, you can hardly blame her."

I said, "Come have some rejuvenation fluid, Grandma. Actually, I find older women quite delightful."

I watched her come towards me and take the glass I held out to her and sink into the other chair, kicking off her damp shoes and tucking her feet under her. I noted that, while she was wearing her by now somewhat travel-creased brown suit, and her pink sweater, she had on her fragile new nylons. Her heavy brown hair in its new soft arrangement still did nice things for her face. But I was disturbed by the realization that these things no longer mattered. I mean, after a couple of days in her company I had stopped judging her by how well or badly she was dressed, or how well or badly she combed her hair, or even how she might not be quite as narrow as she should be in the middle. I knew her too well now—liked her too well, damn it—to worry about such minor external details.

"Tell me about prison," I said.

Her face changed. "I don't think that's a very pleasant subject for the cocktail hour," she said stiffly.

I shook my head. "You can't dodge it forever. You've told me practically everything else. It's time you got rid of that, too, by talking about it. What made you decide to kill yourself in there, with a couple of years of your sentence already behind you?"

She licked her lips. "If I wanted to be analyzed, I'd go to a shrink," she said stiffly. Then she shrugged. "Oh, all right, I'll satisfy your morbid curiosity. But I've already told you. Walter came to see me. Walter Maxon."

I frowned. "I don't understand—"

She made an angry gesture. "Of course you don't understand! You're not a woman, a woman who was . . . was once considered rather attractive, locked up in a bleak, destroying place like that for endless years. They thought I was stuck-up," she said.

"Not surprising."

She shook her head. "I don't think I was, not really, except about the educational nonsense—I'd *been* educated, thanks. But otherwise I was simply scared shitless, trapped in that dingy environment with that kind of angry street mentality I couldn't really understand, the kind I'd met only a few times before in the line of business. We didn't get many clients like that, but there were a few."

"Willy Chavez," I said. "That hired gun you and Baron defended."

"Yes, Chavez was like that, and I never understood his mental processes at all." She drew a long breath. "But there in Ames we weren't attorney and client any longer. I wasn't the fine lady lawyer any longer, merely visiting the dirty jail on business. I was one of them now, I was inside right along with them, just another convicted criminal serving her time, even though it still seemed like a crazy nightmare. No, a mad horror show!" A shudder went through her. "See the gently brought-up, carefully educated, always so well groomed and handsome and self-confident young professional woman. . . . Watch her terrifying transformation into a lank-haired, stoop-shouldered female convict shuffling around dully in an ill-fitting uniform, scared, scared, scared in that ghastly place she's been sent to waste her very best years, years she'd expected to devote to her brilliant career and her blissful marriage. Scared of all the cheap tough women she's got to live with now; but more scared of what's happening to her beautiful life—that was while she was naive enough to think she still had a life! And most of all scared of what's happening to *her*, mentally and physically, of what the endless regimented days of that unspeakably degrading and stultifying existence are doing to her."

She stopped. Outside, the storm was getting noisier, and the windows rattled to the violent gusts. Madeleine looked at her glass, drained it, and reached for the bottle, but it was too far away. I got up and poured more whiskey for her, and for myself, and took the glasses to the bathroom for ice and water. She waited for me to return and sit down again, before continuing:

"I could stand my folks visiting me when they could, there in the beginning, but then they got too ill to travel and there was nothing to break the dismal routine. Actually, I was just as glad not to have to make the effort to . . . to keep myself looking brave and cheerful for anybody. And the hours passed and the days passed and the months passed, God so slowly—and then Walter came." She licked her lips. "Matt, you can't imagine what it was like! Like seeing yourself in a mirror after being very sick, all gaunt and gray and stringy. . . . I hadn't realized how far I'd come, how far I'd sunk, until I saw the expression on his face! The starry-eyed young admirer who'd worshiped the golden girl from afar! Staring with horror at the ugly changes prison had made in me already, and I still had years and years of my sentence left to go! Of course he covered up very quickly and started talking to me as if I were still the same lovely creature he'd known, but afterwards I stood in front of the mirror in my cell and saw myself as he'd seen me. I saw what I'd already lost in the few years I'd been there. I realized that . . . that all of me, all that really mattered, would be gone long before I got out."

She gulped her whiskey, not looking at me. A blast of storm shook the building, and we both waited, as you do, to see if anything was going to crack under the assault, but nothing did.

"I made up my mind then," she said at last. "Why go through that endless grinding misery, all those remaining years of it, just to be tossed back out into the world at

111

last with nothing, nothing, nothing? No marriage, no profession, no friends, no reputation, no money to amount to anything. And no . . . me. Particularly no me. Just a dull and unattractive lump of a woman who wasn't me any longer, scratching out a drab living for the remaining hopeless years of her life. . . . So I found a little piece of metal and spent weeks sharpening it, and did it, but they got to me in time and it was so messy and horrible that I could never quite bring myself to try again. I just . . . kind of let myself go dead inside and wandered through the rest of those dreadful years in an unfeeling and unthinking daze."

"But you were wrong," I said. "You were stronger than you gave yourself credit for being. You did survive."

"Maybe," she said. "Thanks to you I'm discovering that there seems to be something left inside me after all. Whether it's enough to build a new life . . ." She shrugged.

"It'll be enough," I said. "And I didn't have a damn thing to do with it. You'd have worked your way out of that tailspin you were in all by yourself."

"Would I?" She grimaced. "Don't be so damn modest and upbeat and therapeutic, Matt, and give me another drink; and if you tell me I'm not used to it and can't hold it I'll spit in your eye. You can clean me up if I make a drunken mess of myself. The way you've been cleaning me up, building me up, ever since you picked me up at Fort Ames."

"Let me break out the new bottle," I said.

When I'd refilled our glasses, we sat for a while in silence listening to the blizzard; then she said quietly, "I'm sorry. I didn't mean to be so . . . unpleasant."

I grinned. "You sound as if it were something new."

She glanced at her glass, and drank from it. After a little, she said almost shyly, "I really need this. Tonight. Because I want to ask a big favor of you and I'm embarrassed."

"A favor? What favor?"

She said, "It's a wonderful wild night out there, and it's as if we were the only two people in the world, in here. . . ." She looked at me directly, and I saw her throat work. She licked her lips and said, "I want you to make love to me, Matt, or try. If I can. It's been so long. I have to know if I still after all these years . . . if there really is anything left. Please?"

I said, "No."

She got up quickly and walked to the dresser and looked at herself in the mirror, and drank deeply from her replenished drink.

She said in very even tones. "It's all right. I understand."

"No," I said harshly, "you don't understand at all." I set my glass aside and rose and went to her, and took her by the shoulders; I wanted to shake her angrily, but I restrained myself. "Why the hell don't you snap out of it, Madeleine?" I said, speaking to her face, beside mine, in the mirror. "So you're not a beautiful young girl any longer; who the hell is? You wouldn't be that by now even if you'd never gone to prison. But you've got brains and guts and you can still look better than ninety percent of the women around when you take just a little trouble. You don't have to ask any lousy man to go to bed with you as a *favor*, for God's sake! It makes me sick to hear you!" I drew a long, ragged breath. "Jesus Christ, ever since I set up this cozy one-room deal I've been wondering, as a gentleman of sorts and the guy officially responsible for you, how I'd manage to get through the night honorably, to use a very old-fashioned word, without making an unwanted pass. . . . And you humble yourself and say please love me, mister, when all you have to do is snap your fingers! No, I won't make love to you as a favor, damn it! But if you're really willing, and if you don't feel that you're under any obligation or coercion . . . If the lady will generously permit him to demonstrate

113

his passionate desire for her, the gentleman will be most grateful."

She freed herself from my grasp and turned, and studied my face carefully. She spoke rather stiffly: "It's nice that you're so concerned about my pride as a woman, since I've . . . kind of got out of the habit." Then she smiled slowly. "But you certainly take a lot of words to say yes, my dear."

Suddenly she was in my arms, soft and warm. Afraid to make a mistake that would spoil it for her—well, for both of us—I merely held her for a while, and touched my lips to her hair. At last I felt her arms tighten about me as she gained courage and turned her face up for a real kiss, tentative and exploratory. Her lips had a terrible innocence, reminding me of where she had been and how long it had been for her. Presently I eased her away from me and slipped the jacket off her shoulders and tossed it aside, undressing her tenderly, like a docile child. I started to work her sweater up gently, and she slapped my hands away, making a harsh little sound in her throat.

"Stop patronizing me, damn you!" she gasped. "I'm not a baby and I won't break!"

The lips that found mine once more were suddenly fierce and adult. It was a grown-up, knowing body that moved hard against mine. The hands that drew me against her were those of a married woman who'd been here before and remembered the loving way of it. We fell onto the nearest big bed together fully dressed, learning each other's shapes and movements through the rumpled and displaced and soon partly unfastened clothing, delaying too long with these breathless preliminaries, so that in the end we had to hastily, desperately, help each other off with the garments that had to come off, to hell with the rest. . . . After a long, long time I became aware once more of the storm outside.

"Oh, God!" Madeleine breathed at last. "I didn't know

114

I could still . . . could still feel . . . I was afraid that p-place had spoiled me forever! All those deadly loveless years!" Presently she whispered, "Do you know that I love you?"

"Sure, I'm crazy about you, too," I said.

She giggled, suddenly sounding very young and happy. "Try to say that with a little more conviction! But I really do love you in a way, Matt."

"What way?"

"The way you love a man who does a lousy job the nicest, kindest way he knows how. I know I'm a decoy for you, and decoys often get shot full of holes, don't they? I know you'd sacrifice me in an instant if you thought it necessary. But in the meantime you're just as patient as you can be with the unreasonable and tiresome lady just out of the clink." She drew a long, satisfied breath. "And now, well, that was an awfully small hamburger I had for lunch and I'm absolutely starving, and all that whiskey needs something to soak it up; but I do think I'd better change first, don't you? After that uninhibited little interlude, this skirt isn't fit to be seen in public."

I laughed. "In the middle of a howling blizzard you're worrying about a few creases? Everybody's going to be wet and wrinkled tonight, lady." Getting up and picking up my pants, I tossed a wad of nylon at her. "Pull your tights back on and let's go."

There were already six inches of snow on the level, and big drifts were piling up against the buildings as we dashed across to the cafe thirty yards away, the neon lights of which were almost invisible through the storm. There were many more cars outside now and several big trucks. I noticed that the motel's NO VACANCY sign was lighted. Inside, the cafe's TV told us that the highway was completely closed to the west. There was a pleasant, comradely feeling in the crowded restaurant; we were all stranded travelers together. The steaks were tough but

115

tasty, and the French fries crisp and good. Nobody shot at us coming or going, but I took the usual precautions anyway.

At bedtime, looking almost bridal in her soft old satin-and-lace nightie, Madeleine made it clear that she wanted company in her bed; but then we discovered, laughing, that neither of us was really interested in anything but companionship and sleep. It had been a long hard day. But in the middle of the night I awoke when she stirred in my arms, turning towards me. She moved against me, and I felt her lips touch my face.

"Please?"

It was a sleepy, faraway whisper, and I realized that I wasn't there and neither was she, really. This was the beautiful young wife who no longer existed requesting love from the handsome young husband who'd probably died nine years ago. I drew her closer and let my body obey the sleepy instructions issued by hers. I knew the moment she came fully awake and knew me. I heard her laugh throatily in the dark, accepting the situation and proceeding to show this new and untrained partner how to do what she wanted done. There was no great explosion of long-repressed emotions this time. It was just a friendly and satisfying act shared by two lonely people in the middle of the night.

"Nice man," she murmured at last, and fell asleep in my arms.

In the morning, looking out the door, I saw a foot and a half of snow on the ground, and the drifts were enormous. The skies were still gray, but only a few flakes drifted down; the real storm had passed on to the east. The visibility had improved, and I could see the freeway, somewhat higher than we were, several hundred yards away across the gently up-sloping white plain. The big plows had apparently cleared one lane on each side; traffic was moving single file in both directions. A boy in jeans and anorak was shoveling snow off the motel walks.

"I think we'd better take our time with breakfast and wait until they get things sorted out a bit more," I said, closing the door again.

"What did you say, Matt?"

Madeleine appeared in the bathroom doorway with a comb in her hand. In deference to the weather, she was wearing a plaid wool skirt and stiff new jeans that didn't do much to flatter her; but even so she was a very different person from the one I'd helped into my car in the penitentiary parking lot. That sad slumped figure was only a distant memory. There was a nice glow to her this morning. Her back was straight and her shoulders square.

When I repeated what I'd said, she laughed. "I'm in no hurry to get to Santa Fe, darling, you know that. All that's there for me is a lot of humiliation and a little money. I'll be through here in a moment if you want to shave."

But she gave me time to pull on most of my clothes and tuck the gun away under my belt where it belonged. When she came out at last, I went into the bathroom in my undershirt and plugged in the shaver. After a little I heard her say something to me, unclear because of the buzzing of the machine. A moment later I heard a sound I couldn't identify immediately. Then I realized that I'd heard a door closing; and that what she'd said was that she needed a cup of coffee right away and she'd see me over in the cafe. I knew a moment of sharp anger at her stupidity, or at my own stupidity in not making it absolutely clear to her that she should move nowhere without me. . . .

At the same moment, I *knew*. This was the killing moment. Of course you get those sickening premonitions a hundred times, in my line of work, and ninety-nine times nothing at all happens; but it only takes once. I was racing through the motel room as these thoughts went through my mind unbidden. I threw open the door and saw her walking away along the shoveled path

117

through the snow, a sturdy figure in her heavy clothes.

I looked for the threat I sensed was there and could see nothing. For the moment nothing moved in the snow anywhere around the motel or restaurant buildings, except for water dripping off the roofs. Starting after Madeleine, I looked farther afield. Traffic was still proceeding along the highway. There was only a stalled car in a snowdrift on the near side; but there would be lots of those this morning.

But there was none of the snow on the roof you'd expect to see on a deserted vehicle after a blizzard; and I remembered that there had been no car there when I looked out earlier. I knew what I had then, being an old long-range sniper myself. I started to run. It was a mistake; she heard my pounding footsteps on the path behind her and, curious, stopped to look back, giving the distant rifleman a perfect standing shot. I threw myself at her in a desperate flying tackle and felt a blow on the shoulder that paralyzed my whole right side as we went down in the snow together.

CHAPTER 10

I awoke in a hospital bed more or less straitjacketed. That is, they'd immobilized one arm completely, and when I tried to move it my heavily bandaged shoulder caught fire; but I could work the fingers if I tried hard, although they seemed very far away. The other arm was hooked up to some plumbing—they were dripping stuff into me from a bottle—and when I tried to move it a plump little white-clad nurse threatened me with instant annihilation; but those fingers responded also. I could move my legs and wiggle my toes.

"You must lie still, please," the nurse said. Her soft Spanish accent reminded me that we'd actually made it as far as New Mexico, although a few hundred miles short of Santa Fe. The nurse said, "You have lost much blood, but you will be fine now if you lie still."

I tried to tell her that it was just that a man liked to take inventory occasionally—like after being shot—but they'd given me something and the words didn't come out right. There was a question I wanted to ask, had to ask, but I couldn't remember what it was. I went back to sleep. When I awoke again the nurse was gone and Jackson was standing over the bed with a concerned look on his long farmer-face. I noted that he was wearing a sheepskin coat and heavy boots; apparently things were still pretty wintery outside. Otherwise I had no idea of how much time had passed.

"How are you feeling?" Jackson asked.

I wasn't going to waste my limited strength on that kind of a nonsense-question. If he couldn't see for himself that I couldn't be feeling any way but lousy, he could ask the doctors. They knew more about my condition than I did, anyway. There were more important things to talk about.

"Subject?" I whispered.

"Subject okay."

I drew a cautious breath of relief. That was the question to which I needed an answer. It had been a high-powered rifle, and I knew that the bullet had achieved total penetration as far as I was concerned. I hadn't been certain that it hadn't gone on to reach its intended target in spite of my attempt to knock her out of the line of fire.

I made a feeble left-handed gesture towards the view outside the window. "Where?"

"Santa Paula, New Mexico. Llano County Hospital."

Orientation accomplished, I turned back to business. "Sniper?"

"We got him."

"Alive?"

He said, a bit stiffly, "Yes. Alive. Name: Ernest Maxwell Reis."

I shook my head minutely. "Rings no bells."

"One of Otto Rentner's St. Louis boys, moonlighting. With a nice accurate Remington 7mm Magnum rifle."

I frowned. "Syndicate?"

"We don't think the corporation is really involved. In fact we suspect the tough boys aren't very happy with Maxie Reis right now. They don't like anybody who stirs up government agencies unnecessarily, particularly this government agency. But apparently he was offered plenty to take on an outside job, so much he couldn't resist. Like I said, moonlighting."

"Interrogation?"

"No real answers so far. The I-team is softening him up slowly. They'll get the contact method and some kind of a name out of him eventually." Jackson shrugged. "And probably the name will be Tolliver, like it usually is these days, so that won't help us much. Sorry we weren't in time to prevent—"

I used my limited headshake again. "My fault. Hadn't briefed her properly. Took for granted she understood. . . . Where is she now?"

Jackson hesitated. "Protective custody. Well, actually she was kneeling beside you holding your gun when the sheriff arrived. She was defending you, I guess, but at first nobody knew what had happened or where the shot had come from. Naturally, being literal-minded cops, they jumped to the obvious conclusion without even sniffing the damn revolver to see if it had been fired. Particularly when her papers showed she'd just been released from a maximum-security federal pen a few days ago, obviously a very dangerous female character. We straightened them out when we got there, of course, after turning Maxie over to the interrogation team that

120

was standing by, but it seemed best to leave her locked up for her own safety."

"No!" I tried to sit up and the nurse pushed me down. "No, goddamn you, I told you how she was to be treated—"

Jackson said defensively, "There could be a backup man waiting to do the job while we're patting ourselves on the back and congratulating ourselves on nailing Reis. It's a clean enough little jail. She's safer in there, now that you're out of circulation for a while, until we can make new arrangements for her close-in protection."

I had a sickening vision of Madeleine, still so insecure in her newfound identity, once again being subjected to the indignity of handcuffs, once again being bullied by rude officials, once again suffering the humiliation of being locked up in a cell. I couldn't bear to think of the warm and happy woman of last night being once again transformed into the slaty-eyed, stone-faced automaton I'd once known.

"Safer?" I said harshly. "Suppose you do keep her alive that way, what the hell good will it do her or anybody else if she freaks out completely, being stuck behind bars again? Or maybe they'll just find her hanging from the light fixture; she's tried it before. Get her out of there, damn it! Import some baby-sitters, keep her in your own pocket, but get her *out!*"

I heard my voice continue to speak angrily, and a nurse was coming forward and waving Jackson out of the room; and I went off somewhere leaving my voice still talking, which seemed a little odd, but not very. When I awoke, Madeleine was there. She was sitting on a straight chair near the door. She wasn't reading, and the TV was off; she simply sat there with her hands in her lap in the patient way she'd learned, no doubt, from long and grim experience.

The low room lights told me it was night without my having to make the effort of looking at the window—it had been day when Jackson was there—and Madeleine's attitude told me that she'd been waiting for quite a while; but it took her only a few seconds to realize that my eyes were open. She rose and approached the bed. I noticed that there were dark stains on the dark cloth of her jeans. My blood. She'd exchanged the plaid wool shirt I remembered, perhaps too blood-soaked to wear, for her pink short-sleeved sweater, and it was getting a bit grubby. Her hair could have been smoother.

But this was all quite irrelevant, because she was not the totally defeated woman I'd seen once and had been very much afraid I would now see again, after the police ordeal she'd just been through. Although she was quite tired and a bit dirty, she was calm and in control; in fact she looked straighter and stronger than I remembered her.

"Hero!" she said softly, looking down at me. "Throws himself into the path of the speeding bullet! Do you need anything, Matt? Should I call a nurse?" When I shook my head minutely, she said, "I didn't."

"Didn't what?"

"Freak out. Hang myself from the chandelier. In there, where they just had me."

"That Jackson. Motormouth." I looked up at her for a moment. "Gun girl. Calamity Jane Junior. Belle Starr returns. Crouching protectively over the bleeding body with a loaded six-shooter—well, five-shooter, to be precise."

"Some protection, considering that I've never fired a handgun in my life," she said. "And bleeding is right, all over my brand-new shirt and jeans. But I didn't realize the shot had come from so far away. I thought he had to be somewhere close, using a silencer like on TV."

"Suppressor," I said.

"What?"

"Not polite to call them silencers anymore," I whispered. "They're sound suppressors, just like a dirty old man is a soiled senior citizen these days."

"Funny!" She made a face at my attempt at humor, and went on: "What was I supposed to do, just sit there helplessly in the snow holding your head in my lap and waiting for him to stick his gun around the corner of a building and try again? Maybe if I couldn't hit him with a bullet I could scare him to death with the noise. I . . . I'm just a little tired of being pushed around, darling. And having men I l-like abducted or shot right under my nose." She swallowed hard. "Oh, God, I couldn't stop the bleeding and I thought you'd die before those idiots got an ambulance there!"

"And the cops," I said, watching her.

"Yes, the cops!" she said grimly. "Matt, what makes them that way? The same old muscle routine, so familiar I wanted to laugh. Are they bondage freaks? Do they have nice ejaculations in their pants every time they do that to a woman prisoner? The same damn handcuffs, the same loud mouths, the same total lack of any courtesy or consideration, the same pushy-shovy, the same smelly cell. Cheap thrills for the pigs? Do you want to know something? I could never be a lawyer again even if they'd let me. Not after this last experience. That's twice I've been pushed around and yelled at for something I didn't do; and how many apologies do you think the crummy broad got this time after it was proved she'd been grabbed by mistake? Hell, since they couldn't hold me for attempted murder they wanted to get me for having a gun I wasn't supposed to, being the lousy ex-convict I was! No, I really don't have a great deal of respect for the law any longer!"

I licked my lips, watching her, beginning to understand the change I'd sensed in her, the newfound strength and confidence.

"You wanted to *laugh*?" I whispered.

She looked down at me for a long moment. "Yes, darling," she said very softly. "Laugh! Isn't that . . . weird? I thought, when I shouted for somebody to call the police, that I'd be scared to death of them when they

123

got there. Remember how I wouldn't let you drive fast because we might be picked up for speeding? And I think I told you how I felt, or thought I felt, about ever being locked up again. But it wasn't that way at all! Really, it was rather funny, like watching a jerky old movie that frightened the hell out of you back when you were a kid. Matt, I was the . . . the old professional watching those country clowns trying to intimidate *me*! It was ridiculous! I wanted to tell them they were wasting their time, I knew all about it, I'd been through it in spades. I'd been harassed by experts—government experts—and it would take more than a bunch of small-town fuzzies in big hats to scare me. And then they put me into that cell and slammed the door, *clang*, and I waited for the panic to start, and a little voice said, *Listen, stupid, you did eight whole years in a cage like this, are you going to let a lousy day or two get you down?*"

"Good girl," I whispered.

She smiled down at me. "God, I've been awful, haven't I? It's a wonder you could stand me. I'm so ashamed when I think of the mopy, self-pitying way I've behaved ever since I got out. I guess what I discovered just now is that, well, nobody can really hurt you when you've got nothing left to lose. The first time I was hauled away in handcuffs all those years ago and wound up in jail, I literally went into shock at the ghastly disgrace of it—well, I told you—but what's left to disgrace? Back then I was sick at the thought of how it would affect my wonderful job, my spotless professional reputation, my lovely social standing, my bright and shining future. . . . Well, I don't have to be concerned about any of those things any longer, do I? I don't even have to worry about my appearance; these days nobody expects me to emerge from a dirty *calabozo* looking smart and beautiful. And it's a damn good thing, too, isn't it?" She glanced down at herself ruefully. "Well, I'd better find the motel room they've got for me here so I can wash off the jail stink and try to soak the gore out of my shirt and pants. I suppose I'll have to get used to that if I stick with you, Mr. Secret Agent. Gore, I mean." She hesitated. "Matt."

"Yes?"

She drew a long breath. "About that chandelier. Don't you know I couldn't do that to my life now, after what you just did to preserve it?"

Her gratitude embarrassed me, since I'd done very little to earn it; in fact I'd almost got her killed by briefing her inadequately. "Madeleine, look—"

She laid a gentle finger across my lips. "No, don't waste your strength telling me how it was all in the line of duty and you'd have done it for anybody you'd been assigned to protect. I happen to be the girl it was actually done for. I know how I feel about it, and you're not going to change my mind." She bent over and kissed me lightly on the forehead. "Be good."

I grinned up at her weakly. "I've got a choice? You be careful."

"I don't have to be careful. I have two big men outside to be careful for me. With guns. Don't worry about me. I'll be back in the morning."

She was back next morning and each morning thereafter, spending most of her days with me. The staff of the little hospital, shorthanded, was happy to let her look after me in a nonmedical way; and Jackson, also shorthanded, was glad to have her where he could have an eye kept on both of us simultaneously. When I wasn't sleeping, we spent our time reading the books and magazines she brought, or watching TV, or talking about nothing in particular; but occasionally I'd wake from a nap to find her just sitting there in that patient way of hers and I'd wonder what she was thinking about, if she was thinking at all. Maybe she'd just learned, during the long years of her imprisonment, how to turn off her mind altogether and let the endless, useless penitentiary hours slip by.

But towards the end of the week she spoiled that theory by pulling her chair closer to mine—I was practicing sitting up by that time—and saying: "Matt, I'd like to talk about me a little, if you don't mind."

"My favorite subject, next to me," I said.

"Says the man who hasn't told me a thing about himself since the day we met that I didn't pry out of him with a crowbar!" She laughed, and became serious again: "I've been trying to figure out what I'm going to do. I can't go back to what I was even if they'd let me. Even if I could stomach the law, I wouldn't want to spend the rest of my life playing catch-up with the attorneys who didn't have most of a decade amputated from their careers. Anyway, at the moment it doesn't seem very likely I'll get the chance, so that's out."

I said, "Don't be too quick to toss all your legal training out the window. Who knows, you may wind up all vindicated and rehabilitated before this is over, with a dozen law firms clamoring for your services."

"Well, I'll worry about that when it happens," she said dryly. "In the meantime I'd better figure out what else I'm fitted for. Besides scrubbing floors. Actually, I do know a lot about the law and the courts and the legal system. Not to mention what I've learned about the penal system the hard way. I also know how to dig for facts. I'm a pretty good investigator; at least I used to be. And I know how to organize those facts and write them up so they make sense. I've done it often enough. I think, particularly if I can find myself some kind of a little job near the campus, even if it doesn't pay very much, I've got enough money waiting for me to get a degree in journalism. The question is, if I get it, will any newspaper or magazine hire a female reporter—maybe a police or political reporter eventually, something like that—with a criminal record, particularly my kind of criminal record?"

I looked at her for a moment, with an odd, tight feeling in my throat. "Hey," I said, "welcome back to the human race, Ellershaw Number 210934."

She was a little embarrassed. "Well, I've done just

126

about enough moaning about my lost lovely past. It's time to think of the future, isn't it? But you haven't answered my question."

"I don't really know the answer," I said. "But all kinds of people seem to be getting out of prison and buying typewriters these days; I don't see why you shouldn't. I can ask around and find out what you're apt to run up against. You don't have to be on the staff of a publication, you know. There's always free-lance work; in fact that's what I did back when I was married."

"I remember—to that gentle and nonviolent girl you told me about. But you didn't say what you did for a living during your nonviolent phase."

"It's no way to get rich, but we made out all right. But in your case there's one big catch," I said.

"You mean that even as a free-lance I won't be able to escape my prison background?"

"No. I shouldn't think anybody'd give a damn about that, particularly if you stuck to reasonably nonsensitive and noncontroversial subjects; but you wouldn't, would you? There'd be one controversial subject in particular you couldn't stay away from." I studied her thoughtfully. "Isn't that what's at the back of your mind, Madeleine? Sure you'd like to make a living as a journalist, and I think you could do it; in fact you'd probably be very good at it. But all the time you were writing fascinating pieces about women's fashions, or horse breeding, or hang-gliding, or even crime or politics, you'd be dreaming how to break the great story of your innocence, complete with irrefutable proof that would smash the people who killed your husband and framed you into prison."

She hesitated. "Well, what's wrong with that?" she asked defiantly.

"Two things," I said. "First of all you can't make it alone. You seem to be forgetting: there have been at least two and probably three attempts on your life since you left Fort Ames. If we turn you loose right now to carry out your new life plan, you won't live long enough to get anywhere near your journalism degree, let alone the proof you yearn for—somebody wants you dead, remember? And probably they want you dead precisely because they're afraid that now you're free you'll start digging up stuff they don't want dug."

She said wryly, "I'm not likely to forget that little detail, looking at you in those bandages. It does present a difficulty, since I seem to have decided that there are certain advantages to being alive, after all. And the second obstacle?"

"Not really an obstacle," I said. "Just a point to keep in mind as you plan your future: your secret ambition is a little redundant."

She frowned. "Translate, please."

I said, "What I mean is that the information you were planning to search for eventually, after you got established in your journalistic career, is the information we need right now. We can't wait around for it while you're getting yourself properly educated. At least it seems likely that your innocence, and the guilt of the people we're after, are two faces of the same conspiracy or whatever the hell you want to call it. Prove one and you prove the other. I can't promise exoneration, but I'll certainly do my best to arrange it in return for your help. But there's another problem."

"What's that?"

I looked at her and I looked down at myself and I looked back to her. "A pretty ridiculous undercover team, wouldn't you say, Ellershaw? If things get tough—well, tougher—how would you figure the survival quotient of a task force composed of one feeble one-armed agent and one untrained sedentary dame with a crippled wrist who's in such lousy shape she can't climb a flight of stairs without turning blue in the face?"

Madeleine said resentfully, "Damn it, Matt, I'm not all *that* flabby!" Then she looked down at herself, noting the way she filled the rather handsome blue slacks she

128

was wearing. She sighed. "Oh, all right. Point taken. What do you suggest?"

"We have a choice. We can use me in an advisory capacity for the time being—well, as soon as I'm ambulatory again—and get Washington to send us a husky, healthy, violent young man to stick close to you and watch over you while we start stirring things up in Santa Fe—"

"No!" Then color came into her face, as she heard the unexpected vehemence of her own voice. "I mean . . . well, damn it, I don't want to be wished off on some other macho bastard with a gun; I had a hard enough time getting used to this one."

I grinned. "Flattery, I love it."

"What's the alternative?"

"Instead of a husky, healthy, violent young man, how about a husky, healthy, violent young woman?"

Madeleine groaned. "Oh, God, you mean I'd have to get along with a muscular and very superior female agent, probably with lesbian tendencies . . . ?" She stopped and frowned at me. "Or isn't that what you meant?"

I shook my head. "No," I said. "I meant you."

There was a little silence. We could hear somebody rolling a cart of some kind down the hospital corridor outside.

"Me?" Madeleine licked her lips. "That's kind of a bad joke, isn't it, Matt? I told you, I've never fired a pistol in my life. I was never even taught how to punch anybody in the nose, let alone handle firearms."

"But the basic aggressive impulses are there," I said. "You demonstrated that when I was shot, going for my gun like that. Obviously, unlike my ex-wife, you're not sincerely dedicated to the principles of nonresistance and nonviolence."

"You forget where I've been," she said quietly. "Non-violence wasn't very big in Fort Ames, Matt. Not if you were moderately attractive, and if you were heterosexually inclined and wanted to stay that way. I . . . I discovered very fast that it doesn't take a lot of training to learn what hurts. Just take a finger joint that bends one way, for instance, and bend it the other. And they really don't like it when you use your nails and go straight for the eyes." Her face was bleak with memory. "I found that, dazed and shattered though I was when I was finally delivered to the prison after that ghastly jail-to-jail cross-country ride, I wasn't quite beaten enough to let another woman do *that* to me—I told you I was always very conventional about sex. I guess I went a little crazy at being threatened with this . . . this final indignity. Fortunately I was still a pretty strong girl back then; although afterwards it wasn't easy to live with the image of the former dignified lady attorney rolling on the soapy floor of the prison laundry kicking and clawing and biting and scratching like an animal to protect her stupid virtue. But they learned to leave the snooty bitch alone to go to hell her own way, not theirs. I guess I was a little stuck-up after all. And I learned that peace is something you have to fight for. Call it a paradox if you like." She grimaced. "I'm sorry. I didn't mean to bore you with any more pitiful pictures from the pen."

I wanted to say something sympathetic and understanding, but she obviously didn't need or want my sympathy. I said instead, "On the record, you're a very bright lady who catches on very fast. To just about anything. The mind is good, and there's nothing wrong with the body that couldn't be fixed in a place I know, probably including the wrist. It wouldn't be fun. You might even wish you were back in Ames fighting off those amorous lady convicts; but at the Ranch, as we call it, they'd sweat the lard off you and really teach you how to take care of yourself. And of me, until I've got two functioning arms again. Normally it's a three-month basic course; however, there's some stuff you wouldn't be allowed to study because of security, and some we simply wouldn't bother you with. We wouldn't take time

130

to teach you things like surveillance, electronics, explosives, codes and ciphers, safes and locks. If necessary, I can handle that end of it after a fashion. We wouldn't be making a full-fledged agent of you; we'd only be interested in getting you conditioned and trained to the point where, with a little left-handed help from me, you'd have a reasonable chance of keeping us both alive."

I stopped. She was watching me with a curious intentness, but she didn't speak. A heavy truck went by in the street outside the window. When its noise had subsided, I went on:

"You got your other degrees in record time; you can probably earn a limited field qualification in six weeks if you grit your teeth and really go after it. And by that time, they tell me, I should be getting around okay, although it'll take longer to get my arm back to normal again. I've checked with Washington by phone, and the word is that we can afford the delay if I consider it essential. Whatever it is we're dealing with, it's been going on at least since your husband disappeared, and that happened nine years ago. A few more weeks shouldn't . . . What's the matter?"

She had got to her feet, very deliberately, to stand over me. Her face was pale and her eyes were wide and a little shiny.

"Who do you think you are?" she whispered. "Who the hell do you think you are, Matthew Helm? God?" She swallowed hard. "Just what do you plan to do with me when you get me all created, Mister God?"

I said, startled, "I don't know what—"

She spoke furiously: "You've been sneaking up on it ever since you saw what a broken-down female wreck I'd become in that p-place. Encouraging the trembling wretch to drive a car again. Treating the miserable female ruin to some new clothes and a becoming hairdo. And the goddamned sexual reawakening—okay, so I made the first move, but I don't for a moment think you put us together in that room by accident. I don't suppose

131

you planned the police bit, but you probably had it all fixed up to restore the poor downtrodden creature's self-confidence some other way. And now, with the psychological problems taken care of, comes the convenient program of physical conditioning to make a slim, trim, sexy beauty out of the sloppy, overweight jailbird lady. . . ." She stopped, breathless, glaring at me. "Me Galatea, you Pygmalion. You crummy patronizing bastard!"

She turned and ran out of the room, obviously wishing she could slam the door behind her; but hospital doors are pretty slam-proof. I sat there slightly stunned, realizing that there was some truth in her accusations. Not that I'd planned it all deliberately from the start, as she seemed to think, but I'd certainly taken pleasure in watching her steady comeback. I'd seized every opportunity to hasten the process, and maybe even got a kick out of being such a thoughtful and bighearted fellow. And even now I found myself, after the first shock, smiling rather fondly, if a bit ruefully, at the thought of the fierce pride she'd just displayed, which she couldn't possibly have summoned up ten days ago. Okay, patronizing.

There was a light knock on the door, and she reentered the room without waiting for my response and marched up to my chair rather stiffly.

"Do you want an apology?" Her voice was steady. "All right, I'm sorry, I was out of line. What the hell am I complaining about, anyway? Everybody's spent years tearing me down, why should I object because somebody wants to build me up for a change?"

"You Liza Doolittle," I said. "Me Professor 'Enry 'Iggins."

"You sonofabitch," she said with a reluctant grin. "Well, when do we go? And where?"

BOOK TWO

BOOK TWO

CHAPTER 11

IF somebody ever starts a new country and asks me to select a location for the capital, I sure as hell won't pick a miasmal swamp bordering a semitropical river; but I guess we're stuck with that reclaimed mosquito marsh on the banks of the Potomac. Well, it's almost bearable in spring and fall; and as the taxi transported me away from the hospital in nearby Bethesda—my official excuse for coming east being a medical analysis of my damaged shoulder—I noticed that the trees were budding, tenderly, reminding me, if I needed reminding, that considerable time had passed since I'd fallen, wounded, into a New Mexico snowbank.

It was a fairly long haul into the center of Washington, and I should of course have employed my time usefully in considering the true reason for my being summoned here, and the meeting that had been called to discuss it, towards which I was now heading. However, I hadn't really been given enough facts to work on yet, so I found myself instead thinking about Mrs. Madeleine Rustin Ellershaw, B.A., J.D., and wondering how she was getting along.

I'd seen hardly anything of her after we'd arrived at the Ranch in Arizona. People tend to kind of disappear into that sprawling desert installation, which used to be a fairly fancy dude ranch—Uncle Sam took it over for our use when it went broke. Although I'd missed Madeleine's company, I'd been busy with my own problems of convalescence and rehabilitation. Novices in the training barracks to which she'd been assigned are not encouraged to, and usually after a hard day's work have no desire to, associate socially with the full-fledged agents in residence for refresher courses or therapy. In fact such fraternization is discouraged for security reasons: if the trainee washes out, the fewer faces he's seen, the better. And Madeleine had told me firmly that, if she was going to subject herself to this ridiculous bang-bang, punch-chop-kick, run-jump-climb-scramble-crawl indoctrination course, she certainly didn't want me hanging around watching her make a spectacle of herself.

That had been back when we first arrived; and after enduring a car trip across most of two states with an unhealed bullet wound I was hardly in condition to lope across the desert terrain watching a bunch of neophytes being put through their paces, anyway. Some time later, however, I'd had occasion to look up a certain physical training instructor for advice. An exercise he'd recommended was more painful than I thought it should be and I was afraid it was doing my shoulder more harm than good. I found him with a bunch of young hopefuls just in from some kind of a cross-country conditioning run. Leaving, I saw her sitting by herself a little distance from the rest. She looked up at my approach.

"Checking up on the class clown?" she asked with a crooked little smile. "I don't know what those kids would do if they didn't have Auntie Madeleine around for laughs."

She was a mess, of course, after a hard workout in the sun, lank-haired and sweaty, in a torn T-shirt and grubby blue satin running shorts that, I noticed, hung loose about her hips; she'd had to take in the waistband with a safety pin to keep them up. Her nose was peeling, and there were scabs on both knees. I couldn't help remembering a well-groomed young lady making quite an elaborate production of selecting an expensive wine in a restaurant called Cortez; and her eyes said that she also remembered that shining girl who'd been so sure she had her golden life all arranged.

"How are you making it?" I asked.

"Don't ask," she said. "I suppose I'll get over it eventually, but I still feel as if they've been beating me with clubs; and of course they have, a little. But I'm glad to see you, Matt. They say you're pretty good with a rifle. So tell me, please, when you shoot, do you know when the piece is going to fire or don't you? We've been arguing about it."

I shook my head. "I try not to know. I just keep adding a little pressure on the trigger whenever the sight picture looks just right; I never know exactly when it'll let off. That way I can't flinch in anticipation of the noise and recoil and throw the shot wild."

"Okay, thanks. Just what I wanted to know. Matt."

"Yes?"

"Don't look so worried." She gave me that wry grin again. "It's merely a matter of forgetting that I was supposed to be a highly respectable partner in a highly respectable law firm by this time in my life, not to mention a socially prominent and probably very stuffy and self-satisfied married lady, and letting myself become a tomboy kid again with skinned knees and a dirty face— kind of fun, actually, like a second childhood. I'll have you know I'm keeping right up with those scrawny brats. A few aching muscles won't kill me. I'll be all right, you'll see. . . . Oh, God, here we go again!"

The last I saw of her, she was hitching up her baggy shorts and rejoining her group at a crisp trot that did not betray the painful effort I knew it demanded of her. It was clear that she was driving herself hard, remembering that she'd once quit shamefully under pressure to the point of trying to take her own life; she obviously had no intention of letting it happen again. . . .

Normally, on business, we're fairly careful how we approach the shabby side-street headquarters building in

Washington, always leaving our transportation some distance away and testing for surveillance before we slip inside, never mind how. But today I had the taxi driver stop right in front and wait while I fumbled out my money left-handed—my right arm was supported by a black silk sling. Well, whatever passes for silk these petrochemical days. There was clearly no mystery about me today. It was just old Helm reporting with a bum shoulder after being taking apart like a busted clock by the specialists in Bethesda to determine what bright new springs and gears were needed.

Secrecy was reserved for the third party to the three-cornered conference to be held up in Mac's office, a man who'd make every effort to arrive unseen and depart that way. Call him Mr. Smith to be original.

But he apparently hadn't got there yet, since I had to wait below for a few minutes with the pretty office girls who all carry little capsules under their pretty hair, or wherever girls hide such things, because they have access to information somebody might one day try to get out of them; but you don't get much information out of dead girls. At least that's the theory. Then I marched up the stairs, proud that I could make it without puffing—well, not much—but I'd have taken an elevator if there had been one. It had been a fairly slow recovery, and I was still way off my usual fine Olympic form. The time wasted here on all those tests and X-rays when I could have been working hard at rebuilding the body hadn't helped.

As I entered the second-floor office with the big window that somehow isn't overlooked by any roofs or windows within a thousand yards—quite a trick in that crowded city—Mac rose and came around the desk to greet me. It was a courtesy I'd earned by getting shot. Normally he'd simply have nodded as I came in and indicated the chair in which he wanted me to sit. I remembered to give him my left hand to shake, leaving the right acting helpless.

138

"I just received a summary of the final medical report by phone," he said. "Significant tissue destruction. Poor fusion of the fractured bones, if I recall the terminology correctly. Some nerve damage. Remedial surgery recommended in a month or so, as soon as general health permits. Very regrettable, Eric."

I said, "Well, let's hope somebody sneaks a look at the report and is suitably impressed. I'd hate to be wearing this damn thing for nothing." I slipped my right arm out of the sling and flexed the biceps a couple of times. "Actually, I still wouldn't want to try arm-wrestling one of those healthy young ladies downstairs for a bet of any significance. And I'd hate to get slammed by the butt of a hard-kicking rifle or shotgun. But I guess I can shoot a pistol okay if I have to, since I don't like those thundering Magnums anyway."

It was one of the tricky plays that don't often work, pretending to be more badly shot up than I really was; but the fact that he wanted me to try it was significant, indicating that he thought I'd be needing any advantage I could get, even with Madeleine Ellershaw for a baby-sitter. Or particularly with Madeleine for a baby-sitter?

"Any word from the Ranch?" I asked, putting my arm to rest once more in its tiresome silken cradle. "How's my bodyguard coming along?"

Mac returned to his chair, waited for me to seat myself, and patted a file folder on his desk. "She completed her limited qualification, third out of a class of seven, two of whom failed to finish," he said. "She would have been at the top if she'd had any prior shooting experience, but you can't make an instant soldier, or operative, out of somebody who's been brought up in a gunless household brainwashed to consider the firearm an invention of pure evil. One wonders why parents always seem to feel they're doing favors for their children by making them afraid of things. I was brought up to be afraid of dogs—my mother was bitten by one once. I never quite got over it: something of a disadvantage back when I was revising our methods for dealing with guard and attack dogs."

It was an uncharacteristic digression. He very seldom talked about himself; for having worked for him so long I really knew very little about him. It occurred to me that he was looking tired. The black eyebrows were as fiercely independent as ever, but the face was perhaps a little more lined than it had been. Well, he'd set up the agency from the start as a one-man outfit and now he was stuck with it, although I remembered that once not too long ago when a mission had left me in fairly bad shape he'd suggested that I might consider a desk job as his assistant.

Mac cleared his throat sharply and brought his mind back to the present. "Mrs. Ellershaw was beaten by a Texas boy who grew up shooting jackrabbits on the run, and a state-champion lady skeet shooter. Their marksmanship scores surpassed hers by enough to overcome her superior grades in other subjects." He touched the folder in front of him. "However, quite a commendable performance considering that she was ten years older than anybody else in the class and in deplorable physical condition at the start. Also, she was slightly handicapped by the condition of her wrist, but that disability turned out to be largely psychological. In prison, she'd apparently exaggerated the effects of the injury, to herself as well as to others, using it as a justification for inactivity. It didn't take her long to break the habit once it was called to her attention. Some residual weakness, but I'm informed she's working hard on it. Apparently quite an impressive young woman. Her instructors all commented on her intelligence and determination." He glanced at me. "You can inform Mrs. Ellershaw, when you see her, that if her plans for the future, whatever they may be, should fail to work out, I'll be happy to hear from her."

"I'll pass the word, sir."

Mac paused, and went on: "Of course there are some

140

who question our personnel policies. They do not seem to realize that our work cannot be performed by conventional people with conventional backgrounds."

"No, sir," I said, knowing him well enough to decipher this double-talk. "Has somebody raised a question of security with respect to Mrs. Ellershaw?"

"Would you expect them not to?" His voice was dry. "A sinister female convicted of selling, or helping to sell, our critical scientific secrets to the Russians?" He frowned. "How certain are you that she's to be trusted, Eric? Are you emotionally involved with her, by any chance?"

"Probably," I said. "I'm a sucker for lost kittens, and birds with broken wings, and lovely maidens wrongfully subjected to durance vile. And although prison didn't leave her in very good shape, as that record shows, she's a bright lady with very pretty legs. How could I resist, sir?"

Mac said absently, in his pedantic way, "Technically, a married woman hardly qualifies as a maiden if her husband performed his marital duties properly, and there is no reason to believe that Dr. Ellershaw did not." A buzzer sounded on his desk, but he paid it no attention, still studying me carefully. At last he nodded as if satisfied. "Very well, Eric. I have been backing your judgment of the lady and will continue to do so. But I must ask you now to curb your chivalry and keep your temper. The gentleman who just arrived prides himself on being a rough-spoken character—you will probably recognize him, but his name is not to be mentioned. Considering his current position, we cannot afford to antagonize him. Well, at least not unnecessarily." After a moment, hearing footsteps in the hall outside, Mac raised his voice: "Come in, Mr., er, Smith."

The big man who entered was wearing a shapeless suit of brown herringbone tweed, a blue shirt left over from yesterday, and a rather greasy blue tie. His brown shoes hadn't been polished recently. His white hair needed cutting, and the barber—if he ever got to one—would hardly be able to resist the temptation to do some snipping at the bushy white eyebrows that emphasized the redness of the broad grainy face. The body was bulky enough that the vest had parted company with the pants to let a fold of crumpled shirt leak out. All in all, not a prepossessing figure, and generations of bright young politicians had wept bitterly into their veddy dry martinis at the perversity of an electorate that had stubbornly persisted in sending this dumb red-faced slob to the U.S. Senate in preference to their neat and attractive and highly intelligent selves.

Their trouble was, I decided, that they'd never really looked at the innocent baby-blue eyes that seemed to peer in a startled way out of the wide face, as if shocked at the company in which they found themselves. Behind those eyes was a very shrewd politician who'd held his Senate seat as long as he'd wanted it, and had then retired to remain a political power in his state. Only after the last election had he allowed himself to be called back to Washington, as adviser to a chief executive aware of his own lack of experience in domestic political affairs.

There were no handshakes or introductions; Mr. Smith merely nodded curtly to Mac and turned to look at me. "What's the matter with that arm?" he demanded.

Mac said, "I told you he got shot."

"Let the man speak for himself."

"I got shot, sir," I said, on the theory that a few judicious sirs are never wasted.

"Kinda careless of you."

"My orders didn't state that I shouldn't get myself shot, sir. They stated only that I should prevent somebody else from getting shot. I did."

"Threw yourself into the line of fire to save a pretty-faced Commie spy just out of the pen where she should have been left to spend the rest of her treacherous life."

142

The blue eyes regarded me coldly. "The bitch got to you enough that you'd give your life for her, hey, boy? Did you get to fuck her?"

"Yes, sir."

"Was she any good with a man after all that time in the lezzie house?"

"Quite satisfactory, sir."

"Must have been, since you then let her talk you into bringing her into a top-secret government installation to learn all about our classified training methods."

I said, "Sir, I fail to see the purpose of this discussion. What difference does it make where the lady's loyalties lie?"

His eyes narrowed. "What *difference* . . . ! What the hell do you mean, son?"

"If she was innocent of the crime of which she was convicted," I said deliberately, "as I happen to believe, then she can be quite useful to us in many ways. But if she was guilty, as you seem to believe, then she can be equally useful—as long as I don't let her know she's suspected; as long I show her how implicitly I trust her by arranging for her entry to our training center and even allowing her to go through part of the basic course, learning all about such top-secret weapons as the Smith and Wesson .38 Special revolver, the Winchester .308 sniper's rifle, the Fairbairn commando knife, and the M16 assault rifle, all of which are available, in civilian versions at least, in any large sporting goods store. Really, sir, do you think any unqualified trainee is allowed access to classified materials at the Ranch? We're quite aware of the lady's record. I happen to believe she's been the victim of a miscarriage of justice, but I'm certainly not going to jeopardize our security system for my private beliefs. And if she's guilty, as you think, she's bound to make contact with her husband and his unsavory Communist friends sooner or later; and I'll be right there to take advantage of it. Unless I'm

143

ordered to drop her because of somebody's misguided passion for security."

The little baby-blue eyes glared at me for a moment longer; then the shaggy white head was thrown back for a hearty laugh. Mr. Smith clapped me hard on the shoulder, the bad shoulder. I didn't flinch; let him have the small victory of discovering that the sling was a fraud.

"Good boy!" he said. "Want them to think you're practically helpless, hey? Good idea. As for the dame, you're perfectly right, as long as you watch out she doesn't put a knife in your back when double-cross time comes. And of course we can't afford to drop her; she's one of the few leads we've got to the people we have to track down. It just gripes my soul to have to make use of Commie slime like that."

I said, "But the point is that her relationship or lack of relationship to Moscow is practically irrelevant here. Sure, if she gives me a lead to the missing Dr. Ellershaw and his subversive lady friend I'll follow it up; but from what little I've been told I gather that the primary problem that confronts us has nothing to do with Communism or espionage."

Mr. Smith nodded. "That's right. Somehow those two brainy young traitors, the intellectual lawyer bitch and her egghead scientist husband, got themselves tangled up in something else on the side. Something big. We figure they must have stumbled on some incriminating evidence while they were snooping out scientific secrets to sell to their Russky friends. Maybe they even tried to cash in on it with a little blackmail. But the people we're after took care of them easily enough by tipping off the authorities to their spying activities. The husband lit out just ahead of the handcuffs with the Russky wench who'd been sent to help them, but the wife was grabbed and wound up in the pen where, I gather, they knocked some of the snooty intellectual airs out of her. Well, you'd know all about that, being on such intimate terms

144

with her. She was lucky at that; as a traitor she should have got the chair."

He was needling me to see if I'd react to his sneering remarks; he still wasn't quite sure of me. I waited in silence. Mac waited. After a little, Mr. Smith went on:

"When I say they tipped off the authorities, I'm exaggerating. They didn't have to tip them off; they *are* the authorities. At least they're the Office of Federal Security. Also they're the Centers for Advanced Defense Research. CADRE ONE, outside Santa Fe . . . well, Los Alamos. CADRE TWO, on the Oregon coast. CADRE THREE, on an island off the coast of Maine. All staffed by perfectly respectable scientists, up to a point; just as the OFS has a large contingent of good, honest law-enforcement people from various police departments and the FBI. They're the cover, as you sinister characters call it. But behind them in both organizations is a nuculus"—I realized that he meant nucleus—"a nuculus of very smart and particular folks who just can't stand the way this country is being run by you and me and the man I work for. They're going to fix it up right, their way, all orderly and moral and pure and profitable. Well, profitable for them. The CADRES with their fancy linked computers are the planning and organizational end of it. The OFS is the action end, with its figurehead Bennett, who wets his pants whenever somebody, somewhere, pushes the PEE button. Somebody who calls himself Tolliver. The question is: Who is Tolliver? And where is Tolliver?" The little blue eyes stared at me hard. "We have other people working in other places on other leads. Your job is to wring this Ellershaw bitch dry and find out if our man can possibly be working out of the Los Alamos area; if that's the information she and her husband stumbled across that got them clobbered." He glanced at Mac. "You got no further information out of that gunman you captured?"

Mac shook his head. "No. Just the same name, and the contact method used. I would say that we're going to

145

have to go after the information we need; apparently it is not going to come to us, even using Mrs. Ellershaw as a decoy. I should add that after being interrogated and released by us, reasonably intact, Mr. Ernest Maxwell Reis was shotgunned to death on a dark St. Louis street. However, we don't feel this killing is related to our problem. We think it was merely the syndicate's method of indicating to all and sundry, meaning us, that it disapproved of Maxie's extracurricular activities and had not been involved in them."

Mr. Smith nodded. "Yes. Our impression is that the people with whom we're dealing, although they are not above hiring an occasional killer from the syndicate rank and file when they can't find a suitable independent operator, have no real connection with organized crime. This is a bigger thing than drug smuggling or prostitution or a bit of organized larceny. These people aren't interested in stealing a car or two, or two hundred. They want to steal a whole nation. And they're getting close, gentlemen; they're getting damn close." The big man hesitated, and looked at us with an unexpected hint of embarrassment. "I'm on kind of a spot here," he went on almost diffidently. "I've been making long, lousy speeches about country and flag and motherhood since right after they first run me down with dogs and put shoes on me. And maybe this ain't exactly the right time for a speech, anyway. But I'm supposed to let you know that the Chief don't expect to rank in the history books along with Washington and Lincoln. He tries to get along the best he can, but he's got no idea he's the best president this country ever had. He just wants to be damn sure he don't go down in history for being the last. If you know what I mean."

Mac said softly, "He thinks the situation is that serious, does he?"

Mr. Smith cleared his throat. "I can't begin to tell you where this thing is beginning to pop up. We come across it everywhere. They seem to've been building it for damn

146

near ten years, and it's about ready to roll now. Maybe it was figured as a ten-year plan from the start. We'd sure like to know the target date, at least, but anytime we try to act against these people—even learn something about them—we find ourselves stymied. Things just don't seem to get done. Like a poor old dog I once had. He'd try to do his thing like he used to, he was a pretty damn good coon hound, but he just didn't have it anymore. Those heart worms were bleeding him white from inside; and when we doctored him, something went wrong and a great lump of them broke loose and plugged up his heart and killed him. Well, this country seems to've been pretty well infiltrated by these human worms, and we've picked you people to do the doctoring, giving you the most promising lead we've got, this ex-convict bitch. But we want you to move careful, real careful. No sense saving the nation just to wreck it."

I said, "We're greatly honored, or are we?"

The blue eyes narrowed. "Don't get smart with me, son. Too damn many clever people around. Maybe that's the trouble these days. You folks were picked because the Chief won't have nothing to do with the FBI if he can help it. He hasn't trusted them a bit ever since they started playing those entrapment games a few years back; he says they're supposed to prevent crimes if they can and solve them if they can't, not make them happen. Anyway, they're too damn big. The CIA still isn't supposed to operate much in this country; and it's too damn big, too. Too easy to penetrate a big agency. That makes you the patsy. A small one-man outfit that makes its own rules and keeps its mouth shut."

Mac said dryly, "And which, if things go wrong, can be sacrificed without a major national upheaval."

The white-haired man grinned wolfishly. "You got it, mister." He sobered quickly. "Again I'm on a spot. There's another reason for using you, which you've probably figured out by this time. Well, I've done a few crooked things in my time, if not as many as my enemies

147

like to claim. But I never gave any killing orders before. But here goes: your instructions are to find the man behind CADRE, Tolliver or Taliaferro or whatever his real name is, and take care of him discreetly. That big-nosed bastard Bennett, of the OFS, should also—what's that word you spooks use?—be discreetly terminated. If any other individual seems to be in a position to take over, or just make serious trouble, he should also meet with a bad accident. In fact, kind of fatal. We've got to stop this thing before it moves, and it's no time to pussyfoot around. The idea is, you remove the heads of these snaky organizations and we'll take care of the wriggling, thrashing bodies. Discreetly."

"Discretion is our watchword," Mac said gravely.

"This country's fallen in love with conspiracies," Mr. Smith said. "Personally, I think President Kennedy was killed by a lone crazy with a rifle, and President Reagan was almost killed by a lone crazy with a pipsqueak .22 handgun. But some people are bound to make up conspiracies if they can't find them growing naturally. So let them have their fancy imaginary plots; but they can't have this real one. We can't let it be known that the nation's scientific establishment has been infiltrated and perverted by a bunch of ambitious and self-righteous citizens for their own purposes; and it certainly mustn't get around that to help them they even managed to build up a powerful national law-enforcement agency out of a bunch of half-ass security guards. We can't have the nation's faith in its noble scientists and brave G-men shaken, can we now? That would be like curing the pup of live heartworms just to stop his heart with dead ones. Now get me out of here."

"Yes, sir," I said. "Discreetly."

CHAPTER 12

I don't suppose the plane ride west was any better than the plane ride east had been—they're all lousy these days—but I was getting stronger daily so I was in better shape to survive it, and I had more to keep my mind busy. Besides, you gain two hours going west so it seems like a shorter flight, even though actual air time is the same.

Then the plane was setting down on the Tucson runway a couple of thousand miles from Washington, D.C. As far as I'm concerned, Arizona is what God made with what He had left over after finishing New Mexico—Texas is, of course, all the stuff He tossed out beforehand as obviously useless for His creative purposes. I mean, we all have our little prejudices. The silver Mazda was waiting for me in a protected parking area. The crazy rotary engine started on the second try, after I remembered to pull out the manual choke. It was a bit tricky managing the wheel and the five-speed stick one-handed. I went through the usual preliminary security routines, turned off the pavement onto the familiar little unmarked and unpaved road, and treated the sagging ranch-type gate in a way that let the sniper in the hidden guard post on the nearby ridge know it was all right not to shoot me.

From there it was several more rough miles to the main ranch house. The cottonwoods around it were showing pale green leaf buds; a little later in the spring they'd produce vast clouds of fluffy drifting white cotton and set us all to sneezing, but while I'd doubtless swear

149

at them along with everybody else—assuming I was still here, which wasn't likely—I kind of liked the great honest old-fashioned trees and to hell with the newfangled cottonless varieties they're promoting nowadays.

In the ranch office, a girl with streaky brown-blond hair was beating on an ancient nonelectric typewriter. Her back was to me and she was making enough noise to cover the sound of my entrance. I watched her rise and move to the filing cabinets, a slender and taut and pleasing figure in high heels with her tanned bare arms and legs. She was wearing a crisp white skirt and a thin pink sleeveless blouse. She seemed to be left-handed, and a little clumsy, strange for such a healthy-looking girl. Then I saw the old scars on the left wrist, almost masked by the new tan. At the same time she turned and saw me.

I said, "I'm looking for Mrs. Madeleine Ellershaw. Would you happen to know where I can find her, ma'am?"

She said, "Matt, you dope." After a little pause, she said, "Just a minute. I've got to file this before I forget where it goes."

I watched her sit on her heels to put the papers away in a bottom drawer. She used the right hand now that she was in a hurry, I noticed, without clumsiness. Apparently the left-handed business had been some kind of self-imposed therapy for the neglected muscles and tendons. Madeleine rose and smoothed down her skirt and came over to face me. It was a fairly awkward moment; somehow I knew I wasn't supposed to grab this handsome stranger and give her a hello-again kiss. Nor could I be too enthusiastic about her greatly improved appearance. It would not only have sounded as if I were patronizing her and praising her for being a good little girl and eating all her spinach, it would also have implied that she'd looked pretty dreadful when she'd come here.

Actually, I felt a certain sense of loss. I'd grown very fond of the soft, pale, troubled woman to whom I'd made love one stormy night, who'd been such a comforting presence in my hospital room after I'd been shot. But maybe, I reflected sourly, what I really missed was the sense of superiority she'd given me, the feeling that I was being a great guy for being so nice to a poor, drab, overweight, prison-damaged dame who, whatever she might once have been, really had very little going for her now.

But I was going to have to forgo that easy ego trip. The transformation that had just been wrought in that rather colorless and shapeless lady by six weeks of rugged conditioning was as shocking in its way as the earlier transformation had been, the one that had been wrought in a bright and smart and lovely young woman by eight years of prison. I guess I was really taken aback by the fact that she hadn't turned out at all the way I'd expected. Naturally, I hadn't hoped to rediscover the twenty-two-year-old girl I'd known so briefly a dozen years ago; whatever the Ranch may be, it's hardly the Fountain of Youth. But I had kind of thought I'd find that girl's older sister awaiting me, more mature of course, but similarly attractive in a quiet and well-bred way: in other words, the person she would have become if her life had been allowed to fulfill it early promise. But this was a different person entirely.

Not that she wasn't attractive. The soft flesh that had been allowed to accumulate during the years of confinement and despair, which had blurred the fine features and thickened the slim figure, had been burned away under the hot Arizona sun that had also changed the prison pallor to the smooth golden tan I'd already noted. I'd thought of her as a girl, seeing her from behind; but there was really nothing girlish about her, I realized now. This was an adult and very striking woman, but the shocking thing was not so much what she'd gained as what she'd lost: a certain air of gentility that she'd somehow managed to cling to throughout her troubles, up to now.

The Ranch had done what it was supposed to do. It had taken the wreckage that crushing disgrace and brutal imprisonment had made of a refined young lady and had used it to construct a very handsome but quite unladylike fighting animal.

For a moment I saw her with frightening clarity, sleek and dangerous, like a female puma I'd once encountered on a mountain trail—we'd both decided we had urgent business elsewhere—and I wondered whether I'd really done her a favor by bringing her here. Particularly with a criminal record behind her, it was a risky way for her to be; safer to have left her ineffectual and inconspicuous. We faced each other like that for a long moment, almost like enemies. Then Madeleine relaxed and smiled at me at last, and suddenly there was only a very good-looking woman in her late twenties or early thirties standing there in a summery blouse and skirt, with fingers rather smudged by carbon paper.

"Well, Matt?"

"I'm going to miss that nice plump lady who took care of me in the hospital," I said.

"I wasn't plump, damn it!" She grinned. "Well, maybe just a bit too well-upholstered. Aren't you going to say something nice about me?"

"I wouldn't dare," I said. "You'd think I was patronizing you again. Like: you Cinderella, me Fairy Godfather."

"You louse." But she laughed, unoffended. "Incidentally, if you're wondering what I'm doing in here, the other girl came down with some kind of violent dysentery and had to be rushed into Tucson. I wasn't doing anything after the class went on to the technical and classified stuff, just a bit of jogging, and fencing left-handed when Martinelli had time for me, and trying to learn to shoot a little better when the range was open. And waiting for you to return. So I volunteered my services, and they looked at me very suspiciously, and locked up the heirloom jewelry and the silver flatware and all the secret formulas for terminating the world with a big bang, and turned me loose. God, what a disorganized mess; I'd like to spend six months straightening it out. Their filing system is simply prehistoric, along with their antique typewriter. But anyway, it's nice to know I can still run one of those machines after a fashion. One day I suppose Uncle Sam will stop buying me clothes and feeding and housing me, not to mention teaching me how to kill people, and I'll have to go out and make it on my own." She gave me a look that was almost shy, and went oddly with her new self-possessed appearance. "Matt."

"Yes?"

"It's . . . kind of scary, knowing all that stuff. Do you know what I mean?"

"I know. It's a good way to feel about it. Don't stop."

She licked her lips. "It's like . . . well, owning an attack-trained dog you're not quite sure you can control. But when I think of all those poor, helpless, untrained, unarmed women walking the streets afraid, never making eye contact with anybody lest they be jumped and raped . . . I always wondered why a man like you would go in for work like this. But that's part of it, isn't it? Not having to be afraid of *anybody*."

"Don't get too cocky. If a hundred-and-twenty-pound girl meets a two-hundred-and-twenty-pound man who knows the same tricks, too bad."

She laughed quickly. "Do you want to give it a try, buster?" She glanced at her watch. "Well, I'd better log you in and lock up here and show you your room. We're over in Cottonwood Cottage, very cozy. I've got the keys right here. My turn to supply the booze."

Many of the dude-ranch rooms had been in the big, hotel-like main building known as the Lodge, but there had also been a number of single and double cabins, and we'd kept them and retained the original names: Aspen, Birch, Cottonwood, Pinon, Tamarisk, Willow, Yucca. Cottonwood was a two-unit cabin. Madeleine unlocked the first door we came to and put the key on the little table just inside.

153

"Come next door as soon as you're ready," she said. "Don't be too long; I'm thirsty."

When her door opened to my knock, after a suitable cleanup interval, I was a little surprised to see that she hadn't changed her costume. I guess I'd expected her to be eager to show off her glorious new figure in something glamorous and intimate and sexy. Well, to be perfectly honest, in spite of our no-kiss meeting, I'd been assuming in my smug male fashion that we'd simply pick up where we'd left off the night before I was shot.

Seeing her still in her office clothes, becoming though they were, and noting the separate, if neighborly, accommodations she'd arranged for us, I decided that I'd better take nothing for granted. The situation had altered considerably since that snowy evening, and certain people had altered considerably also. The signals were pretty clear: the strong, slender woman before me felt that our relationship was in need of clarification, if not a complete overhaul.

She said, "I made a fire; it still gets a little chilly around here after sundown. Sit down and let me make like a hostess."

"What did you do to your hair?" I asked, settling into a deep chair in front of the big stone fireplace.

"It just got that way. All that sunshine. Well, the girl in the beauty shop—I got into Tucson under protective escort a couple of times—thought it was very chic and wanted to emphasize it a bit, so I let her." She brought me a drink and stood over me. "If you feel it's too gaudy for what we'll be doing, I've got a rinse that'll turn me into an instant mouse."

I shook my head. "No. I want to talk it over with you and get your ideas, but my feeling is that our best bet is to walk boldly into the cage, meaning Santa Fe, and stir up the animals. Flashy car, flashy blonde—well, semi-blonde—gent with arm in conspicuous black sling. All part of the image we'll be projecting, if you agree that the best way to tackle our problem is to attract attention rather than avoid it. But before we get on that subject, I'd better bring you up to date. Not to be corny or anything, but I've got good news and bad news."

She sat down gracefully in the opposite big chair. "Give me the good news first, please."

"I'm supposed to let you know that the bossman was very impressed by your training record. For an old lady of thirty-four with a bum wrist you did real good. I'm supposed to let you know that we can use your special talents. We get a lot of wild, bloodthirsty kids, but good-looking dames with legal training don't wander in the door every day." I looked at her across the low round cocktail table that separated us. "I'm not selling anything, Madeleine. In fact I think you'd probably be better off carrying out your journalistic plans, when the time comes. This kind of work isn't for everybody, and I'm not a bit sure it's for you. But I thought you might be pleased by the official compliment."

She said quietly, "Thank you, Matt. Yes, I'm pleased and flattered. May I think it over?"

"As long as you like. It's an open offer."

"And the bad news?"

"Double-headed. First, if you've got any sense at all you'll be scared—I am—when you learn the dimensions of this thing we're being asked to go up against. Second, you'll be mad when you learn the attitude of the people who're asking it. One of them, anyway. Do you want to hear it all now, or after we've had another drink and maybe dinner?"

"I thought we'd have dinner right here in front of the fire," she said. "Let me call the kitchen and get things started, then we can talk."

Room service is provided at the Ranch for people in residence who, for one reason or another, aren't supposed to be seen too much; or for people who aren't supposed to see too much, like who's currently using the big dining room. However, unless you're on a special diet for medical reasons, you take what they're dishing out that day; there's no menu. The only official choice is coffee, tea, or milk. Unofficially, however, you can get a bottle of moderate wine, if you try hard and have a certain amount of seniority. But it seemed that a feminine voice with a nice way of saying please could accomplish the same purpose; I could hear her promoting a certain California Cabernet with apparent success.

"Like old times," I said when she returned.

"Oh, the wine," she said. "I always do seem to take over in that department, don't I? But I'm afraid what they're bringing is hardly Château Margaux. Now you can pour me another martini from that pitcher and spring your bad news on me."

I told her of the meeting in Washington, holding nothing back, not even the fact that I'd been asked if I'd got to fuck the lady and, if so, how she'd performed. She'd been watching the fire as she listened; now she turned to look at me.

"Well, what did you tell him?"

"That you were quite satisfactory, of course," I said.

"Thank you for the testimonial." Her voice was tart. Then she smiled faintly. "He's kind of an old blowhard, isn't he, your Mr. Smith. I suppose he's who I think he is; we got some news even in prison."

I noted that she was no longer stumbling over the word. I said, "Yes, but let's leave his real name out of this. . . . Goody, that sounds like food at the door."

The dinner was roast beef, and the wine seemed quite adequate to me, but I'm hardly a connoisseur. Madeleine wrinkled her nose over it in a critical way; then she grinned at me quickly across the table. Clearly we were both thinking the same thing: barely two months earlier she'd been a different woman in a different place, a place where nobody—she least of all—had worried about the difference between imported and domestic wine.

She drew a long breath. "Well, it looks as if the fate of the nation rests upon our shoulders, doesn't it, Matt?"

I said, "Hell, it always does. You'll get used to it."

She laughed. "Don't be so cynical in front of the green troops; they might think you don't take the mission seriously. Matt."

"Yes?"

"May I make a suggestion? When we get to Santa Fe, it's pretty important that we're convincing and, well, a little dangerous-looking, isn't it? Just as you said a little while ago. Well, I've been thinking about it while you were away, and I know the character I'd like to play—I even got together some clothes for the part. If you'll let me do it my way."

I said, "Don't be so goddamn humble, Ellershaw. You know damn well you're going to do it your way. It's mainly your show, and I'd be a fool to argue with you about how it should be performed. Tell me."

She said, "Of course what I'd love to do is return home in a chauffeur-driven Rolls and emerge gracefully all glittering with diamonds and dripping with sables—wearing an umpty-thousand-dollar Paris gown, of course—and look down my aristocratic nose at all the crummy peasants who'd gloated over my . . . my downfall. But first of all that would be too expensive to be practical, and second of all, even if it were feasible, it wouldn't accomplish much except to reinflate the ex-convict lady's punctured ego. It wouldn't scare the people we're after into betraying themselves by making another move against us. If I deliberately give the impression, at your agency's expense, that I've somehow managed to land in the lap of luxury since my release from the pen, there'll be no real driving motive for me to seek vindication, or revenge, will there?"

"Sounds reasonable," I said. "Carry on."

She swallowed something in her throat; clearly her homecoming was something she still couldn't contemplate without emotion.

She said, "Even if . . . even if I come back to Santa Fe now, after serving my sentence, looking just reasonably presentable, pretty much the same woman who was

157

hauled away to stir, only eight years older—well, looking about the way I do this minute—my return will have no real impact. The few people who remained my friends and were sorry for me when it happened, and maybe actually believed me innocent, will be relieved to see that I haven't suffered too badly from my incarceration. Those who just loved seeing the hotshot lawyer girl knocked off her high horse will be disappointed that I show so few effects of my prison ordeal. But nobody'll be particularly afraid of me. It will just be the same Madeleine Ellershaw back again after having—whether as innocent patsy or guilty accomplice—paid eight years of her life for her folly in loving and trusting the wrong man. And everybody knows that, whatever may have happened to her, Mrs. Ellershaw was brought up to be a real little lady who couldn't possibly do anything crude and vengeful no matter what the provocation."

"Makes sense," I said. "But what's your point?"

She drew a long breath. "Matt, what we need is a truly shocking change in me that'll make them sit up and take notice. Well, we had one that was shocking enough, but thanks to you and this outdoors torture chamber of yours, that flabby, pasty-faced dame is gone. She wouldn't have been much good for menace, anyway; she wouldn't have scared a sick mouse."

"So what do you suggest?"

"Let's face it, I'm not a real little lady any longer." Madeleine pushed her empty plate aside and leaned forward earnestly. "After Fort Ames and this place, I'm not any kind of a lady. I've . . . lost faith in all the things that supported me before: my upper-class family, my careful upbringing, my expensive education. They couldn't keep me out of prison, and they didn't do me a damn bit of good while I was in there. But now I have something very simple and primitive to sustain me instead: the fact that I can toss any bastard across the room who annoys me. Or blow his brains out with a gun. Or spill his guts with a knife, or break his neck barehanded. It scares me,

158

as I told you, but it gives me confidence, too. So let's use it, damn it!" Her voice was suddenly harsh. "Let's show those sinister creeps who framed me, who'll undoubtedly be watching, what a cheap, crude, vengeance-hungry female animal their damned maximum-security correctional institution has made of the nice, bright, polite young career girl they ruined and sent away to prison. My idea is, you're the conscientious trainer trying to restrain me, trying to keep me off people's throats, and I'm your savage killer-Doberman-bitch straining at the heavy leash, just panting for blood. What do you think, Matt?"

"Colorful," I said. "But promising, if you're willing to make yourself look that bad."

She said rather grimly, "You're forgetting the dismal dame who was dragging herself homewards so humbly before you got shot. After facing the idea of coming home like *that*, I find anything an improvement. This way I at least get to spit in their eyes. I've got it all set, the way I'm going to dress; I'll show you in the morning." She laughed. "You won't like it, but as you told me once under similar circumstances, I'm not putting on this act for you." She hesitated, and glanced at me a bit uncertainly. "Matt?"

"Yes?"

"I don't mean to be a take-charge girl. Slap me down if you want to. After all, you're the professional here. I'm just a wet-nosed amateur."

I grinned. "I just love that phony humility; you know you'd bite my head off if I really—" I was interrupted by a soft knock at the back door of the unit, which led out to a little patio where the dude-ranch guests used to sunbathe in private. When Madeleine glanced at me quickly, I said, "I called somebody from my room and told him to stop by, somebody I want you to meet. I'll let him in."

The young man who entered when I opened the back door was wearing a sports shirt and slacks. He was very

159

pretty, and his hair was very pretty, too; one of the blow-dry boys. He could have been the star of any current TV show—John Wayne, where are you now that we really need you?—except for his eyes. They were brown eyes, and they were opaque and deadly as he stepped inside expecting a trap because he'd been trained to expect traps everywhere. Then he saw me clearly and saw that I matched the description he'd been given. The wary tension went out of him and suddenly he was just a nice young fellow with smiling brown eyes.

"Eric?"

"I'm Eric," I said. "This way."

We didn't shake hands; this was business, not friendship. I followed him into the big room, where Madeleine stood by the fireplace, waiting.

"Madeleine, this is McCullough," I said. "Take a good look at him. You know Jackson, and young Marty, and after all those days nursing me in Santa Paula, you can probably recognize some of the other men who were watching over you. That's the first line of defense. McCullough, here, is the second, with a backup crew. I thought you'd better see what he looks like so you don't shoot him by mistake some time when things get a bit hairy. Now that you're a dangerous lady with a limited hunting licence . . . I mean field qualification."

Madeleine nodded. "Hi, McCullough."

"Mrs. Ellershaw."

"Okay, McCullough. That's it," I said.

"I'll be around," he said. "Good night, ma'am."

There was a little silence after he'd gone, then Madeleine whistled softly. "Am I right in thinking that he's not as sweet as he looks?"

"We hope not. One of the new ones. Like me, he's been recuperating from a few anatomical perforations."

"I haven't seen him around."

"There are quite a few things around this place you haven't seen. And people." I grinned. "Old soldiers like

160

me don't worry too much about showing their faces around. I mean, we're known, we're in dossiers all around the world. Our covers were blown long ago, and sometimes it works just as well that way. When a miscreant hears that Horrible Helm is after him he just lies down and dies, or cuts his throat obligingly, saving me a lot of trouble. But often an unknown face is needed, and we try to keep the new young ones, like McCullough, from being spotted too soon. So they don't wander around this place openly and ogle the pretty girl trainees, unlike some people." I studied her for a minute, and said, "Well, it's been a long day and planes make me tired. I think I'll thank my hostess and retire to my own quarters, if she doesn't mind."

Madeleine looked a little surprised. I was aware of her gray eyes following me questioningly as I picked up the sling I'd discarded to eat and put it back on. She didn't speak until I reached the door.

"Matt?" The question that had been in her eyes was in her voice also. Then she came quickly across the room to me. "Was I so obvious, my dear?"

"I got the message," I said. "Just a friendly dinner in front of the fire for old times' sake. But no cozy shared bedrooms, no slinky negligees, no seductive smiles. You made it pretty clear: I was not to take you for granted now because of anything that had happened between us in the past. All seigneurial privileges revoked, right?"

She licked her lips. "I didn't mean . . . Oh, God, you must think I'm an ungrateful bitch!"

I said, "Let's leave gratitude out of this."

She spoke breathlessly: "I've been regimented for so long, Matt! I . . . I've belonged to other people for so long. They took me away from me; they left me no say in what was to become of me. For years I've had no rights in myself, in my own body, do you understand? And now . . . now at last I'm free enough and strong enough to take myself back from all the people who've owned me and controlled me. Including you. Even you. I don't want you to think for a moment that I don't appreciate—"

"To hell with appreciate," I said. "I think it's swell. Just put me on the list for when you're ready to be courted properly, Mrs. Ellershaw."

She smiled slowly. "Right at the top," she said. "Thank you, Matt. Thank you for being so understanding."

Tired though I was, I took quite a while to get to sleep. Being understanding always gives me insomnia.

CHAPTER 13

IT'S roughly five hundred miles from Tucson to Santa Fe. With an early-morning start, we were passing Albuquerque, sixty miles south of our destination, by three in the afternoon, with the Rio Grande off to our left and the Sandia Mountains, the steep west face of them, towering on our right. They once flew an airliner into that five-thousand-foot wall of rock and had a hell of a time getting to it afterwards; but of course there wasn't much left to get to.

Half an hour later we came up over the top of the great black escarpment called La Bajada—the descent or drop, obviously named by folks traveling the other way—and saw Santa Fe ahead, nesting in the foothills of the tall Sangre de Cristo mountains, the southernmost extension of the Rockies proper. I glanced at the woman behind the wheel, who was showing no signs of weariness although she'd been driving since daylight. She was costumed for her new role: still another Madeleine Rustin Ellershaw for me to get used to. The girl was a real chameleon.

There had been the proud young lady lawyer so long ago, and more recently the beaten ex-convict, and the comfortably unspectacular and undemanding lady who'd watched TV with me in the hospital, and the taut, self-possessed, suntanned woman who'd greeted me with some reserve upon my return from Washington. Now I had a defiantly sexy tight-pants broad on my hands, in too-snug jeans that weren't very clean, and a cheap white knitted shirt that was little more than a glorified T-shirt, also very tight, so that her fine breasts flaunted themselves arrogantly through the thin, strained material. No brassiere, of course: nipples boldly on display. There were high-heeled sandals at one end of her and a considerable amount of makeup at the other, particularly around the eyes.

It was sleazy, provocative kid stuff in a way; and the fact that she was very obviously not a kid but a mature and handsome woman—boldly handsome now, with that blond-streaked hair—made it all the more disturbing. I hated to see her do this to herself, but then, as she'd said, she wasn't dressing for me. She glanced at me with a little half-smile as she drove us towards the distant city we'd taken so long to reach.

"Don't look so disapproving, darling," she said. "You should be getting used to it by now."

I said, "I'm grateful for small favors. At least you didn't go in for the floppy pantaloons or baggy knee-britches and bloomers they all seem to be wearing this year."

She laughed. "After all the work I did getting my ass trimmed down to size, I wasn't about to drape the sleek new femme fatale in those lousy manure sacks even if they are fashionable at the moment. Anyway, I'm not supposed to be fashionable. I'm supposed to be a bitter female ex-con angrily rejecting the wealthy fashionable world she used to know before it has a chance to reject her." She drew a long, rather shaky breath, and studied the view ahead. "There it is!" she said softly. "Santa Fe. There were . . . times when I thought I'd never see it again. And times when I didn't really want to, when all I wanted was to crawl into a hole somewhere far away where nobody'd recognize me." She grimaced. "Well, it's supposed to be very good for the character to face up to things. I should have one hell of a character by the time all this is over. But . . ."

"But what?" I asked when she hesitated.

"Stay close and hold my hand when I need it, please. It's going to be rough; and even though I've had lots of practice, I don't really know how much more humiliation I can take."

We spent the night in a convenient motel, one of the older ones just a few blocks from the city's main plaza. It was a pleasant, rambling place with tree-shaded grounds, which hadn't changed very much in all the years I'd known it. In the morning I couldn't help remembering that, long ago, as a respectable free-lance photojournalist, I'd occasionally brought my wife to dinner in the restaurant where Madeleine and I were now breakfasting. Afterwards, leaving the car parked in front of my unit, we hiked the few blocks downtown to keep the appointment I'd made by phone when we got in the previous afternoon—Madeleine had also called her parents' lawyer and set up a meeting after lunch.

We had to pause briefly on the way to our destination for her to gape, aghast, at a tall new bank building—well, tall for the town. Originally a picturesque southwestern desert village of low adobe houses, often little more than mud huts, Santa Fe keeps fighting to stay that way, or at least stay looking that way; but this was a relative skyscraper.

"I didn't know they were allowed to do that!" Madeleine protested.

I glanced at her, a little amused but also rather

touched. In spite of what had been done to her here, in spite of where she'd spent the past eight years, in spite of the indignities and dangers that undoubtedly lay ahead of her, she could still be distressed by what had happened to her quaint old hometown during her enforced absence.

"I gather nobody else did, either, until they did it," I said. "Come on, let's go say hello to the cops."

The police station was just across the street from the new bank. The shabby, two-story, territorial-style building—meaning that the pseudo-adobe walls were topped with brick—hadn't altered much in spite of the changes in its surroundings. I felt Madeleine grow tense as she approached it, and thought she was simply experiencing a recurrence of the old prison fear of uniformed authority that she'd conquered once. Then I realized that this was probably the building to which, expensively dressed and bejeweled for a festive dinner with her husband, unable to believe what was happening to her, the young Mrs. Ellershaw had been brought under arrest with those *things* shining on her wrists to be rudely questioned and thrown into a cell on the last day ever of the good life she'd once known.

But that would have been the wing that housed the city jail. We entered the administration wing instead, and after a little wait outside the office barricade were admitted to the presence of the Chief of Police, Manuel Cordoba, a compact, dark-faced, uniformed man with a mustache, whose eyes widened slightly with recognition, and some shock, at the sight of Madeleine. She was still in yesterday's cheap and provocative costume, a little more grubby for a day's wear; but since spring mornings are chilly at Santa Fe's altitude of seven thousand feet she was also wearing, open, an inexpensive ski jacket she'd bought while costuming herself for the part she planned to play here. The quilted garment was a strong, almost luminous, shade of violet.

I saw her take note of the chief's stare. Her lips grew

tight and narrow. She'd know, of course, that it wasn't that Chief Cordoba didn't see lots of women in jeans, tight and loose, clean and dirty; in fact it seemed likely that a large percentage of the females he encountered in the line of business were jean-clad ladies. But he was obviously recalling the well-groomed young professional woman whom, almost a decade ago, he'd undoubtedly met in the course of his normal police duties.

I said, "You may remember Mrs. Ellershaw, Chief Cordoba."

He nodded. "I remember."

I said, "Having served her full sentence, Mrs. Ellershaw is not required to report to the authorities, but we thought it best to let you know she was in town."

He nodded. "We were notified of her release from the Federal Correctional Institution at Fort Ames. That was a couple of months ago, wasn't it? I thought she must have decided not to come back to Santa Fe after . . . what happened here. But since all formalities have been complied with, it is, as you say, no official concern of mine as long as her presence creates no law-enforcement problems here."

It wasn't exactly a gracious welcome, and I felt Madeleine draw a sharp breath, preparing to speak; but I forestalled her.

"That's just the trouble, Chief," I said. "Somebody's trying to kill her; presumably somebody who apparently feels more strongly than you do about having her come home." I touched the sling supporting my right arm. "I stopped one bullet aimed at her the hard way, but there's no telling where the next one will go."

His eyes narrowed. "What do you wish from me?"

"Nothing," I said. I looked at him hard. "I mean that literally, Chief."

He studied me for quite a long time. "I remember you, too, of course, Mr. Helm," he said at last. "You used to live here. We try to keep track of our more prominent citizens."

"I wasn't very prominent," I said. "Just another camera snapper and typewriter pounder. The town is full of them, along with the artists and craftsmen who seem to gravitate here."

He said, "That may be, but at one time you gained a certain prominence in our records, Mr. Helm. You may not remember me, but when I was a younger officer there was a kidnapping here. A small child, not yet walking, snatched from her crib. Name: Elizabeth Margaret Helm. Parents: Elizabeth and Matthew Helm. There were also two people killed at this time. A man was found shot several times with a certain .22 pistol. He was quite dead. The weapon was found beside a woman who'd been very badly abused, also dead. Quite coincidental, of course; nothing to do with the abduction case. It was officially announced that, although she'd received injuries that were crippling and disfiguring, the woman had somehow managed to reach a gun and shoot up the insanely jealous lover who had hurt her so badly. He had staggered away to die. She had then, unwilling to live with what she had done, and what had been done to her, turned the gun upon herself. That is what appeared in the newspapers."

I was aware that Madeleine had glanced at me sharply; she was now listening very carefully.

I said, "But the papers were wrong."

Chief Cordoba nodded. "We had been asked to cooperate by disposing of the case in this manner. The request had come from Washington." He shrugged. "The kidnapping of a small child is an inexcusable crime; we were willing to overlook a few . . . irregularities in the recovery procedure. Actually the man, one of the kidnappers, had been deliberately shot to death by a certain individual to keep him from interfering in what was to happen or endangering the kidnapped child. The woman, his female accomplice—I believe the woman was in fact the brains of the operation; the man merely served as muscle—had then been skillfully and ruthlessly interrogated by the same, er, mysterious individual. Shortly, we got a telephone call asking that police officers with personal knowledge of a certain barrio should go there circumspectly and free the little girl from a certain address. I was one of those officers."

I said, "I remember, Chief. And my wife and I were very grateful for your efficiency, and still are. At least I know I am, and I'm sure she is, although I haven't seen her lately."

He nodded. "I did understand that Mrs. Helm was no longer, er, Mrs. Helm. In fact, she left Santa Fe within the year, with the children, did she not? And the agency in Washington that had requested our cooperation was one with which you had formerly been connected, wasn't it? It is my understanding that, after your divorce, you rejoined that organization and now reside in Washington, although you still spend your vacations here from time to time."

"It is a pleasant city," I said. "And you are well informed."

"And you ask me to do nothing to protect Mrs. Ellershaw?"

Abruptly, we were back in the present, after a tour through the painful past.

"That's right," I said. "Protection has already been arranged. I just wanted you to be aware of the situation, Chief, in case anything happens. I'm carrying, and so are some agents who are working with me on this. I'd like to be sure that your officers don't get, well, officious, if there's any trouble. Here." I took a card from my shirt pocket left-handed and laid it on the desk. "If you want confirmation from Washington, call that number, please."

He didn't touch the card. "Do I gather that there's more involved here than the threat to Mrs. Ellershaw?"

"That's a question I'm not permitted to answer," I said. "Officially, I'm here on behalf of the United States government to investigate the possibility that the lady's civil rights may have been very seriously violated; that she may even be innocent of the crime against her country of which she was convicted. The attempts on her life—there have been others—tend to support this hypothesis. It seems possible, now, that somebody had reason to want her put out of circulation for a long time and took steps to arrange for her false arrest and conviction; somebody who, now that she's free again, is still afraid of her and wants her silenced permanently."

Cordoba hesitated. "As a policeman I must point out—you will excuse me, Mrs. Ellershaw—that there could be other, less favorable, explanations."

Madeleine spoke for the first time since entering the office. Her voice was harsh: "I know! If there's an innocent explanation and a guilty one, I know damn well which one a fucking copper will go for every time! God, don't I know!"

Chief Cordoba's eyes narrowed again, as much with surprise as her coarse way of speaking as with anger. I put my hand on Madeleine's arm.

"Easy, easy!" I spoke to the chief: "I must ask you to excuse her. She's under considerable strain; it's tough on her, coming home like this after being . . . away for so many years."

Madeleine said, "Damn you, Helm, don't talk about me like I was a nut in a shrink's office! I'm a damn sight saner, particularly about cops, than back when I was an innocent career girl entertaining this weird notion that the law and the people with badges had been put there to protect *me*. God, what a laugh! If I hadn't been so fucking naive, I might not have let the bastards rob me of eight years of my life."

I said sharply, "Mrs. Ellershaw, the chief and his department had nothing whatever to do with what happened to you. Don't take it out on him."

Chief Cordoba said quietly, "It is all right. I understand. But I do think the . . . lady should remember that it was a federal case from start to finish. We were never involved."

Madeleine said, more quietly now, quite softly in fact, "That's perfectly true, Chief. God, how true it is! My husband was lured from our house right here in your town, kidnapped, and murdered; and you and your department were never a bit concerned, never a bit involved. If you had been, if you'd solved that crime as you should have, I'd never have gone to prison, would I? So don't try to pass the whole buck to the feds; and don't expect me to love and respect you, any of you, after the way you let Roy's murderers go free. But I bet you're hell on kids smoking pot."

That stung him. "The rumor was very carefully investigated and nothing was ever found to substantiate it!"

I said quickly, "We're wasting your time with ancient history, Chief. But there's one more thing I'd like to bring to your attention before we go."

When he spoke, after a little pause, his voice was stiff and resentful: "What is that, Mr. Helm?"

"I must advise you that we're not the only federal agency involved."

"I see."

I went on: "Naturally, the organization that investigated Mrs. Ellershaw's alleged crime, and supplied the evidence on the basis of which she was prosecuted, isn't going to be pleased when it learns of our activities. They have, shall we say, a vested interest in Mrs. Ellershaw's guilt. They may ask for your cooperation in, well, making the investigation tough for us. That will put you on a fairly awkward spot. May I suggest a policy of benevolent neutrality? Let us feds fight it out, and keep your own department from getting mixed up in it. That's what I meant when I said I'd like you to do nothing."

He said, "Go on, Mr. Helm. I'm listening."

"The Office of Federal Security is a fairly big agency these days," I said. "It seems to have considerable clout, so there may be some pressure. I hope you will resist it.

There will be no pressure from me, from us. However, if you call that phone number, you'll find that my instructions come from fairly high up, I think high enough to satisfy you that your best bet is to play this one strictly hands-off." I took Madeleine's arm and started to turn away.

"Mr. Helm."

I looked back. "Yes, Chief."

"One question. Is Mrs. Ellershaw . . . carrying?"

I said, poker-faced, "Heavens, Chief Cordoba, for her to have a gun, just out of the pen, would be very illegal, wouldn't it?" I shook my head. "No, she doesn't have one and wouldn't know how to use it if she did; her parents had very strong feelings about firearms. I can shoot pretty well left-handed if I have to, and as I said, I have some agents around to help me keep her safe. Anything else?"

"Yes." He looked at me for a long moment. When he spoke again, the formal Hispano act they like to pull on the dumb Anglo was gone. "How much of this crap do you expect me to believe, friend?"

I gave him a slow grin. "I hope you don't believe any of it. If you believed it, that would make you pretty stupid, and I'd like to think you're an intelligent man."

He stared at me unsmiling, and said, "I never heard that civil rights were the concern of your rather, if you'll excuse me, obscure agency."

I said carefully, "What you mean is, you'd like to know what's really going on. Join the club, Chief. I'd like to know too. All I'm doing is following instructions. Nobody's bothered to tell me what it's all about either." I gave him another grin. "Let's just say I've been ordered to set off a few firecrackers in the zoo. The people who sent me are very interested in learning which of the big local carnivores are gun-shy, and how high they'll jump. I hope you'll see your way clear to simply watching the show without interfering."

Outside, the sunshine was very bright after the gloom

171

of the little office, but the breeze was chilly. Hot, summery Arizona seemed a long way off, up here in the high Sangre de Christo foothills. Madeleine shivered and zipped up her bright quilted jacket as we stood for a moment on the sidewalk outside the police station. I waited. At last she threw me a sharp glance, as if expecting some kind of an unfavorable comment, and started to walk in the opposite direction from which we'd come. I strode along beside her without speaking.

"That bastard!" she said after a little. "Offers to protect me, more or less, but makes damn sure I'm not carrying a gun to protect myself."

I said, "You did fine. Shook him up a bit without, I hope, really making an enemy of him."

"Matt, did she really divorce you because of *that*?"

"Cut it out, Ellershaw," I said. "Irrelevant, incompetent, and immaterial, I think you lawyers say."

She spoke quietly: "You can't have it both ways, my dear. You know practically everything there is to know about me; don't shut me out when I try to learn a little about you. That was you, wasn't it, that certain mysterious individual who shot that man to death and then . . . interrogated that woman to find out where the little girl was being held. Your little girl."

I cleared your throat. "Okay. Fair is fair, I guess. Yes. They were trying to force me, through my kid, to do something for them, but we don't play that game, ever. Which you might remember if you're ever dumb enough to let yourself be taken hostage. We'll do our best to blast you loose, but we'll make no deals."

"I'll certainly keep it in mind," she said. "And you're stalling."

"The woman's name, the name I used to know her by, was Tina," I said. "She was in the business, our business; she was pretty tough; and I had to get very rough before she'd give up the address."

"And for that, your wife left you? For saving your

172

child, *her* child? My God, what kind of a woman was she?"

"A very nice woman," I said. "A very nice, sensitive woman who'd never been told what kind of work I'd done before we met—security was very tight back then and I wasn't allowed to tell anybody, not even my wife—and who suddenly discovered she was married to a man she didn't know, a violent stranger whose touch made her want to throw up. She walked in on it, you see, although I'd asked her to stay home and wait. It was pretty gory, and she'd never encountered anything remotely like it in her sheltered New England life. I told you once: a gentle and nonviolent girl."

"Would she rather have seen her baby dead?" Madeleine asked contemptuously.

I shook my head. "You don't understand. Intellectually, Beth could accept what I'd done as necessary for our kid's survival; but emotionally . . ." I shrugged. "And before you pass such a quick and arrogant judgment on her, remember that you're appraising her from the viewpoint of a hardened graduate of Fort Ames Penitentiary, not to mention that other place where you've just been learning how to cut people's throats. The young lady I took out to dinner twelve years ago might not have been quite so ready to accept a man with blood on his hands."

After a moment, she said, "I'm sorry. It's really none of my business, anyway."

Her voice had an absent quality, as if she'd suddenly lost interest in the subject; she was looking ahead as we walked along a street lined with trees. I noticed that they displayed very little in the way of leaf buds yet. A few thousand feet of altitude, and a few hundred miles of latitude, made a considerable difference in the seasons.

"Are we going where I think we're going?" I asked at last.

She said, "Yes, it's right up ahead."

"I know. I was there once, remember?"

She stopped in front of a two-story house set back from the sidewalk, flanked by large cottonwoods, in a grassy yard all its own, one of the few such private oases of greenery remaining in that part of town. She looked down at herself, and glanced at me a bit uncertainly, almost shyly.

"Do I look all right?" she asked.

"No," I said honestly. "You look all wrong, but isn't that what you want?"

She nodded. "Will you let me handle it, Matt? I'm going to make a paranoid spectacle of myself—I want to check out some wild and impossible theories that used to come to me in prison when I was feeling particularly downtrodden, betrayed by the whole world—at least my whole world. All I want you to do is look embarrassed and try to hush me, and apologize for me if it seems indicated, just as you did back there at the police station. Take your cues from me, please."

"It's your show," I said. "Carry on."

She hesitated, and glanced down at herself, and gave a rueful little laugh. "Do you want to know something funny? Even after everything that's happened to me, I still find it very hard to go in there looking like such a tramp. God, I remember how carefully I used to check my hair and lipstick and nylons every morning before I started up this walk. So let's get it the hell over with before the lady loses her nerve."

She squared her shoulders and turned up the neatly swept concrete path towards the massive building. It was an old residence—almost a mansion—that had been lovingly converted to offices in the days before it became fashionable to bulldoze everything flat and cover the solid old foundations with flimsy modern structures. I saw her make her high-heeled, tight-pants walk deliberately vulgar and provocative as she mounted the steps to the covered porch—*portal*, in the local idiom.

Mrs. Madeleine Ellershaw walked straight up to the heavy old front door; but before marching inside she

174

paused very briefly to touch—reminiscently, sadly—the discreet brass plate, nicely polished, that read: BARON AND WALSH—ATTORNEYS AT LAW.

CHAPTER 14

THE reception room was large and luxurious and rather old-fashioned, as befitted the building. For waiting clients—one sensed they'd never have to wait long in this well-run place—there was a comfortable sofa with a couple of deep chairs to match, and a low table supplied with a few reasonably current magazines, but not so many that the place looked like a dentist's waiting room. More like a well-lived-in den or study. There were real rugs on the floor instead of the usual synthetic wall-to-wall stuff. I saw one little Navajo number in the corner, about five by seven, that I'd have liked to have if I'd had anyplace to put it, but it would have given my sterile, furnished Washington apartment a bad case of artistic indigestion. It's only a convenient place to sleep between assignments, anyway.

The receptionist at the antique-looking mahogany desk in the alcove by the fine old stairway was a self-conscious beauty with a lot of pale gold hair pulled back severely to a big roll at the nape of her neck. I recalled from my long-ago forays into fashion photography that you could call it a chignon if you wanted to be fancy. She was wearing a severe white silk blouse, the kind with a built-in ascot-looking arrangement of the same material at the throat. The jacket of a severe gray suit, on a hanger, was neatly suspended from an old-fashioned

175

coat tree in the corner. She was presumably wearing the equally severe gray skirt of the suit—that area wasn't visible as she sat behind the desk—but I didn't think she'd have interested me greatly even if she'd left it off. I mean, there's a rumor to the effect that the ones who make a production of looking untouchable usually aren't; but my own minor researches in the field indicate that it's generally a lot of work to find out and hardly ever worth it when you do.

She raised her delicate, carefully drawn eyebrows as Madeleine marched up. She'd obviously appraised at a glance the roughly dressed female who'd just entered, and decided not to waste on her the gracious smile of welcome reserved for important clients.

"Ye-es?"

Madeleine said, "I want to see Mr. Baron and Walter Maxon in Mr. Baron's office. As soon as possible. Would you arrange it, please?"

"I'm afraid that without an appointment—"

Madeleine glanced at me. "Shit, I tried to be polite, I even said please, you heard me," she said harshly. She put her hands on the desk, leaning forward. "Get on the phone, Blondie! Tell Mr. Baron there's an unsuccessful case of his downstairs, one of his few failures, and if he tries to give her a runaround she's going to commence dismantling the fucking premises starting with the bleached number with the penciled eyebrows!"

I said hastily, "Take it easy, take it easy."

I turned to the girl and dropped my ID folder on the desk in front of her, open, to show the pretty badge-thing inside, so carefully designed to impress people. I picked it up, flipped it closed, and put it away.

"Helm, Matthew Helm," I said. "Mrs. Ellershaw and I really would like a conference with the attorneys she mentioned, as soon as possible. Government business. Would you arrange it, please?"

"Mrs. Ellershaw?" Clearly recognizing the name, the blond girl threw a startled glance at the jeans-clad woman on the other side of the desk. "Well . . . well, as a matter of fact Mr. Baron gave instructions weeks ago that anytime Mrs. Ellershaw came in she was to be shown right up if he wasn't with a client, but she didn't give her name, so how could I know?" The receptionist's voice was resentful. She went on with some satisfaction: "Anyway, there *is* somebody in his office right now. But I'll let him know the minute he's free—"

"Madeleine! My God, Madeleine!"

There was a quick pounding of feet on the carpeted stairs as a youngish man threw himself down them and came hurrying up to us.

"Hello, Walter." Madeleine's voice was soft.

"Gosh, it's good to see you!" the man said breathlessly. "I . . . we were beginning to think you'd decided not to come home at all. I was going to try to find you as soon as I could get away. . . ." He stopped, and reached out impulsively to take both her hands. "Let me look at you. Hey, you look great!"

The funny thing was, he meant it. He clearly wasn't even noticing how she was dressed; he was remembering only the distressed, disintegrating woman in prison uniform with whom, several years ago, he'd talked so awkwardly in Fort Ames. It was obvious that he'd looked forward to this meeting with considerable trepidation, wondering what shape she'd be in—if she'd even be recognizable after her long imprisonment. His relief at seeing her whole once more, tanned and healthy, was rather touching.

"I . . . I got your letters," Madeleine said. "I'm sorry I hardly ever answered them. There wasn't anything to write about, in that place. But thank you; and thanks for sending the things I asked for. . . . Walter, this is Mr. Helm, who's, well, kind of looking into my case for the U.S. government, a little late. Mr. Helm, Mr. Maxon."

We shook hands. He was a very boyish and sincere-looking young fellow—well, the record I'd read gave his age as thirty-five, but he didn't look it. He was almost

177

too good to be true; but his emotions upon seeing Madeleine had been revealing and, I thought, genuine. I decided to take him at face value for the time being. He was a little under six feet and a bit heavy, almost plump; if he didn't start fighting it soon he'd have a real problem around the middle. He had mousy-brown hair cut moderately short but not short enough to make any kind of a crew-cut macho statement, and he wore a neat blue suit and big horn-rimmed glasses.

"It's a pleasure to meet you, sir," he said. "It's about time somebody looked into—"

The receptionist, who'd picked up the phone, interrupted: "Mr. Baron will see you now, Mrs. Ellershaw."

Madeleine turned towards the stairs. A white-haired woman in an obviously expensive suit and blouse was descending with the care used by those whose knees aren't quite as reliable as they once were; she glanced at Madeleine as they passed, and then looked back quickly, frowning. Abruptly, she drew her jacket about her and buttoned it carefully as if to protect herself from contamination. She swept out of the place holding herself very straight, her squared shoulders expressing disapproval.

I heard Maxon, beside me, mutter, "Old biddy!"

But Madeleine hadn't even noticed; she was looking up at the man who'd come to the top of the stairs to greet her. I'd got a glimpse of Baron once in court, twelve years ago when I'd come here to get some information out of his client, Willy Chavez. I remembered that the senior active partner of Madeleine's firm—Walsh had been retired as a lawyer even back then, although I'd gathered he still had a voice in running the firm—had looked like quite a sizable specimen, but he'd been sitting down at the time. I hadn't realized how big he'd be standing up: a great gray grizzly of a man as tall as my own six-four and a great deal wider. Also, thank God, a great deal older, nearing seventy now, according to our information, so I could probably handle him if I really had to, but it wouldn't be fun. I don't mean that I had any specific reason to think I might ever have to tackle Mr. Waldemar Baron, attorney at law, but men who are in my line of work—and lots of men who aren't—do tend to make that instinctive appraisal of anybody new and husky and masculine: *Can I take this large bastard or can't I?*

It was clear that he'd been quite handsome; he was still a striking man, even though the creases and jowls of old age were getting the better of the strong bony structure of his face. Like Walter Maxon, whose role model he obviously was, he was rather formally dressed for Santa Fe, in another dark blue suit complete with white shirt and silk tie, and highly polished black shoes. The big horn-rimmed glasses perched on his sizable nose gave him an earnest, scholarly look despite his size. The eyes behind the glasses were steel-gray and didn't miss the fact that I was there, with Maxon, although they didn't have time for us at the moment.

As Madeleine reached him, he swept her into his arms and hugged her affectionately. "It took you long enough to get here, girl! I was beginning to think you'd done something stupid, like crawling off to hide under a rock somewhere, instead of facing down a little community disapproval right here where you belong." He held her away from him. "Well, you look better than I expected, except for being dressed like a tramp."

Her sudden laughter was sharp and bitter. "God, it's like coming home! You're still on that sartorial kick?" She freed herself irritably and laughed again. "Actually, the main reason I came back here is that Joe Birnbaum wants to see me about my folks' estate, although why it couldn't be handled by mail I have no idea. And you forget, Waldemar, I am a tramp, a cheap ex-convict tramp. Why shouldn't I dress like one? What else is there left for me to be, after what you let them do to me?"

"Let them?" He stared at her for several seconds. When he spoke again, his voice was soft: "There were no recriminations after the trial. You were"—he stopped

179

and swallowed—"you were so nice about it, you broke my heart. You'd trusted me to save you and I'd failed you, but not one word of blame did I get from you. And now you've decided . . . Well, I deserve it, but you didn't give me much to work with, my dear. You wouldn't take my advice and accept the rather favorable bargain I'd thrashed out with the prosecution. . . . Ah, let's not stand here on the stairs reviving ugly old memories! Come into my office. . . . You, too, sir. I gather you have some mysterious government business to discuss, but there's no reason we shouldn't do it comfortably. I'll see you shortly, Walter."

"I want Walter present," Madeleine said.

Baron started to speak, stopped himself, and shrugged. "As you wish, my dear."

He tried to put his arm around her shoulders as they proceeded along the upstairs corridor, but she shrugged it off impatiently, bringing a look of sadness to his face. But I didn't feel there was anything sexual involved. It was more like a parent's conciliatory advance being rebuffed by a sulky child. Well, I'd already gathered that she'd been Baron's personal protégée, selected very young from, presumably, a number of other youthful legal prodigies, and carefully groomed and trained by him for a place in the firm. There would inevitably have been some emotional involvement on both sides, certainly respect and perhaps real affection; but I'd never had a hint of anything beyond that, and I got none now.

Baron's office was a big, light, high-ceilinged room that might once have been the master bedroom of the imposing house. The design of the large rug on the floor looked vaguely familiar, and the name Aubusson popped into my mind, but I wouldn't want to vouch for its correctness. The massive desk was quite old and quite ornate, but the chair behind it was an anachronism: a husky modern swivel armchair, metal, gray. Well, a man Baron's size would want something solid and comfortable to hold him. Probably his two-hundred-odd pounds had splintered a few of the flimsy antiques bought on the advice of the interior decorator, and he'd got mad, ordered up the biggest and toughest thing the local office-supply store had in stock, and plunked it down in the middle of all the fancy decor and to hell with appearances.

There was a gold-framed mirror on one wall, and there were a couple of large, dark, old-fashioned paintings on the others, in which the sprightly nymphlike ladies were more or less covered by diaphanous white garments that drifted about them gauzily and rather interestingly. The gentlemen were more substantially clad, in an old-fashioned way, and looked rather stuffy and unenterprising. I mean, a girl dressed like that expects something to be done about it, doesn't she? Get with it, boys!

We took our places in front of the desk, like kids settling down before the teacher. Baron seated himself in the gray metal chair and placed his hands flat on the big desk, a gesture clearly meant to bring the meeting to order.

"Perhaps it's as well that Walter's here," he said deliberately, "since we've spent some time discussing your problem, Madeleine. And I hope Mr. Helm—that's the name, isn't it, Helm?—won't mind if we get a little personal business out of the way before hearing what he has to say."

"Never mind me," I said. "Carry on."

Baron went on: "As I was saying, at the time of your release some weeks ago we considered what could be done for you, my dear. The suggestion I'm going to make has been cleared with the other partners. There was some opposition from Homer Walsh, who felt that you—your case—had caused the firm enough unfavorable publicity already, all those years ago, and that your presence here would rake it all up again; but we managed to win

181

his approval. What I'm trying to say is . . . well, we can offer you a position of sorts if you care to accept it."

I saw Madeleine swallow hard, clearly affected; but her voice was harsh when she spoke: "A position of sorts. What sorts?"

Baron showed some embarrassment. "Of course, it's impossible under the circumstances for us to employ you in anything resembling your previous capacity. . . ."

"I see!" Madeleine laughed sharply. "The janitor's quit and you need somebody to wax the floors and scrub out the johns; a grateful cleaning woman who'll slip in nights to do her work so she won't be recognized and give the place a bad name!"

I caught the quick little glance she threw me; and I knew she was apologizing for using the poor-downtrodden-scrubwoman line I'd heard before—but Baron hadn't.

Disregarding her sarcasm, he said calmly, "We have the biggest law library in the state, but nobody's been responsible for it, so nobody can find anything in it. It will take several months for you to learn how it should be organized—I believe there's a seminar on the subject coming up in Denver to which we'll send you, if you accept the job. This will provide you with something to do, and a modest salary, while I investigate what can now be done about your situation. I had to make certain you were actually coming back here before I made any moves on your behalf."

There was a little silence. At last Madeleine drew a rather shaky breath and murmured, "God, you're good, Waldemar. I'd forgotten how convincing and persuasive you can be. I'd forgotten how you had me believing in you even while those damn steel doors were clanging shut behind me for eight years! If I let you, pretty soon you'll have me thinking it didn't even happen. . . . But I already have a job. I have the job of finding out who hired you to do a job on me!"

"Madeleine!"

She went on inexorably: "Or, hell, let me kid myself that I didn't misjudge you that badly. Let me keep on telling myself that there isn't—wasn't—money enough in the world to *hire* you for that. But you'd do just about anything for this precious firm of yours, wouldn't you? And if somebody got something on you that, made public, would mean the end of everything you and Homer Walsh had built up here, I'm sure they could blackmail you into sacrificing your pet girl genius—at least she thought she was a genius, which made it easy for you—the precocious little new-hatched lawyer you'd worked so hard at turning into a tough practicing attorney. And the fact that . . . that she considered you her friend would make no difference at all, with the survival of the firm at stake!"

It was Walter Maxon who burst out, shocked: "Madeleine, you're crazy! You can't believe this!"

"Can't I?" she demanded. "At first I couldn't, of course, sitting in that lousy cell watching myself deteriorate day by day, trying to face the fact that I'd never again be the bright girl wonder. . . . trying to accept that by the time they let me out there'd be no way back for me, even if there had been something to come back to, which there wasn't. But it was just something blind and accidental that had happened to me, like being hit by a runaway truck or struck by lightning. I did find myself wondering a bit, occasionally, but I told myself it was too easy to get paranoid in there, and I'd better get a good hold of my sanity and stop suspecting everybody. The whole world couldn't possibly be conspiring against me. But it was, wasn't it, Waldemar? At least *my* whole world was, all that was left of it, with Roy gone. You."

Waldemar Baron said gravely, "I'm sorry you feel this way, Madeleine, but I suppose it's perfectly natural that your mind should have found a scapegoat during your

183

long prison ordeal, somebody to blame for everything that had happened to you."

She laughed harshly. "It isn't my mind that's shooting at me, Waldemar!"

"Shooting at you!" That was Maxon again. "My God, you must be imagining—"

I interrupted: "I don't know about the lady's accusations, Mr. Maxon, but I do know there have been several attacks on her person. I've got a hole in my shoulder to prove it. So let's leave her imagination out of this. She may be wrong, but she's not hallucinating."

Madeleine had paid no attention to this exchange. She was still staring bleakly at the man behind the desk.

"You shouldn't have done that," she said to Baron. "Sent those men to kill me. If you'd just left it alone, you'd have been perfectly safe. I . . . I wasn't good for much when I got out. And I didn't *really* suspect anything; I hadn't put it all together yet, even in all those years. If you'd left me alone, I'd simply have wandered off somewhere in my dull and hopeless way and never troubled you again. But Mr. Helm's agency got wind of the fact that I was to be assassinated and wanted to know why, and somehow in the line of duty he managed to stick all the jagged pieces of Ellershaw back together—well, almost all; I guess there'll always be a few chips missing, a few cracks showing—and I started asking myself the questions I should have asked years ago, and here I am."

In the ensuing silence, we heard somebody walking down the hall outside the office, although the footsteps were muffled by the deep carpet.

"Here I am," Madeleine said softly, "wanting to know why you want me dead. Here I am wanting to hear about the clever railroading job that was done on the naive young girl attorney who thought she was so bright and sophisticated, and had the illusion that she was surrounded by loyal friends. That dumb, innocent girl whose husband learned something he shouldn't have, presumably up in that scientific security-fortress he worked in up Conejo Canyon. What it was is beside the point—"

Waldemar Baron stirred. "We all know what your husband did up there, Madeleine. We all know what he stole up there. There was never any question raised about *his* guilt—"

"And why wasn't there?" Madeleine leaned forward in her chair. "Why was my high-powered attorney so busy trying to browbeat me into confessing to something I hadn't done that he never explored the possibility that my husband hadn't done anything either—anything subversive and illegal, that is? You never for a moment considered the possibility that the whole case against me, against us both, might be a put-up job, as phony as the hair of that snow queen you've got reigning downstairs these days! Why didn't you?"

"But you yourself accepted his guilt, my dear!"

She said, "Ah, there's the real cleverness of it! Yes, I accepted, numbly, the possibility that Roy could have taken super-secret laboratory reports, or whatever they were, for some crazy idealistic reason of his own—I resigned myself to it in my dazed way, as I resigned myself to a lot of things. Everything except my own guilt; I *knew* the truth about that. But I didn't seem to know anything else anymore. My . . . my lovely serene assurance was gone; my wonderful young confidence in myself and my judgments. Nothing was the way it was supposed to be. My safe and beautiful world had suddenly become a terrifying place where people grabbed me rudely and put manacles on me and shoved me around as if I were some kind of an animal and yelled outrageous accusations at me and locked me up in filthy places stinking of urine and disinfectant. . . . You knew, didn't you, Waldemar? You had me all figured out; you knew exactly how to break me. You set me up so carefully, and then you had them tear me down so brutally, knowing what it would do to me—the precious little rich

185

girl who'd grown up so very intelligent and competent in lots of ways, but who'd never had a rough hand laid on her in all her sheltered life, or a rude word spoken to her. You knew that kind of treatment was the one thing I couldn't possibly cope with!"

Abruptly, Waldemar Baron heaved himself out of his chair, a little painfully the way old men do, although he'd displayed few signs of his age previously. He walked to the diminutive bar in the corner and poured himself a drink and stood there with his back to us.

"Psychological demolition!" Madeleine said softly. "Build her up so the shock will be that much greater when you smash her down. I was suddenly very busy those last few weeks, wasn't I, Waldemar? Those last weeks when Roy was so troubled but I simply didn't have time for him because in addition to my own work I was forever being asked please wouldn't I take over this or help out with that. And of course, being me, ambitious me, I was delighted, even though it meant working my ass off. I thought it was a measure of how good I was, what a solid place I'd made for myself here, how much I was trusted and relied upon! And then a fantastic bonus to tell me my efforts were recognized and appreciated— and that very night the crash: total disgrace, total disaster. Arrest and jail; and nobody to help but a boy just out of law school who didn't know his anus from a prairie-dog hole. Sorry, Walter. But don't try to tell me, now, that it was a coincidence, that it just happened at a time and in a way that left me no defenses at all!"

Walter Maxon started to speak and checked himself. Madeleine stood up and walked deliberately to the window and stood looking out. She spoke with her back to us:

"It was Mangle Madeleine Week, it was Smash Ellershaw Month; and it went on and on. Husband gone, career in ruins, bills and creditors and total financial disaster, home gone, dreadful newspaper and TV publicity, unbelievable public snubs and insults; and every time I seemed about to catch my breath and get some kind of a grip on the situation, I'd receive another dose of the kind of brutal treatment I simply couldn't deal with: another trip downtown for interrogation, another shocking humiliation session, with my lawyer telling me that of course we must cooperate in all ways with the federal authorities, my dear. Yes, you did a good job on me, Waldemar. You made sure I was in a total beaten-down daze right up to the trial and through it, too punch-drunk to really know what kind of a legal job you were doing for me. And it wasn't much of a job, was it? I keep remembering Willy Chavez."

Walter Maxon stirred. "Chavez? Who . . . ? Oh, I remember, but that case was before I came here. What does Chavez have to do with this?"

Madeleine didn't look his way at all. She continued to stare out the window. Her voice reached us: "Chavez was guilty as hell, Waldemar, but you got him off anyway on a clever technicality. I was innocent, but you didn't get me off. And now that I'm, well, functioning again after a fashion, I'd like to know why the great Waldemar Baron couldn't find any clever technicalities with which to keep his own associate out of prison. And while I was too . . . too shattered at the time to actually remember much of what happened in court, I've recently studied the transcript—Mr. Helm had an abridged version he let me read—and it was a very lousy job you did of defending me, wasn't it? A lot of noise, a lot of drama, but so little substance that even the jury saw through it and decided that I simply had to be guilty if my well-known attorney couldn't do better than that for me." She paused, and drew a long breath, and went on: "And then at last it was over, and I was hauled off across the country by way of one foul, bug-infested little jail cell after another—more of your treatment, Waldemar?—and finally I was put away in that place and you were safe for eight years. But now they've let me out at last, not quite a bag lady or a mental case, although it was close, so I have to be killed. . . . Walter."

187

The younger man started. "Yes, Madeleine."

"When you came back from that visit to Fort Ames, what did you tell them about me, about how I looked?" When Maxon hesitated uncomfortably, she turned on him. "You didn't tell them the truth, did you? You're a sweet boy, Walter, and you couldn't bear to describe the gray wreck of a woman you actually saw in there; it would have seemed disloyal, wouldn't it? So you told them all, when you got back here, that I was doing fine, just fine, bearing up beautifully, still the same brave lovely person as always. . . ." She laughed softly, seeing the truth in his face. "You were being kind, but I'm afraid you passed the sentence of death on me, my dear. You got somebody worried. If I'd actually recovered from the initial shock of my conviction, as you reported, if I was standing up unexpectedly well to all the degrading prison routines, if I was still—or again—an intelligent, thinking woman instead of the useless zombie they'd tried to turn me into, then I'd be a menace when I got out, wouldn't I? A danger that had to be removed."

Waldemar Baron swung around to look at her, and she turned a little to face him. He spoke without expression:

"Do you really believe all this, Madeleine?"

She didn't answer the question. Her face was quite pale as she said, "I could have understood your having me murdered, Waldemar, if enough was at stake. I mean, the life of one lousy girl lawyer as against the welfare of the firm . . . But the way you did it, the cold-blooded, unspeakably cruel way you did it! Wearing me down like that, breaking me, humiliating and humbling and crushing me, grinding me into the dirt! Damn you, I loved . . . No, it wasn't love, but I honored and trusted you; and in the end you even let them send me to that hell-place to be totally destroyed! How could you do it to me? How the hell could you do it?"

She whirled and ran out of the room.

CHAPTER 15

AFTER the door had closed, Waldemar Baron stood staring at it for a little while; then he seemed to come awake abruptly. He asked me what I wanted to drink, and told Maxon to fix his own, he knew the way. Actually, it was a little too early for the first drink of the day as far as I was concerned, but it was no time to be arguing about booze. After putting a glass into my hand, Baron moved to the chair in which Madeleine had been sitting, swung it around one-handed, and sat down facing me. He gave me a faint, cynical smile.

"I suppose you're waiting for me to tell you, sadly, what a poor unbalanced woman she's become, Mr. Helm, making such wild and unfounded accusations against someone who's never had anything but her good at heart."

I said, "I don't know about her accusations or your heart, sir, but Mrs. Ellershaw has just spent several weeks at a facility of ours going through a rigorous course of physical rehabilitation, preceded by a psychological testing program designed to find out if she was likely to break down under the pressure. I can assure you there's nothing whatever wrong with the lady's mental or emotional balance; in fact she passed all tests, and the course, with flying colors."

"I see." He studied me for a moment longer, and rose again, and went to the desk to pick up the telephone. "Did you check Mr. Helm's credentials, Cassandra? I see. . . . Yes, thank you, my dear, that's very good.

189

Thank you." He put the phone down and returned to his chair and studied me for a moment. "The Chief of Police, Mr. Cordoba, says that you seem to be quite legitimate, although there's some mystery about what function your agency actually performs."

I said, "We sometimes wonder ourselves, sir."

He said, "It's been a long time. I will retire soon. Perhaps I've been looking for someone to take my confession before I do—"

Walter Maxon said sharply, "Waldemar!"

Baron looked at him for a moment, and shook his head regretfully. "I appreciate your faith, Walter, but Madeleine is perfectly right. I deserve every ugly word she threw at me."

Maxon started to speak again, and stopped. We sat in silence for a little. Everybody started when the telephone rang. Baron made a little gesture, and Maxon rose and picked it up, and listened.

"No," he said. "No, he's in conference and can't be disturbed. Later."

Baron waited for him to return to his chair, and spoke quietly: "Let us consider, first, what I did not do. I'm afraid Madeleine gives me credit for greater wickedness and ingenuity than I'm capable of. I certainly did not set out deliberately to shatter her self-confidence or destroy her self-esteem. There was, of course, no deliberate program of working her to exhaustion so she'd be more vulnerable; and it was simply unfortunate that the only one of us available the night she needed legal help was rather inexperienced. I don't know what horrors she was subjected to on her way to Fort Ames, but I assure you I had nothing to do with them." He cleared his throat. "And I hope you'll believe me when I swear that if there have been attempts on her life, as you say, they were not organized by me and I know nothing whatever about them. It's natural that, under the circumstances, she'd evolve the theory that all her disastrous troubles are connected; all the result of a great elaborate conspiracy concocted by a master villain. By me. But as I said, she's endowing me with a greater capacity for evil than I actually possess." He paused briefly, and went on: "However, this is all peripheral. Her central thesis is perfectly correct. I did allow her to be sent up, quite deliberately."

Walter Maxon started to speak impulsively, and checked himself. He licked his lips, and asked quietly, "Why?"

"For the reason she stated. She's an intelligent person and she knows me quite well. She knows there is only one thing that could cause me to betray the trust of a client and . . . and friend, as I did."

Maxon asked softly, "Blackmail?"

Baron nodded. "A firm like this is very vulnerable. It was demonstrated to me, quite convincingly, how we could be destroyed in a very brief space of time if I did not agree to what was asked of me. There were large corporate clients who were already uneasy because of Madeleine's troubles. . . . Well, never mind the details, but there were also, I'm afraid, specific instances where we had, as they say, sailed a little too close to the wind. At least it could be made to look as if we had, and with one of our attorneys—a photogenic and newsworthy young female attorney—already indicted for a serious crime, the publicity would have ruined us."

"Exactly what were you supposed to do?" I asked.

He shrugged his big shoulders heavily. "Exactly what I did do. She was to be rendered harmless. A confession would be satisfactory. With her husband already missing under incriminating circumstances, she would be no further threat to anybody as his confessed accomplice. No matter what she dug up later she wouldn't get anybody to take her seriously, not after admitting her guilt, not even if she were treated leniently by the law and allowed probation or a suspended sentence. But her credibility had to be destroyed by a confession, I was told; that was mandatory. Either that, or she must be tucked away safely in a penitentiary after a conviction that would serve the same purpose." He grimaced. "So I concentrated on getting the best bargain I could out of the prosecution. . . . But you know what happened. She wouldn't accept any agreement that involved a guilty plea. She left me no choice at all. The evidence against her wasn't really overwhelming and I could probably have created doubts in the minds of the jurors. . . . And there were legal maneuvers I could have tried that might well have proved effective. I simply did not try them. You know the result. I have found it a hard thing to live with, these past eight years."

Maxon started to speak again, but changed his mind, improving my opinion of him. At least he knew when to keep his mouth shut.

I spoke to Baron: "How were the demands presented?"

"By telephone."

"And you threw to the wolves an innocent young woman of whom you were rather fond on the strength of one mysterious phone call?" When he didn't speak, I said, "I see. There had been other cases. They were called to your attention. Object lessons, so to speak."

He nodded. "The voice listed three examples. I could investigate them, if I liked, before making up my mind. One didn't require investigation. It involved a client of ours who'd apparently persisted with a suit after being warned to settle. Of course we'd had no suspicion at the time, although I'd noticed that he seemed to be under heavy pressure of some kind. We won the case for him. Three months later he shot himself, after some rather messy private affairs were made public—he was a man whose reputation for rectitude was very important to him. I checked out the other two situations. They were farther afield—one was in another state—but both had ended in disastrous publicity for the individuals and organizations involved."

"Did the caller give a name?" I asked. When Baron hesitated, I said, "A name like Tolliver, perhaps?"

"I see!" Baron nodded slowly. "So that's what you're really here about. Chief Cordoba considered that story about civil rights a bit thin. Well, I'm happy to learn that something is being done about it at last; and I'm relieved to have my own sin off my chest. What . . . what do you plan to do, Mr. Helm?"

"About you?" I shook my head. "Legal ethics don't concern me, Mr. Baron. Mrs. Ellershaw will want her reputation cleared eventually; what further compensation she'll require for the career and the years that were stolen from her is up to her."

He said, "I would have done my best to make it up to her in any case."

I said, "However, I think for the moment it's best to leave the situation as it stands. Her exoneration can come later. You can thrash it out with her then. For the moment, helping us, she'll be more effective in her present status as a lady still trying desperately, and perhaps hopelessly, to regain the good name and the civil rights that were taken from her by the court's decision." I glanced at Maxon. "I hope we can count on your cooperation, Mr. Maxon."

He hesitated. "I'll do whatever Madeleine wants."

I said, "She's agreed to help us out, and I think she'll appreciate any assistance you can give us, even if it merely involves sitting on your hands and keeping your mouth shut. You've probably already gathered that this is not a simple case of one young woman being ruthlessly crushed when she got in somebody's way. It's not even a local phenomenon. It's nationwide, and it's been building for nine or ten years, maybe even longer. We suspect that the focus of the infection is somewhere in this general area. If your active help is needed, you'll be asked. In the meantime I hope you won't make any grand gestures that'll louse things up for us, like stamping the tainted dust of Baron and Walsh off your shoes, with loud speeches of moral condemnation."

"I understand."

I looked back to Baron. "I think we've got certain things in common, sir," I said. "You'd like to preserve your firm and your reputation while at the same time setting right, as far as possible, the injustice for which you were responsible. As far as Mrs. Ellershaw is concerned, she's very bitter at the moment, as you've heard, but I think she can be persuaded to be reasonable. However, there's still the mysterious Mr. Tolliver, and he may not like the way you're now giving aid and comfort to someone he's gone to considerable lengths to eliminate, one way or another. So it's in your interest to help us identify and deal with him, so we can get him out of your hair." I paused, watching him. "You didn't happen to recognize the voice, by any chance?"

Baron hesitated briefly. "He used some kind of a distorting device on the phone that made it sound tinny and unnatural. But . . ."

"Yes?"

The big man cleared his throat. "Mr. Helm, I may be absolutely wrong in my suspicions. I have no evidence at all. . . . But you say that this national conspiracy, or whatever it is, has been developing for some ten years, and that it's run from somewhere around here?"

I shrugged. "That's the assumption upon which I'm operating. There are undoubtedly agents and teams investigating other possible areas, but I was told this was the most promising lead we had. Whom do you suspect, Mr. Baron?"

He shook his head doubtfully. "I hate to make wild accusations, but there's a certain individual who arrived in Santa Fe about a dozen years ago. . . . The voice on the phone used some seagoing turns of speech that seemed familiar. I don't want to discuss this with you further. I never even said it—and you, young Walter, never heard it. But I suggest, Mr. Helm, that you take a good look at a certain Admiral Jasper Lowery. Good day, sir."

Going to the door, I looked back. Baron had risen to

watch me leave. I could read nothing in his expression; but he certainly was big, standing there in his fine, high-ceilinged office in the sunlight from the big windows.

"Mr. Helm. Just one more thing."

"Yes, Mr. Baron."

"When you speak to Madeleine of this . . ." He paused, and went on: "It would be frivolous to talk of regrets or apologies. But please assure her that the interim position I offered is hers if she needs employment and can bring herself to work here again; and that I will in any case find a legal remedy for her situation, regardless of the cost to myself or the firm, whenever you feel the time is appropriate."

Leaving, I wondered what the two men remaining would have to say to each other, Madeleine's devoted young admirer and her reluctant old betrayer. It should make for an interesting conversation. Downstairs, I saw no sign of her, and I turned to the blond receptionist to ask the question; but before I could speak, my troubled lady emerged from the alcove behind the stairs with her face freshly washed and her lipstick freshly applied and her hair freshly combed. She let me hold for her the quilted jacket she'd taken off; and she zipped it up as we emerged on the portal, although the day had warmed up considerably while we were inside.

"Well?" she asked at last, as we started for the street.

"Great performance, Mrs. Barrymore."

Her face was pale with the strain of the scene she'd just been through, but she tried to shrug in a matter-of-fact way. "It wasn't as if I hadn't played the part before. All I had to do was remember all the awful, whiny, poor-little-me routines I put on for you right after I got out, and edit them slightly for a new audience."

"A little more than that, wasn't it? You threw every-thing at him but the sink, suspicions you'd never hinted at before."

Her shoulders moved awkwardly under the violet ski jacket. "You needed a paranoid lady; you got one. I mean, you can suspect anybody if you try hard enough; so in order to shake them up, as you wanted, I dredged up all the ugly disloyal little thoughts I'd never really allowed myself to . . . Matt!" She stopped to stare at me, her face suddenly quite bloodless under the Arizona tan. "Matt, I wasn't *right*, was I?"

I said, "Mrs. E, you hit the jackpot."

"Oh, no!"

She'd stopped, beside me. I stopped and turned to look at her. "You really didn't know?"

After a lengthy silence, she said almost inaudibly, "Maybe I didn't want to know. Maybe I never let myself know. Tell me what he said."

I said, "Well, the word is you exaggerated just a little. He was not responsible for the crucifixion of Jesus Christ, or the assassination of Abraham Lincoln, or the Johnstown Flood. He didn't even plot to drive you insane by having you sample the lousiest, dirtiest jail cells clear across the country. And he most certainly had nothing to do with the recent attempts on your life. But he damn well did allow you to be sent up, kind of by default."

She licked her lips. "I guess I must have realized that when I looked over the transcript you lent me. I just didn't want to face it." She turned away from me and started walking again. I saw her throat work convulsively, and her voice had a choked sound when she spoke again: "Go on. Tell me everything."

Keeping pace with her, I gave it to her more or less verbatim, ending up with: "So you've got employment of sorts if you want it, and exoneration when you want it."

She didn't seem to hear me. She said softly, "I used to worship him, Matt! I mean, really. If . . . if some time when we were working together he'd asked me to please slip off my shoes and panty hose and lie down on the couch and haul up my skirt, I'd have been a little sad because it would have meant the end of a working relationship I treasured, but I wouldn't have hesitated for a moment, at least not before I was married. Of course he never did. One of the hardest things I've ever done in my life was to walk in there today, like that, and say all those terrible things to him. But I must have known subconsciously. . . . I must have needed to *know*, one way or the other."

I said, "Of course you realize that you're free now."

She glanced at me sharply. "I don't understand."

"We've got no strings on you anymore. You don't need us anymore. It was kind of understood that we'd clear your reputation, if at all possible, in return for your help. Well, it's cleared. All you have to do is go back to Waldemar Baron and tell him to put the legal machinery into motion, and there you'll be, a respectable citizen once more, entitled to the abject apologies of the society that misjudged you so wickedly and mistreated you so cruelly."

She looked at me sharply, disturbed. "Matt, do you really think I'd do that, leave you in the lurch?"

"No," I said. "But I had to make sure you understood that you could if you wanted to."

She laughed. "And you're forgetting the fact that somebody's trying to kill me and I do need you, to keep me alive."

I grinned. "There's that minor problem, to be sure." I glanced at my watch. "Well, I feel we've made some progress, thanks to you. We know considerably more than we did this morning, and if Baron's to be believed about the voice he heard on the phone, we even have a possible lead to the mysterious Mr. Tolliver. How about a good lunch to celebrate? The Cortez is only a couple of blocks from here."

Her face was strained and preoccupied once more. "I suppose it really is a triumph of sorts, but I don't feel much like celebrating, Matt; and I'm not really dressed for . . ." Then she glanced at me sharply. "More of the shake-em-up campaign, Mr. Helm?"

"The idea was to display you in all your old haunts,

197

shockingly coarsened and hardened by your years in the pen, bitter and vengeful and dangerous. Wasn't it? And if they turned away customers in jeans, these sloppy days, they'd lose half their clientele. But we'd better get there fast before the business-lunch crowd descends on the place."

CHAPTER 16

THE maître d' of the Restaurant Cortez, who was also the proprietor, was named Alfredo Hernandez: a tall, lean, hidalgo-type character, black-haired, with a neat black mustache and a neat black suit. He was very good indeed, recognizing Madeleine immediately and addressing her by name, showing every indication of pleasure at greeting an old customer, even one whose appearance and style of dress showed distressing changes. I noticed that he carefully made no reference to how long she'd been away—the only hint he gave that he was quite aware of where she'd been.

He also recognized me, although I'd never been a regular; and he said that certainly we could have a booth along the wall, Mr. Helm, this way, please. He maneuvered the heavy, half-round table out of the way to admit us to the semicircular settee, returned the table to a comfortable position, and summoned a waitress to take our drink orders.

"Whatever you're having," Madeleine said when I asked her preference. "Well, a good quick jolt is indicated, I guess. A vodka martini."

"It must be ESP," I said. "Two vodka martinis, please."

We sat in silence waiting for the drinks to arrive, watching the place fill up. The decor was turn-of-the-century red-leather-and-plush-and-velvet; you half expected Diamond Jim Brady to swagger in with Lily Langtry on his arm, but, coming from outdoors yourself, you wouldn't really be able to see him, or her, until your eyes became used to the low light level inside. Very cozy illumination. When a trio of pants-wearing middle-aged ladies stopped by our booth, I thought they were simply pausing to let their eyes get properly accommodated so they could make their way to the table indicated by Hernandez without bumping into anything. Then I saw that the leader of the group was staring at us with an expression of cold disapproval.

The woman was rather tall and bony, but quite handsome, and her expensively tailored black pantsuit didn't look too bad on her narrow body. Well, if you like pantsuits. There was a frilly white blouse. Her graying hair was very carefully arranged about her thin face. I thought she was about to address Madeleine; but after a long moment she turned away in a very pointed manner and spoke to her friends instead, saying loudly:

"Well! I suppose Alfredo is obliged to let in anybody who doesn't create a disturbance, but one would think an ex-convict would at least have the decency to ask for the back room if she *must* patronize a respectable restaurant!"

They swept on, leaving the people at the nearby tables staring our way curiously, or carefully not staring our way curiously. When I looked at Madeleine, there were lines of strain around her mouth, but she spoke with the same dreadful clarity the tall woman had used:

"In case you didn't know, Mr. Helm, that mouthy old bitch is Adelaide Lowery. Her mother used to run a cheap boardinghouse in Annapolis, which made it easy for her to grab herself a future admiral. You know the kind of *noovow reechies* from the East who move out here; and before they've got their fucking bags unpacked

199

they're acting like their ancestors came down the Santa Fe Trail by wagon train. Instant old-timers, we call them. . . . I think the waitress wants our orders. What are you eating?"

We both took the day's special: sauerbraten. When we were alone once more, Madeleine glanced towards the table where the tall woman had settled and was now conversing very brightly with her friends.

"Did I sound like a vulgar felon type, I hope?" Madeleine shivered slightly. "Brrrr, it's like jumping into an icy pool, coming home like this; the first shock is pretty breathtaking. But I guess you can get used to anything, even being a . . . a second-class citizen, fair game for witches like that." She swallowed hard. "God, after that little exchange, I feel as if I were sitting here naked. Talk to me, Matt."

"You talk to me," I said. "Tell me about the Lowerys. I suppose that's the wife. Kind of a coincidence running into her like this, when I heard the name for the first time only half an hour ago."

Madeleine shook her head. "Actually, it's not so strange. She eats here every day, holds court you might say."

"What do you think of Baron's suggestion? Could her husband, this retired admiral, be the Tolliver we're looking for?"

"I suppose it's possible." Madeleine frowned, thinking hard. "The Lowerys hit Santa Fe—I think it was the year you and I met on the Chavez case—like the hordes of Attila the Hun. Socially speaking, of course. They really took this town by storm. I mean, one day nobody'd ever heard of a Lowery, and the next day everybody knew the name." Madeleine hesitated. "But shouldn't we be asking ourselves whether Waldemar really thinks Admiral Lowery is this mysterious and intimidating voice on the phone, or just wants us to think he thinks so."

I glanced at her sharply. "When you start suspecting a guy, you go all the way, don't you? Of course you've got

200

a point, but it's the best lead that's been offered us so far, because it's the only lead. To hell with Baron's motives in suggesting it. We can't afford not to check it out. So give me the Lowery story as far as you know it, please. . . ."

There was a pause while the waitress put our lunches in front of us, and offered rolls around, and asked about coffee. Later. Madeleine tasted her sauerbraten and nodded approvingly.

"Jasper Lowery," she said, after swallowing. "Rich boy, old New England money, went into the Naval Reserve during World War II and was sent to Annapolis to take some kind of courses at the Academy. That great Santa Fe social arbiter and aristocratic southwestern beauty, Addie Krumbein as she was then, was helping her ma sweep the floors and make the beds in the tacky rooming house where he stayed. Propinquity had its way. If I sound prejudiced, it's because I am; and not just because of the lovely welcome-home she just offered me."

"Explain, Mrs. Ellershaw."

"It's hard to like somebody who hates your guts," Madeleine said. "Well, maybe I did act a little too unimpressed when I first started seeing her around at social functions behaving as if Noah had dropped her family off here when he passed by in the Ark. I mean, one gets tired of these phony Old-Santa-Feans. It's a goddamn cult. Maybe my trouble is that my family actually did come down the Trail way back before New Mexico became a state. The first Rustin hit here about 1895, if I remember right."

"You were just a kid at the time, of course," I said.

She grinned and stuck out the tip of her tongue at me; then she sobered quickly and I could see her reminding herself that she was a mature and dignified woman who'd known great hardship and suffering. But the martini was doing its work, and she was relaxing again after the strain of her encounter with Baron, and the shock of the insult she'd just received. The color was returning to her face, and I found myself thinking that, regardless of how she was dressed, she was by far the most attractive woman in the restaurant.

"So you can see that it was a great triumph for Adelaide when the cocky young bitch who'd snooted her wound up behind bars as a common criminal," Madeleine said. She grinned wryly. "But I'm not the only jailbird in the family. As a matter of fact we're quite proud of my great-uncle, who spent ten years in prison for shooting a man. Self-defense, he said, but the jury didn't agree. Very dangerous family, we Rustins."

"Let's hope so," I said. "It's got a lot of survival value. Let's hear more about the Lowerys."

"Jasper must have been a pretty competent young officer. The Navy let him switch from reserve to regular and kept him on after the war, and kept promoting him, although I don't think he ever really functioned as an admiral; it was one of those courtesy promotions they often give them when they retire them. Anyway, I met him socially a few times, back before I was sent to . . . back when they first came to town. He likes to tell the ancient story about the old salt who, on the beach at last, throws an anchor over his shoulder and hikes inland; when he finally reaches a place so far from the water that a local yokel asks him what he's doing with that funny-looking pickaxe, that's where he puts down his roots. In Lowery's case, Santa Fe."

"Does he do anything here except collect his Navy pension and count his old New England money?"

She shook her head sadly. "I don't know where you keep yourself when you come to town on vacation, Matt. Don't you ever read the papers? Plural. Back in the good old days there used to be only one, remember?"

"That's Admiral Lowery? The *Daily Journal*?"

"That's him. When he got here, the old Santa Fe *New Mexican* was the only paper in town. Way back when Lew Wallace was governor, he probably read the *New Mexican* every afternoon after he'd settled his problems

202

with Billy the Kid and done his daily writing stint on *Ben Hur*. Lowery started up the *Journal* a year after he got here. The *New Mexican* had never been what you'd call rabidly liberal, but the *Journal* quickly made it look like *Pravda West*. However, the *Journal* turned out to be sprightly and interesting to read, if you didn't mind suffering an occasional attack of apoplexy at the reactionary editorials. Lowery was no newspaperman himself, but he picked good newspapermen to run his paper, and let them run it as long as they followed his basic political guidelines." She hesitated. "Well, they don't have *completely* free hand; there's a little nepotism. Like a rather amateurish social column entitled "Today with Adelaide." At least it was amateurish when I last read it; maybe she's improved with eight years of practice."

"Anything else?"

"No, but I have an unworthy hope that Waldemar is right about Jasper Lowery. I suppose it's too much to expect that his wife's done anything to be arrested for herself, but I'd get a big kick out of seeing her visiting her so-important husband in the same jail they had me, with the newspaper and TV people yapping and snapping at her just the way they did at me." She made a little grimace of distaste. "Oh, God, I used to be such a nice, kind, charitable little girl, and just listen to me now!"

Then she looked up, quickly and warily, as a man stopped by the booth. He was tall and rather fragile-looking, slightly stooped, with a wispy white mustache and a pink expanse of scalp that didn't have too much white hair around it. And very sharp old blue eyes beneath white eyebrows.

"It's good to see you back, Madeleine."

Her defensive attitude relaxed. She drew a long breath, and smiled up at him. "Thank you, Judge. This is Mr. Helm, from Washington. Helm, Judge Harlan Connors."

His answering smile was gentle. "Keep your chin up, young lady. It'll be a little rough for a while, but don't let

them grind you down. A pleasure to make your acquaintance, sir."

I watched him move away, walking carefully as befitted his age. When I glanced at Madeleine, her eyes were
shiny.

"That was sweet of him," she said huskily. Then she
sniffed, and groped in her purse for a Kleenex.

"Are you okay?" I asked.

"I guess . . . I guess I just can't stand people b-being
n-nice to me." After a few more sniffs, and some dabs
with the tissue, she swallowed hard and sat up straight,
facing me. "I'm okay, Matt. Don't worry about me. I'll
make it, if you'll buy me a nice big gloppy dessert and to
hell with my gorgeous new figure. . . ."

Later, leaving, we had to make our way through the
now crowded restaurant to the entrance hall, and past
the little knot of people still waiting there to be seated. I
could sense that my companion felt as if she were running a gauntlet, even though most of the patrons clearly
didn't know her at all. Even if they were locals who'd
seen her picture in the newspapers eight years ago, they'd
forgotten. However, there were a few who obviously recognized her but made a point of pretending not to, and a
couple who recognized her—a pair of lawyers just coming in—and made a point of greeting her a little too
heartily.

"God, Old Home Week!" she breathed as we emerged
in the dazzling New Mexico sunlight. "It's awful of me,
Matt, but I find the ones who're friendly almost as hard
to take as the ones who aren't. They're all so obviously
wondering just what it was like for a nice, well-brought-
up girl like me, from a good family, to be locked up in a
dirty dungeon all those years; and was I homosexually
molested by my depraved fellow inmates or wasn't I; and
just what kind of a degraded female creature have I been
transformed into by my brutal penitentiary experiences,
really?"

I said, "Tell me about Homer Walsh. I had the impression he was retired; but judging by what Baron said, he still has a voice in the affairs of the firm."

Madeleine grinned abruptly, walking beside me. "Don't you want to help me feel sorry for myself?"

"You're doing fine all by yourself," I said.

"Good man. Keep slapping me down whenever I start my martyr act. Homer Walsh had a very bad auto accident and wound up in a wheelchair; that was the year after I joined the firm. A thin, dark, intense little man, and a very good trial lawyer, but he never practiced law again after he got well—I gather that, apart from being crippled, he's never been *really* well since. But he's still a partner, kind of an inactive partner, and he does have some say in the policies of the firm. At least that was the way it was when I . . . left, and I gather it's still that way."

"What about Walter Maxon?"

"Walter's a very nice boy, that's his trouble. Nice and a little shy. He'll never be a real cutthroat lawyer, but he's conscientious and totally honest. Perhaps that's why Waldemar's apparently been pushing him along faster than he really deserves; he wants somebody obviously square and straight right there to pick up the pieces, and the firm, if things go badly for him, after what he was forced to do to me." She grimaced. "What Walter really needs is somebody to tell him what a wonderful guy he is, and keep on telling him and telling him."

I said deliberately, "It's fairly obvious that, with your husband nine years missing, you could have the job anytime. Even legally, with just a little red tape."

She said, "Maybe, but it's kind of optimistic of us to arrange my future, Mr. Helm, before we're sure I'm going to survive this perilous undercover operation I'm engaged in for you and the U.S. government."

"I'll do my best to see to it," I said. "And when it's over I think that guy's going to be right there waiting for you loyally—like he's been for eight years—and you'd better have made up your mind whether or not you want what he offers you. Meaning him."

She said with sudden sharpness, "Want? What does *want* have to do with it, Matt? I had what I wanted, everything I wanted, and it was all snatched away from me. Even if I'm given every possible break from now on, even if the old verdict is set aside and my name is cleared and all my rights as a citizen are restored, with all those years lost to me I'm going to have to pass up all the great things I wanted for myself and settle for what I can get—what I can get that I can still make some kind of an endurable life out of. What I *really* want . . . God, I don't even know what it is any longer! And I used to be so sure, so blissfully sure!" She shook her head abruptly. "Whine, whine, whine! You're neglecting your duties, Mr. Helm. You're supposed to kick the self-pitying bitch in the pants where they're tightest—and that's pretty damn tight—whenever she goes into that sad routine. What's next on our agenda?"

"Well, as soon as possible we'd better check out that Conejo Canyon installation. I've got the names of two scientific guys who knew your husband there before he vanished, and who're still there. One's more or less running the place now. But it's a forty-mile drive to Los Alamos, and you've got that appointment with your folks' lawyer, Birnbaum, in less than an hour. We'll have to see how much of the afternoon is left when you've finished with him."

But when we reached the motel, we found a handwritten note awaiting her at the desk. She glanced through it and gave it to me to read. *My dear Madeleine: Unfortunately I find myself tied up in court this afternoon, how about ten tomorrow morning? Looking forward very eagerly to seeing you again and most sorry for the delay, your Uncle Joe.*

Madeleine took it back from me when I'd finished. "I used to call him that when I was a little girl, although there's no real relationship," she said. "Well, what do we do now? . . . Oh, God, look at that!"

She was staring at the nearby newspaper-vending

machine. The enormous headlines showed black through the slightly beat-up plastic: PRESIDENT SHOT! That was the *Journal*, making you read the paper to find out if the shooting had been fatal or otherwise. The *New Mexican*'s giant headline was equally terse, telling what had happened but not to whom: ASSASSINATION FAILS!

CHAPTER 17

MAC said, "You would have been notified immediately if it had concerned you, Eric."

"Yes, sir," I said, making a face at Madeleine over the phone. We were in my motel unit, and she was half rereading the newspaper stories and half listening, sprawled in one of the large chairs by the window in the unladylike fashion that seems to go with jeans. "Yes, sir," I said. "But I would like to protest, sir. Here I am in my rusty tin suit playing knight errant or something to a distressed lady while there's work of national importance peculiarly suited to my talents and training. . . ."

It had not been the crime of a wild-eyed gent with a cheap rifle and a political grievance, or an unbalanced youth with a target pistol trying to attain some kind of national importance, any kind, as long as it made the headlines. It had been a systematic and well-organized commando raid, somewhat similar to the Sadat assassination, executed by six men with automatic weapons of the submachine-gun persuasion, exact make unspecified. The chief executive had survived through the devotion of a couple of Secret Service men who'd thrown themselves

207

into the line of fire and hustled him back into his car, taking a good many bullets in the process. Fortunately, while one of the men had died on the spot and the other was in the hospital fighting for his life, those feeble little 9mm slugs don't have all the penetration in the world, and only one had got through to the man they were protecting, inflicting a minor wound.

The other Secret Service men in attendance had not only been badly outgunned, they'd been handicapped by their consideration for the innocent bystanders, something that never concerns us. I mean, if you ask us to protect somebody in public life he gets protected, and to hell with the women and children and stray dogs; which is probably why we're so seldom asked. In this case, however, on request, we'd had two riflemen covering the scene, one from a rooftop two hundred and fifty yards away, the other from a high window at about four hundred. They'd started cutting down the commandos the instant they revealed themselves. There had been only the initial burst of fire before the attackers started dropping mysteriously—in the melee down in the street nobody'd heard the distant reports at first. With two down and then, in the time it takes to operate a bolt-action sniper's rifle, another two, the final pair had tried to run for it, but had been smashed to the pavement in their turn by the heavy rifle bullets. Of course there had been some breakage. What with the close-in 9mm automatic fire, and several of the long-range .30-caliber projectiles richocheting and breaking up after perforating their targets, seven people in the crowd had been hurt, two fatally.

Mac said severely, "We have enough brainless snipers available; we don't need another. What we need is somebody with intelligence enough to stop this conspiracy at the source, which means, of course, finding the source. Are you making any progress?"

"Yes, sir," I said sourly. "But I wouldn't want to say in what direction."

"There seems to be less time than we'd hoped," Mac said. "Indications are that these people may have completed their initial infiltration, if we may call it that, of our society and are now starting the action phase of their campaign. The confusion following the violent death of the President was presumably expected to give them the opportunity to make their political move, whatever it may be. Well, we'll try to parry it if it comes, and in any case to keep him alive. A man in the White House who's humble enough to admit he's no rival to Washington or Lincoln is a jewel to be preserved. We've had some who thought they belonged on the shining throne of heaven right alongside, or perhaps a little ahead of, the Almighty. Your job is to see that we don't have to shield him too long, since the advantage is always on the side of the assassins."

"Yes, sir," I said, and the line went dead.

Madeleine was looking at me curiously. "You're envious," she said.

I said, "Those boys got to shoot. All I've been getting is shot at."

"Is that *all* you've been getting?" she asked slyly. Then a little color came into her face, and she said quickly, "I'm sorry, that was uncalled for, considering the lady's current chastity program."

"The Lily Maid of Astolat," I said. "Come on, Lily Maid, let's go visit some geniuses."

Fifteen minutes later, after I'd made a couple of preparatory phone calls, we were on the four-lane interstate heading north up the Rio Grande valley. Another twenty minutes saw us turning west on the twisty two-lane blacktop road that leads to Los Alamos. We crossed the Rio Grande, which was running silty and yellow as always under the old-fashioned, steel-girdered highway bridge; but the water was not too high yet, since the winter's snowpack hadn't really started melting up in the mountains. Leaving the river behind, we drove up through the Jemez foothills. It had been a silent drive so

209

far, but now Madeleine, at the wheel, turned her head to glance at me.

"Any instructions for the chauffeur, Boss? As I recall, that's kind of a nasty hill ahead, just the kind I'd pick if I were planning a fatal accident."

I said, "Just go up it fast. We'll be on the outside most of the way, and you don't want to give anybody a chance to pull alongside and nudge us over the edge and into the canyon. Particularly not that blue pickup that's trailing us."

She nodded. "Yes, I've been watching him. . . . Matt."

"Yes?"

"There's something I want to say before . . . before anything happens; and I don't want any interruptions while I say it; and no answer is required." She was looking straight ahead through the windshield as she spoke. "In other words, just shut up and listen. The President of the United States has just been shot. You have a bullet hole in your shoulder. We're being shadowed right this minute. We're obviously bucking something pretty big, and I don't think it's too melodramatic to consider the possibility that . . . that I might just possibly be killed sometime during the next few days. . . . No, goddamn you, shut up!"

She glared at me fiercely, and returned her attention to the road, making the right-hand turn that would take us up the canyon to Los Alamos. The road straight ahead was the big-truck route that went the long way around and came in by the back door.

Madeleine said, "What I want to tell you is, if it happens, don't brood too much about it. Don't blame yourself. What I'll be losing is something I didn't even have that day you picked me up at Fort Ames. For all practical purposes, I was dead then, ready to slink off to some kind of a bleak and hopeless half-life, and quite possibly eventual suicide. At least now I've had a little chance to live again, and if I get dead again, permanently this time, it's just too damn bad. It would have been nice

210

to see what I could do with this new life you've helped me find, but at least you won't remember me as that dough-faced zombie dame in that awful brown suit. I've had a chance to be me again—kind of whiny and complainy, I know, but still me—and that's worth everything that happens next no matter how bad it may be."

After a little, I cleared my throat and said, "I wish we didn't need you so badly. Somehow, you seem to be the key to things around here, at least the only key we've got. Otherwise I wouldn't risk—"

She shook her head, a little impatiently. "I'm trying to tell you, don't worry about it! I'm alive again, I'm having a good time, I'm even being allowed to help my country a little after being convicted of betraying it. What more can a girl ask? Nobody lives forever, and there have been times when I didn't even want to. So driving a nice car on a lovely, sunny day like this with a . . . a man I kind of like beside me is all I need. My God, there were years and years when a pleasant drive in the country was so far out of reach I didn't even dare let myself dream about it!" Before I could respond she laughed and said, with a quick and deliberate change of mood: "I don't really think anybody's going to run us off this road, with all the Armco barriers, or whatever they call them, that they've put up since I last drove up here. You can't even see down into the canyon any longer for all that fencing."

It was really a rather claustrophobic ride, roaring up the steep, winding little mountain road between the rock wall and the steel protective barrier that allowed only occasional glimpses into the valley below.

I said, "Just the same, I'd rather not put them to the test, if you don't mind."

"Do you have some reason to believe that there'll be . . . that somebody's going to try to kill us today?"

I said, "When I called him just now, and let him know where we are heading, our guardian angel, Jackson, seemed to think it was a distinct possibility. He's under the impression that somebody won't like us snooping

211

around the Center where your husband used to work, and that they may try for us either coming or going. Keep your eyes open for his signal. He's got plans for some kind of an escort to see us through, if things get hairy."

But there were no signs of Jackson or his people as we surmounted the last rise and topped out by the fenced-in strip of the Los Alamos airport, passing the building that used to be a guard post where all visitors were checked into and out of the town, back in more secure and suspicious days.

Now the barriers and guards were gone—the security blanket no longer covered the community as a whole, only the individual installations—and this was no longer the legendary Secret City; it was just another shiny-new little western town, planted on the side of the mountain where there used to be nothing but pines and piñons and a rambling school for boys. We took the right-hand fork where the road branched; and the blue Chevy pickup went off to the left and was seen no more, at least for the moment. Madeleine guided us through the center of the town and out into a residential area that soon gave way to empty scenery, mostly standing on end.

"I drove up here with Roy a few times on weekends when I wasn't working and he had short errands to run at the lab," she said reminiscently. "We had a Mercedes, that's how fancy we were. It was one of the things that had us pretty broke, but we'd told ourselves that he needed a good car for all the commuting. Of course I still had my beat-up little Fiat for popping around town. Whenever I came up here with him, I had to wait for him in the visitors' lounge just inside the gate; that's as far as anybody gets without the proper impressive clearance, unless they've changed the procedure. I think we turn left on a dirt road just ahead. . . . God, they've got it all paved now! Ellershaw is years behind the times, as usual."

We started climbing again, along the bottom of a nar-

212

row canyon, where a turbid creek ran beside the black-top road. I wondered what made it so murky—up that high in the mountains, the streams usually run pretty clear—and why there was steam coming off it although the day was not cold. At this time of the afternoon, the rock walls shaded the road except when it twisted in exactly the right southwesterly direction and let a shaft of sunlight find its way to the bottom of the cleft.

Suddenly, a turn brought us out into a sizable mountain meadow—well, it had probably been quite a pretty, grassy, open place once. Maybe you could even have picked wildflowers there; but now it was all paved parking lots and blocky gray buildings, and tanks cylindrical and spherical, and some oddball structures I didn't recognize and undoubtedly wasn't supposed to. This was all crammed into the limited space between the high perpendicular cliffs. There was no visible creek running through the area, but a giant culvert emerged from the hillside to the left and dumped steaming, cloudy water into the old stream channel. Presumably it had been used for cooling some highly secret experiments. I didn't particularly want to know about them. If I did find out, somebody would probably try to shoot me for such a dreadful breach of security; and my still-weak shoulder was evidence that I had enough hostiles to cope with already.

There was a tall chain-link fence topped by several strands of barbed wire on overhanging brackets. I could see no break in the fence except at the road ahead, where a small guardhouse flanked the opening and a red-and-white-striped lifting-type barrier blocked it. There were also a couple of uniformed gents armed with M16 assault rifles. There was a series of signs along the approach road graded from STOP 1500 FEET AHEAD to just plain STOP!

When Madeleine brought the Mazda to a halt at the last red sign, one of the guards stepped forward to look at her; then he bent down so he could see me in the right-hand seat.

I said, "We have an appointment with the Scientific Director, Dr. Johansen. My name is Helm. This is Mrs. Ellershaw."

"Identification, please."

I let him look at my pretty badge thing. Madeleine showed her driving license. The man walked over to the little building and checked a clipboard hanging from a nail beside the door and came back to us.

"You may proceed to Parking One, Mr. Helm. There'll be somebody waiting to escort you to Building A, our administration building. However"—he gave Madeleine a quick, cold glance—"however, you'll have to let the, er, lady out at the guest house just ahead. I think you'll both understand why we can't allow her beyond that point. She'll have to wait for you there, Mr. Helm."

I regarded him for a moment. He was a big, red-faced character in a neat blue uniform. It wasn't the uniform of any of the armed forces with which I was acquainted; but he'd certainly been there, probably in the Marines, and I'd have bet that he'd served as M.P., or I guess the Navy calls it S.P. for Shore Patrol.

"What's your name?" I asked.

"What?"

"You heard me," I snapped. "Name. Rank, if you've got any in that monkey suit. Serial number or whatever they tattoo on your ass in your half-baked security outfit. Come on, amigo. These aren't state secrets I'm asking for. Talk!"

"Look, mister . . . !"

I spoke to Madeleine. "Get us the hell out of here, Mrs. E. We'll find a phone in Los Alamos. I'll call Washington and find out who goofed. . . . No, hold it just a minute, I still want this monkey's name!"

He shifted a bit under my stare and said, "Look mister, I'm just following orders."

"No, you aren't. Do you want to bet me money that your standing orders or regulations or whatever the hell you call them give you the right to refuse to identify

214

yourself to an agent of the United States government, or even a private citizen? That's not classified information, buster, so give!"

"Wohlbrecht," he said in a surly voice.

"Wohlbrecht, what?"

"Wohlbrecht, Arthur."

"Wohlbrecht, Arthur, what?"

He glared at me and I glared right back. Although I had worn an officer's uniform once, a long time ago, I never got much practice commanding troops—they used me for other purposes—but I've run a few operations since where instant obedience was necessary to the success of the mission, not to mention the survival of everybody involved including me. I can play bullyboy as well as the next guy; and this character had learned real discipline once. He was an easy mark. It came grudgingly, but it came.

"Wohlbrecht, Arthur, sir!"

I stared at him hard a moment longer; and he looked away at last. He knew damn well why I was doing it. He'd pushed a little and I'd pushed right back.

I relaxed and gave him a big friendly grin. "Okay, Art. I'm Matt. Now we've made faces at each other, let's see if we can't solve the problem sensibly. You see, I'm responsible for Mrs. Ellershaw's safety. Totally responsible. That means I can't leave her waiting in any lousy guest house, not even with one of your boys looking after her. Not even if you've got combat records like the Angel Gabriel and are armed like a bunch of Hollywood *bandidos*. Now, I could go back to square one and call Washington all over again and get things straightened out, but that would cause a lot of trouble for everybody. So what do you suggest? Like maybe having the Scientific Director come to the guest house to confer with both of us, along with the other gent we want to see? Or maybe you can arrange to get us special limited clearances of some kind, both of us, just as far as the building we want, if you send a man along with us to make sure

215

Mrs. Ellershaw doesn't slip a nuclear reactor into her jeans when nobody's looking. . . ."

That was the way it was eventually done. We had to make the ride in one of their jeeps, of course, since there wasn't room in my jazzy two-seater for a chaperon. Wohlbrecht escorted us himself and turned us over, at the front door of Building A, to a young fellow in slacks and sports shirt, saying, not too grudgingly, that he'd be waiting in the parking lot to ferry us back to our car when we were through in there.

Our civilian escort took us upstairs and deposited us in an outer office where a pretty blond girl in a pink sweater was beating on an electric typewriter. She looked as if she might be a younger, and perhaps slightly less self-satisfied, sister of the elegant snow queen presiding over the reception desk at Baron and Walsh. She paused in her typing to use the phone, and said the Director would see us in a minute, please be seated. We sat down side by side on a rather hard little couch by the door.

"What was that all about?" Madeleine asked at last.

"What was what all about?"

She said, "You don't usually push people around like that, Matt. Making him call you sir, for heaven's sake."

"It worked, didn't it? We're here, aren't we?" Then, a little shamefaced, I said, "Besides, they've got to learn, Mrs. E. I let it pass when Chief Cordoba pulled it because we couldn't afford to antagonize him, at least not yet; but we don't have to take it from a lousy security jerk."

She looked at me for a moment. "Take what, Matt?"

"I'm supposed to be protecting you. That makes it, I feel, my job to remind them that you're a lady, ma'am. They've got to learn a little ordinary courtesy. They've got to understand that, no matter where you've been, you're not to be referred to as an er-lady."

Madeleine smiled slowly. "I suppose I should say it's just something I'm going to have to get used to and it

216

was stupid and childish of you to resent it, but . . . thank you, Matt."

After a wait of fifteen minutes, we were admitted to the presence of Scientific Director Oscar Johansen, Ph.D.

CHAPTER 18

THE pompous look of the man awaiting us behind the big desk in the inner office came as no great surprise. Dr. Johansen had telegraphed his character very clearly when he'd shown himself willing to compromise his own security system rather than condescend to leave his office and go out to meet us in the guest house, so-called; and had then deliberately kept us waiting to demonstrate his resentment.

Well, the information that had been passed to me through Jackson indicated that Dr. Oscar Johansen hadn't really been a topflight physicist who could play scientific ball in the same league with Dr. Roy Ellershaw and the second man we'd come here to meet, Dr. Kurt Grunewalt. Perhaps realizing this, Johansen had switched over to administrative duties some years ago—or perhaps he'd been switched over—and obviously he'd done pretty well in his new field of endeavor.

He was now in command here, in overall charge of the scientific projects in which he'd previously participated, and of the scientists who'd previously been his colleagues. Top dog—but he'd know they were laughing at him in the small back rooms of the Center where the real work got done: the little man who hadn't really been able to make it in the laboratory so he'd got himself kicked upstairs to an office from which he got to tell other men to do the things he was incapable of doing himself.

He didn't rise to greet us when we entered, but remained seated behind his desk: a heavy, florid, blond man with thinning fine hair carefully brushed to cover the places where there wasn't much left. Small, pale-blue eyes. White shirt, blue tie, crisp white laboratory coat presumably worn to indicate that his impulses were still soundly scientific. Big meaty hands with a big ring on one, presumably indicating graduation from an educational institution of which he was proud. Enough after-shave to be noticeable.

I won't say I never trust a man who goes in heavily for deodorant and cologne and professional manicures. Never is a long time, and I've known some very dainty male characters who turned out to be as tough and competent and likable as anybody. But a guy who's all that bothered about how he looks and smells is starting from behind as far as I'm concerned, and I could tell at a glance that Dr. Johansen wasn't ever going to catch up to a point where I'd find him even tolerable.

The office was strictly business, however, a point in his favor—one of the few points in his favor—with gray government furniture and gray government filing cabinets; and a window with a view of a gray government structure of complicated design, involving a lot of large twisted pipes with unnerving little plumes of steam leaking from them here and there. You kind of expected the whole crazy sci-fi thing to blow when the pressure rose just a little higher, taking you with it. I brought a chair forward and seated Madeleine, and then did the same for myself, without invitation.

"I wish to make it perfectly clear," Dr. Johansen said, "that the responsibility for bringing a known security risk onto these premises is entirely yours, Mr. Helm, and that of your superior who forced this meeting. I have put my protest on record, in writing."

I ignored this nonsense and asked, "Where's Dr. Grunewalt?"

"Oh, yes." Acting as if it were a minor detail that had slipped his mind momentarily, he picked up the telephone. "Linda, tell Kurt we're ready for him now, please." He put the phone down and said, "This is a busy installation, Mr. Helm. You can hardly expect the personnel to stand around awaiting your pleasure."

I said, "Tell me about this busy installation. As Scientific Director, are you responsible for the operation of the entire plant?"

He said, "Well, of course, construction and maintenance are outside my jurisdiction except in a very general way. Naturally. Also finance and purchasing. And security; although of course we're all responsible for security in a sense. But basically these functions come under the Administrative Director, Mr. Snelling. I organize and correlate the actual scientific work of the Center. May I ask where these questions are leading?"

"Questions? I've only asked one so far." That was childish, I suppose, but I found the man hard to take. I went on: "I'm trying to get a picture of the place at the time Dr. Ellershaw worked here."

"It's grown considerably since then. There are two new laboratories since Ellershaw's time. Unfortunately, all we can find room for in the limited area available to us here."

"When you say laboratories, do you mean new buildings?"

He nodded. "For security's sake, each project is housed in a separate facility. Personnel cleared for Lab Beta, for instance, have no access to Lab Epsilon." He threw a malicious glance in Madeleine's direction. "I mention Beta because that's where Project LS used to be located—the research program that Ellershaw attempted to betray to our country's enemies in such a callous and mercenary fashion."

"That's a lie!"

219

Madeleine was on her feet. I rose hastily and put my hand on her arm to restrain her. As she glared at Johansen and started to speak angrily, she was interrupted by a light knock on the door. A small dark man entered. He stopped just inside the room, sensing a crisis.

"Perhaps I should go back out and knock again."

"No, no, Kurt." Johansen was obviously relieved at the interruption. "Find yourself a chair. This is Mr. Helm from Washington. Dr. Kurt Grunewalt. And no doubt you remember Ellershaw's wife."

It was a contemptuous introduction that was supposed to remind everyone of what Roy Ellershaw had done, and of where his wife had been spending her time recently, but Grunewalt stepped forward quickly to take Madeleine's hand. He was no taller than she was: a wiry little black-haired gent—although he was well into his fifties, there was no visible gray in his hair—with a big nose and sharp brown eyes in a dark, narrow, inquisitive face. Unlike the administrator in the room, who was dressed like a TV scientist, the true scientist present was wearing baggy gray flannel slacks, a rather limp blue sports shirt, and an old gray sleeveless sweater with some snagged places in it. He bowed over the hand he held, in a formal European way.

"I don't believe we ever met socially, Mrs. Ellershaw," he said, "and I'm afraid we last saw each other, in the courtroom, under rather unfortunate circumstances. I suppose it's too much to hope that you bear me no ill feelings for my testimony."

Madeleine hesitated, and shrugged. "You told only the truth, didn't you?"

"Yes. The exhibit I'd been asked to identify . . . I could say nothing else."

"Then I've no grounds for resentment, Dr. Grunewalt, although it was . . . another nail in my coffin. But they had me pretty well boxed in already, even without your evidence." She gave him a reluctant little smile. "Anyway, it was a long time ago."

Grunewalt studied her a moment longer, in a regretful way, and turned to shake hands with me.

"Mr. Helm. I understand you work for the government —as do we all, of course. How can I be of service?"

I glanced towards the man still seated behind the desk and said, speaking to both of them: "You should be aware that we're not at all satisfied, in Washington, that Mrs. Ellershaw's civil rights were given proper consideration before and during her trial. There's reason to believe that she could be—I'll put it no more strongly than that at the moment—that she could be the victim of a serious miscarriage of justice. We're therefore reopening the investigation originally carried out by another agency, and trying to determine just what happened here at the time of her husband's disappearance and her arrest, and in the weeks immediately preceding. Since you two gentlemen were reasonably well acquainted with Dr. Ellershaw—at the time, you were working on the same project with him, I understand—I'm starting with you. Please understand, this isn't a formal inquiry. If I should come up with sufficient evidence of error, my findings will be turned over to our Legal Department for appropriate action, at which time you'll be asked to make your statements in the proper form. In other words, right now we're just exploring the possibilities, informally."

I was aware that Madeleine's lips were firmly compressed, not with disapproval, but to conceal her amusement at this verbose legalistic double-talk; but fortunately she had the only legal training in the group. The other two obviously didn't know any more about law or legal procedures than I did.

Johanson said uneasily, "But . . . but after eight years . . . !"

Grunewalt laughed. "Mrs. Ellershaw has good reason to be even more clearly aware of the length of time that has passed than you have, Oscar. For my part, if a mistake was made, a terrible mistake, I'll be very happy to help correct it as far as possible."

"Yes." The big man behind the desk spoke hastily. "Yes, of course, we're all happy to cooperate."

"But I would prefer to cooperate sitting down," said the smaller man. When we were all seated, he said, "Where would you like to begin, Mr. Helm?"

"Well, let's start at the end, just to get the record straight. This laser shield, I believe it was called, that you were all working on, the LS-system that was so important to the nation's defense that the Russians were falling all over themselves to steal or buy it . . . I don't want to trespass on any realms of desperate security, but perhaps you can answer the question: Is it in operation now?"

I looked at Johansen, but he made no response. I turned to Grunewalt, who shook his head. "No."

"No you can't answer, or no it isn't, Dr. Grunewalt?"

"No, it isn't."

"Can you tell me why, if it was such a great defensive invention? There's been plenty of time to install it or whatever you do to a gadget like that—distribute it, deploy it—hasn't there?"

Johansen cleared his throat warningly. "Kurt, I'd like to remind you that, regardless of what Mr. Helm's investigations turn up eventually, at the moment Mrs. Ellershaw has no security clearance whatever; quite the contrary."

"Clearance, schmearance!" Grunewalt made an impatient gesture. "Who in our field, in this country or out of it, doesn't know that, with Roy gone, Project LS was a disastrous failure? The problem was always the outlandish energy requirements of the system, Mr. Helm. I could find no way of solving it—or shall we say that none of the solutions I dreamed up proved practical? And your contributions were no more useful, Oscar. But Roy, our button-pushing enfant terrible, set up a model of the system in his beloved computer, don't ask me how. Although I can use it for ordinary calculations, even fairly intricate ones, when it comes to such complex theory I still find myself completely intimidated and inhib-

222

ited by a machine that can think. I leave the true electronic magic to the younger generation; I'm still an old-fashioned pencil-and-paper man at heart. But Roy could think nowhere else but at his console; he played it like a musical instrument. And he was making progress."

Madeleine, who'd been listening in silence, gave a sudden ugly little laugh. "Progress! Just *progress*?" She stared at Grunewalt incredulously. "Do you mean to say that I was punished, ruined, for supposedly having in my possession some pieces of paper describing a lousy national-defense system that didn't even *work*? That might never have worked even if Roy had stayed available to work on it? Goddamn it, at the trial they made it sound as if I were a female Benedict Arnold opening the gates of the lousy fort to the British—except that in my case it was supposed to be the whole damned country I'd exposed to the dirty Red Russians! But what you're saying is that the priceless secret stuff they claimed to've found in that bank box of mine wasn't really good for anything but toilet paper!"

Grunewalt cleared his throat. "Actually, my dear lady, it wasn't even suitable for that. Computer printouts make very poor bathroom tissue."

"And for *that* I was shamed and vilified and had my life totally destroyed!"

Johansen said stiffly, "Regardless of the material involved, there had obviously been a major breach of security."

"Security! Oh, my God! Do you know what kind of a stinking kennel they locked me up in for your dirty security? For eight whole years! I . . . Oh, Jesus, Helm, lend me your hanky, I can't seem to get a Kleenex out of these lousy tight pockets."

We waited for her to blow her nose and wipe her eyes; then I went on to ask the kind of questions I'd be expected to ask. I learned that the scientific threesome composed of Grunewalt, Ellershaw, and Johansen had divided the work of Project LS among them according

223

to their aptitudes. Inspiration, calculation, and organization, was the way Grunewalt described it. He, Grunewalt, was the misty-eyed middle-aged dreamer who came up with the wild ideas; Ellershaw was the hardheaded young computer whiz who put those ideas into language the machine could understand and tested and refined and elaborated them electronically; while Johansen . . . well, Grunewalt was diplomatic, but I got a distinct impression that he and Ellershaw could have got along quite well without the big blond man and used him mainly for scientific housekeeping, the routine work of the project.

I learned a little about the layout of Laboratory Beta, and the security procedures employed. I learned that both Johansen and Grunewalt were married and had homes nearby, in a development in the bedroom community of White Rock, just down the hill from Los Alamos. I learned that Grunewalt had actually not been at the laboratory during the critical few weeks preceding Roy Ellershaw's disappearance; he'd been sent to the East Coast to work with a certain Dr. James Finn at CADRE TWO, where a special nuclear research program was in progress at the time. Purpose of visit: to determine if Finn's work with nuclear energy might possibly be applicable to Project LS.

"Was it?" I asked.

Grunewalt shook his head. "You know how they are. Any energy problem that arises, they think they can solve it by either fission or fusion. Finn was actually developing a miniaturized long-term power source for . . . well, I suppose that's still classified. He was dealing in milliwatts, where we needed megawatts and plenty of them. His work was quite fascinating, and caused us to revise some long-held ideas about critical mass; but I was happy to be ordered back here . . . that is, of course, until I learned what I'd been called back for. The place was a shambles; that stuffed shirt Bennett, of the Office of Federal Security, had men crawling everywhere and was asking insulting questions of everyone; Roy was missing; and I was asked to identify certain computer printouts, hard copies, that had been found where they shouldn't have been—well, to confirm Oscar's identification of them."

"Which you did then, and later in court."

"There was no possibility that I could be mistaken, Mr. Helm."

I said, "You'd better explain it to me in simple terms; I don't know too much about computers. But a printout is a printout, isn't it? Infinitely reproducible? And I don't suppose we're talking about a little personal computer with a memory all its own. For all the separation of facilities you boast about here, for reasons of security, there's one place it all comes together, isn't it? In the single giant memory of the big master computer that, I've been given to understand, serves not only this whole installation but also CADRES TWO and THREE at the far sides of the continent."

Johansen had a tolerantly amused look on his face. "Yes, yes, Mr. Helm, you're quite correct in what you're thinking. It would have been theoretically possible for someone who could decipher the access code to break in from another terminal and, to put it melodramatically, steal Ellershaw's program and print it out, but . . . Tell him, Kurt."

Grunewalt spoke in a kindly way: "The possibility was, of course, thoroughly explored at the time. However, Roy was, as I've said, a real computer genius; I doubt very much that any protective code he devised could be broken."

"But it could be compromised, couldn't it? By somebody who talked too much at the wrong time?"

Grunewalt laughed. "Oscar or myself, you mean, since we were the only others who knew it? But you are barking up the wrong tree. The fact is that it was not the contents of the hard copies that led me to identify them with such certainty; even though, as a matter of fact,

225

experts established that they had actually been run off at our terminal and no other. Apparently those printers produce material that is unique to them, as do typewriters. But the printouts in question also carried numerous penciled notations in Roy's handwriting indicating possible ways in which the program could be modified and rewritten to explore . . . No, Mr. Helm. Those printouts definitely came from the terminal in Laboratory Beta, by way of our security safe. As a matter of fact there were some notes in my handwriting, too; we'd worked on them together before I left for the East. There was no doubt whatever of their origin."

After which, of course, as a conscientious investigator, I had to ask questions about the safe and who had access to it. That pretty well completed the interview. I glanced at my watch as if preparing to leave, but settled back and asked, as a casual afterthought:

"Just to make sure I have it all straight, in Dr. Ellershaw's time there were three separate scientific laboratories here, each operating independently on different projects, except for the computer linkage. Is that correct? And now, since Dr. Johansen tells me two more have been built, you can house five separate research programs."

Johansen said quickly, "No, you are mistaken. We have only sufficient facilities to carry out four independent projects at any given time."

I said innocently, "It's been a long time since I had any contact with the Greek alphabet, but you mentioned a Lab Epsilon. Alpha, Beta, Gamma, Delta, Epsilon. Five, unless you skipped a letter somewhere."

There was an amused laugh from Grunewalt. "Oh, you're referring to the Monkey House."

"The what?"

"We've had a bunch of mad social scientists grafted onto us since the earliest days of the Center. Social engineering. Community interaction. Political interrelations. Whatever the currently fashionable jargon may be.

226

Apparently they're trying to quantify human behavior and study it computerwise, if I've got the verbiage straight. They were originally in Lab Alpha, but they outgrew that little building, so it was turned back to us and Delta was built especially for them—we got Epsilon at the same time, as a consolation prize of sorts. Obviously somebody has some real political influence in that research group; but I wish they'd stop calling themselves scientists and giving science a bad name. Institute for Advanced Human Managerial Studies, indeed!"

"I see," I said. "Well, I guess that takes care of it. I certainly thank you both for your cooperation. . . ."

Wohlbrecht was waiting in his jeep when we crossed the parking lot with our security escort. He drove us to the Mazda and bid us goodbye very politely, but I had no idea whether I'd gained his respect by calling him down, or made a lifelong enemy who was merely smart enough to hide it until he got a chance to strike back. Not that it should matter, since it seemed unlikely that we'd meet again, but I don't like leaving human booby traps behind me.

Then we were driving away along the steaming, murky creek that had probably been a nice little trout stream once.

CHAPTER 19

I guess we both had a sense of escaping from a trap as we drove away from all those weird scientific structures stuffed into that gaping erosion wound in the side of the mountain. However, the narrow, dark exit canyon with its poisonous little stream—at least I wouldn't have wanted to try drinking the stuff—wasn't exactly reassuring either, so it wasn't until we turned onto the open main road again, heading back towards Los Alamos in the low afternoon sunshine, that normal human relations were resumed.

"Well, I think we got somewhere," Madeleine said. "Back there. We learned a few things. That Johansen creep is really a creep, isn't he? *And* he was one of the three people who had access to that safe where the print-outs were stored."

I nodded. "And let's note that not too long after your trial, just long enough not to attract unfavorable attention, Dr. Johansen found himself happily transferred from a scientific job he wasn't very good at to an administrative position of considerable prestige and power that was right down his alley. Does anything come to mind? Like Mr. Bennett, the minor security official who wound up as head of one of the nation's top law-enforcement agencies only a discreet interval after your husband disappeared?"

"Another payoff, Matt?" Then Madeleine nodded and said, "Yes, of course. Somebody had to get that LS-Project computer material out of the laboratory safe for the people who were going to pretend to find it in my safe-deposit box, instead of what was really there. And if Roy didn't take it, and Grunewalt was two thousand miles away . . ."

"Right. Two little Indians from three little Indians leaves one larcenous little redskin, if you'll excuse my racism, ma'am. Our sweet-smelling Scientific Director who didn't want to meet us so badly."

Madeleine said, "And the fact that Dr. Grunewalt *was* sent off to CADRE TWO is also significant, don't you think? They got the only other honest man, besides Roy, out of Laboratory Beta so Johansen could operate more freely. Steal more freely, is more like it."

"Yes," I said, "but I think you're overlooking the most

228

important thing we learned in there. I think we're on the track of what it was your husband got hold of that made it necessary for him, and you, to be eliminated."

She nodded slowly. "Yes. I think I know what you mean, but I'll let you say it."

I said, "We had a long discussion back there of the fact that somebody else could have stolen Dr. Roy Ellershaw's secret computer material but didn't, during which it came out that he was considered a super computer whiz kid, even by his very bright colleagues, right? Which I didn't know, although you probably did. So how about the possibility that, in exactly the same way, he could have stolen somebody else's secret computer material and did? We heard he was so good it was unlikely that anybody could break a code he'd devised. Was he so good that he could break somebody else's code if he got intrigued enough to try it? And if so, whose?"

Madeleine licked her lips. "You're thinking of the Monkey House, aren't you?" When I nodded, she said, "Roy was certainly curious about what was going on in there. He mentioned more than once that all the real scientists at the Center used to speculate about it, in a patronizing way. They had a kind of protective feeling about the big CADRE computer, *their* computer, and they wanted to know what kind of silly, pseudo-scientific games the political and social so-called scientists were playing with it. Advanced Human Managerial Studies, for God's sake! And the people in Alpha were apparently pretty rude to anybody they met around the place, say in the parking lot, who asked casual questions. They got quite nasty when anybody wandered too close to their sacred building. If one of them got Roy mad—he was pretty even-tempered, but he didn't like being pushed around—he might have thought it a good joke on them to crack their protective code, or whatever you call it, and run off a hard copy of their ridiculous attempts at computerized social scientification, and hand the stuff back to them with a flourish—so much for their childish

229

security! It would have been a challenge to him. He did love to play with that machine, if you can call it a machine, and see what it could do. And what he could do." She cleared her throat. "Only, when he did break the access code, and saw the material that was coming up on the screen—"

When she stopped, I said, "When he started getting it out it didn't look so ridiculous after all. In fact we can safely guess that it scared hell out of him, judging by the disturbed way you say he acted during those last weeks. So he kept probing the computer memory, digging away, gradually breaking through whatever electronic defenses they'd put up to protect their stored information; and in the meantime he got hold of Bennett, thinking that he was being a good citizen by letting the Office of Federal Security know that things were going on up Conejo Canyon that shouldn't be."

Madeleine said grimly, "Only that slimy Mr. Bennett saw a chance to cash in on the information, and for a price—or maybe he was already on the payroll, we still don't know which—he let the people in Laboratory Alpha know that somebody was raiding the master computer for their stuff. But they didn't panic; after all, they had Bennett to let them know if things were going critical. They let Roy dig away for several weeks, whenever he had computer time to spare from his real work, while they laid their plans and made their preparations. To make it look good, they even brought in a sexy Communist lady, Bella Kravecki, and had her get friendly with us: the supposed payoff woman, our contact with the enemy. When they were quite ready to strike, bingo! No more Dr. Ellershaw. And pretty soon, for all practical purposes, no more Mrs. Ellershaw either, at least not for eight long years. The Great Conejo Canyon Spy Case. Closed."

We were entering Los Alamos now. I said, "Which brings up a question. The question."

"Yes," she said, "it does, doesn't it?"

230

"Just what the hell *were* they doing in Lab Alpha that they had to go to such lengths to hide it? Whatever it was, we know that a few years later they got Lab Delta built larger so they could do more of it. Advanced Human Managerial Studies. . . ."

Madeleine said, "I hate to change the subject, but we've got another interesting question, Matt. Blue Boy is back." She gestured towards the rearview mirror. "That pickup truck that left us when we got into town on the way up."

I leaned forward for a look at the right-hand mirror. "I see him."

"Maybe I should take the back road out of here. It's a little longer, but it's good and wide and not perched on the side of a cliff."

I shook my head. "Jackson said just stick to the regular route and watch for a signal; he'd see that we got through."

"If you say so, Boss. There's the intersection. One left turn coming up." Presently she said, "We've still got company behind. . . . My God, what's that monster semi doing up ahead? This isn't the truck route. Okay, he's stopping; he must just have made the wrong turn back there."

We were passing the little airport now, and she guided the Mazda around the big eighteen-wheeler that was just slowing down and pulling out onto the shoulder. The trailer was labeled in large letters: INTERMOUNTAIN EXPRESS. A couple of hundred yards ahead, parked, was a black van with psychedelic decorations involving scarlet streamlines and golden flames, a real hippie truck, if the word isn't obsolete. As we approached, all its lights went on, and off, and on, and off again.

"There's our boy," I said. "Speed up and give him some space to tuck in between us and the pickup so he can take it off our backs."

Madeleine dropped down a gear and hit the accelerator; the Mazda leaped ahead obediently, and the black

231

van lurched into motion and cut in front of our unwanted escort, the driver of which leaned angrily on his horn. The driver of the van honked back contemptuously. I sat twisted in my seat to watch the show. It all happened very rapidly: the incensed pickup driver, perhaps thinking of the steep and winding downgrade ahead, where passing would be impossible, tried to get around while the road was still straight, and the driver of the van let him come almost abreast and then simply took him off the road and into the shallow ditch where I lost sight of them as our road turned and dipped down into the canyon.

"What happened?" Madeleine asked.

"Scratch one blue pickup," I said. "I think we're free and clear. . . . Oh, Jesus!"

"What's the matter?" Her eyes went to the mirror, and she gasped. "Oh, my God! Do you think it's chasing us? Let's get the hell out of here!"

Behind us, the big semi had lunged into sight. It seemed to fill the whole little mountain road as it thundered after us, gaining speed. Madeleine's hand went to the gearshift lever; I grabbed it.

"Easy, easy!"

"But—"

"No rush, sweetheart. He looks ferocious, but there's no way a heavy rig like that's going to catch a sports car on this hill, so what's the point . . . ? Goddamn it, watch your driving!"

She cut hard right to make room for a big sedan that had appeared around the curve ahead. It whipped past, horn blaring; looking back I saw it squeeze past the oncoming truck, just barely.

"Please don't yell at me, Matt."

"Sorry. You watch ahead, I'll watch behind. Slow down a little, let him get a little closer. . . . That's fine, hold that while we figure things out. Obviously he's the beater."

"Beater?"

232

"Sure, he's coming through the forest stomping and yelling and beating the bushes, driving the game to the guns waiting silently up ahead. In this case, down ahead. . . . A little faster now, don't let him get too close. That's it, you're doing fine."

"You mean they've got an ambush . . . ? But what can we do? If we let him catch us, he'll mash us flat and roll right over us, won't he?"

I said, "Remember the scenic overlook about halfway down? We'll try to shed him there, hoping they'll let us get that far. . . . Ease off a little. Don't get too far ahead of him yet."

"Tell me what you want me to do."

Her face was pale and shiny and her hands gripped the steering wheel fiercely as she threw us around the curves with an occasional glance at the rearview mirror; but she was holding position ahead of the onrushing semi quite consistently now, speeding up as it gained momentum in the straights, slowing a little so as not to pull away from it in the curves the little Mazda negotiated easily while the giant rig astern had to scrub off speed in order to lurch around with its great tires screaming at the very edge of adhesion. I had to hand it to the man behind the wheel, he was handling all those tons in a very professional manner. I saw the sign ahead: SCENIC OVERLOOK 1 MILE.

"Ready now," I said softly. "Remember, goose it as soon as you're around the curve; you want room enough to brake hard. And do your heavy braking while we're still on the pavement. The parking area itself is gravel; if you hit it too fast we'll slide right through the Armco and off into space before you can get us stopped."

"But I've got to get over to the left. . . . What if there's a car coming the other way?"

"Then there are going to be a lot of squashed people all over the road, including us," I said.

"Gee, thanks loads!"

I grinned tightly. "You've got to learn to play the

233

odds. If you know there's definitely a guy behind trying to kill you, and probably some guys ahead trying to kill you, you can't be bothered with the minor statistical possibility of meeting a stranger on a blind curve. It's one of the lesser risks, let's say. . . . Okay, here we go!"

She was getting very good with her downshifts; and the Mazda leaped ahead as she accelerated through the curve, leaving our oversized pursuer out of sight for the moment. Then the parking area was coming up, ahead and on the left, and the brakes went on hard, and the semi was coming around the curve astern like a runaway locomotive, roaring down on us as we lost speed.

"Good," I said. "Come left now . . . slower, slower . . . you're doing fine . . . no, don't worry about the fucking mirror, keep your eye on the . . . Ease off a little and let her roll now, tease him along, waggle your pretty tail at him. . . ."

I guess I'm not a very nice guy. My original idea had simply been to get clear, assuming that the driver astern, knowing that he had another hard curve to negotiate with his enormous vehicle, would have to let us go—but he wasn't letting us go. Towering over us only a couple of car lengths astern, hypnotized by the pursuit like a hound after a rabbit, he was following us over to the left as we approached the parking area. Already he was out of position, and it seemed like a hell of a fine idea. . . .

"Now!" I said. "Hard left, downshift, and floor it the minute she hits the gravel. Spin her out!"

With the massive truck bumper almost upon us, the Mazda lunged aside. Madeleine slammed the lever across and hit the gas hard. The rear end broke loose and we were spinning and sliding across the little parking area perched on a point of rock with a spectacular view, in which nobody was interested at the moment. A top-heavy sedan or pickup might have rolled, but the low-slung sports car simply skittered sideways over the gravel like a hockey puck. . . . And the driver of the semi, realizing his position, was trying to make a retrieve, too late. He was too far out, too-far left. As he tried to come right and pull his big rig back to safety the left front tire of the tractor hit the gravel and he lost it completely and went sliding across the gravel bent clear out of shape, as the hotshot drivers say, totally out of control, with the tractor at a crazy angle to the bulky trailer. Sparks flew as the rig brought up against the steel barrier, but only for a moment. The supporting posts, never designed to resist such an impact, pulled right out of the mountainside, and the eighteen-wheeler went over the edge, taking a long ribbon of steel with it.

I became aware that, sliding broadside, we'd come to a halt well short of the barrier. Madeleine was hunched over the steering wheel with her hands covering her face. I got out and pulled my arm out of the annoying sling and went around to open her door. She let herself be helped out, and tried to cling to me.

I said, "Later. Let's get the hell out of here before we indulge in hysterics."

Her giggle had an uncontrolled sound. "I can't *stand* all that mushy sympathy!"

She stumbled around the car, and I eased back the driver's seat for my longer legs and folded myself into it. Our doors slammed shut almost simultaneously. I took us out of there fast, and back up the mountain the way we'd just come. When we topped out at the airport, the van and the pickup were still in the ditch, locked together, and the drivers were standing nearby arguing hotly. Although it seemed incredible that so little time had passed, there were no police or wreckers or ghoulish spectators on the scene yet. I made a left turn at the intersection beyond, where we'd turned right, earlier, to Conejo Canyon. A little farther on, at the next intersection, I turned westwards.

Madeleine looked up dully. "This isn't the way to Santa Fe."

"That's right," I said. "These are clever people. They set up that pickup as a decoy to take out our escort. They

235

could have thought of setting up another ambush on the back road, just in case. But I doubt that they'll be covering the road west across the mountains. It's a considerable detour. We'll have to drive clear over into the next big valley, and then almost down to Albuquerque before we can pick up the interstate and come back north, but I don't feel like playing any more games today, and I don't think you do, either."

It was quite a climb, on another twisting little two-lane road; but there were no indications that we were being followed by anybody, friendly or hostile. For the moment we were on our own. It wasn't a bad feeling. The high country was quite lovely, and I saw that Madeleine was recovering, beside me, and enjoying the mountain scenery.

"Can we stop?" she asked at last. "That's a pretty place up ahead."

"Sure," I said, and pulled up among the trees, far enough so the car couldn't be seen from the highway. "What did you have in mind, Mrs. E?"

She laughed. "Well, I was promised an opportunity to have some hysterics, remember. But first of all I've got to pee very badly, if you must know. Don't go away, I'll be right back."

Being better equipped for the purpose—as the little girl said enviously, watching her little brother, it's *such* a handy thing to have on a picnic—I had my own bladder problems solved and was back at the car before she returned. I watched her come towards me and felt a kind of possessive pride at the attractive picture she made even in her shabby jeans. I mean, hell, I'd practically built this handsome wench from scratch, hadn't I? I warned myself to cut it out; she'd hate me if she ever got a hint I felt that way. I was taking too much credit, anyway. The good stuff had been there right along, just badly disorganized by her devastating experiences. She'd merely needed a little help in putting it back together.

236

She stopped in front of me. "We killed that man, didn't we, Matt?" she said quietly.

I shook my head. "As far as I'm concerned, he killed himself. We didn't ask him to come chasing after us."

"But at the end, there, you deliberately had me tease him, tempt him, let him think he could catch us and finish it right there." She shook her head quickly. "No, I'm not blaming you, my dear. Because I . . . I loved doing it to the great big bully in his monster truck!"

"Good girl," I said.

"No," she said. "No, I'm not a good girl, not any longer. Not at all the sweet young lady I used to be, the gentle and sensitive person who died in Fort Ames, or maybe even earlier in one of those dreadful jails into which they stuck me on the way there. That's what made me so sick just now, Matt. Not just the reaction, but the knowledge that I *liked* seeing that truck falling down into the deep canyon with that man in it! It was a . . . a wonderful triumphant rush, almost a sexual feeling, knowing that we'd beat the bastard at his own game!" Her face seemed to crumple and her eyes grew shiny with tears. "Oh, God, Matt, what have they made of me? What have you made of me?"

Then she was in my arms, crying. I tried to hold her in gentle brotherly fashion and let her work her own way through it; but her distress was too disturbing and her nearness was too tempting. Soon I found myself touching my lips to her hair and, when she raised her tear-wet face questioningly, to her lips. The kiss was tentative and passionless at first; but soon it became something very different. Her breathing changed, and I felt her breasts pressing warmly against me as she drew me against her hard, her nails digging fiercely into my back; and my own hands moved downwards from her slender waist to possess the smooth roundness of her buttocks, finding them, although I'm normally a lace-and-satin man at heart, very pleasing and exciting under the taut rough cloth of her jeans. . . .

CHAPTER 20

SHE drove us away from there in silence, and I said nothing, because it had been a fine thing that really didn't need talking about. I just hoped she wasn't hurt or angry at the impulsive way we'd broken her stern nonintercourse pact. Then I heard her laugh softly, and I knew everything was all right.

"I've still got pine needles in my hair," she murmured. "No self-control, no self-control at all! And you weren't much help, Buster!"

"What do you want me to say, that I'm sorry?"

"If you do, I'll slug you. It was a dumb idea anyway, that one of mine. My God, with people trying to kill me all over the place, I'd better do all the living I can while I'm still around to enjoy it."

"Sir Matthew at your service, Milady."

"Service?" She laughed again. "Keep it clean, darling. Now tell me how the hell we get out of this lovely mountain wilderness. . . ."

We stopped for dinner at a little Mexican restaurant in the town of Bernallillo, just before picking up the interstate north. The food was chile—hot, but we put out the fires with adequate quantities of cold Mexican beer. It was a pleasant starlit night by the time we'd finished, traffic was light on the four-lane highway, so it was an easy enough drive; but sitting in the copilot's seat with nothing to do I found myself yawning repeatedly. It had been a long day.

But it wasn't through with us yet. When Madeleine stopped the car under the sheltered breezeway in front of the motel office, and I went inside to check for mail and messages, a young man coming out—Marty—brushed against me and spoke a couple of words in a lipless way. I went on to the desk and found nothing there for us. I went back and got into the Mazda.

"Brace yourself," I said. "Welcoming committee of some kind. Your room."

"Oh, my God," she said. "Do you think, if I ask nicely, they'll give me back my nice quiet cell in Fort Ames?"

I said, "It seems a kind of simpleminded way for anybody to lay for us, but we'd better give it the full-dress treatment anyway, if only for practice."

"Matt, am I supposed to be scared all the time?"

"If you weren't scared, I'd worry about you," I said. "When we go in, don't brandish any weapons unnecessarily, and don't shoot anybody you don't have to, including me."

Actually, of course, I did worry about her. She'd done very well so far, but you always worry when you're working with one of the new ones; and this one, I couldn't help remembering, had been brought up to be afraid of guns. If she'd been brought up to be afraid of golf clubs, I wouldn't have been happy having her behind me with a number two iron or, heaven forbid, one of those terribly dangerous woods. But it really went quite smoothly.

She stopped the car in front of her door. We got out on opposite sides and strolled up the walk together. I spoke clearly, "Let me make like a gentleman, doll. Where's your key?"

I felt the small tug at my waist, left side, as I slipped the key she'd handed me into the lock. We'd worked out all the moves pretty carefully; and I was wearing a left-handed FBI-type holster high on my belt back under my jacket. Usually I prefer the gun more in front, rigged for a cross draw but available to either hand; but at present we didn't want anybody getting the idea that I might possibly consider using my poor useless right hand, and

this made it easier for her, too. As long as she was somewhere to my left, front or back or side, she could get at
the weapon; and still I'd been telling Chief Cordoba the
gospel truth when I said she wasn't carrying, as the jargon goes.

In an obvious emergency she would, of course, simply
go for it. Otherwise the signal for her to arm herself was
any term of endearment. As long as I called her Madeleine, or Mrs. Ellershaw, or just plain Ellershaw, or Mrs.
E, or Convict #210934, nothing was supposed to happen,
but if I called her sweetheart or honeybunch, or dear or
darling, or doll, she was supposed to go to battle stations
soonest. I'd been afraid it might have an inhibiting effect
on our relationship, having her grab for a loaded
revolver whenever I whispered tenderly that she was my
own true love; but as we'd demonstrated a few hours
earlier, that fear had obviously been groundless.

"Excuse me," I said politely, entering the room ahead
of her.

I elbowed the door clear back with my left arm. I'd
already pressed the release, and the little sleeve gun had
slipped down into my right hand, concealed by the black
silk of the sling. We moved into the room like that, and I
was ready to throw myself aside to clear the field for her
weapon while bringing my own into the open to lay
down a barrage of nasty little jacketed .25-caliber
slugs—I didn't have much faith in the accuracy of the
lousy little palm-sized automatic, but even a small bullet
just whistling past your ear can be distracting. Madeleine, with her heavier .38-caliber artillery, was supposed
to really mow them down while I and my popgun were
holding their amused attention.

The cause of all this activity was curled up in one of
the big chairs by the room's front window sound asleep:
a small dark-haired girl I'd never seen before in my life.
There was a purse on the low round table between the
chairs; and what seemed to be a camera case, one of the
light canvas jobs that had replaced the heavy leather

gadget bags we used to lug around when we wanted to look professional.

I signaled to Madeleine to keep the intruder covered, and moved forward to check her luggage for weapons, and found none. She continued to sleep soundly. I stole silently away to inspect the bathroom, empty, and my own adjoining room, ditto. Returning through the connecting door, I found Madeleine still watching the little girl, who was still slumbering like a baby.

"Cute," I whispered.

"So's a coral snake," Madeleine breathed. "Mr. Helm, let me introduce you to Miss Evangeline Lowery, spoiled-brat daughter of Admiral Jasper Lowery and his gracious wife Adelaide, whom you've already met."

"How do you know she's a spoiled brat? She can't have been more than thirteen or fourteen when you last saw her."

"Well, she was impossible then, why should she improve? With a mother like that?"

I grinned. "I think you're just prejudiced against Lowerys in general. You were probably pretty impossible at fourteen, yourself. But what the hell's the kid doing here?"

"We could try asking."

I felt the .38 being returned to my left hip. As Madeleine moved forward, I returned the sleeve gun to its clip and went over, belatedly, to close the outside door. The sleeping girl started when Madeleine touched her, and sat up abruptly. She stared blankly at Madeleine, and glanced at me, and looked back to Madeleine, frowning as if she'd expected someone quite different from the suntanned and healthy-looking but rather cheaply and carelessly dressed woman before her.

"Mrs. Ellershaw?" she said uncertainly.

When Madeleine nodded, the little girl gave a toss to her head to settle her short dark hair into place, finishing with a couple of quick pats. I saw that she had a rather intriguing snub nose and freckles. She stood up and hauled at her nicely tailored and obviously expensive dark-blue slacks and tucked her crisp blue gingham shirt into them. Her waist was tiny. She located a pair of neat little blue shoes with rudimentary heels, and stepped into them.

"Sorry about that, Mrs. Ellershaw," she said. "I must have dozed off; I didn't think I'd have to wait so long. You remember me? Vangie Lowery?"

"Yes, I remember you. What do you want?"

Vangie Lowery hesitated, and seemed to lose her youthful assurance. Her mouth quivered. "Set him free, Mrs. Ellershaw!" she breathed. "Oh, turn him loose, please! Don't keep him worshiping at your feet forever! Oh, damn, where's the crummy john in this crummy place?"

She was sobbing loudly as she dashed across the room and disappeared into the bathroom, slamming the door behind her. When I turned to look at Madeleine, she had moved to the table to examine the kid's blue sailcloth purse.

"What was that all about?" I asked.

Madeleine shrugged. "Walter Maxon, I suppose. She had a terrible crush on him. Followed him around like a puppy. He was dreadfully embarrassed. It seems a long time for a childish fixation to last, but I can't think of anybody else I'm holding in thrall at the moment." She smiled at me across the room. "Present company excepted, of course. Are you enthralled, Mr. Helm?"

"Mesmerized," I said. I grimaced. "Lowerys for breakfast, courtesy of Brandon and Walsh. Lowerys for lunch, courtesy of Adelaide. Lowerys for dinner, courtesy of Evangeline, known as Vangie. Do you have a feeling somebody's trying to send us a message, Mrs. E? A message that reads Lowery, Lowery, Lowery?"

"We still haven't actually met Admiral Jasper."

I said, "But I get a distinct impression that we're supposed to, expected to, don't you?" I frowned. "Anything interesting in her purse?"

"A press card. Surprise, surprise. She's a reporter-dash-photographer for, guess what, the Santa Fe *Daily Journal*."

"So that's how she got in, waving her credentials at the maid or somebody," I said. "Seems like Daddy Lowery's got the whole family on the payroll. The question is, if she didn't come here just for personal reasons, if she really wants an interview for her paper, do you want to give it to her?"

Madeleine shrugged. "Why not? Isn't that what we're after, publicity?"

"Better think about it a bit," I said. "It could get kind of rough. The way she seems to feel about you, you can be sure she won't write you up nice. Are you prepared to appear in print as a foul-mouthed broad calling down obscene curses upon those who framed her into prison, she claims, although she was really innocent as the snow is white, she claims. With a deadpan recap of all that overwhelming trial evidence to show what a pitiful liar you are. With pictures of you looking as old and hard and jail-worn as the camera can make you. And for contrast, an old professional portrait from the files, with the smiling young subject looking very smart and lovely and refined. Mrs. Ellershaw before prison versus Mrs. Ellershaw after. Can you take that?"

Madeleine said quietly, "After Fort Ames, I should be able to take just about anything, shouldn't I?" She shook her head quickly. "Don't worry so much about me, darling. This is exactly what we want. It's why I got myself up like this, isn't it? Turn the little bitch loose on me and let her do her worst."

The kid emerged from the bathroom at last. Except for some pinkness about the eyes she'd done a good job of reconstruction. She marched right up to Madeleine.

"I suppose you think I'm an awful little fool, Mrs. Ellershaw," she said, "but I thought maybe, if you really understood what you were doing to Walter . . ."

"Doing?" Madeleine's voice had changed, becoming

harsh and vulgar. "I've never done a fucking thing to your Walter, dearie. Hell, I answered a couple of his letters with short notes of thanks, since I was brought up to be a polite little girl; I was even taught to curtsy, if you can believe it. But that was early in . . . in my sentence, while I was still remembering what it was like to be a human being. I also let him come to see me once because he wanted it so bad and I thought it might help me to have a little contact with . . . with the outside world. But it didn't. You try being locked away like that for years, just sitting in a cage watching your life run away uselessly, and see if you want people coming to gawk at you through the bars like in a fucking zoo."

The little girl licked her lips and said stiffly, "It's been doing terrible things to him all these years, Mrs. Ellershaw. He still thinks you're innocent; and he feels it's his fault you were convicted because of the way he failed to protect your rights the night you were arrested. . . . And all these years imagining dreadful things happening to you in there, and finally that curt little note—he said your handwriting was very shaky—asking for some clothes to be sent because you were getting out at last, but telling him so definitely that you did not, repeat not, want him to come and meet you. Naturally, he figured they'd hurt you so badly, left you in such awful condition, that you couldn't bear to be seen by anybody you'd known before. . . . But you look all right to me, Mrs. Ellershaw. Not exactly what I expected; but there doesn't seem to be a great deal wrong with your condition."

Madeleine's lip curled. "Expected? What the fuck did you expect? Did you think I'd still be the dainty young glamour girl of Baron and Walsh after spending eight years in the asshole of the federal prison system? For something I didn't do—but you don't believe that, do you?"

The little girl hesitated, and squared her shoulders bravely. "No, Mrs. Ellershaw, I do not. I think Walter is just blinded by . . . well, let's call it heroine-worship. And

244

his own sense of guilt. But the fact that he should have done better for you that first night doesn't make you innocent. Actually, nothing that happened that night affected the final result of your trial, did it? And I've read all about your trial, and talked to people, and frankly I can't see any way you *can* be innocent."

Madeleine laughed harshly. "Tell me all about it, honey," she said. "No, on second thought, don't bother. Tell him." She waved a hand in my direction. "Miss Lowery, Mr. Helm. Helm is from Washington, and I'm sure he'll love to hear how I'm really guilty as hell, even though I've seduced him into reopening my case with my gorgeous gowns and gracious manner, not to mention my refined fucking language. Get me a drink, Helm, will you? And let's all sit down, for Christ's sake. Why are we standing around like telephone poles?" She dropped carelessly into a chair, her jean-clad legs sprawling wide. "You didn't come here just to ask me to let your boyfriend out of my clutches, did you, Lowery? You do want an interview with the glamorous lady spy; you want her reactions upon being released at last from the grim penal institution in which she wound up spending damn near a quarter of her life to date. Or did you bring all that crap that's cluttering up my table just for show?"

Vangie Lowry turned out to be a rather clumsy and inexperienced interviewer; she even had trouble working the little tape recorder she produced out of one of the numerous pockets of her camera bag. However, she was very sneaky with her camera and flash. She went for the low-angle shots that make them look all prognathous jaws and apelike nostrils, and the bottom-lighted shots that can make Mother Teresa look like the Auschwitz lady—or was it Belsen or Buchenwald?—who specialized in lampshades made of human skin. A very wicked little girl.

"Thank you very much, Mrs. Ellershaw," she said at last, smiling sweetly as she gathered up her belongings.

"I'm sorry to have taken up so much of your time, and I do appreciate your cooperation. Well, er, goodbye."

After she'd gone, and the sound of her car had dwindled down the drive, I closed the door and looked at Madeleine, who was standing by the big window staring bleakly out into the night.

"Don't silhouette yourself against the light like that," I said. When she let the curtain fall and turned to face me, I asked, "Are you all right?"

She shook her head minutely. "What do you think? Am I supposed to enjoy making myself look and sound like that, with the help of a little creep like that?" She hesitated. "Matt?"

"Yes?"

"Do you mind if we don't . . . I seem to be suddenly feeling kind of depressed and antisocial."

"I think I can restrain the raging beast within," I said dryly. "Anyway, I have to slip out for a moment. I'll make sure your protection is in place out there, but maybe you'd better keep this handy just in case."

I slipped the snub-nosed Smith and Wesson out of its holster and gave it to her. I was glad to see her check the loads, as you do routinely with any weapon that's given you—people have died from assuming that a gun was handed to them loaded or, for that matter, unloaded.

She said, with a return of the old bitterness: "Like I said before, once I was a nice little girl. If somebody'd handed me a gun I'd have screamed in horror and dropped the nasty thing on my foot."

"The dinosaurs were nice, too," I said. "At least I suppose other dinosaurs thought so. But they became extinct because they couldn't adapt to changing circumstances." I grinned. "Try not to become extinct while I'm gone, Mrs. E."

Outside, the night was cool and clear. I walked deliberately towards the street, waiting for a sign; then a shadow moved near one of the parked cars. I gave the unobtrusive signal that meant I didn't want an escort and he should keep his eye on the subject and forget about me. Then I walked for a while. When I was reasonably sure there was nobody behind me, I made another signal and a car pulled to the curb beside me and stopped. I got in. McCullough sent the car away.

"You're clear," he said.

"I thought so," I said. "What the hell happened?"

"Nothing happened."

"We almost got run into an ambush."

"There was no ambush." His young voice was cold. "We took care of it before you were a quarter of the way down that hill; you'd have had a clear road if you'd kept going. We thought of doing something about the semi, like with a rifle bullet or two, but then we figured if you couldn't keep ahead of a big clumsy rig like that, in a fast sports car, to hell with you."

I grinned. "Okay. Sorry. So Jackson let himself be sucked in by a decoy, but our backup system worked. Good enough." I glanced at him. "Did you get anything out of the men who were laying for us?"

He said in the same cold voice, "We didn't have a hell of a lot of time from when we saw what was up to when you started down that toboggan slide."

"Not enough time to waste time taking them alive."

"You got it, mister."

I glanced curiously at his handsome young face. He was one of the icy ones, and in a way I envied him; he'd never have to worry about getting emotionally involved with a troubled lady he'd been assigned to protect. She'd always remain strictly a subject to him. It was the safe and professional way to handle it. But ice is pretty brittle, and he'd crack some day; the cold ones always do. But that was in the future. Right now he was the right man for the job.

"Find me a pay phone," I said. "And keep up the good work."

"That's what I'm here for," he said.

The phone booth was in the lobby of La Fonda Hotel,

the big old one on the Plaza. Legend says that an exuberant gent rode a horse into the lobby once, but that was before they got it all cluttered up with little newsstands and giftee shoppees. Mac answered immediately, once I'd gone through the preliminary nonsense with the pretty girl on the switchboard—at least she had a pretty voice; I hoped the rest of her lived up to it.

"Yes, Eric?"

"Reporting. I think we may be gaining on something, but I don't know what." I told him what had happened today, with emphasis on what we'd learned, or thought we'd learned, at the mysterious Center up Conejo Canyon. "Advanced Human Managerial Studies, for Christ's sake!" I said irritably. "Look, isn't it time somebody broke down and said what the hell's going on? Presumably, since they tried to kill the President, they've got somebody in mind to take his place? Or maybe not exactly his place, since we did get a hint that he was afraid of being the last *elected* chief executive, right? So who's in the wings, waiting to step on stage, King John the First of America? Or Emperor Jim, or Dictator Hank? And who the hell's behind him, and just what are they after? There's got to be a political party of some kind, doesn't there? A lot of people with a lot of influence, more influence every day, who don't like the way the country's being run and think they can do better. So the man said. But, Jesus Christ, what do they really want, and who are they, and where are they?"

"Where?" Mac said. "I think you'd better assume that they're everywhere, Eric. Remember that poor ole hound with the heartworms all through his bloodstream. As for who they are, and what they want, you don't need to know that. And neither do I. Or so we've been told, repeatedly. Don't think I haven't asked those questions, too."

I said, "Okay. But pass the word. Since they won't tell me who the bad guys are, or even the good guys, I'm assuming that anything that moves in the bushes is hostile if I didn't put it there myself, and I'm taking it out. And I don't want any complaints later."

"Just do the job you were sent out there to do and there will be no complaints," Mac said.

The hike back to the motel stretched my muscles nicely after the long drive, but it didn't do much for my mental state. I felt trapped and frustrated by all the secrecy. Not for the first time I envied the boys in the military, where you got to wear a conspicuous, unmistakable blue uniform and shoot at the guys in conspicuous, unmistakable gray. Or whatever. In this angry condition, I barged into my room heedlessly, and brought up short seeing that the bed had been disturbed since I'd left. The little stainless steel automatic—a Bauer, if it matters—slid into my hand.

"Don't shoot me, please. I'm turning on the light."

The sudden illumination showed me that not only had the bed been disturbed, there was somebody in it: my depressed and antisocial lady, in her soft and pretty old nightgown, the expensive satin one with all the lace on it.

She gave me a slightly tremulous smile. "May the silly wench change her silly mind?" she asked.

Chapter 21

AWAKENING, with daylight in the room, I had to disentangle myself gently before I could sit up. By that time she was awake, too—if she'd actually been asleep—looking up at me gravely from the pillow. Even allowing for the fact that the girl always looks even lovelier afterwards, kind of sweet and soft and young no matter what her age, this was, I thought, a very good thing to find in my bed.

I was aware that I'd never got around to locating my pajamas, let alone putting them on; and we'd never got her nightie off, either—it was somewhat disordered and crumpled now after valiant active service. I leaned over and kissed an exposed breast, done to a nice golden brown, I noticed, and carefully returned a displaced shoulder strap to its proper location and function.

"An investigation is in order," I said sternly. "Candidates at our super-secret training facility are not supposed to have enough leisure time to get themselves smooth allover tans. We must get to the bottom of this."

She said, unsmiling, "If that's meant as a pun, it's pretty bad. Even if it isn't meant as a pun it's pretty bad. And the bottom of me is just as tanned as the top—you're welcome to investigate—and I got it that way while waiting for you to get back after the course was over. And I'm not going to tell you where, because if I did you'd spend all your time at the Ranch trying to get a peek at the nekkid girl agents, wouldn't you? And now that we've got that important matter disposed of. . . . Matt," she said softly, with a total change of expression, "Matt, you've got to help me."

Startled, I looked down at her lying there beside me. "Help you how?"

"This isn't any good, for either of us. We've got to stop it."

I said, a bit stiffly, "I thought it was pretty damn good, myself. I regret that the lady found it unsatisfactory."

She shook her head quickly. "Please don't be stuffy! The lady found it . . . very beautiful, you know that. I think she made that very clear. That's why we've got to stop it. Because it's taking us both where we shouldn't go. At least it's taking me where I don't want to go. Or maybe I should say, it's making me what I don't want to be."

"And what is that?" I asked.

"A depraved female with a criminal record, in tight pants, who sleeps with men under bushes and in tacky motel rooms." She shook her head again. "I know, I know, I'm making it dirty now, I'm spoiling it, and I'm very sorry, my dear; but I've been lying here thinking it out, trying to find out what I really want—"

"And I'm not it," I said.

"That's right, Matt. You're not it. You don't need a wife, let alone a jailbird wife, and even if you were crazy enough to ask me, I don't need a sinister secret agent for a husband. What I really need . . ." She stopped, and swallowed hard. "The trouble is, I'm a coward."

"Sure," I said. "Sure. I remember being told all about that scaredy-cat dame crouching in the snow beside my unconscious body brandishing a cowardly revolver in her trembling hand. That's the same yellow broad who went through the basic course at the Ranch with flying colors, and only yesterday did a job of driving under very hairy conditions that would make Andretti and the Unser boys sick with envy."

She allowed herself a faint smile. "Oh, that," she said. "I guess maybe I've got a little physical courage hidden somewhere, enough to get by on normally, although the way I gave up completely and tried to kill myself, back there in Ames, doesn't make me any Joan of Arc, does it?"

"Anybody can be worn down in time," I said.

She shook her head once more. "But I'm not talking about that. I'm talking about the other kind of courage, the kind of . . . of inner strength and confidence that enables you to face. . . . Matt, I'm not only a coward, I'm a snob; and I can't take too many days like yesterday. I remember that nightmare year of humiliation, of being a public spectacle, between the time I was first arrested and the time I was tried and sent off to serve my sentence. Yesterday brought it all back: being publicly insulted by the Lowery woman, seeing the ghoulish expressions of all those people in the restaurant, being sneered at contemptuously by Dr. Johansen, and even

251

treated like trash by that cheap security guard.... While you were still asleep just now, I was lying here figuring out what I must have now to make a reasonable new life for myself. And I decided that what I desire more than anything else in the world . . ." She stopped and swallowed hard. "What I really yearn for, Matt, is respectability."

I started to speak and stopped. Outside, somebody started a car and drove it away. Madeleine gave a hard little laugh.

"God, isn't that ridiculous?" she said harshly. "But you've got to remember the kind of girl I was, the way I was brought up. The fact is, I simply can't bear to be a . . . an untouchable, like this. I want my lousy respected upper-class status back, damn it! You can snicker anytime. Isn't that a tacky little ambition for a girl who was once going to set the whole world on fire?"

I looked down at her, lying there, so torn between the shining world she'd lost and the shabby world in which she found herself.

I spoke very carefully: "Since the subject of matrimony was mentioned earlier, let's explore it a little further. Is there any possibility that you'd feel respectable enough as Mrs. Helm?"

After a startled moment she said, "Matt, you dope, I wasn't hinting . . . My God, you gave me back my life in more ways than one, you don't have to marry the girl!" She frowned at me. "Are you serious?"

"It can't have escaped your notice, particularly since last night, that I find you attractive," I said. "And I don't normally propose to ladies in jest, ma'am. I'll admit I haven't given the subject the consideration it deserves. I've had a few other things on my mind, like keeping us both alive; but the more I think about it, the more intriguing I find it. At least I'd like to discuss it with you; but you said flatly that you didn't need a government agent for a husband. Is that a firm decision?"

"Oh, God, Matt, you're making me feel awful!"

"I see," I said. It was strange, I reflected, how you could regret the loss of something you hadn't even known you wanted. "So it is a firm decision."

She licked her lips. "You're making it very hard for me. . . . Oh, damn it, I'll be blunt. As Mrs. Helm I'd be the mysterious wife—with a prison record, yet—of a mysterious man who's always disappearing to do mysterious, and probably very disreputable, chores for the U.S. government. Very strange couple, my deahs; not quite, quite, don't you know? Matt, that isn't what I want. That isn't what I need: to keep on being a subject for gossip and curiosity and speculation the whole rest of my life." She shook her head quickly. "Not even if a very nice man is included in the package. No."

There were many things I could have said, but I didn't say them. She was a bright lady, and she'd have said them all to herself already. She'd obviously been unable to argue against the bitter hurt and shame of coming home a despised ex-convict; and if she couldn't convince herself, what chance had I?

"So what's the battle plan now?" I asked.

She glanced at me warily. "No arguments, Matt?"

I grinned. "You're thinking I can't want you very much to give up so easily. You don't understand. This is where I display my true nobility of character for you to remember if your plans ever change. This is where, if the dumb female I happen to want wants something or somebody else, I give the idiot wench all the help I can. All the time knowing that she's making a terrible mistake of course; she'd be much better off with wonderful me. And hoping she'll come to her senses and realize it."

She swallowed hard. "Now you're making me cry."

"No law against it. But you'll have to supply your own hanky, this birthday suit is a little short of pockets."

She sniffed a couple of times, and gulped a bit. Then she said, with careful steadiness, "First, I want to be cleared, exonerated, vindicated. Totally and completely.

There'll always be a . . . a stigma, of course; prison is prison no matter how you got there. But maybe in time people will forget, if I do nothing conspicuous to remind them."

I said, "Even if Waldemar Baron doesn't come through as promised, I think we can probably manage to arrange that. So let's take it from the point where you're a full citizen again with your reputation publicly rehabilitated and all your civil rights restored. That won't be good enough?"

"No, Matt. You know it won't. I'll still be a public freak, a curiosity, a woman with a past, somebody people whisper about."

"Move one state over and not a soul will recognize the name."

"No! I have that much pride at least. I'm going to find it—what I'm looking for—right here where I lost it. I'm going to cram myself down their lousy throats and make them accept me again, all the ones who rejected me. But to hell with all my big career ambitions. It's been going on too long, Matt, and I'm too tired, and too far behind after all the lost years, to make a fresh start and try to catch up. I just want . . ." She paused, and drew a long breath, and went on: "This is very cold-blooded and you'll despise me for it, but I intend to marry a certain very straight and respectable young lawyer—I think he's willing, or I can make him willing—and be the best wife to him I possibly can, and the best mother to his children if it comes to that; and maybe one day when I walk into a store the manager won't even remember that the dame was once notorious. He'll just remember she's the rather attractive, or at least well-preserved, spouse of a prominent citizen and pays her bills on time. That's all the ambition I have left, Matt."

"Sure." I leaned over and kissed her on the forehead in chaste brotherly fashion. "You want a Maxon, lady, we'll get you a Maxon. But I think we'll have a better chance of tracking down a good specimen if we don't let ourselves starve to death. There's a meal called breakfast you seem to have forgotten."

"Matt."

"Yes, Madeleine."

She reached out to touch the healing scar on my naked shoulder, the nasty-looking place in front where the late Maxie Reis's expanding 7mm rifle bullet had emerged, taking a bit of me with it. The entry wound behind was merely a cute pink dimple.

Madeleine licked her lips. "I'm . . . not thanking you very well for saving my life."

I was a very patient and forbearing fellow, but I didn't have to take that kind of crap. "That," I said, "was a stupid and insulting thing to say, Mrs. Ellershaw; and don't ever let me get the idea that you're considering entering my bed, or my home, for some screwy notions of girlish gratitude. Maybe you'd better get out of that slightly beat-up glamour gown and into some jeans. You're not so pretty in pants, but you seem to make more sense."

That left a certain coolness between us; and at breakfast we discussed the day's plans in a very businesslike manner. She had her ten o'clock appointment with the lawyer, Joe Birnbaum, of course; and after that—well, after lunch—she'd initiate me into the mysteries of certain state buildings where old property records were stored. Since I wasn't about to let her wander around those offices alone and unprotected, I might as well help. She'd show me how to assist her in searching for the mining property in which we were interested.

"But it's an awfully long shot," Madeleine said dubiously. "Now that I've had time to think about it . . ."

I said, "You're feeling pretty negative today, aren't you?"

"It's . . . kind of a negative world, Matt. I just keep forgetting it now and then. And this property search . . . I mean, even if the shaft we're looking for does exist, it doesn't have to be recorded as a mine. There are a lot of

255

big ranch properties with old forgotten diggings on them, for instance. And anyway, the whole theory is based on a crazy lady's crazy dream."

"It's been nine years," I said. "Nine years since young Dr. Roy Ellershaw told the girl he'd married that he was just stepping out of their pleasant home for a moment and would be right back to take her out to a gala celebration dinner. Nine years of lonely hell for the wife he left behind. Would he have left you to face all that by yourself, Madeleine, if there had been any way he could possibly get back to you?"

She shook her head. "No. We've been through all that. No, Roy is dead. I know that. But the mine and the shaft . . . that's stretching intuition or ESP or whatever you want to call it pretty far."

We'd both got up, finished with our meals, and I took her bright ski jacket from the back of her chair and helped her into it. She was still wearing the same skin-tight jeans, and the same high-heeled sandals, but today she had on an elaborate white Mexican wedding shirt, prettily ruffled and rather becoming. However, instead of buttoning it up properly like a modest señorita, she'd left it hanging partly open in front, in sexy peek-a-boo fashion. Of course, the idea of buttoning any shirt or blouse tidily, even if it was designed to be worn that way, seems to be considered positively subversive these days— wearing a necktie comes under the heading of high treason, of course. Madeleine's heels rapped smartly on the tiled floor as we headed through the lobby towards the motel's front door.

I said, "Alive or dead, your husband didn't vanish from the face of the earth. He's got to be somewhere. So, assuming he's dead, as we both think, let's look in the likely spots where he wouldn't be found under normal circumstances. Even if we disregard your dream, a mine shaft ranks pretty high among the places a body could stay hidden indefinitely in this country."

"Well, all right," she said ungraciously. "By all means,

let's go look for your hole in the ground. As soon as I've seen Joe Birnbaum and learned what kind of a two-bit heiress I . . . Oh, my God! That lousy, jealous little bitch!"

She'd stopped to stare at the morning paper visible behind the transparent cover of the vending machine by the front door. One of the smaller photographs on the front page showed a face that was recognizable as hers, but only barely.

I dropped a quarter into the slot, opened the machine and took out two papers, and gave one to her. Brought up honest, I put in an extra quarter for the extra copy I'd taken, and closed the machine. Then, not looking at Madeleine but hearing her paper rustle as she opened it, I unfolded my own to read the story, noting that the admiral's offspring had even got herself a byline, by God. Well, I guess it helps when your daddy owns the rag.

"MONSTROUS INJUSTICE" CLAIMED

by Evangeline Lowery
The Daily Journal Staff

SANTA FE—Former Santa Fe attorney and society figure, Madeleine Rustin Ellershaw, recently released from the federal penitentiary at Fort Ames, Missouri, after serving an eight-year sentence for crimes related to the national security, has returned home, she says, to set the record straight. . . .

That much was pretty straightforward, but then it got rough. There was a résumé of the events preceding the trial, and of the trial itself, which gave the impression that the pretty young wife of Dr. Roy Ellershaw, left behind to take the rap by her fleeing genius husband and his seductive Commie accomplice, had been caught red-handed with stolen top-secret scientific documents in one hand and a fistful of rubles in the other. Mrs. Ellershaw would be remembered as a smart and popular young

257

member of a prominent local family, employed by a well-known local law firm. Now disbarred from her profession, and displaying the grim effects of her long incarceration, Mrs. Ellershaw, 34, had been interviewed in her cheap motel room dressed in soiled jeans and T-shirt. Brandishing a drink in her hand, Mrs. Ellershaw had loudly proclaimed her intention of proving that she'd been framed by the prosecution, betrayed by her own lawyers, and railroaded into prison by an impressionable jury and an incompetent judge.

The photograph heading the column showed an aging, angry woman with a raddled face and untidy hair. There was also, much as I'd predicted, a smaller cut showing a glamorous young Mrs. Ellershaw at the time of her marriage, in glorious wedding attire. I'd forgotten what a lovely young girl she'd been. Even though I knew the tricks that had been used for the more recent shot—and, for that matter, for the super-flattering wedding portrait —I found the contrast between the two pictures heartbreaking. When Madeleine made a little sound beside me, I glanced her way apprehensively.

But she was laughing wryly. "'Brandishing a drink in her hand,'" she said. "What the hell was I supposed to brandish it in, my foot? But the kid isn't as dopey as she looks. She writes a mean story, doesn't she? And takes a mean picture? God, don't I look *awful*?"

"Madeleine—"

She laughed again. I could detect no hysteria in the sound. It was good, healthy, if somewhat rueful, laughter.

"Relax, Matt. I'm not going to kill myself again. As a matter of fact, as far as this story's concerned, it couldn't be better, could it? Not only for you, but for me."

"I don't understand."

She said quietly, "People don't like seeing people kicked around, Matt. Normal people don't, not really. The vicious little brat has done me a favor. Yesterday I was a dangerous spy and traitor in the eyes of a lot of folks who just knew I'd been in the pen but didn't really remember the whole story. But now it's all out in the open again, and I'm merely a poor loving girl who stupidly helped out the husband she doted on, a treacherous fiend who then deserted her for another woman."

She drew a long breath, and folded up the paper deliberately, and tossed it into a nearby waste receptable. She took mine and did the same thing to it.

"Don't you see, darling, I'm no longer a sinister female menace," she said. "I'm just a pitiful dumb wife who, even if she was technically guilty as her husband's accomplice, has paid for her crime; and who might just be an innocent patsy like she claims. And who, now that she's come crawling home broke and shabby, leaving her youth and her looks behind in prison, is being picked on by a great big powerful newspaper that ought to have the decency to leave the poor thing alone—hasn't she been punished enough already?" Madeleine glanced at me. "Matt, I'm sorry. I woke up so damn depressed and kind of took it out on you. But I'm all right now." She looked at her watch and took my arm. "It's getting late, let's go see Uncle Joe."

CHAPTER 22

As we walked downtown together, I asked myself how I'd managed to survive so long without understanding other people at all, particularly people of the opposite sex. I glanced at the woman marching along beside me at a brisk pace more suited to her practical trousers than her impractical high-heeled shoes, and wondered a little resentfully why being made love to by me last night should have left her in despair, while being slandered and ridiculed in the public press this morning seemed to have cheered her up tremendously. But I reminded myself that there are times when even I don't make much sense to anybody, even myself.

It was another fine New Mexico day. The climate at the elevation of Santa Fe is all you can ask for, neither so hot in summer as to really require air-conditioning, nor so cold in winter as to demand a lot of heavy clothing. And it was early enough spring that the yearly plague of tourists hadn't yet descended on the town and filled up all the parking spaces and slowed traffic to a crawl.

It occurred to me that I was thinking like an old resident, not a visitor currently domiciled in Washington, D.C. I found myself recalling the pleasant, faraway domestic time when I'd actually lived here. There were, I recalled, a great many things to be said for matrimony. I wondered what my former wife was doing, and if she was still getting along well with the man with whom she'd replaced me, actually not a bad guy. I wondered how the kids I'd seen so rarely were making it, and how they were handling the sex-and-drug problems that seemed to be common to young people these days. And I wondered as I walked what my life might have been like if, all those years ago, I'd been allowed to retire from violence permanently, as I'd tried to do; if I'd managed to stay right here playing husband and daddy. . . .

I felt a hand on my arm. "Don't look so grim. I said I was sorry. I didn't mean to be such a manic-depressive bitch."

I shook my head. "Not you. Just playing with might-have-beens. This town sometimes does it to me. I don't really know why I keep coming back. Maybe it's not such a hot idea. Maybe when something's over one should just get the hell out. For good. Maybe you should think about that."

"I know," she said. "But if I ever go, I want to go on my own terms. I don't want to feel that I was driven out. . . . Here we are."

It looked like a single, long, rather ancient adobe structure right on the sidewalk—actually, I remembered, it was a historical edifice with a plaque to prove it—but an archway let us through the first array of shops to reveal that the building was actually a great hollow rectangle surrounding a pleasant courtyard with flower beds and flagstone paths: a plaza, in the local idiom. There were small stores, art galleries, and professional offices.

Madeleine led me along one of the paths through the flower beds, across to a door on the far side of the open space. The brass plate on the door read: JOSEPH P. BIRNBAUM—ATTORNEY AT LAW. It was apparently a fairly large suite of offices. Around the corner to the left was a small gallery displaying some of the bright, delicate, decorative black-velvet paintings the Indian artists seemed to favor at one time, although I thought they'd been phased out in favor of the Fritz-Scholders type of rugged redskins, a much more intriguing art form. Off to the right, beyond another archway that, I remembered, led out to the parking lot behind, was an architect's office and an antique store.

"Easy now, baby," I said as Madeleine, still ahead of me, reached for the knob.

She glanced at me sharply, shocked. "Matt, what . . . ?"

Then she checked herself, and stepped aside to make way for me. I felt the tug at my hip, and the sudden lack of weight in the revolver-holster as she acted on her endearment cue, a little belatedly. I pressed the catch to release the stainless-steel automatic into my hand. Holding it concealed, as before, I turned the doorknob cautiously with my free hand and shoved the door away from me hard, letting it slam inward, hoping I wasn't scaring an innocent legal secretary out of her nylon panty hose. I heard Madeleine, behind me, gasp at the sight of the shambles revealed by the open door.

In a moment we were inside, and I had the door closed. I set the dead-bolt lock to make sure it stayed

261

that way. I stepped quickly off to the left, waving Madeleine off to the right; no sense making an easy double shot for anybody, although there was nobody in sight, just a thoroughly torn-up reception room. The upholstered furniture had been slashed open and ripped apart by somebody who enjoyed destroying things with a knife. Photographs and paintings had been yanked from the walls and smashed. All the drawers from the bank of files behind the secretary-receptionist's desk had been hauled out and emptied, and the desk drawers as well. On the desk I saw, only slightly askew, a small, neat nameplate: MRS. PATRICIA SILVA.

"Matt, how did you know . . . ?"

"Never mind it right now," I whispered, just as she had whispered, although after the slamming-open of the door our presence couldn't be a secret to anybody in the place. "Which is Birnbaum's office?"

She gestured with the .38, straight ahead beyond the desk. She spoke in more normal tones: "Right over there. It's big. Windows on the parking lot. Two more offices, smaller, at the end of this room—over there—for the young lawyers he takes on from time to time. Bathroom between them."

"And what's the door at this end, over behind those files?"

"That's the storeroom for clients' papers—kind of a vault, really. It's like musty library stacks in there. It should be locked. . . ."

"No, stay put," I said as she started forward. "You cover me, I'll do the exploring. I've had more practice."

"Matt, how did you know something was wrong?"

"My left ear itched." I grinned at her briefly. "Once early on, as the British say, I went through a door carelessly and got a leg shot out from under me, even though I'd had a feeling something was wrong. So now I respect any little warning tickle. Like I think I said once before, why should you have all the ESP in the outfit? Watch those doors while I check in here."

The storage-room door wasn't locked. Well, to be accurate, it was locked but the key was in the lock—part of a sizable key collection on a split ring, not the kind you'd usually leave hanging in locks. We hadn't seen it because of the out-jutting file cabinets. I opened the door and found that the dark storeroom beyond, crowded with metal shelves, had been just as thoroughly scrambled as the outer office, to the point where there was no possible way, short of a complete inventory, of learning what, if anything, was missing. Which could have been the idea. I came out to find her still standing warily where I'd left her, gun ready.

"Another disaster area," I reported. "Cover me while I check the back offices and the can." I grinned tightly. "Professional note: make sure of the unimportant spaces first so nobody can jump out of them at you when you finally get around to concentrating on the important ones." The two small offices and the bathroom were empty. They had also been torn apart, but less thoroughly, as if the searchers hadn't had much hope of finding anything back there. Or as if they'd been tiring of their labors when they got that far; and you could see why. Emerging, I drew a long breath, and said, "Stay right here. Holler if anybody comes."

I went through the door into Birnbaum's office the way it says in the book, latest revised edition. I could have saved myself the trouble. The two people in the big comfortable room—well, it had been comfortable before the rip-it-apart boys had got at it—were no threat to anybody, at least not to anybody with a strong stomach. Lawyer Birnbaum himself wasn't so bad. He was merely dead, slumped over his disordered desk without a mark on him. I could see part of his long, dark, face; probably a sensitive, intelligent, and friendly old face in life. The hair was gray, wavy, and hardly disordered at all. His skin was still quite warm to the touch, but not as warm as it should have been.

The woman sprawled in one of the deep chairs provided for clients was a different story. She'd been a short woman with a comfortably upholstered body and a comfortable round face. The heavy hair, only slightly streaked with gray although she'd been in her fifties, had been pulled back to a neat bun at the nape of her neck, but it had mostly escaped confinement now and was straggling wildly. She'd been wearing a neat brown trousers-suit and a white silk blouse with a bow at the throat; but the bow had been yanked apart and the blouse wrenched open. Blouse and jacket together had then been forced off her shoulders and down her arms, binding them to her body. The straps of her businesslike brassiere had been cut with a knife, and the garment dragged downwards to free her generous breasts. It was now a twisted rag around her middle—a bloodstained rag, because the tip of her right breast had been sliced away leaving a circle of raw flesh about two inches in diameter from which, as long as she was alive, the blood had poured freely, soaking her clothes and the chair in which she sat. But it had stopped bleeding now.

I moved closer to determine the cause of death: a skillful knife-thrust into the neck that had severed the spinal cord. A gagging sound made me whirl to see Madeleine behind me, her face white and sick.

"I told you to stay put," I said. "Use the bathroom if you're going to puke; don't mess up the scene of the crime."

"I'm . . . all right. Don't be so damn tough-guy, tough guy. Some people haven't seen as many mutilated bodies as other people."

I nodded. "Good girl. Just a minute while I take a quick look around."

I went over and rechecked Joseph P. Birnbaum as carefully as I could without moving him. There was a wall safe, open, in the alcove beside the big stone fireplace; I guessed the legal-looking papers and envelopes strewn on the rug below it represented its former contents. I sniffed, and approached the fireplace, and found the smoke-smell stronger there. A considerable amount of paper had recently been burned there and the ashes hammered apart with a poker that had been left lying on the hearth. I saw something crumpled and brownish more or less intact at the rear of the fireplace and used the poker to fish it out cautiously: a scorched, wadded-up manila envelope of considerable size, say 10×14. Laying down the poker, and carrying my find, I returned to Madeleine.

"Let's get out of here. Watch out for that blood on the rug."

Following her out into the reception room, I found myself glancing back uneasily with a feeling that there was something I'd overlooked. Then I realized that I was trying to locate the little piece of meat that was missing. Sick. I closed the door behind me. Madeleine turned abruptly; and I held her for a moment as she fought for control. She drew a long, ragged breath and freed herself.

"Oh, God, poor Uncle Joe! Poor Miss Pat!"

"You knew her?"

"Of course. A nice widow lady. She came to work here right after her husband died in an auto accident. She was still . . . quite young and pretty back then, in a plump, girlish sort of way. Very bright, very competent, very kind, very pleasant. His wife was an invalid, a whining, demanding bitch. We always thought they'd eventually . . . I hope to God he at least slept with her occasionally so they got something out of it. All those years!" She swallowed hard. "Why would somebody *do* that to her? And what happened to him, could you tell?"

I said, "Presumably they were trying to force the safe combination out of him. All this"—I waved a hand at the shambles around us—"was probably done as much to terrorize them as to determine that the stuff the goons were after wasn't anywhere but in the safe. Obviously the show was run by a guy who likes busting things up and throwing them around and slashing them with a knife.

I've met a few like that." Something stirred in my mind as I said it, and I tried to recapture a memory, but it wouldn't come and there was no time to work on it. "He was using the search as a way of softening them up, making sure they knew they were dealing with a ruthless gent who wanted something badly and would stop at nothing. Then, when they'd been properly impressed, the pressure really went on: the elderly gent slammed down behind the desk with a gun at his neck watching his middle-aged lady having her clothes wrenched apart and cut apart, seeing her thrown into a chair, seeing the knife at her breast; he trying to gasp out the safe combination but not getting it out quite in time to save her because he was starting to have trouble with his breathing and because he was dealing with a hasty guy who *likes* using that knife. . . . But the old man got the number out at last in spite of the agonizing pain in his chest. Then he put his head on the desk and died. He did have a heart condition, didn't he?"

Madeleine nodded somberly. "Yes, he'd had a coronary . . . oh, years and years ago. Fifteen years? He'd made a good recovery from that; but then he had another one and almost died at the time of my trial. Even after . . . after I was sent to Fort Ames, I heard from my folks that he was still in the cardiac ward just barely making it. He was a very tough old character, but it would have left him pretty vulnerable, wouldn't it? And an experience like this . . . !" She shook her head. "Shouldn't we be calling the police?"

"As soon as we've figured out what to tell them. And what not to tell them. They'll want to know why it was done; what the murderers were trying to find. Did find. They'll want to know if it had anything to do with us, with you."

She licked her lips. "Did it, Matt?"

"It could have," I said bluntly. "We can check. They burned a considerable amount of rather flimsy paper and were careful about hammering apart the ashes, but the

266

manila envelope was more fire-resistant and didn't really matter to them anyway. Here it is."

I smoothed out the heavy envelope on Mrs. Silva's desk, a little embarrassed about the ashes I was spreading around. I reminded myself that the place was a mess, anyway, and the lady was dead. A corner of the envelope had been burned away, and there were blackened places where the fire had tried to catch but hadn't quite made it. But the writing, done boldly with a very black felt-tipped pen, was quite legible: CONFIDENTIAL MATERIAL—DO NOT OPEN! *Upon receipt of legal proof of my death this envelope must be delivered intact and unopened to my wife, Madeleine Rustin Ellershaw, appearing in person to receive it. Signed: Roy Malcolm Ellershaw.*

There was a long silence; then Madeleine sighed deeply. "I wondered why Uncle Joe was so insistent on my coming here; I couldn't really see why the estate business couldn't be handled by mail." She shook her head. "Poor Roy. Everything he did for me was wrong, wasn't it? If he'd just left Uncle Joe some loophole—but there never was any proof of death."

I said, "I suppose it was a problem in legal ethics. Your husband was the client in this instance, not you, even though Birnbaum had known you since you were a kid. With your trial coming up, it seems likely that Birnbaum fought with his lawyer's conscience about opening the envelope in spite of the client's strict instructions, to see if there was something inside that would help your case. . . . Whether that moral conflict brought on his second coronary or not, we'll never know; but by the time he was functioning again, after a fashion, it was all over and you were already in prison. And he was a sick old man and couldn't bear to face that decision again. Until enough years had passed that Roy Ellershaw, the client, could be considered legally dead, and his wishes could be obeyed at last."

"And whether or not it would have helped me, it's

burned now," she said grimly. "So I can't even use it to help me now."

"The experts can do very fancy things with ashes nowadays, but I wouldn't be too optimistic," I said. "That must have been the reason you had to be killed when you got out of Ames. The people with whom we're dealing, call them the CADRE people, must have learned somehow that your husband had left you more than what was found in your safe-deposit box, maybe even a whole second copy of the Monkey House computer stuff. It's quite possible that the stuff Bennett stole from your bank made reference to additional material awaiting you elsewhere, but obviously it didn't say where. So they presumably searched all the likely places where Roy Ellershaw might have cached something for you—it would be interesting to see if there were some unexplained burglaries or break-ins eight or nine years ago—but it never occurred to them he might have approached the lawyer representing his parents-in-law. Until you got back here and made a beeline for your Uncle Joe; and somebody started wondering, just like you, why Mr. Birnbaum had been so insistent upon your coming in person to clean up some estate matters that could undoubtedly have been handled by remote control. So they sent out the wrecking squad and hit the jackpot."

"So in a way I'm responsible for bringing this . . . this disaster upon two nice people." Her voice was bleak. "I'm gaining on it, aren't I? Yesterday I helped send a man crashing to his death in a canyon, and today I'm accessory to two murders. And now we had better call the police."

I said, as she reached for the phone, "Don't trouble yourself. I think they're here." I'd heard heavy footsteps outside. "At least we've got company coming, and it sounds official. Let me have that .38 back, quick."

I tucked it away, and returned the .25 to its arm clip. Somebody was trying the knob even as I moved towards the locked front door.

"Open up! Police!"

"Hold your horses, I'm coming," I shouted. "Take it easy coming in, Officer. Federal government here."

Whatever that might mean. One of these days—or years—I'm going to have to learn how a real FBI-type G-man does it. I got out my fancy identification folder. It made me a little clumsy getting the door unlocked one-handed, but you never know with cops. They do get nervous, and I wanted the situation perfectly clear from the start. I didn't want to have to shoot one just to stay alive. . . .

The door slammed back the instant the bolt was clear. Well, I'd anticipated that and stepped back, but the husky uniformed gent who charged in wasn't holding a gun, as I'd expected. It would have slowed him down a bit, and we'd have had to go through the up-with-the-hands routine, and the assume-the-position-against-the-wall routine; but he just grabbed the wrist of the left hand in which I was displaying my ID and wrenched it around behind me, ignoring the leather folder that dropped to the floor, swinging me around roughly at the same time. Holding me there facing away from him, my arm twisted up between my shoulder blades, he gave me a nasty one-handed pat-down and found the .38 on my hip and yanked it free.

"I've got this one." His voice was harsh with strain. "Put the cuffs on the woman."

"Already have." This one was just a voice, with a slight local accent.

"Close the door."

"Already have."

The one behind me released his hammerlock. "You! Straight ahead. Hands against the wall. High!"

I said plaintively, "Officer, I'm not wearing this sling for show, I can't raise my—"

"Forward march! You'll be surprised what you can do when you really try!"

"Matt, watch out!"

269

It was a warning cry from Madeleine. I threw myself down but not quite fast enough; the baton or billy club or whatever they call it nowadays glanced off the back of my skull hard enough to make my extremities tingle as if they'd been frozen and were just coming back to life. I almost lost the little automatic as it slipped into my hand; then I was rolling away and coming back up. . . .

The big cop was on top of me, ready to take another vicious swing at my head; but his face changed as he saw the .25. I fired three times and saw dust fly off the front of the blue uniform. Not a very good group, I must admit: one slid off far enough to nick the shiny badge worn over to the side, but maybe that was the one that did the work. You never know with those feeble little bullets. Anyway, he came down hard, the nightstick flying out of his hand—apparently he hadn't taken time to use the thong properly. The whole room was a bit hazy, and I was having trouble maintaining single images of things—they wanted to split in two; but I saw the other policeman across the room hunched over, clawing at something wrapped around his face.

He was holding a gun, but he dropped it so he could use both hands to free himself. I realized that the moment his attention was distracted and he'd turned to assist his partner, Madeleine must have dropped her handcuffed arms over his head. Even as I crouched there, waiting for my vision to clear so I could shoot safely without hitting her, I saw them go down together. She threw herself aside in a twisting way as she fell, applying all the weight and leverage she could. Even across the room, I heard the ugly tearing and cracking sounds as the spinal bones and ligaments fractured and ripped. I realized that she'd quite literally wrung the man's neck, but it must have been very hard on her handcuffed wrists. But the trainers at the Ranch would have been proud of her.

The waves of dizziness were getting worse instead of better. I heard the sound behind me, but my reactions were slow, and I didn't get around quite in time. I just got a glimpse of a strained and hating white face, and of another bulky blue uniform, and of another raised nightstick—or maybe he'd picked up the same one from where it had fallen instead of using his own. As if it mattered. The club came down.

Chapter 23

THEY'D cleared the broken junk off a slashed-up sofa in one of the small back offices and spread a small rug on it and put me on it. A doctor of sorts had come and said that my brains weren't leaking out of my skull anywhere that he could see, but I'd better be kept quiet and taken to the hospital for observation as soon as possible. Then he'd gone on to his real clients, the ones who weren't breathing.

I hadn't bothered to tell him about the throbbing ache in my side where one of the later cops to invade the premises had kicked me. There's really nothing much that can be done about broken ribs—if they were broken—but the medical profession always feels obliged to try, and the cure is usually worse than the disease. I thought I could manage to live without all that tape and benzocaine. At least that was what they'd used the last time I'd let them. They've probably figured out something even more smelly and uncomfortable by now.

After the first rush of eager law-enforcement officers, the lid had gone on; and now only a limited number of let's-solve-a-murder boys and girls were wandering around the gory premises. I could see them as they passed the open door of the room in which I lay. A young cop was watching over me and pleading with me silently to wiggle a toe so he could get to kick me, too: goddamn cop-killer! Fortunately they were all slightly inhibited by the fact that somebody'd picked up the ID I'd dropped. Otherwise I'd undoubtedly have been resisting arrest until there was nothing left but a bloody pulp.

For my part, I was fighting my aches and pains in my usual forbearing and Christian manner by making sure I remembered a certain face, the one I'd stomp on if I ever met it in a dark alley with nobody looking. It belonged to the uniformed gent with the fast shoe with the hard, hard toe. I planned to learn his name before I left here. I mean, I'm a pro, and I don't go around seeking personal vengeance when there's work to be done; but if somebody drops it into my lap afterwards, when I have time to spare, who am I to question the generosity of the gods—if you want to call them that—who watch over unpleasant men like me?

Besides, we like to have the word get around. If enough guys, in or out of uniform, have it firmly impressed upon them that we're not forgiving Christian gentlemen, or ladies, and that it's not very wise to get in our way when we're working—if you don't regret it now, you will later—our work will be easier. We have problems enough with the real enemy, whoever he may be at any given time, without being gratuitously given the boot treatment by any sand-country copper with an itchy toe. At least it gave me something to think about besides my pounding head and throbbing side.

Then the waiting was over and Chief Manuel Cordoba came marching in, in full regalia, a sturdy and confidence-inspiring officer of the law if you were sucker enough to have confidence in a policeman. At the moment I had none. It wasn't quite fair, of course. In a sense I was blaming them all for my own abysmal stupidity. I was the jackass who'd loused up a job and lost a lady through my incredible idiocy in putting her, not to mention myself, at the mercy of some armed goons instead of blasting their heads off the instant they came crashing through the door like that. Just because they were wearing pretty blue suits, for Christ's sake! How naive can you get?

Cordoba came up to the sofa and stood looking down at me for a moment. Then he waved my young uniformed chaperon out of the room and closed the door behind him and returned.

"Well, what have you got to say for yourself, Helm?"

"Where's Mrs. Ellershaw?" I whispered.

His voice was harsh. "We'll get to Mrs. Ellershaw. At the moment, you're the major problem, you and your fast gun and your fancy Washington connections. . . ."

He was bluffing hard. He knew he was on a bad spot—how bad remained to be determined. I shook my head. That was a mistake, but I could live with it. It wasn't as bad as some I'd made.

"I'm not important," I said. "You're not important. Your men aren't important. We're all alive and doing well, with a few deserving exceptions. What about Madeleine Rustin Ellershaw? Several attempts on her life already on record. Last seen in handcuffs in the same room with a gent in police uniform who was beating on me with a club, description follows. Five nine or ten. Brown hair. Blue eyes. Age around four oh. Weight around one nine oh. He's put on a little weight since I last saw him; and he was a patrolman when I last saw him, but that could have changed, too. Name: Philip Crisler. I don't see him here. Where is he? And where is Mrs. Ellershaw?"

"How do you happen to know Officer Crisler?"

I looked at him grimly. He was wearing a very handsome sidearm with ivory grips, presumably acquired before the recent save-the-elephant campaigns. For practicality, it wasn't quite as bad as mother-of-pearl; but it was still slipperier than good old checkered walnut.

I said, "Easy, amigo. Are you thinking clearly? Maybe

you should have a lawyer standing by. You're voluntarily admitting that you're acquainted with this murderous criminal who definitely attacked a federal officer and probably kidnapped a woman who was assisting the U.S. authorities. You're even admitting, by implication, that he was wearing a police uniform legitimately. Are you sure you want to go on record with all that?"

He snorted. "Listen, Helm, you've killed one of my men, and your ex-convict female accomplice seems to have killed another, although God knows how a woman could have done *that*. . . ."

I said sharply, "Chief, you keep making it worse for yourself! Now you're confessing that those two homicidal characters were your men, too, not just goons masquerading in police uniforms! Hadn't you better reconsider a little? Do you really want to take all the credit for this bloody mess?" I stared at him hard. "Do you want a little advice? If you don't care to take it from me, call it advice from Washington."

He started to speak angrily and checked himself. "What advice?" he asked.

"You've got three choices," I said. My head was aching badly, but I tried not to let it show. I went on: "First suggestion. If by any hopeful chance you're holding Mrs. Ellershaw in jail for some reason, or in secret custody somewhere, produce her. Then perhaps we can settle everything else in simple, friendly fashion."

He licked his lips. "We haven't got the woman. We don't know where she is." He glared at me. "And we want her for resisting arrest and committing homicide upon an officer of the law."

I sighed. "You're trying to fight it, Chief, but it can't be fought. Any policeman or detective with a few brains can read what happened in this place. Sure you could have the evidence altered to frame me if I were a helpless, independent private eye like in the books, but we both know I'm not. Neither helpless nor independent. And, hell, maybe you're even an honest officer; it has happened. So you're stuck with it; and in case you haven't had time to familiarize yourself with it, I'll run it past you quickly the way it will go into the record, the way it actually happened—"

"The way *you* say it happened!" That was automatic. He drew a long breath, and said, "All right. Go on."

"This is the way it reads, amigo. After politely admitting the police to the premises like a good citizen, I was savagely clubbed from behind by Cop Number One, presumably because he didn't want to use a noisy gun on me. Let's not discuss my stupidity in letting him catch me off guard. I thought we had a deal, you and I, and you were keeping your department from taking sides in this hassle, which was my mistake. . . . Did you say something, Chief?"

He glared at me and didn't speak. I pushed myself up a bit, heroically concealing the agony of my poor fractured ribs, if that's what they were.

"All right," I said, "so I treated these fine law-enforcement officers the way I normally treat policemen, with wary respect, and got half clobbered for my pains. When I decided at last to take defensive action to keep my brains from being completely scrambled, and took care of Cop Number One, Cop Number Two hauled out his piece to avenge his partner. Mrs. Ellershaw jumped him to save me, and took care of him; but then Cop Number Three, Crisler, entered the fray and that's all she wrote as far as I'm concerned. God knows where he came from. I suppose he slipped in from the parking lot, using the outside door to Birnbaum's private office. I suppose I should have been ready for that, but somehow I have this picture of bluebellies always hunting in pairs, like hungry coyotes. You will excuse me for being slightly prejudiced at the moment, I'm sure. But I'll admit it wasn't the brightest day of my life."

"Listen, Helm . . . !" He checked himself. "You still haven't said how you knew Crisler."

I said, "You won't like it. Years and years ago, even

before that kidnapping incident we both remember involving my little girl, I had a fender-bender problem up a lane near where I used to live. The other guy came roaring out of his driveway without looking; but when he called the police from his house a young cop friend came to the rescue in a patrol car. Crisler. To protect his buddy-buddy, Crisler wrote me up for every crime since the sinking of the *Maine* in Havana Harbor in 1898. I was keeping a low profile at the time, I wanted to be an inconspicuous citizen, so I didn't argue; I just got old Judge Marty Martinez to dismiss the charges afterwards. But I made a note of the name and the face. I always do." I stared at him hard. "And don't try to tell me that no cop ever did a favor for a friend in this town, or any town. My ribs hurt, and I'd hate to go into paroxysms of uncontrollable laughter."

He answered my stare with a glare of his own, but it wavered after a moment. "Your ribs? I thought it was your head. . . ." Then he stopped.

"Right on, man," I said. "One of your fine upstanding guardians of the law gave me a couple of good kicks in the side while I was lying out there half unconscious." He didn't speak. I went on: "You've checked on me and you know where my orders come from. Pretty high up, right? Or you wouldn't be here and I wouldn't be here. I'd be in a cell being beat on in relays because cop-killers always seem to be unruly fellows who have to be subdued by force, right? Now shall we get on with the listing of your possible courses of action, Chief?"

"If you wish." His voice was expressionless now.

I said, "Here's my next suggestion: just pull that fancy ivory-handled piece you've got on your hip and shoot me dead."

"That's a strange thing to say, señor."

"Why strange?" I said. "I'd call it obvious. Don't try to tell me you haven't thought of it. Don't try to tell me you don't wish, at least a little, that one of your boys had got slightly trigger-happy before you got here. Don't tell me

276

you haven't considered the possibility that, with me out of the way permanently, a terrible case of mistaken identity of course, and Madeleine Ellershaw also gone, perhaps never to return . . ." I found myself pausing here, and clearing my throat for some reason, before I went on. "With both of us out of the way, you might still be able to salvage something out of this bloody mess. That's assuming, of course, that you still insist that you have complete control over your department, and that Officer Crisler was operating under orders from you, as were his two pals. Which is what you were more or less saying just now when you implied they were all your men. But were they? Are they? Do you really want to assume full responsibility for them and their actions, *all* their actions?"

"Mr. Helm . . ." He paused.

"I know, it's hard to admit," I said. "But your final choice, and you'd better make it fast, is to backpedal a bit and admit that you don't have complete control of your department anymore. They aren't all your men, really; and these three rogue cops were operating under orders from somebody else. Somebody perhaps using the code name Tolliver, representing a powerful secret organization that seems to have infiltrated a lot of law-enforcement agencies in this country and even created one of its own: the Office of Federal Security." I looked at him for a moment. "I think it's too late for benevolent neutrality, Chief Cordoba. Pick your side. Either use that pretty gun—they'll pay you well for it, either in money or political influence—or sit down and relax and let's talk this over sensibly."

He stood looking down at me for a long moment, his dark face expressionless; and it happened the way it sometimes does regardless of the shade of the skin or the color of the hair or the language spoken by the ancestors. I don't say that we became friends in that instant; but there's a relationship between fighting men that the nonviolent ladies and gentlemen of the world can never understand, which may be why they fear us and pretend to despise us as old-fashioned and obsolete and dreadfully immoral—macho is the buzzword they're always throwing around, very derogatory. Cordoba smiled faintly.

"But how would I dare draw my weapon, Mr. Helm, when you've had me covered from that sling ever since I walked into this room?" He shook his head. "It's very foolish of you. Even if you have no faith in the police, perhaps with some reason, you could never hope to shoot your way out of here, you know that."

I shrugged. "In my business, when you've got your back to the wall you don't waste time figuring the odds. If your life is at stake, you just blow away the guy in front of you and grab his weapon if yours is going dry and start walking and keep firing. Eventually you're either out of there or dead. And if you're dead, they'll remember you, those who're left standing. They'll remember how hard you were to put down, and how many you took down with you; and maybe they won't be quite so eager to tackle the next guy from your outfit who comes along. We call it public relations, Chief."

"But clearly my men were careless, to leave you armed," he said.

I shrugged again, and it was still a mistake. "They found the .38 from my holster where Cop Number One had dropped it; and I looked pretty damn helpless, so they didn't bother to search me further. And frankly I have no memory of tucking the little sleeve gun back up where it belongs; and I'd appreciate your not mentioning it to anybody, and soft-pedaling the caliber of the bullets your medical examiner comes up with. That way, maybe I can surprise somebody else sometime."

There was a knock on the door. Cordoba went over and opened it, and spoke to the man outside for a minute or two, and came back. His face was grim.

"What was Mrs. Ellershaw wearing?" he asked.

A wave of sick anticipation hit me, but I refrained

278

from asking the obvious question. "High-heeled blue sandals. Blue denims. White cotton wedding shirt. Quilted ski jacket, kind of violet-colored. No hat."

"An empty police car has been found on a dirt road just outside town. Tire tracks nearby indicate where a heavier vehicle, probably four-wheel drive, had been parked for a while before being driven away; so apparently there was a change of transportation. Caught on an inside molding of the patrol car was a scrap of violet cloth. It would have been hard to snag a garment in that place accidentally, I'm told."

I drew a long, rather shaky breath. "So she was still alive and thinking clearly up to that point. Leaving signs for us to follow. I presume it was Crisler's official car that was left behind. Any signs of Crisler?"

He nodded. "Officer Crisler was lying in the bushes nearby. He had been killed by a skillful knife-thrust to the neck, very much as Mrs. Silva was killed. There were traces of blood on his shoe; and I will be very much surprised if the shoe does not match a partial footprint we found in the office next door, near the dead woman's chair, that was not made on his most recent visit here, after the blood had started to congeal. It would seem that Officer Crisler was the second man involved in tearing this place apart earlier, and killing those two; he must have returned to help his colleagues deal with you, while the first man, the one in charge, waiting in the car unwilling to show himself. And then the first man, the knife specialist, disposed of Crisler after he had delivered the woman and served his purpose." Cordova grimaced. "At least that is one old grudge you can erase from your account books, Mr. Helm."

"That makes me feel just great," I said. "Considering that the lady I was supposed to protect is now riding around the boonies helplessly handcuffed, at the mercy of a wild man with a knife."

279

CHAPTER 24

AFTER that, Chief Cordoba pumped me quite thoroughly about the case and, since we needed his cooperation, I let him. It was a rather frustrating experience. He was not, of course, willing to accept the idea that a man listed in the records as a fugitive was dead because his wife had dreamed that he was. And he certainly wasn't going to buy the idea that an innocent woman had spent eight years in prison; no policeman likes to admit that such things can happen.

Nor could he accept the notion that his turncoat cops might have been influenced by mind-bending techniques developed surreptitiously in a secret government laboratory behind chain-link fencing and barbed wire. Advanced Human Managerial Studies, bullshit! As a matter of fact, I wasn't quite sure I believed that one, either. Why go all sci-fi when a little dough will do the job? I didn't think a man like Officer Crisler would come very high. Nevertheless, the session wasn't a total loss. Cordoba might laugh at my crazy brainstorms, but I noticed that he didn't laugh very loudly. He'd remember them if events occurred to confirm them.

Interrogation complete, Cordoba drove me back to the motel himself. I guess he didn't want to trust me with any of his men, or vice versa. I didn't know whether he was afraid that they'd go for me if they got me alone, or I'd go for them; but either way he was probably correct. Certainly, the way I was feeling at the moment, if anything in uniform—whether the uniform was blue, green, or purple with orange zebra stripes—had laid a hand on me, or more particularly a foot, I'd have shot it dead on the spot. I'd done my stint as departmental punching bag and football, thanks.

The chief wanted to take me to the hospital, but I wasn't having any of that. I wanted to be near a phone where I could be reached by anybody who had a message for me.

"Do you expect a ransom demand?" Cordoba asked, when I explained this. He frowned. "But what will they ask for? They have already destroyed the documents they feared."

I said, "They'll ask for something very valuable, amigo." I grinned. "One way or another they'll ask for me."

"You?" He frowned at me uncomprehendingly.

"It's a whole new ball game," I said. "Figure it out. Crisler and his knife-wielding partner must have reported that the dangerous papers, whatever they were, had been found and carefully burned. Yet the two of them were sent back here to help out a couple more rogue policemen. Help them do what? Well, it was known that Mrs. Ellershaw had a ten o'clock appointment, remember, and it could be assumed that her diligent bodyguard would accompany her. So it seems likely that we were still the target; but with a difference. Let's note that after the previous earnest attempts on Mrs. Ellershaw's life with shotguns and rifles, they used the handcuffs on her this time. Obviously, now that she's no longer a threat she's to be preserved, at least temporarily, presumably for bargaining purposes. But it's clear that the orders concerning me were quite different. That first club that was swung at my skull wasn't kidding. It would have killed me if I hadn't been warned in time to duck a little."

"I see," Cordoba said softly. "You feel that your death is now considered desirable?"

I said, "Handcuffs for her, club for me, what does it look like? As an experienced officer of the law, you must

281

know that it's only in the movies that you go bashing people on the head you don't want dead. Crisler and his club weren't kidding, either; but he couldn't quite get a solid swing at me, the way I was weaving around due to the effects of the first guy's blow. And even after he'd managed to knock me out he presumably had to leave me for the moment to deal with Mrs. Ellershaw—perhaps she even came to my defense again—and by the time he had her subdued there were probably sirens screaming and people beating on the door asking what all the fuss and shooting was about in there. So all he could do was get the hell out the back way fast with his prisoner, leaving me alive. That could be why he wound up with a knife in the neck. He hadn't done the job he'd been sent to do; he hadn't disposed of me."

Cordoba said carefully, "No offense, señor, but what would make you so important now?"

I said, "Certainly no offense, señor; and I'm afraid you're flattering me. I'm still only of secondary importance. First there were the hidden documents, or computer printouts, or whatever, perhaps with a covering letter from a dead man, that his wife had to be prevented from acquiring and employing to damage this CADRE outfit. But with that taken care of, they could turn to problem number two, just a minor difficulty: a government agent who's been making a persistent nuisance of himself and whose association with Mrs. Ellershaw has apparently brought him too close to the heart of the organization for him to be ignored. So terminate with extreme prejudice, as the Langley lads like to say. Using the lady as bait if necessary."

Cordoba started to ask a question, and checked himself, which was just as well. He didn't want to know how I was going to solve the problem. Always assuming, of course, that I could figure out a solution.

"Any help I can give, you have only to ask," he said. "The department owes you that."

I gave him a crooked grin. "Don't stick your neck out too far, Chief. You mean any *legal* help, don't you?"

He gave me a sharp glance and didn't answer. He left me in front of the motel. I entered the main building, walking carefully so as not to jar my injuries unnecessarily. I asked the dining room to send to my room a pitcher of vodka martinis, a bacon and tomato sandwich on white toast, and a pot of coffee. Cream and sugar, yes. Back in my unit, after limping through the landscaped grounds and suffering no attacks upon my life, I found that the big double bed nearer the door, which had got fairly thoroughly disordered last night by two affectionate and active bodies, looked smooth and virginal once more. The bathroom was beautifully sterile, with all glasses protected from contamination by plastic armor. The telephone was silent.

I considered lying down to rest, but that would have involved getting up again when my lunch arrived, a painful prospect. I compromised by seating myself cautiously on the bed to make a couple of local calls, using certain code words specifically designed for crisis situations. I debated calling Washington as well, but I had nothing to say that could be said over an unsafe line. Then I said to hell with it and called anyway. As always, I got through to Mac without significant delay.

"Matt here," I said when I heard his voice on the line, using my real name to let him know I didn't trust the connection.

"Yes, Matt," he said. "I have a report to the effect that you've encountered some trouble."

"Not much," I said. "The priceless secret documents that might have saved the nation, or at least restored the girl's reputation, have been burned; the heroine herself is in the hands of the brutal enemy; the hero has a dented skull and a couple of bent ribs; but otherwise things are going great, just great. I want an I-team standing by. How soon can I have it?"

283

"There is an interrogation team in Denver."

"Put them on the road and tell them to goose it, please. What's the general situation, sir?"

"Not very good, Matt. In fact, rather critical. There's been another attempt on the life of the prominent gentleman in question, although in this instance we managed to avoid publicity. We have identified the probable replacement, a rather gaudy military character; but of course he would be taking orders from a committee of wealthy and powerful civilians. The word CADRE is appearing here and there in association with this movement to save the nation from the degenerates who are leading it to destruction. Indications are that, having failed for the second time to remove the chief executive in order to take advantage of the confusion following his death, CADRE is considering an open coup d'etat. And I hate to say it, but I am not at all certain that it would fail."

"What about our mysterious friend, Mr. Tolliver?"

"He seems to be the active power behind the throne. Well, the throne they hope to establish, or dictatorship, or whatever. Have you any clues to his identity?"

"Well, somebody seems to think I'm getting too close; otherwise why bother to try to kill me?"

"But close to whom? What about this lawyer, Baron?"

"Hell, Tolliver could easily be Waldemar Baron, but he could just as easily be his junior partner Maxon—I never trust these meek-and-mild characters too far. Or he could even be a rather intriguing police chief they've got here, named Cordoba, who plays the dumb Hispano character very well. But everybody seems to be steering me towards a naval gent named Lowery who owns one of the local papers; and sometimes it's best to ride along with the tide, so to speak, so I think I'll tackle him first."

"Keep in mind that we probably don't have much time left."

I said, "As the old Athenians used to say, I will return with my shield or on it."

"I believe you're thinking of the Spartans, Matt."

He was probably right, damn him. I hung up, hoping that if anybody was listening, the conversation would have shaken him up a bit, particularly the part about the interrogation team, and left him wondering just who I had in mind for the rack and thumbscrews. But I wished I had something better to do than shake the trees and see what fell out of the branches. I continued to sit there, since moving was no fun at all, wishing I had a job in which I wasn't expected to cope with a national emergency after being beaten to a pulp; but of course we stoical heroes of the underground services just naturally ignore such insignificant handicaps. That wasn't the worst that was expected of me, anyway.

When the knock came on the door, I got up without groaning too loudly, pleased to note that the drastic change in altitude produced no noticeable dizziness: perhaps my cranium wasn't seriously shattered after all. But I still wasn't functioning as well as I might. Expecting a waiter, I was taken by surprise—the way we aren't supposed to be—when the door was shoved open roughly the moment I unlocked it. Hastily, I stepped clear, reaching for the .38 left-handed; but it was only Walter Maxon, boy attorney, unarmed and distressed and disheveled.

"Where's Madeleine, what's happened to her?" he demanded breathlessly. "My God, hasn't she suffered enough without . . . You were supposed to be protecting her!"

I looked at him grimly. "So were you, nine years ago. She doesn't seem to have much luck with her protectors, does she?" I saw a man with a tray behind him, and said, "Hold everything, let me take care of the waiter." When the food was on the table by the window, and the bill signed, and the waiter gone, I went into the bathroom for an extra glass, which I had to skin like a squirrel before I could fill it with ice and liquor. Sometimes I wonder what's so terrible about a few germs. "Here, sit

285

down and have a drink and relax," I said, handing it to Maxon. "Where did you hear about it?"

He was all dressed up in his dark three-piece lawyer suit, of course—it was still a business hour of a business day, although it seemed to have been going on forever— but he wasn't in good professional shape at the moment, not by the sartorial standards of Baron and Walsh. His white shirt was leaking out between his vest and his pants, his starched shirt collar was unbuttoned and looked wilted, and the knot of his expensive blue silk tie was at half mast. His sandy hair was tousled, making him look like a rumpled, dressed-up schoolboy. He sank into a chair and gulped at the liquor thirstily.

"I . . . I've been going crazy ever since I read that vicious story in the paper this morning!" he said. "I came over here right away to reassure her; she must have been terribly hurt by it, and I wanted to tell her that none of her friends would pay any attention. . . . Anyway, she wasn't here, neither of you was here, and I had to stop by the police station on business and I heard . . . My God, after everything she's been through, to be subjected to savage libels and violent . . . What are you doing about it? She's your responsibility! If anything happens to her . . . !"

After this incoherent speech, if it could be called a speech, he drew a long breath and gulped some more martini. He was hitting the sore spots, and I was tempted to ask him just what the hell he would have done if attacked by a pair of apparently legitimate policemen, but to hell with that. As he'd said, her protection had been my responsibility, not his.

"Blame is easy," I said. "But I haven't heard any constructive suggestions, let alone any offers of help."

"Help? Of course I'll help, just tell me what to do!"

I'd done the liquor-and-ice bit for myself. I lowered myself cautiously into the second chair at the small round table by the window.

"For a start, tell me about Admiral Lowery, if you've

286

met him," I said. "Never mind the history, I've got that. And a physical description. But I need to know what makes him tick. A lot of Navy officers are pretty arrogant, humorless bastards; and he's kind of small, like his daughter. That would tend to make him even tougher to deal with. Little guys with rank and money tend to be pretty pompous and self-important."

"But what has the admiral got to do with . . . ?" He checked himself. "Well, all right. Yes, of course I've met him. No, he's very reactionary in his politics, of course, as you'd expect of a military man with a lot of money. But I wouldn't really call him pompous. He's got a lot better sense of humor than his wife with her social ambitions, let alone his daughter. . . . Christ, I always knew Vangie was, well, a bit unreasonable on the subject of Madeleine, but I didn't realize she was pathological! To write an article like that about somebody who's already been hurt so badly . . . !"

I said, "Let's skip Vangie Lowery, at least for the moment. Back to her daddy. Tell me if he's in town; and if he is, make a guess as to where I can find him."

"Right now, probably at home. It's a morning paper, so he doesn't usually go there until well after lunch to see how next morning's edition is coming along. Oh, and yes, he's in town, all right. Vangie said he okayed her story himself and if I could find anything actionable in it I was a better lawyer than Mr. Rath, the attorney they use, who'd also checked it before they went to press with it." He drew a shaky breath. "She was right, of course. It isn't libel to call somebody a convict when they've been convicted, even if the verdict was totally wrong and the sentence was positively savage—locking up a . . . a lovely and sensitive person like that for eight whole years in a brutal place like that without parole!"

I ignored the impassioned oratory. "I gather you've spoken with Miss Lowery this morning. Where?"

He licked his lips. "Outside the police station. She'd been checking on a story for the *Journal*; she was coming out when I went in. We . . . had an argument."

"Can you get in touch with her?"

He looked startled. "Oh, no, I couldn't possibly . . . ! I mean, it wasn't just an argument. I got so angry I did something pretty terrible, Mr. Helm. I couldn't possibly call her now. In fact, I wouldn't be a bit surprised if she has me arrested."

I said, "Seems unlikely. She passed up her best chance, right there outside the cop house, didn't she? What did you do, haul off and slug her?"

"How did you know?" He stared at the floor. "I must have been a little crazy! I never dreamed I'd ever raise my hand against . . . But that article, just gloating over Madeleine's . . . over what prison had done to her! And those pictures that made her look so . . . And the way Vangie seemed to feel no guilt at all, just standing there taunting me. . . . I just couldn't help myself! I really struck her quite hard, Mr. Helm, hard enough to knock her down. Actually I think I wanted to kill her. And she picked herself up and ran off crying and I stumbled into the station; but before I could remember what I'd come for they all started milling around and the chief rushed out. I knew something serious had happened somewhere in town and I got one of the desk officers I knew to tell me in confidence. . . ." He swallowed hard. "Why do you want me to call Vangie? I mean, if it's really important . . . I said I'd help. She could be at the paper; she mentioned that she was going there. But she'll probably hang up on me."

"It's important," I said. "Tell her to come here as fast as she can. Tell her I may have a story for her."

He hesitated. "Look, you're not going to *hurt* her, are you?"

I regarded him curiously. "Says the man who just smacked her in the puss. No, I'm not going to hurt her. I just want her here for a little while." I pointed. "Phone's over there between the beds. I'll eat my lunch, such as it is, while you talk with her."

Even as we looked at it, the instrument in question made a sharp jangling sound. After a moment I heaved myself out of my chair and limped over to pick it up.

"Helm?"

"Yes. What do you want?"

The voice at the other end of the line did not identify itself, but as it began to speak rapidly I recognized it anyway. It belonged to the man named Jim Dellenbach who was currently known as Scarface, thanks to the front sight of his own revolver as applied by me. Dellenbach said that a certain lady was being held in custody by the Office of Federal Security. Unfortunately, he went on with malicious satisfaction, circumstances did not permit confinement under civilized conditions, and she was really quite uncomfortable and would remain that way, underground, tied hand and foot in the dark to suffer hunger and thirst and the indignity of soiling herself helplessly, until I'd shown myself willing to cooperate fully by withdrawing all our agents from a case that we'd had no business sticking our long noses into. . . .

In a way it was a relief. It was out in the open now. We weren't even pretending to be polite and friendly colleagues in government service, not that we ever had. But now we were two federal agencies openly battling each other for survival, and maybe for the nation's survival, using every dirty weapon in the book including the old buried-alive routine. I said, what I was expected to say, of course, that certainly I'd cooperate in every way I could. The only person who possibly believed me was Walter Maxon, listening; but then he was a very naive young fellow. Maybe.

CHAPTER 25

THE porno shop was on a rather public corner and clearly marked. The sign was quite gaudy, in fact, with big red letters on a yellow background: ADULT BOOKS. I drove past and parked the Mazda up the block and hiked back, feeling conspicuous and rather wicked as I went inside. I told myself that for a man who'd just shot a policeman to death, and had a lady friend kidnapped, to be sensitive about being seen in the company of a little obscene literature was pretty ridiculous.

I arrived first, according to the arrangements made over the phone; and I spent my waiting time, as instructed, in front of the shelf marked BONDAGE. Most of the magazine covers featured, in living color, lovely young girls with sexy figures who were elaborately gagged and tied up in humiliating positions with unnecessary amounts of rope. The facial expressions of these abused young ladies were truly pitiful; but I noted that, while total nudity sometimes obtained, the usual costume seemed to be the standard porno uniform of high heels, sheer stockings, and sexy garter belts—and that the nylons were always perfectly smooth and totally intact no matter what dreadful suffering the poor girl was enduring.

As it happens, I've witnessed and even directed a number of real-life female-captivity situations in the line of duty, and I couldn't help remembering that it's practically impossible to overpower and tie up a struggling, scratching, biting, kicking wench who doesn't want to be overpowered without causing some deterioration of her costume, particularly her fragile hose. If the lady offers any resistance at all, she almost invariably winds up with distressingly sagging and laddered stockings. I decided that, since none of the pretty prisoners depicted on these magazine covers had been disturbed enough about their predicaments to sustain any visible nylon damage fighting to escape, I wasn't going to worry about their cruel bondage. Besides, a study of the clumsy knots employed indicated that any enterprising dame with any Houdini instincts whatever could have freed herself in short order.

Careful analysis of my own reactions indicated that none of these pictures did a thing for me. Apparently it was not my form of perversion, which was not to say I didn't have any. I yawned and, waiting for my contact as arranged, reviewed the rather instructive little scene in which I'd just participated in my motel room.

You had to hand it to Walter Maxon, I reflected. For a mild-looking young man, he apparently packed a mean punch when aroused. When she'd arrived at his summons—to his considerable surprise—Vangie Lowery had displayed a left eye that was swollen almost shut and badly discolored. There was also a large Band-Aid on the heel of her right hand. He had reached her at the *Journal*; but she must have stopped at home to make repairs before going there, since she presented herself to us in immaculate, tailored white linen trousers that had obviously never made violent contact with the ground, and a short-sleeved blue jersey blouse, and high-heeled white shoes. She was rushing the spring season a little, but she was a trim and pretty sight except for the spectacular shiner. Surprisingly, she wasn't a bit self-conscious about it.

"Isn't it a beaut?" she said to me cheerfully as I opened the door for her. "I'm just happy he didn't sock me in the mouth; I'd have been spitting teeth for a week. Hi, Slugger."

291

Maxon was staring at her in dismay. "Gosh, Vangie, I didn't mean to—"

She made a face at him. "Stop it! At least have the courage of your lousy convictions. You thought I needed a poke in the eye so you poked me in the eye. And knocked me down. And ruined a pair of slacks. And left me with a bleeding hand where I'd tried to break my fall and a big bruise on my fanny in addition to this eye. I was a real disaster area when I sneaked into the house to change, I can tell you; but the worst part was knowing that . . . that you should have kicked me a couple of times, hard, when you had me down. Mr. Helm?"

"Yes, Vangie?"

"That woman. She's really innocent, isn't she?"

"We're working on that assumption. As you were told. What made you change your mind about her guilt, if you have?"

Vangie shrugged. "Maybe I didn't. Maybe I've always suspected, deep down, that she probably hadn't done . . . I mean, Walter has always been so sure she wasn't guilty; and he's a lawyer and not really a dope, although he sometimes acts like one. Maybe it just took a poke in the eye to make me understand that I was just clinging stubbornly to any reason I could grasp for despising her. And then hearing rumors that she'd been kidnapped right after my lousy piece came out. . . ." Vangie licked her lips. "Is it really true? The police are being very hush-hush about what happened."

I said, "It's true. When the time comes, I'll see that you get the whole story."

"At the moment I couldn't care less." Vangie drew a shaky breath. "Look, Mr. Helm, can't we do something to get this tragic bitch back? Damn her, she's always getting herself into these awful spots. Who can compete with the lovely lady saint brutally hauled into court and convicted of false charges, the dainty princess cruelly confined in the dungeon vile, or the tormented beauty trembling in the hands of the wicked beasts? Jeez, an ordinary girl just hasn't got a chance!" She was totally ignoring Walter Maxon; he might not have been present. She looked at me gravely. "I suppose you had me come here because you thought I could help. How?"

I looked down into the small disfigured face and realized that there was a very real young woman behind the cute snub nose and the freckles and the ugly swollen eye, not just a spoiled little brat making a breathlessly romantic game of pursuing a somewhat older man, and of hating the somewhat older woman with whom he was obsessed. When I told her what I wanted, she looked disappointed.

"That's all? Just stay here until I get a phone call?" She frowned at me. "A call from whom?"

"You'll know him," I said. "After that, you'll be free to go."

"Mystery, mystery!" She grimaced. "Oh, all right, I'll play. But if you're not going to finish those potato chips . . . I never got any lunch."

"Help yourself. I'm afraid we've cleaned up on the martinis, but there's coffee in that fancy thermos jug if you want it," I said. I turned to Maxon. "As for you, if you still want to be helpful, I've got a legal-type job for you. We're looking for a hole in the ground that could hide a dead body. Madeleine was going to search the public records for any suitable mining property within, say, fifty miles. You should know how to look; maybe you'd be willing to take over now that she's . . . not available. Here's a list of the owner names to watch for."

He frowned. "A dead body? Whose . . . ? Oh, that's right, she thought her husband had been murdered, but she never managed to convince the authorities. But what made her think of a mine—"

I interrupted: "It's too long a story, and you probably wouldn't believe it if I told you. Okay, it's a long shot, but it should be checked, particularly now that there's a possibility that a live body may be hidden in the same place. Gloating over Madeleine's predicament, the guy on the phone was just a little too specific about the crummy, dark, underground conditions under which she was being held."

Maxon's face was pale and eager. "Do you think there's a possibility we can discover where . . . ? I'll get right on it!"

I said, "Incidentally, don't get mad when you see your own name on the list of suspects. We're trying to be fair to everybody."

When I left them, he was studying the slip of paper I'd handed him, and she was sitting at the low table sipping coffee and munching the potato chips I'd left on the sandwich plate. Neither of them was paying any attention to the other. . . .

Alone in the pornography emporium now, I found that I didn't really like facing that solid shelf of captive Kodachrome lovelies, remembering a lady who was suffering the discomforts and humiliations of real bondage, not just posing for a photographer. It was a relief to see Jackson enter, carrying an attaché case. He stopped at the counter to get change for the quarter machines, and walked past me towards the dark little corridor marked MOVIES.

"You're clean, just give me a minute," he breathed as he passed. "Booth two."

I gave him his minute, and followed. When I entered the second booth of the four back there, he was watching the screen, upon which a handsome woman in high black leather boots with high heels, black tights, and a black leather garment that looked like a bullet-proof corset was doing very mean things to a naked man. I was happy to see it. Equality of opportunity. I'd thought only women got to suffer in that place.

"Did you get it?" I asked.

"It's in the case."

"Well, let's have it."

Reluctantly, he took his attention from the screen and picked up the case and started to unfasten the catches;

then he stopped, having spotted the gleam of the .38 in my hand even in that darkened place. But, hampered by the case, there was no quick response he could make.

"Helm, what the hell?"

"If you throw it at my head, you're dead," I said. "Just keep holding it like that with both hands on it, in plain sight. Where's your sidekick, young Marty?"

He licked his lips. "We just learned from the police that Marty has been found dead in the trunk of his car in the parking lot behind that lawyer's office; apparently he was killed several hours ago. That's why you were allowed to walk in on two dead bodies without warning. Helm—"

I shook my head, silencing him. "So Marty wasn't in it with you and had to be taken out when things got tight. Was he starting to get suspicious? How long did you think you could get away with it, amigo? Once or twice, okay, but it was getting kind of ridiculous."

He licked his lips. "I don't know what you're talking about!"

"My escort!" I said softly. "My bodyguard. Was I supposed not to notice that nothing has worked right since the day I picked up Madeleine Ellershaw at Fort Ames with you supposedly watching over us? Oh, you did keep that shotgunner from taking a crack at her that day—but dead, so he couldn't talk. And next day you let us walk right into the arms of Mr. OFS Bennett. And Maxie Reis was allowed one good shot at her. That should have been enough. And you put on a nice show at the top of that Los Alamos hill, but we still wound up with fifty tons of semi chasing us. Hell, the only person who *wasn't* allowed to sneak up on us without warning in spite of your valiant protective efforts was little Miss Lowery, who wasn't going to hurt us anyway!" I grimaced. "And today young Marty died very conveniently so we could be found associating with a couple of stiffs and dealt with appropriately by a couple of outlaw cops."

In the silence that followed I sensed a change in him,

as he switched his attitude from denial to defiance.

"Outlaw?" His voice had changed, too. "Isn't there some question about what's law and what's outlaw these days, Helm? I don't really think you're in a position to make the distinction, a lawless establishment mercenary like you!" He laughed harshly. "You're a little late with that gun, my friend. There are going to be some changes. Very soon we'll be the law and you'll be the outlaws, you and those who still support this decadent, dirty, drug-ridden society. We're going to make this country fit for *decent* people to live in!"

"Decadent and dirty?" I said, and glanced at the screen where the black-leather-clad lady, having roped the naked gentleman to a post, was sticking spring-type clothespins on all his obvious anatomical features including the most obvious one. It seemed an odd way for either of them to get their kicks. "If you don't like decadent and dirty, what the hell are we doing here?"

He cleared his throat. "One must know the evil in order to combat it."

I said, watching the screen for a moment, "I don't think much of the plot, but the action is terrific. But there are some people waiting outside to keep you comfortable until the I-team gets here."

That shocked him. "You have an interrogation squad coming? You *knew*—"

"You've been under surveillance ever since Santa Paula," I said. "I had plenty of time in that hospital to figure things out, amigo. To figure you out. I've been saving you; I thought you might come in handy some day. Now you're going to tell us where they're holding Mrs. Ellershaw. The easy way or the hard way. I don't give a damn which; but those I-team boys just love hurting people and are very good at it. I'm sure they're licking their chops and hoping you'll be stubborn."

I saw the fear in his eyes, even in the vague flickering light from the screen where the nude gent was still having a very rough time and, I suppose, enjoying it immensely.

But that was why I'd left Jackson on the job and let him think himself unsuspected, because when I started really checking on him, I'd learned that his record showed that he could be cracked. It was, in fact, why he'd been relegated to this kind of support duty, because he had cracked once. Knowing that it could happen to anybody, certainly to me, I didn't venture to judge him; but Mac had decided that he was just a little too vulnerable to pain to be trusted with first-line assignments. Apparently the shame of this demotion had festered inside the man, leaving him susceptible to being bought, whatever had been used to buy him—perhaps just an ideology that turned him on. Or maybe they'd used their Advanced Human Managerial Studies on him.

Now he was pale and sweating, once more facing the kind of interrogation he knew he couldn't stand.

"Helm, I swear I have no idea where—"

"Who does know?"

"Bennett. He's been looking for a chance to get back at both of you, remembering the way you humiliated him in front of her in that motel back in Missouri or wherever it was. He's going to leave her securely tied up somewhere, some secret place he knows but didn't say; leave her there unattended to die eventually if you don't come through with what he wants. They want."

I said, "I know. I got all that over the phone, complete with threats. Who's he using?"

"The Bobbsey Twins. Jim Dellenbach, the big blond one, the one you gunwhipped back there—"

"Yes, I recognized the voice."

"And Roger Nolan, the handsome dark one you put to sleep in the john, remember?"

"I remember. But there's another one, the one who did the knife work on Birnbaum's secretary, not to mention on a certain cop who'd served his purpose. Who's he?"

Jackson shook his head. "I don't know. I wasn't told about anybody else."

297

"What about the heavyset older guy, Burdette?"

Jackson hesitated. "Burdette doesn't run that kind of errands."

"Burdette is special?"

"Hell, they have to keep a token pro around the joint, don't they? That bunch of half-ass amateur night watchmen?"

He was trying to tell me something without saying it; and I thought I knew what it was. But there wasn't time to go into it now. I looked at him grimly.

"Again, the sixty-four-dollar question, friend. Where?"

"I swear I don't know where they're holding her! I swear it!"

I studied him for a moment longer in the flickering darkness. It had been worth a try; but I thought he was telling the truth. One hope down the drain.

"Shhh, not so loud," I said. "Let's go."

The naked man was still suffering happily on the screen when I left; I hoped the lady in the black boots was getting her jollies, too. As we passed the bondage section, the tied-up girls on the magazine covers grimaced at us with phony terror as we passed—there was also a big-boob section for those who were turned on by bosoms; and there were other shelves devoted to fellatio, cunnilingus, and various forms of homosexual entertainment. Outside, the sun was bright and the world looked surprisingly normal; not that I've got any strong objections to abnormality, even assuming that somebody knows what it is. Jackson's lined farmer face looked perfectly normal, too; but he started apprehensively when two men stepped out from behind a parked car to seize him by the arms.

"Careful," I said. "I haven't frisked him. Better check him for death pills, too, or you may lose him."

"We'll take care of it."

"I think he's told me as much as he knows."

"The boys who are coming will check it out."

I shrugged. "He's all yours."

298

I watched them put Jackson into the rear of a rental sedan, one on each side of him. The driver took them all away. I couldn't help remembering that Jackson and I had recently done a job in Chicago. Although we'd never got to be exactly friends, we'd functioned well together. Goddamn it anyway.

But the thought of Chicago reminded me of the attaché case that was now tucked under my sling-hampered right arm. I opened it and took out the large envelope that was lying on top of the miscellaneous stuff inside. Two men came up to me as I stood there. One was Pretty Boy McCullough, with his goddamn blow-dried hair and his cold, cold, boyish face. He didn't even give me the satisfaction of punching him in the nose for showing satisfaction at the clever way we'd kept Jackson on a string and reeled him in when we needed him. I didn't know the man with McCullough, a rather plump and pleasant-looking young fellow. I made them wait while I checked out the contents of the envelope. Then I tucked it under my arm and handed the attaché case to McCullough.

"You might as well look through this, although it isn't likely he was carrying anything around that would help us."

McCullough took the case. "This is Bob Wills," he said. "He'll work with you tonight; just let him know what you want."

"And you?"

He gave me his flat gray stare. "I have a lead I'd like to follow. If you don't mind."

He wasn't supposed to have leads. I was supposed to have leads. And if he did have leads, he was supposed to bring them to me so I could follow them.

"A lead to Mrs. Ellershaw?"

"Not exactly."

I reminded myself that too damn many operations have foundered because the captain of the ship got stuffy about his own importance.

299

"Go to it," I said. "Anybody who's got a lead is a long way ahead of me."

"What's the situation? Have they made contact?"

I nodded, and spoke to both of them: "It's the old coffin routine: *While you stall, mister, your pretty lady's lying in her own filth buried in a black place where you'll never find her, slowly dying of thirst and starvation.* So we'd better find her."

"What do they want for her?" McCullough asked.

I frowned at him. "What the hell does that matter? You know the standing orders. We never go that route no matter who dies. If we did, we'd be patsies for anybody who wanted to wave a gun at anybody."

His eyes were steady on my face. "Yes. I just wondered if you remembered."

I said grimly, "Thanks, I don't need that crap from you. Go chase your clues, whatever they are. Mr. Wills and I have work to do." I stared at McCullough hard, until he turned and walked away; then I addressed the other man: "Did you bring the rifle?"

"The seven millimeter Maggie you got shot with? Yes, Jackson hung onto it, with official permission, after grabbing Maxie Reis. We got it from the trunk of his car right after you called; I guess he hasn't had time to miss it. We checked the sighting—four hundred yards on the nose—and made you a rough trajectory table out to six hundred. Pretty tight-shooting gun; Reis knew his business. Two boxes, forty rounds, of fresh ammo, 150-grain soft-point expanding. It doesn't kick too badly, but it's quite a hunk of artillery just the same. With a muzzle velocity over thirty-one hundred that Magnum load will damn near tear your arm off." Then he stopped abruptly, shocked by what he'd just said.

I grinned and rubbed my right shoulder reminiscently. "Don't remind me. It damn near did. Well, keep it handy and don't bounce it around too hard. I may want to shoot at somebody later, and it would be nice if I hit him. Now here's what we do. . . ."

An hour later I was navigating the Mazda one-handed up the sweeping drive that led to the rambling Lowery hacienda, in an expensive development several miles outside town set in rolling hills dotted with twisty green desert junipers where the real estate was sold by acres—lots three acres minimum. It was called El Gobernador Estates, if it matters.

CHAPTER 26

I'D called ahead and Admiral Jasper Lowery was expecting me. He opened the front door himself, a wiry little man with a weathered face and the very pale blue eyes you quite often see on sailors, not quite so often on other kinds of outdoorsmen, although I remembered that the old cowboy who'd taught me how to ride had had the same sun-faded eyes. Crisp short gray hair whitening at the temples. Faded Navy khakis kind of frayed by numerous old punctures at the collar tabs where the captain's eagles had once been pinned. He'd never worn the rear-admiral's stars on active duty, I remembered; that had been a retirement promotion.

"In here, Mr. Helm," he said.

He led me through a living room that made no pretense of being southwestern. The furniture, as far as I could identify it, was all New England and quite old. All it needed was a quaint old spinning wheel—but that wasn't fair. It was actually a rather formal and handsome room appropriate to the social aspirations of the mistress of the house.

The admiral's own tastes were reflected in the study into which he ushered me. This was nautical as hell, with

301

half models of several modern warships displayed on one wall, presumably ships on which Lowery had served. There were also full models of a number of modern sloop-rigged racing yachts—maybe he'd served on those, too—and of a very handsome old topsail schooner. Lowery smiled as he saw me looking at the rakish two-master, in the place of honor on the mantelpiece.

"The old *Evangeline Lowery*. She didn't smell as pretty as she looked. She was a slaver, Mr. Helm, fastest ship ever to run the Middle Passage with a cargo of black ivory; and don't tell my wife I told you. She prefers to have people think the family fortune was founded in more respectable ways. Drink, sir?"

I shrugged. "If no obligations go with it. This isn't a social call, Admiral."

He looked at me for a moment. "Fair enough, Mr. Helm. The offer still holds."

"Scotch if available."

He nodded, and poured two Scotches from an expensive-looking bottle, and gave me one. "Now, what can I do for the United States government?"

I said, "It's not quite as simple as that, sir. There are some personal elements involved. I'd like to show you a few photographs. Perhaps at the desk. . . ."

"As you wish." He seated himself in the big swivel armchair behind the rather cluttered desk, and swept a clear space in front of him. "Carry on, mister."

I selected a glossy 8×10 print from the envelope I carried, and glanced at it to make sure I had the right one even though looking at it still hurt after the time that had passed. I turned it around to face him and laid it before him. He glanced at it casually, and grew quite still.

"Her name was Eleanor Brand," I said. "We met on an assignment. Later, we kind of lived together for a while. Until a man who wanted me to do something for him thought she'd make a good lever to use against me."

302

Lowery drew a long breath and studied the photograph carefully. It showed a young woman lying dead in a city street with one shoe missing and considerable amounts of blood on her dress.

"So you refused and the man killed her," the admiral said softly, without looking up.

"Well, the actual killing was done by his son and a friend, but the basic instructions were his, yes. A daughter was involved, too. Here's exhibit number two, dated a few weeks later." I laid the second photograph before him. Taken in a disordered bedroom, it showed a chunky dark man in gory white pajamas lying on his back on the floor with half his face torn away by the submachine-gun fire that had also riddled his body. "There's the man who gave the instructions," I said.

Lowery nodded slowly. "In Chicago, wasn't it? I've seen that print before, or one very much like it. They called it the Lake Park Massacre, I believe. It got enough national coverage that we even ran a brief story in the *Journal*. The man's name was Jimenez, if I remember rightly. He'd been president of one of those little Central American countries and wanted his old job back."

"Correct," I said. "He thought he could use my marksmanship skills to help him; we'd worked together once in the past. Here's a picture of one of the younger murderers he sent to do the job. I was sorry about the dog, it had never done anything to me, but nobody wants to go up against a trained killer Doberman so the boys took him out, too." I let Lowery look for a little at the dead man and the dead dog sprawled side by side on a dark lawn; then I put down a final 8×10 from the envelope. "And here is the son, who helped with the killing; and the daughter, who conducted the negotiations and, when they were unsuccessful, passed the death sentence by phone. When the shooting started, they tried to flee the house in their nightclothes. God knows where they thought they were going. As you

303

can see, wherever it was, they never got there."

Like the previous photograph, it was a stark black-and-white outdoors flash shot, rather shocking, showing a pretty, dark-haired young girl in a dreadfully stained nightgown slumped lifeless against a fence with the bloody head of a handsome dead young man in her lap.

The admiral looked at me across the desk. His voice was expressionless: "I remember the story quite clearly. The attack on the well-guarded Jimenez estate outside Chicago was apparently staged by a disciplined commando group recruited by a soldier of fortune named Bultman, but he was never apprehended."

I said, "I know lots of soldiers of fortune, sir. I can even get in touch with Bultman if I ever need him again. He's a very good man, if somebody feeds him the right instructions and information. Somebody with a good motive for turning him loose to kill."

That wasn't quite fair to Bultman, who was quite capable of operating on his own and had done so frequently; but in the case in question, while the money had come from elsewhere, I had actually supplied him with the data he'd needed to do his job. Lowery was studying me across the desk.

"What are you trying to say, Helm?"

I shook my head. "Please, Admiral. Let's not play dumb-dumb games. You know that Mrs. Ellershaw is missing. You know, I'm sure, that she came to Santa Fe under my protection. I'll throw in something you may not know: I'm rather fond of the lady, in fact I've asked her to marry me." Using the marriage proposal in this way made me feel a little cheap; but it was no worse than the way I was using the ugly death picture of Eleanor Brand; and my feelings were beside the point, anyway. I went on: "As I've just demonstrated, I hope, I don't like losing pretty ladies I'm fond of. I try to make certain, as far as my official duties permit, that things happen to the people responsible. In this case my official duties and my private desires run parallel. My agency wants Madeleine

Ellershaw back. I want her back. You would be well advised to help me retrieve her, sir."

We spent a moment glaring at each other across the desk. Somewhere in the house somebody was running a vacuum cleaner, presumably a maid. I doubted that the admiral's lady condescended to do her own housework, after all the beds she'd once made in her mother's Annapolis boardinghouse.

When Lowery started to speak, I forestalled him: "Let's get the bullshit out of the way. Am I trying to threaten you? Yes, I'm trying to threaten you. Do I know that you're an important man who can get me fired with one phone call to Washington? Yes, I know that you're an important man who can get me fired with one phone call to Washington. Maybe. But even if you can, what the hell good will it do you, Admiral? Fired or unfired I'm still the same man, my lady is still missing, I'm still mad, and I've still got a gun and a lot of nasty friends. And I'm going to get Madeleine Ellershaw back if I have to reduce the population of New Mexico by fifty percent. Do I have to tell you who goes first, considering the story you ran in your paper this morning?" I stared at him a moment longer. "Do you know where your daughter is at this moment, Admiral Lowery?"

That brought him to his feet. "You bastard! If you've laid a hand on Evangeline—"

I said, "Mrs. Ellershaw has just spent eight years in hell. Plus one in purgatory beforehand. She's earned the right to be left alone. What's your brat earned, Lowery, except a good spanking for that cheap story she was jealous enough to write and you were callous enough to print?" He started to reach for the desk phone, and I dropped a slip of paper on top of the gory photographs on the desk. "Try that number. Ask for Room 117."

He looked at me for a moment, and sank back into his chair, and punched out the number on the phone. "Room 117, please. . . . Evangeline? Are you all right?" I saw him relax noticeably. He listened for a moment and said, "I see. That's fine, my dear, I'll see you at the paper shortly." He replaced the phone and looked at me searchingly. "She says she's all right."

"She is all right. Free as a breeze, too. Probably just getting into her car to drive back to work."

"What are you trying to prove, Helm?"

I said, "You disappoint me, sir. All these rhetorical questions! What am I trying to do, say, prove? You know the answers. Your daughter didn't have to be sitting in my warm and comfortable motel room drinking my coffee and munching my potato chips, at liberty to depart at will. Isn't it obvious to you by this time that I'm trying to do this politely? Do you have any doubt that I could have grabbed her just as easily and started sending you fingers and toes and ears and noses in the mail—well, just one nose, I guess, and a small one at that. Instead, because I was told that you were a sensible man with a reasonable sense of humor, I'm giving you a chance to come through before I start hurting people."

He licked his lips. "This is incredible! You're incredible, Mr. Helm. You're supposed to be an agent of the United States government."

I laughed at him. "Who the hell do you think is holding Mrs. Ellershaw? Tell the Office of Federal Security about the duties and responsibilities of federal agencies. What we've got here, Admiral, is your federal agency against my federal agency. You've got a hostage, Madeleine Ellershaw. But I've got your family anytime I want them. Hell, you offered them to me, why the hell shouldn't I take them?"

He looked shocked. "Offered?"

"Maybe you didn't know you were doing it. Maybe you thought it was some kind of a game you were playing, driving the dangerous unwanted dame out of town by having her insulted by your wife in a public restaurant and smeared all over the morning paper in your daughter's story. Or making it look as if she'd been driven out of town, so when she disappeared everybody'd assume that the poor broken ex-convict dame had simply found her reception in her old hometown too unpleasant and had sneaked away in her shame, forgetting her loud and unconvincing protestations of innocence." I shook my head. "You can't have it both ways. If you're willing to use your family against us, why the hell shouldn't we use them against you?"

"But I never expected . . ." He stopped.

I said, "Admiral, if you push hard enough, if you hurt people badly enough, sooner or later you'll always find yourself facing an angry man, or woman, with a gun. In this case, me. Can you get Mrs. Ellershaw back for me? I'm not asking if you will, that's another question, just if you can."

He looked at me across the desk. After a moment, reluctantly, he shook his head. "No."

I said, "I was given to understand that you might be the big cheese in these parts, as far as a certain sinister organization is concerned."

"Sinister?" His head came up angrily. "There's nothing sinister about us! All we want. . . ." He checked himself.

"All you want is to purify the country, according to my last informant," I said. "Well, fine. Go ahead and purify all to hell. At the next elections, use your money and influence and newspaper to put in your pure candidates and kick out all the impure bastards currently contaminating the political scene. Not that I'm particularly eager to be purified, but if you can get enough people to vote your way I'll go along with purification, at least until the election after that. But when you try to circumvent the elective process by force and assassination and subversion, backed up by computerized trickery, whatever it is that's going on up in those CADRE installations of yours, to hell with you. And when you frame an innocent woman into prison for your convenience, and try to kill her after she gets out, having already murdered her husband to protect yourselves, to hell with you. Do anything you like with your money, even to buying votes; at

307

least that shows a certain respect for the vote, being willing to pay for it. But play it within the system, mister. The people will decide when they want a new system, and I don't think it will be one run by you and your kind. And don't ever try the guns; you're not good enough. Guns are my business. You can buy me and sell me a hundred times over, but when it comes to the real crunch it's the bullet that counts; and I'm the bullet specialist around here. So it would be well if you kept your hand away from that desk drawer, sir. What have you got in there, the old service .45? A great old firearm, but you'll never make it."

There was a long silence; then Admiral Lowery slowly relaxed in his chair and smiled. "I was told you were a wild man, Mr. Helm."

"I can guess who told you. How's my friend Burdette these days?"

He didn't answer that. He said, "I can't give you Mrs. Ellershaw, on my word of honor. I can't even tell you where she is. I don't rank highly enough in this organization, yet, to have such knowledge of . . . of current operations. Here I'm just an ordinary seaman, following orders."

"That makes two of us," I said. I studied him for a moment. "So, to change the simile, you're just the screaming baby they tossed out of the sleigh to keep the wolves— me—busy long enough so they could whip up the horses and get away. And you agreed to this?"

"I . . . swore to do my part when asked, without question," Lowery said.

"God, it sounds like a college fraternity. Did you slice your thumbs and mingle your blood when you made this fancy oath? And was Vangie asked if she wanted to join this crusade of yours? And give her young life for this pure cause of yours if it came to that, as it may? Or your wife? I assure you, Admiral, that if Mrs. Ellershaw dies, she won't die alone."

He licked his lips. "You mean that, don't you? If it

308

happens, you'd even retaliate against a young girl who's never done anything against you?"

"I don't call that hatchet job she did on a woman I've asked to marry me exactly nothing. If she's mean to people, she can hardly complain if they're mean to her. She uses her daddy's newspaper, I use my Smith and Wesson .38. There's a difference?"

Actually, I had no idea what I'd do if Madeleine were murdered; but since it would accomplish nothing, I doubted very much that I'd take it out on the kid. Or the mother, for that matter. But Lowery didn't have to know that.

He cleared his throat. "Maybe we can work out a compromise. I can't help you with the woman, but I think I know how I can arrange for you to . . . have somebody else. That self-important stuffed shirt Bennett. He may know where she is. Making him talk is your problem."

I kept my face straight. Apparently there were useful strains and jealousies inside the great purification crusade. A military man accustomed to command might be willing to humble himself for a cause in which he believed, but he'd still find Bennett's arrogant pomposity hard to take, maybe even hard enough that he'd be willing to indulge in a spot of betrayal.

"Where?" I asked.

"I'll have to make it look as if I'd seized the opportunity to set a trap for *you*," he said. "I . . .we have a cabin well up the road to the ski run. It's lonely enough that you should be able to operate without attracting attention, particularly since it's too late for the skiers and too early for the summer climbing-and-fishing crowd. I'll call and say I lied to you when you came storming in here with your threats, and told you that the woman is being held captive up there. I'll tell them that they'd better ambush you, and dispose of you permanently, when you stage your dramatic rescue of a prisoner who isn't there, since you obviously have no intention of yielding to their demands, whatever they are. Our demands. I think Bennett will grab the opportunity to deal with you himself. I've been given to understand that you've made a fool of him on a couple of occasions. Is that good enough?"

I grinned. "Pretty sharp thinking, Admiral," I said. "You win either way. If Bennett traps me, and kills me, your family is safe. If I trap Bennett and he talks, as he will, your family is safe. I bet you fought some tricky naval actions in your time, sir. Okay, it's a deal, but I'll want to see some pictures of the cabin, and a topo map of the area if you have one. . . ."

CHAPTER 27

IN addition to being picturesque in its own right, in spite of what progress has done to it, Santa Fe has a number of tourist attractions, including a well-known opera for the entertainment of musical summer visitors. And then there's the ski area in the mountains above the town, for the athletic types who arrive in winter. The Chamber of Commerce keeps trying to get the fifteen-mile access road to the run widened and straightened, but the steep Sangre de Cristo Mountains don't take kindly to being straightened; and a few flatlanders fall off every year, mostly Texans—I suppose because there are more of them. To those of us who grew up driving in that kind of country it seems like a perfectly safe and comfortable thoroughfare, just a little more stimulating to drive than most, although it was even more fun before it was paved, back when you could slide the corners dirt-track fashion.

310

I'd left the conspicuous Mazda at the motel and hitched a ride in a flossy four-wheel-drive station wagon called Eagle, distantly related to the old utilitarian jeep. It was well after dark when we got the word. Bob Wills drove. He'd turned out to be more difficult to work with than his boyish appearance suggested, rather impatient and critical, and he was getting on my nerves a bit; but then I always prefer to work alone, given a choice. I guess I'm not really a leader of men at heart.

Here, of necessity, we had a small military operation going; and I didn't know any of the friendly forces Bob had recruited, numbering five. Two rode in the rear seat of the Eagle. A third drove the battered old International pickup, vintage uncertain, that followed behind us at a discreet distance. The remaining two were already on station. They'd just let us know by radio that the fish were in the net and we could man the winches and crank them in anytime. Bob wanted to do it now.

"All we have to do is sneak in and pick them off one by one, damn it," he said. "Wally's got most of them spotted already, the way they've set up their so-called trap for you around that cabin. These are good boys, Helm, they know the mountains, and they can work in the dark. Those creeps will never know what hit them."

I said, "Maybe, but I don't want to wind up in a firefight. It's a still night, and any shooting up here on the mountain will be heard clear down in town. We've already presented the city police with four dead bodies— well, two weren't ours but some people would like to give us credit for them, anyway. Five if you include Marty. I've managed to smooth all that over after a fashion with the Chief, but I don't want to have to deal with the county sheriff and the state cops as well. And the bottom line, as they say, is that if there's a lot of wild firing in the dark the man who knows what I want to know may wind up among the dead and the whole operation will be wasted; and so will a lady I'd kind of like to keep alive. Where's this ambush spot your man picked out for us?"

"Well, if we're going to do it this way, at least we should block the Aspen Ranch road above, in case they decide to go out that way."

I said, "The word is that Bennett rode up comfortably in a Mercedes; and he'll never get it out that way. That little dirt road is rough enough any time of year; now in the spring it's strictly four-wheel-drive country. And it's a considerable detour, so if he did pull a fast one and slip out that way in the heavier vehicle he's got up there, it would mean he was onto us and ready for us and we'd have a battle we can't afford before we could take him. Anyway, we can't spare the men; we've got barely enough to do the job here. No, either it works as planned, and they come back down this way and stumble into our hands all unsuspecting, or we go back to the goddamn drawing board and try to figure out something else."

"If we wait them out, it'll be a long night for the lady," Bob said.

"It'll be a long night for everybody," I said, wincing as a bounce of the car hurt my side. "How far did you say it was to the place where we can set up our deadfall instead of walking into theirs?"

When we got there, it looked good; and I had them back the Eagle up into the little dead-end stub of a road up a side canyon that other people had used for parking and picnicking. Then I had the heavy old pickup parked in front of it ready to go. I limped around a bit and checked that the vehicle wouldn't be hit by the lights of a car approaching down the steep main road; in the dark there was a good chance it would pass unnoticed until the time came for it to do its stuff. Good enough. Now if everybody behaved exactly as I hoped, we had it made. The sides of the canyon rose black against the sky around me, and a few stars twinkled up there in a cold and remote fashion.

After a final conference with Bob Wills, I made my cautious way back to the ambush site and asked the driver of the International to please join his friends in the

Eagle. I told him I wanted his vehicle for snoozing; he could have it back when action-time came. He grinned, a nice enough guy, and went back to the station wagon. I struggled up to the pickup's high seat and tried to make myself comfortable on the cracked pseudo-leather up-holstery. The space was too short for my legs, and my ribs hurt, but I reminded myself that somewhere else somebody else was even less comfortable. *It'll be a long night for the lady.* You have to work with all kinds, but why did I have to be saddled with a mouthy sonofabitch tonight?

Once it's set and running, there's never any point in wearing out the brain cells thinking about the operation. If you haven't got it figured out right by that time, it's too damned late. And there was no point whatever in worrying about Madeleine Ellershaw, what kind of shape she was in by now, what kind of conditions she was enduring, and how she was enduring them. If she was still alive—and what if she wasn't? So I thought about her anyway. . . .

"Helm!"

I realized that, thinking about her, I'd fallen asleep. I sat up groggily. The door of the pickup opened and I could see a dark silhouette, a bit chubby, recognizable as Bob Wills.

"What's the word?" I asked.

"No word, but—"

I said, "For Christ's sake! Did you wake me up just because you were lonely?"

"Look, damn it, it's well after midnight. We're just wasting time sitting here doing nothing!"

I said, "Amigo, if you can't learn to do nothing for reasonable periods of time, you'd better take up tennis or some other sport where you get to hop around like a flea in a frying pan. Either they come or they don't. Either we'll get them or we won't. Now go play cards or mastur-bate or something and let me sleep. Close the fucking door as you go out, please."

The truck door slammed. I heard his angry footsteps recede. It occurred to me that I wasn't having much luck of late with my subordinates, if you could call them that: Jackson under interrogation, Marty dead, McCullough off on a private mission I probably shouldn't have authorized, and myself saddled with this nervous character who obviously considered me a superannuated incompetent, and could be right.

It was getting to be kind of a rat race anyway, with all these people milling around; who the hell did I think I was, anyway, Eisenhower supervising Operation Overlord? The fine old lone-wolf feeling, me against the world, was all too often missing these days of committee operations. Maybe it was time to pull out while I was still in one piece—well, more or less—and marry the girl if I could get her out of this alive and talk her into it, and settle down to . . . well, hell, it didn't matter what, really. Danger pay had been piling up in banks and investment accounts for years. I could live a long, long time, even married, on what I had put away.

Suddenly I was awake again, realizing that I'd been asleep again. I was sitting up, yawning, when the head of the driver of the truck I was using for a bedroom appeared at the window.

"Mr. Helm?"

"Time to go?" I asked, opening the door and checking my watch. Three forty-five.

He nodded. "We just had Wally on the two-way. They're giving up on you up there, and pulling out. Three cars. Well, the Mercedes, and the big old crew-cab Ford pickup with a camper shell that we knew about. And a four-wheel-drive GMC Carryall stuffed full: Wally counted nine piling into that one. Nine that we didn't know about. Must have come up that back road and parked well above the cabin and filtered in without Wally's seeing them."

What he left unsaid was that if we'd made the attack

Wills had recommended to me, we'd have been outnumbered well over two to one, with nine unexpected marksmen popping at us from behind the trees. Disaster Alley.

"What's the order of withdrawal?"

"Ford first, GMC second, Mercedes bringing up the rear. Friend Bennett is letting the troops break trail for him, I guess, just in case there should be somebody waiting along the road with a nasty gun."

I said, "Good, then we won't need the roadblock above. Just the one below, to isolate the Merc and keep the two lead vehicles from coming back to help after they've passed. They'd have a hell of a time turning those big heaps around on this narrow road, anyway. Tell Bob . . . no, I'll tell him. You get ready here. You've got your part all straight?"

He nodded again. "I block the road when I get the word from Jack that Bennett's car has passed the bend just above us." He tapped the walkie-talkie he held. "I just checked it out. Communications loud and clear."

"Did Wally say where Bennett was riding?"

"Rear seat, left side. Behind the driver."

"Does everybody know that, in case there should be shooting? We don't want to hurt the poor little fellow. At least not with a bullet."

"Everybody's got the word. They'll be careful."

I said, "You'd better ride out the crash in the cab. If you try to get out, and they're coming fast, they could hit the truck and shove it over on top of you before you're clear."

"I know, sir. I'll be all right. This old wreck is built like a tank; that's why I picked it off the second hand lot."

I eased myself to the ground and looked at him for a moment. I decided that I'd leave the encouraging handshakes and noble before-the-battle speeches to General Eisenhower, wherever he might be. I just gave him a kind of salute and he grinned at me, and mounted to the seat of the pickup in an agile and painless way that made me

315

jealous. I started back towards the Eagle, but saw Bob Wills getting out of it carrying a walkie-talkie of his own, and a submachine gun of some kind that gleamed menacing in the dark. It didn't seem like exactly the right weapon for capturing a man alive and talking; but if I criticized him now he'd probably get mad and start tossing around hand grenades and vest-pocket nuclear devices. For the same reason, seeing that the other two men had already gone to their stations, I didn't check what instructions he'd given them, lest he think I was being critical. I'd just have to hope he'd got things organized right in his prima-donna way.

He passed me without speaking. We'd worked all this out earlier; and I followed him past the parked truck and up the road to a point from which we could shoot out the tires of Bennett's car, we hoped, in the unlikely event that it came around the last curve so slowly that it managed to avoid collision with the International, which would be blocking the road by that time, and tried to back uphill out of danger. Scrambling up the steep slope in the dark, to the patch of brush we'd picked for cover, was no fun at all. As I eased myself onto a suitable rock up there, I heard the motor of the truck start up, roar a bit, and settle down to steady idling.

"Jack, come in," Bob Wills said into his set. To me, he said, "Jack's around the curve, a couple of hundred yards above us."

"I hear you," said a tinny voice. "Nothing in sight yet. Saw a shooting star, though. Is that supposed to be good luck or bad?"

"Never mind the heavens, concentrate on matters terrestrial."

"Matters terrestrial. Wow! Aye, aye, sir!" After several minutes, the tinny little loudspeaker addressed us again: "We're in business. Headlights up the canyon. Two sets so far. . . . Still just two pairs of lights. Getting closer, okay here they come. I'll give you mark as the second one passes so you'll get an idea how long . . .

Mark! I repeat, that's the *second* vehicle, the three-quarter-tonner. No sign of the sedan yet."

In the silence that followed, I heard the growling sound as the driver of the waiting International jazzed his idling motor a bit to make sure of it. Then a set of headlights swept by below our hillside perch, and another. I could hardly make out the dark bodies of the vehicles, let alone the faces at the windows.

"Twenty-four seconds," Bob Wills said.

"Get ready, here comes the Merc," said the radio. "Coming, coming, coming . . . Mark! Nothing else on the road. Leaving post, heading down to lend a hand. Out!"

Wills was staring at the parked pickup truck below us, still motionless. "Get *out* there, you dumb jerk!" he said angrily, but he didn't say it into his set.

But the pickup driver, with a clear knowledge of how much time he had to work in, was in no hurry. He waited a few seconds longer, then he eased his clumsy old vehicle forward and halted it where it would block the highway completely. I heard the parking brake go on and the engine stop. His timing was good. We caught the loom of headlights around the curve above us, sweeping out over the canyon as the Mercedes made the turn and headed down towards us at a fair rate of speed for that road, perhaps trying to catch up with the rest of the convoy that had pulled a little ahead of it.

The pickup seemed to materialize magically across the road as the headlights hit it. The sedan was already below us. Tires screeched and the car went into a skid to the right, heading for the hundred-foot drop-off on that side of the road. I beseeched the driver silently: *Get off your brakes, you dumb prick!* One of these days I'm going to invent a car without any brakes. It'll kill fewer people than the ones we've got, at least in high-speed situations with stupid auto-jockeys who lock up everything tight and lose control whenever things get a bit hairy. Either the driver heard my soundless plea or a measure of sanity returned; his wheels started rotating again, his steering recommenced functioning, and he got himself aimed left towards the rear end of the pickup, the light end, the hillside end.

But he'd overcorrected in his panicky counter-reaction to his first panicky reaction. His left wheels rode up the steep bank and flipped the Mercedes onto its side a moment after it had smacked the back end of the pickup and spun it halfway around. I was already sliding down the rocky slope to the road, stoically ignoring my aching side, heroically interposing my body between Bob Wills' automatic weapon and the wrecked car, just in case he should be irresistibly tempted to give it a burst.

I tried to remember which military greats had been shot in the back by their own men. Charles the Twelfth of Sweden, for one; but there had been others. Stonewall Jackson?

CHAPTER 28

THE interrogation van was a blunt, boxy, windowless vehicle with a red paint job that had faded, as had the lettering on the side: GARCIA AND KETTENBERG— PLUMBING. When I opened one half of the rear double door, and hauled myself inside, Bennett was sitting on the narrow cot at the side in his underwear and socks, a costume that left him little dignity. They hadn't had to work on him very hard, and there wasn't a mark on him except for a patch of white tape on his forehead at the hairline where he'd hit something when the Mercedes flipped; but his shoulders sagged, his body looked shrunken, and his face was that of an old man with a

318

faint silvery stubble of beard and dull staring eyes.

"Tell me about the Orosco Grant," I said. "Orosco with an 's' or Orozco with a 'z'?"

"With a 'z'," he said.

"Size?"

"Several thousand acres, but parts are still under litigation. You know these fucking Hispanos, suddenly rising up now and claiming that their innocent ancestors were screwed by the sneaky Anglos—after they stole the land from the Indians in the first place!"

There was nothing in that for me. An easterner himself, he was merely parroting what he'd been told by his landowning local associates.

"Access?" I asked.

"I already told them—"

"Tell *me*."

"Turn east off the freeway on State 470. Seventeen miles. Barbed-wire fence, left side. Padlocked gate. Key—"

"I have the keys they took off you. Go on."

He continued to speak mechanically, as if repeating a speech he'd made several times to another audience, as of course he had. They'd have made him repeat every detail endlessly until they were sure they had the truth, as far as he knew it.

"Dirt road," he said. "You'll need four-wheel drive crossing the arroyos. Two arroyos. Deep sand. Proceed nine and a half miles from the gate into the Gabaldon Hills. The old Higsbee Mine."

"Landmarks?"

"Las Dos Tetas. The mine is kind of between them. Actually, the diggings are in the one to the south. Two round knobs closer together, a little higher than the surrounding hills."

"What's left at the mine after all these years?"

"Not much. A couple of old buildings. Falling down. Piles of dirt. Hole in the hillside, tunnel. Branches. First branch tunnel on right."

319

"Alive?"

Apprehension flickered in his eyes. "We didn't hurt her!" he said defensively. "She was alive when we left her there!"

"Yesterday?"

"Yesterday."

"Is there a shaft, a deep vertical shaft, or whatever it's called in mining parlance?"

He hesitated. "Yes. End of main tunnel. I was told that years ago, when they were working it, they thought they had a rich strike in one of the lower strata, but it petered out."

I watched him closely. "It sounds like a convenient place to dispose of her body if she happened to die on you."

His eyes betrayed him again. "We weren't going to harm her!"

"Twenty-four hours tied up in the dark with the rats doesn't count as harm?" I stared at him grimly. "What were you supposed to do with me if you caught me up at that mountain cabin, Bennett?" He started to speak, and stopped, and looked away. I said, "Then you have a good idea what I'm supposed to do with you, once we've wrung you dry."

His eyes widened fearfully. "But I've told you everything!"

"Not yet you haven't," I said. "But you will. And if you do, and if the boys don't have to work too hard for it, and if we find Mrs. Ellershaw alive and not too badly damaged, thanks to your information, well, I'm allowed a certain amount of discretion in carrying out my orders. Keep it in mind."

Leaving, I glanced at the equipment that cluttered up the inside of the van. Apparently they did most of their work electrically. The inside of the mobile torture chamber was covered with soundproofing, not too neatly applied. Outside, there was bright sunshine, and it was warmer than it had been. A cool morning had come and gone while we cleaned up the mess on the mountain and delivered the warm body in question to the I-team and let them work on it. The afternoon was now getting balmy; summer was obviously on its way. The van stood at the curb by the green strip of park that runs along the Santa Fe River. Three men were sitting at a nearby picnic table drinking beer. Seeing me emerge, one rose and came up to me.

The man in charge of the I-team looked quite ordinary. They usually do. Very few of them have werewolf fangs and pointed, tufted ears. This one was dressed in a faded, flowery sports shirt, frayed jeans, and the kind of tricky jogging shoes that have taken the country by storm. He was a somewhat older McCullough type, with the kind of boyish/girlish appearance the longish hairdos give the prettier ones these days, even into their thirties and forties. But I didn't like his eyes. Well, hell, maybe he didn't like mine. We all have our little specialties. Who was I to criticize?

"Satisfactory?" he asked.

"So far." I told him what I wanted.

"No problem," he said. "Not with this one. Very cooperative."

"Meaning you had a problem with the last one I gave you?"

He shook his head. "He never got this far, friend. These damn suicidal types!"

I drew a long breath. "They lost him?"

"So I was told. I never saw him."

I started to speak angrily, to say I'd warned them to be careful. Obviously Jackson, fearing pain as he did, had had an extra little dose of oblivion hidden out somewhere, and they'd missed it, searching him. Well, at least he'd had the satisfaction of outwitting us all in the end. In any case, it wasn't this man's fault.

"Well, try not to lose this one," I said.

An hour later I was rolling down the four-lane highway in Bob Wills' fancy FWD Eagle, which he'd been very reluctant to lend me, although it was in a sense a company car. Well, I'd been equally reluctant to let him, in return, use the Mazda, which wasn't. God save us from all temperamental agents, present company excepted. I'd left Wills with careful instructions: he was to keep certain people covered, and act in certain ways if certain things happened, and he was not to come blundering after me helpfully under any circumstances. Until tomorrow. If I wasn't back by then he could buy himself some shovels and hire a jeep and take a crew out to bury the bodies, if he could find them.

"Goddamn it, Helm," Wills had said. "You talk as if the country out there—this Whatchamacallit Grant—is just crawling with war-painted Apaches, or Navajos, or whatever the hell kind of hostile Indians you used to grow out here! Bennett says he simply took the woman to the mine and left her tied up there unguarded, doesn't he?"

I said, "He may even be telling the truth, as far as he knows it. But I'm not going to gamble my life, or Madeleine Ellershaw's, on what Bennett thinks he knows. If you were in the same outfit with him, and had to use him, would you tell him any more than you had to? So remember what I told you: stay clear. If it's easy, one man can do it. If it's hard, maybe one man can still do it. But in either case a lot of superfluous characters raising dust all over the desert will surely get her killed, and me as well."

Now, driving south along the freeway all by myself, I felt it all drop away. It was a lovely feeling. To hell with critical subordinates. To hell with tame torturers I'd had to use to save Madeleine's life, because they were better at interrogation than I was, even though my conscience told me that if I had to get information by such means the least I could do was get my own hands bloody. This way I was like the kind of hypocritical creep who loves steak but wouldn't dream of going out and murdering a poor little steer—or deer—himself. Or herself. And to hell with fantastic nationwide plots and science-fiction garbage and Advanced Human Managerial Studies.

I had a very good notion of what was waiting for me out there in the Gabaldon Hills. Who was waiting for me. The double-trap technique. He'd let me avoid the clumsy ambush arranged by Bennett—perhaps he'd even guessed that Admiral Lowery had suggested it under duress—and now he hoped I'd be feeling very self-satisfied and clever, and very safe, so I'd come marching boldly into the real trap, baited with a captive lady, that had been waiting for me right along.

I made the turn at the elaborate cloverleaf that seemed like a highway department overreaction to such a small state road. I drove the seventeen miles along the rough narrow pavement and found the gate in the barbed-wire fence—*bobwahr*, they call it over in Texas. I unlocked the padlock with one of the two keys that had been taken from Bennett's collection. The other was supposed to unlock Madeleine's handcuffs if she was still wearing them; but it seemed overoptimistic to think that far ahead yet.

I snapped the lock shut again conscientiously after driving through the gate. Range etiquette requires that you leave all gates as you found them; and it makes no allowance for battered ribs. This was wide-open country now, forty-acres-to-a-cow country, with the Sangre de Cristo Mountains, where I'd spent the night, tall and sharp against the northern sky, and the Gabaldon Hills low and dark and rounded ahead. The road was two ruts across the dry land on which grew, out here on the flats, only scraggly tufts of grass and an occasional cactus. I passed two side roads, if you could call them roads— barely more than tire tracks—that Bennett had neglected to mention, and kept plugging towards the beckoning hills.

The Eagle promptly stuck itself in the sand in the first arroyo. I realized that I'd forgotten to lock the front hubs; hell, I'd even forgotten to get power to the front wheels, wherever that control might be. My own old go-anywhere vehicle, which I'd recently traded in on the Mazda, had had full-time four-wheel drive, a great institution, but it uses a little more gas in order to keep turning that forward drive-train even when you don't need it, so they don't go that route these economical days. But it had got me out of the habit of switching over when the going got tough. I struggled out of the car and found that there were no locking front hubs. Nor could I find an extra shift lever anywhere in the screwball machine. When all else fails, read the instructions. I got the manual out of the glove compartment, and it directed me to a simple little switch on the dashboard, to be operated a certain way under certain conditions. . . .

With all four wheels pulling, she came right out; and the second arroyo was no problem at all, although it was a wide, sandy wash with a little trickle of water down the middle. There must have been a shower back in the hills. There were no permanent watercourses out here. Anyway, I knew where to come if my canteen ran dry.

I could now see my landmarks ahead: the two identical round hills known as the Dos Tetas. Well, some men will see two tits in practically any pair of rocky humps, particularly if they've been away from home for a while. That southwestern country is lousy with geological protrusions that reminded some lonely man of a woman's breasts.

It was time to leave the road. I cut to the right across country along the base of the hills. After a couple of miles of broken-field running, or driving, I found a suitable valley going the right way and followed it upwards into the hills until it became an impassable little gorge and to hell with it. Hiking time had come. I got out of the car and discarded the black sling that had served its purpose as well as such tricky disguises usually do; well, I don't suppose Mac had expected it to work miracles. I hung the canteen over my shoulder and struggled into the small nylon backpack that held some energy snacks, a flashlight and some patent light-sticks for cave exploration, and a change of clothes for the lady, in case over twenty-four hours of real bondage, as opposed to the porno variety, had left her in no condition to meet her public.

Then I picked up, and loaded, the 7mm Magnum rifle I'd inherited, kind of, from the man who'd used it to put a hole in my shoulder although that hadn't been his real purpose. It was a plain-Jane Remington job off the shelf, but some work had been done to accurize it, to use the shooters' jargon. The trigger pull, for instance, was lighter and crisper than they usually come from the factory; and the bolt worked very smoothly indeed.

The big telescopic sight on top was a $3\times$-$9\times$ Redfield variable. Being conservative where weapons are concerned, I'm not too fond of these slightly complicated zoom-type scopes. Although I'll grant the tremendous advantages of optical sights in general, I still think the single-power jobs, having less glass and fewer adjustments, are less likely to shake apart under heavy recoil. But Maxie Reis had gone for flexibility, and I had to admit that there had been nothing wrong with his shooting that a motionless and unobstructed target wouldn't have cured.

I climbed out of the cleft, leaving the station wagon at the bottom, and looked around to make sure—well, reasonably sure—that I'd know where to come to find it again. The altitude—over a mile, even out here away from the mountains—pulled at my lungs, accustomed to half that elevation at the Ranch. My side hurt and I still had a trace of a headache, not to mention a couple of noticeable knots on my skull; and I felt fine, just fine. It had been a long and not very direct trail we'd followed from Fort Ames, but the end wasn't very far ahead now. This was what it was all about; and to hell with the pretty vine-covered cottage with the pretty wife waiting in the doorway to kiss me welcome home from my pretty, safe, dull job. I was a hunter again, in my own kind of country, not a male nurse or a bodyguard or a goddamn field marshal sending armies into battle. It was good to be back at work.

I slung the rifle over my uninjured shoulder and wondered if the other would take the recoil if it had to, but what the hell. It wasn't as if I were planning to spend a week trapshooting at Vandalia or rifle shooting at Camp Perry, if they still held the big matches there. The 7mm Remington Magnum isn't really a hard-kicking gun—not compared to the .30-caliber jobs and up—and if one or two or three shots didn't do the job here, the job probably wouldn't get done. I set off towards the bosom-like hills ahead at a deliberate gait; no sense in arriving all sweaty for the long wait that would probably follow.

When I got there, I scouted the approach very carefully in case some surprises had been left out there for me to fall over, or into, but I could find none. Easing myself to the top of the final ridge at last, I saw a kind of twisty little valley rising up to the cleft between the two stony breasts. The road ran up the valley to the two remaining ramshackle mine buildings—the wood was silvery with age—set among the heaps of stuff dug out of the mine all those years ago. Tailings is the word that comes to mind, but it doesn't have to be right.

The mine itself was in the side of the hill to my right as I lay there studying the situation. I couldn't really see into the tunnel entrance, but I could see the ancient timbers framing it. The thought of the woman lying helpless inside the hill somewhere, if nobody'd lied to me, was too disturbing to consider at the moment; nor did I allow myself to remember that I don't really like crawling around in the bowels of the earth, as I'd have to if everything went well.

Nothing moved, except a little scraggly grass waving in the late-afternoon breeze. I would have liked to see a jackrabbit hopping around over there, or a prairie dog peeking out of a hole in friendly fashion. It was a hell of a bleak, dead place. I wondered how much gold they'd got for all their digging, if it was gold they were after. Silver? With a moderately long-range weapon, he might be waiting somewhere on the breast/hill to my left, covering the mine entrance in the opposite hillside. He could control half a mile of the approach road from there, and the whole little valley. He could probably arrange to have a good field of fire even if I circled and came in from the other side. I didn't know what was over there and didn't intend to find out; I'd had enough hiking for the day. Circling wouldn't fool him. He knew his business; he'd be ready for me either way I came. Why wear out shoe leather, and myself, being fancy?

But the record didn't make him a long-range man. So it was seventy-five to twenty-five, say, maybe even eighty-twenty, that he was waiting with an automatic weapon, M16 or equivalent, in the brush up on the right-hand hillside over the mine entrance. He couldn't see as far from there, but he could take me anytime between the moment I hove into sight around the shoulder of the hill and the instant I disappeared into the tunnel below him. If he let me get that far, which wasn't likely.

That was, of course, assuming that I was coming at all. I mean, coming the way he expected. He had a certain image of me: I was supposed to be a hell-for-leather guy, a Wild West character smashing through the batwing doors of the saloon with two six-guns blazing. Well, there were times for that kind of dramatic headlong stuff, and he'd certainly seen me indulging in it, but there was no law saying I had to make a habit of it. I'd waited out one man this morning; I could wait out another this evening.

I looked around and found that luck, and the shape of the terrain, had brought me to a perfectly suitable spot. Moving to any of the other little knobs or ridges around wouldn't improve my position much and might warn the man awaiting me that company had arrived. I slid back cautiously to where I'd left my canteen and the little pack, and ate a chocolate bar washed down with water, and resumed my position just below the crest behind a convenient clump of brush. I slipped my arm into the rifle sling, which I'd already adjusted to my own dimensions, somewhat longer than those of the previous owner. Then I waited.

It was the deadest damn hollow in the hills I'd ever watched, and I've watched a few. There wasn't even a hawk or buzzard in the sky above it. I'd arrived just before four o'clock. Five o'clock passed, and six. The sun approached the rounded Gabaldon Hills, and hung just above them for a while, turning larger and redder, and dropped behind them. The light started fading fast.

I picked up the rifle at last. I shouldered it, lying there, using the taut sling for rigidity, target fashion. The fancy variable sight had one big advantage: in order to provide light enough for the highest magnification it had an objective lens large enough to give fantastic illumination at the lowest. Set to 3×, it brightened up the darkening view remarkably when I peered through it. But, sold on my own clever deductions, convinced that he'd appear on the hillside above the mine because that was the logical place for him to be, I almost missed the first stir of movement on the opposite slope. I only caught it with my naked eye, when I took a momentary rest from squinting through the telescope.

But there he was, clear and sharp when I swung the gun that way and lined up the scope. He was taking some precautions but not many—hell, he'd been waiting all afternoon under the hot sun, probably, and nothing had happened. Now, reluctant to give up but badly discouraged, he was moving in closer, to where he'd be in position in case I got tricky and made my approach in the dark. But it had been a long dry day and he really had no faith that the tiger would come to the helpless bait he'd staked out for it, not any longer. It had seemed like a good idea at the time, but it just hadn't worked and to hell with it.

He made his way downward with the care of a man

who's carrying a heavy weapon and too much personal weight. I put the cross-hairs on him and followed him down. He slipped, started to slide, caught himself by a scraggly bush, and stood there for a moment, panting. Maxie Reis's rifle fired without my giving it any orders.

As I'd told Madeleine once, if you do it right, the gun always goes off kind of unexpectedly. There was a ringing pause; then the man four hundred yards away started rolling helplessly down the steep slope. I tracked him down, and he knew I was tracking him. He didn't stop at the bottom to look for his lost weapon, or examine his wound, or catch his breath; he just got to hands and knees and started crawling desperately towards the cover of the nearest mine building, dragging one leg. To hell with Maxie Reis. To hell with Bob Wills. Handing me a rifle shooting damn near two feet low at four hundred!

Well, that's why I try to make a point of sighting in my own guns; it just hadn't been feasible in this case. I held the cross-hairs over the distant crawling figure by the requisite amount, and led it enough to compensate for its awkward forward movement, and fired again. The movement stopped. After a moment he fell over on his side and lay there. I fired a third time at the still target to make absolutely sure of it. The recoil hardly bothered my shoulder at all. Then I drew a long breath, and started to slide back down to where I'd left the pack and canteen, and checked myself. I asked myself uneasily why I'd figured it so wrong. Why had my man been parked on the wrong hillside?

I resumed my position at the crest, put my arm back through the rifle sling, replaced the spent cartridges, and settled down to wait some more. It was dark, for all practical purposes, when I got my answer: there *was* a man with an automatic weapon hidden exactly where I'd expected one, in the brush above the mine entrance. At least the telescopic sight, with its ridiculously large objective lens, picked up a dark shape rising from behind a bush over there, holding something that gleamed faintly.

In the moment of hesitation, while the unknown gent was looking around warily to determine if it was safe to come down, I put the dim, dim cross-hairs in approximately the right place. The Remington shattered the evening stillness with its whiplike Magnum report. There was the same breathless little pause while the bullet covered the distance; then the distant man was falling and rolling, winding up in front of the mine entrance behind a hump of tailings where I couldn't see him.

It took me an hour to make the final approach. I didn't worry about the first target. I'd had three good shots at that, all hits. But the second target, in near-darkness, had been a much shakier proposition. But when I could see him at last he was lying in front of the tunnel entrance where I'd expected to find him. I studied him for a while from the corner of the ruined building I'd used to cover my advance. He didn't move and I couldn't see his gun anywhere, but to hell with it. I was a pro, not the International Red Cross. I aimed the rifle roughly at the center of the sprawling black shape over there, and pulled the trigger. The muzzle flame was spectacular in the dark; the report was deafening. The body jerked, and an arm fell outwards in a tired fashion, and the hand released something that shone faintly in the night.

Moving forward cautiously, I kicked away the mean-looking knife and looked down at the body of the man who'd presumably tortured and killed Birnbaum's secretary, Mrs. Silva, and skillfully executed Officer Crisler. The second 7mm bullet had done the job—it occurred to me that I'd wound up firing more shots than I'd expected, but my shoulder was still holding up under the pounding. There was something familiar about the dark dead face, but the name didn't come to me immediately, not until I'd got out the flashlight for a good look.

Then I found myself being wrenched backwards in time to a long-ago year when I'd bought a dinner for a lovely young girl attorney to thank her for making arrangements for me to question a killer in his cell; a killer who'd later been turned loose due to the legal efforts of the firm of Baron and Walsh. The dead man at my feet was Willy Chavez, still mean enough with a bullet in him to wait with his knife to gut the man who'd shot him. In a sense we'd started with Willy and now we were ending with him, I hoped. A circle of some kind had been completed.

Well, there would be plenty of time to make sense of it later. The open mine shaft was waiting; but before diving in there I moved to the other body, and turned it over, and shone the light on the heavy dead face of Phil Burdette. There was, of course, no pleasure in the victory now. There had been a certain sense of achievement earlier, immediately after the shooting; but the trouble with the lonely game we play is that, unlike chess, checkers, or Pac-Man, there's seldom anybody to share your triumph when you win. Asking a dead man to admire my fine marksmanship wasn't very rewarding. And there was no way for him to express his admiration for my cleverness in figuring out that a dodo like Bennett couldn't possibly be running even a Johnny-come-lately law-enforcement agency like the OFS. Bennett simply had to be a figurehead who'd blackmailed his way into a position of prestige and power with what he'd found in Madeleine Ellershaw's safe-deposit box, but who'd been willing, even happy, to leave the real work and responsibility of the agency to a true professional. Burdette.

"Adiós, compadre," I said softly to the dead man on the ground, as one pro to another.

Then I got the spare clips out of his camouflage coverall; he was dressed like a real commando type, although he was hardly built like one. I found the gun he'd dropped on the hillside above. An M16, as I'd anticipated, it was a better weapon for what came next than the slow and awkward bolt-action rifle. Making sure the premises were secure behind me before entering the mine—if she was still alive in there, she could wait a few minutes longer—I checked out the buildings and found

331

one empty; but there was a little 4WD Japanese pickup truck tucked away in the other. The key was in the ignition lock, so we had transportation out of here without wandering around the hills in the dark looking for a lost Eagle. I unloaded the Remington and put it, along with pack and canteen, into the bed of the diminutive truck. Then I went and found Chavez's weapon where he'd dropped it; it's only in the movies that you leave a lot of stray firearms scattered around the scenery. I unloaded all weapons except the one I was using and hid the ammunition, except a spare clip in my pocket, behind a loose board, so that at least somebody'd have to hunt a while before using this artillery against me.

I was stalling; I didn't really want to know what was lying inside that mine. Christmas was gone and I didn't believe in Santa Claus anyway. What the hell had he done for me recently? But the time had come, and, carrying the assault rifle, I made my approach according to the rules. Willy Chavez's presence still bothered me, and I sensed that I was overlooking something simple and obvious. Although I couldn't take time to figure it out, at least I could take the normal precautions. I hoped there weren't too many spikes and splintery timbers to receive me as I made the final dive inside. My hope was rewarded; all I got was a lot of dust and a twinge in my side. I lay there for a while, listening, and heard nothing. Gun ready, I shone the flashlight down the tunnel and saw nothing but a long dusty hole in the ground, apparently going on forever beyond the reach of the light. A second dark hole opened up to the right about twenty yards ahead. Rising cautiously, so as not to crack my already battered skull on the low ceiling, I drew a long breath.

"Madeleine?" I called. *"Hey, Madeleine!"*

The pause that followed was endless; then a faint voice answered me. "Matt?"

I knew a violent surge of an emotion I didn't allow myself to identify. It was no time for sentimentality, with

332

two dead men outside; but I'll have to admit that, while I took a few precautions, I made the final approach in a rather hasty and unprofessional manner. When I hit the light I couldn't see her at first among the rocks and debris that littered this side tunnel; then I realized that the dusty object lying against the left-hand wall was not geological in nature. In fact it moved a little.

I hurried forward and knelt beside her. Her ankles were tied and her wrists were still handcuffed. Ropes secured her fore and aft, as the sailors say, to the old uprights supporting the mine roof at this point. About ten yards farther on the whole business had collapsed to block the tunnel. I broke a light-stick I'd taken from the pack and stuck it in a crack in the rock above her and put away the flash, looking down at her in the weird greenish chemical light.

Her eyes were open, looking up at me. She'd apparently thrashed around a lot, trying unsuccessfully to free herself, covering herself with the dust of centuries—well, decades. She didn't look a bit like the kind of immaculate girl captive you see on TV, with the careful hairdo just slightly disordered and the pretty dress perhaps slightly torn at the shoulder. Well, they never do.

Her parched lips moved in her incredibly dirty face. "What took you so long?" she whispered.

I leaned over and kissed her gently. "Sorry about that." I wrinkled my nose. "You don't smell so good, Mrs. E."

"What the hell did you expect, leaving me here for weeks?" She grimaced. "Matt, why am I always such a disgusting mess whenever you find me? Ever since you picked up that revolting female zombie at Fort Ames . . ."

I said, "Does it really matter, as long as I do find you? Let me get those handcuffs off first. What the hell did they do to your wrists?"

"The handcuffs cut into me. I did that when I . . . You remember. That policeman who was going to shoot you."

333

"Yes. I owe you one for that. Just lie still, damn it. Let me get those ankles before you start thrashing around. Okay. Anything broken that you know of?"

She shook her matted head. "No, but I don't seem to have any feet. At least I can't feel them."

"You will," I said grimly. "All right, let's sit you up, carefully. How does that feel?"

Sitting, she made an attempt to cover herself with her torn and filthy wedding shirt, since the zipper of her equally filthy ski jacket had ceased to function.

"I'm all right, Matt. Really. Just awfully dirty. But if you brought some water . . . well, I guess I'm kind of awfully thirsty, too." Then her streaked face twisted with pain. "Oh, God, I think my feet are coming back to life. Jesus!"

I put the M16 into her lap. "You sit there and hold that; they taught you how to use it, remember? I've got a canteen and some clothes for you. I'll be right back, and we'll get you cleaned up a bit."

"Please don't leave me here!" It came out as a panicky cry. Then she controlled herself, abashed. She looked down, and took the gun I'd given her and checked it, and looked back up at me. "Sorry. I hate hysterical women. Trouble, Matt? I heard some shooting outside."

"There was a kind of welcoming party, but it's taken care of. At least I think so, but the old ESP is kicking up a bit. You're not really in top combat form at the moment, so just sit tight. I'll be right back."

"Don't be too long, please. I've had about enough of this lousy black hole in the ground."

I took out the revolver, less cumbersome than the assault rifle in these close quarters anyway, and made my way back towards the main corridor, if you could dignify that wormhole in the hill with such a fancy name. I was getting a kink in my back from the effort of reducing my six feet four to the midget height required in here. I hesitated, not liking the business of emerging from a lighted tunnel into a dark one; then I went out low and fast, or

334

started to. A metallic gleam ahead checked me; instinct threw me back and down heedlessly, with a clear picture of a double-barreled shotgun aimed my way around the corner where the two tunnels met. Once you've seen those big twin muzzles from the wrong end, you never forget them.

The shotgun fired, making a thunderous crash in that confined space that I was only dimly aware of because I'd landed wrong, on a fallen boulder, on my injured side, and the pain was unbelievable. I couldn't move and I certainly couldn't breathe; one attempt to draw a breath convinced me that I'd have to find a new method of oxygenation or, hell, just strangle quietly and peacefully. I'd lost my gun and, paralyzed by the breathtaking pain, couldn't make myself grope around to find it, or even go for the little automatic that was still up my sleeve.

Stupid, I thought numbly, taking care of the two outside so carefully, checking everything so meticulously out there, and then getting too eager to rescue the girl to take a good look down that obvious tunnel where a third enemy had been waiting all the time, letting his associates die unassisted, just waiting, waiting for me to come to him. . . .

I was dimly aware that the man with the shotgun was in the entrance to our side tunnel now, taking deliberate aim to finish me. The elderly, handsome face pressed to the fancy stock was that of Waldemar Baron, Attorney at Law, the man who'd deliberately confessed to a serious breach of legal ethics so he wouldn't be suspected of even more serious crimes. Well, who else would Willy Chavez be working for around here but the lawyer who'd saved him from the chair, or at least a life sentence? But I still couldn't see a busy and highly visible public figure like Baron being the mysterious Mr. Tolliver in his spare time. Not that it mattered now, with the side-by-side muzzles of the expensive shotgun steadying for the final shot. . . .

The M16 opened up behind me, full-auto. I heard the wicked little metal-clad projectiles snapping past and smashing into the body of the man in the tunnel entrance. Stuff was sifting from the ceiling in the eerie glow of the light-stick: dust, little stones, even a big rock somewhere, jarred loose by the reverberating reports of the GI weapon. Baron fell forward on top of his gun which, miraculously, did not fire the second, still loaded, barrel when it hit.

I decided it was time to give respiration another chance. It was a mistake. Something was really very wrong inside my chest. Then the coughing started, tearing me apart, and I passed out.

CHAPTER 29

I wound up in the hospital all taped up, of course; mummified, practically armor-plated from navel to nipples. They get as big a charge out of doing that to you as Jackson had got out of his two-bit porn movies. But even before that they did nasty things to my rib-punctured lung and stuck needles into me just about everywhere and even had me trapped in a plastic tent for a while breathing some kind of gas they pumped in, presumably oxygen, but you couldn't prove it by me.

Fortunately I wasn't really around while all this was happening. I was off somewhere watching the silly character in the bed from a considerable distance and not greatly concerned with his pitiful sufferings. But even during this period of dissociation something kept nagging at me, the sense of a job unfinished, and a possible answer came to me, and I crawled back into the body that was affording them such a lot of professional entertainment and asked for McCullough. At first they pretended they couldn't understand what I was saying, then they told me I wasn't well enough to have visitors, and finally they got him for me, with his jeans and girlish hair and icy eyes. He didn't give me any nonsense about how happy he was I'd made it, and how great I looked, and how I'd be out of there as good as new in no time at all. He just waited to find out why he'd been summoned.

"Tolliver," I whispered. "I've got a hunch—"

He took something out of his pocket, a newspaper page, and unfolded it, and put it into my hands. "Maybe we had the same hunch," he said.

I didn't have to search for the name. The obituary was the longest on the page, as befitted the prominence of the dead man, who'd died of a heart attack in his home at the age of seventy-two. I read that he'd been a lifelong resident of Santa Fe, the son of well-known Santa Fe citizens, named; and that he had been a successful attorney and partner in a prominent law firm, named; until an automobile accident had confined him to a wheelchair. There had been a wife who'd predeceased him by fifteen years, named, and three children, named, who'd produced several grandchildren, named. The deceased had been a veteran of World War II. Graveside ceremonies would be performed on a certain date—already past—at a certain time at the Santa Fe National Cemetery. Arrangements were through a certain mortuary.

The name at the head of the column was WALSH, HOMER WILLIAMSON. The mysterious senior partner of Baron and Walsh whom I'd never met, and never would meet now. I folded the paper carefully and gave it back to McCullough.

"Agent Orange?" I asked, with professional curiosity.

He nodded. Officially, the orange capsule that fits our new little automatic hypo is known as Injection C, but the color had made the other name inevitable. This is the

337

one that takes a little while to work but can't be detected in the body after death. Agent Red is instantaneous but detectible; and Agent Green just puts them to sleep temporarily, as Jim Dellenbach's partner, Nolan, had discovered back in Missouri.

McCullough said, "I confirmed first, of course. It wasn't hard. Mr. Walsh was really quite proud of his secret achievements as the mysterious Mr. Tolliver. He was aching to boast about them to somebody outside his organization if he died for it. As he did."

I licked my lips. It was still hard to concentrate. "How did you come to suspect . . . ? Hell, never mind the details. It got done. If you want a pat on the back, you've got one."

He grinned. "All that gaudy praise, I can't stand it. Well, they want me back in Washington. Bob Wills will be around in case you need somebody. See you around sometime."

"Not if I see you first," I said. "I hate independent young bastards who figure things out for themselves instead of showing proper deference to the senior agent in charge."

He grinned again. If he didn't watch out, it could become a habit. He made a very rude gesture and went out. I watched him go and decided that how he wore his damn hair was his business; but if I ever got so concerned about how my head looked I'd leave the stuff comfortably short and invest in a set of fancy wigs suitable for every occasion, like some fairly tough, sword-bearing gents of a few centuries back.

After that, perhaps due to the relief of knowing that the mission had got completed, even if not by me, it was suddenly all over except for the long healing, and the hope that someday in the distant future I'd be released from my adhesive-tape corset and permitted to draw a real breath again.

I was even allowed to submit myself to the terrible strain of picking up a telephone and calling Washington.

338

Mac said he'd heard I was probably going to live and he approved; but there was a small problem of my having delivered the wrong merchandise before I was disabled. I said there had been a mistake in the original order. The shipment had been correct as delivered; and I'd committed myself to having the item ordered in error returned to stock. All of which double-talk was meant to indicate that Burdette had been the right man; and that Bennett was a lightweight and no threat to the national security, and that since he'd come through with the information I wanted he should be turned loose with a kick in the pants.

Mac brought me up to date on other matters. It seemed that, coincidentally, at just about the time I'd had my unfortunate and almost fatal car accident, cause and location carefully unspecified, a terrible thing had been happening in the hills some distance outside Santa Fe. A certain prominent attorney out hunting jackrabbits on his own property had stumbled upon a government agent—thank God not one of ours—engaged in some kind of a mysterious investigation of a deserted mine on the place. Curious about his presence, the lawyer had gone in after him. There had apparently been a misunderstanding in the dark, fire had been given and returned, and both men had died, proving what dreadful things guns really were.

I wondered how they'd managed to conceal three unmistakable long-range rifle-bullet holes in one of the bodies; but a short-range shotgun blast will tear things up so badly that little things like that tend to go unnoticed, particularly if the examiner has been instructed not to look too hard. I wondered what had happened to Willy Chavez's body, but he was the kind of man who wouldn't be missed much. A lot of bodies have disappeared out there on the desert without a trace.

I asked what else had been happening, and Mac said I didn't really need to know. He said he'd been told, quite firmly, that he didn't need to know, either. We'd done our part, we'd accomplished our mission, and that was all that should concern us. Curiosity about a certain program of Advanced Human Managerial Studies was being strictly discouraged. However, I might be interested to learn that in line with current governmental economy directives, the three Centers for Advanced Defense Research were being closed down as an unwarranted drain on the national science budget. In another move in the same money-saving direction, the nation's undercover and law-enforcement agencies had undergone a certain amount of consolidation. The Office of Federal Security had been abolished and its duties and responsibilities had been assumed by the FBI, which was having a little trouble determining exactly what they were.

Later, they let a cop come in to see me, a chunky uniformed man with a broad Indian face. I recognized him, of course; I'd made a special effort to memorize that face. He said his piece very nicely: Chief Manuel Cordoba had suggested that it would be appropriate for him to come in and apologize for kicking me. He'd seen his *primo* lying dead beside me—the word means cousin, or perhaps first cousin, but in those parts it's used very loosely—and he'd lost his temper, he was very sorry. I said I understood and it was perfectly all right. I watched him march out stiffly. Like hell I did and like hell it was. But Cordoba was a smart man. He knew that, having received the apology, I'd do nothing further about it, even if I should happen to meet Officer Saiz in a convenient dark alley sometime when I had heavy boots on.

Still later, Bob Wills appeared. "The sling," he said.

"What?"

"I heard you were griping about that rifle shooting so low after we'd checked it out for you. But you shot target-fashion using the rifle sling, right? Downward pull on the stock. Well, the fore-end. But we'd sighted it in from a rest, the way Maxie Reis had used it. Upward push on the fore-end. Some rifles just happen to be very

340

sensitive to variations in fore-end pressure, that's all."

He was very self-righteous about it, and it wasn't worth arguing about. "It's okay. The job got done," I said.

"Here's what you wanted," he said, placing a large, well-filled manila envelope on the bedside table. "What do I do about Scarface and his pal?"

"Dellenbach and Nolan?" I said. I grimaced. "That's right, I shot off my mouth, kind of, about what I'd do to them if they ever molested Mrs. Ellershaw again. So chop off their right hands and turn them loose." I saw him looking shocked, and grinned. "Hell, let them go. Consistency is the hobgoblin of little minds, somebody once said, I forget who."

"Emerson?"

A little surprised, I regarded him more closely. Well, it's hard to tell by looking who's read a book and who hasn't.

"If you say so," I said.

He shrugged. "Hell, I'm just guessing. It sounds kind of like Emerson, but it could have been six other guys. Well, take care."

"You too."

It was next day before they came. I'd been expecting them. I'd been aware that she'd often been in the hospital room watching over me, as in Santa Paula, back when things were critical; but I hadn't seen her since, and I knew her very well by this time. The fact that once I was over the worst she hadn't felt able to drop in casually meant that she had something to tell me I wouldn't like. She was waiting to be sure I was well enough that it wouldn't interfere with my recovery.

They made quite a handsome couple together. The glowing face of the man let me know I'd guessed correctly. He was dressed very properly as became a respectable young attorney whose prospects with his firm had become quite bright with the removal, through accidental shooting and natural death, of a couple of superannu-

341

ated partners. But Walter Maxon was all business at first. He wanted to let me know that—although it was old stuff now—he had investigated the property records as I'd asked and learned that the old Orozco Grant had been purchased a good many years ago, before there had been any of this recent title trouble, by a group of investors that included Waldemar Baron, who'd also done the legal work on the deal. Having relieved himself of that information, he stood there fidgeting uncertainly for a moment before delivering his big news.

"Lainie and I are getting married. I hope you don't mind."

I didn't look at Madeleine. She'd never before allowed herself to be called anything but Madeleine in my hearing, although she'd told me that in prison they'd called her Elly for Ellershaw, but clearly her proud fiancé had invented this diminutive as a token of affectionate possession and she was willing to go along with it. She was watching me steadily, gravely, silently; but I sensed very clearly that she was asking me not to spoil it for her.

"Mind?" I said heartily. "Why should I mind? I think it's great." I held out my hand. "Congratulations, amigo, and my best wishes to both of you."

"Thank you. Well . . . well, Lainie has some kind of business she wants to discuss with you privately. I'll wait outside."

Then he was gone and I allowed myself, at last, to look at the woman I'd known as a shabby ex-convict, and a sweaty trainee at the Ranch, and a grimy kidnap victim. And in between times an intelligent and pleasant companion and, occasionally but not often enough, a loving bedmate. But this was still another Madeleine Rustin Ellershaw: a serene and confident and beautiful woman in a smart black dress and smoky sheer stockings and high-heeled black pumps. I frowned at the dark, unspringlike costume; then I understood.

"Mourning?"

Madeleine nodded. "A little late, nine years late, but it

was, after all, a funeral, and I felt like making a . . . a final gesture." Her voice became strained. "Not that there was much left to bury."

"So your husband was there after all?"

She nodded. "At the bottom of the mine shaft, just as we thought. It's a little eerie, isn't it? How we could guess so right on the basis of a crazy dream. The identification is positive, never mind the gruesome details. They released the . . . the body at last yesterday. We had the funeral today." She hesitated. "Roy wasn't alone. She was down there too. Bella Kravecki. At least the skeleton was feminine; they haven't confirmed that identification yet. Poor girl, she thought she was being brought out here just to make the espionage frame-up look good—our supposed Commie contact girl—but after she'd served her purpose, Waldemar apparently had her killed right along with Roy to keep her quiet." Madeleine hesitated, and glanced at the door through which Walter Maxon had gone. "Thanks, Matt," she said softly. "You did that very nicely. Thank you."

"My pleasure, ma'am," I said.

She stood by the bed looking down at me, obviously arranging in her mind what she had to say to me, to get it absolutely right. I saw that there was a much greater change in her than could be accounted for by just a clean face and a handsome dress. The predatory hunting female I'd recognized at the Ranch, full of hate and anger for what had been done to her, was gone, being no longer needed. This was a calm and civilized lady dismissing by an act of will all the previous ugly incarnations that had been forced upon her, and the people associated with those incarnations. Like me.

But I was glad to note that her voice was a little unsteady when she spoke at last: "On . . . on the personal level there isn't much to say, is there? We like each other, but we aren't kids to talk about love. And is that what we have between us, anyway?" She shrugged. "I don't know. I don't think you know. And I don't think I'm strong

343

enough or brave enough, after everything that's happened to me, to embark upon the great adventure of finding out. So let's talk about the other thing, the fact that you're probably disappointed in me now, and feel that I'll be . . . well, wasting myself as the very proper wife of a small-town lawyer, after all your careful training and guidance." She shook her head quickly. "But I wasn't really born to fight and kill, my dear. It was something that had to be done, for my sake as well as yours, vengeance if you like, payment for the years they'd stolen from me. Retribution. Nobody should be allowed to do what they did to me and get away with it; and if that's contrary to the gentle Christian ethic I was taught as a girl, it's just too damn bad. Anyway it's done now. Finished. I can live with it now; with everything that's happened to me. I can put it all behind me and forget it. I can start a new life, and this is the life I want. I'll make him a good wife, you'll see."

It was a humble statement on the face of it; but I wondered if Walter Maxon knew what he was letting himself in for, because I had a hunch this very bright lady would wind up subtly guiding him, without his knowledge, to achievements he'd never hoped for, the achievements she'd once hoped to attain for herself. But perhaps I was selling the man short. Possibly one of the reasons he'd loved her so long and loyally was that he'd sensed in her the driving qualities he lacked; and knew they'd work very well together, a team to be reckoned with.

I said, rather pompously because there was a certain amount of hurt involved, "As I just told your Walter, you have my very best wishes, Madeleine. I hope it all comes your way from now on; you've earned it." I started to reach for the envelope on the nearby dresser, but the corset wouldn't let me, so I just waved a hand at it instead. "That's for you. Call it a wedding present now. . . . Open it." I watched her as she looked inside. I said, "Computer printouts. Membership lists for the various

344

regional CADRES; they had the country divided into about a dozen units. Organization tables. Infiltration plans. Tentative final-strike plans, to be developed further. Remember, this is what Roy Ellershaw got out of the big CADRE computer nine years ago, so it's obsolete in a sense, or we wouldn't be passing copies around. But it showed us the general shape of the threat and gave us enough names to work from. Of course it's still highly classified, I don't have to tell you that. Burn after reading and all that stuff."

She nodded. "How did you find it? I thought they'd destroyed. . . . We saw the ashes in Uncle Joe's fireplace."

I shook my head. "Wrong copy. That one *was* destroyed; the backup copy. This is the original material your husband gave you piecemeal, in sealed envelopes, to put away into your safe-deposit box, and Bennett found there. I had a hunch a guy like that wouldn't hand over his blackmail material trustingly, no matter what high government position he was promised. He'd keep it hidden somewhere for insurance. We got the hiding place out of him, and a confession, with a little, er, persuasion and a promise of immunity. There's also a covering letter from your husband. I think you should wait until you're alone to read it. It's kind of between the two of you, and I regret the necessity for snooping. The guy seems to have loved you quite a lot." I watched her close the envelope again, and said, "Anyway, copies are in the hands of the authorities, along with Bennett's statement admitting the substitution he pulled to frame you, and the money he planted on you; and of course there's also the discovery of your husband's body for them to consider. Supporting evidence of sorts. The wheels of bureaucracy are turning in their usual ponderous fashion. Pretty soon you'll be a respectable lady again with all the marks against you officially erased."

She was silent for a moment; then she whispered, "Damn you, Matt, how can I ever repay—"

"Cut it out," I said. "We made a deal of sorts, and you

345

more than kept your part of it. That careful training and guidance you mentioned wasn't wasted no matter what you choose to do about it now. It served its purpose, didn't it? With your help, at the risk of your life, we got where we needed to go. Functioning as my bodyguard as planned, you saved my life at least twice, maybe three times—I gather that, even beat-up as you were, you did a hell of a job of getting me back to civilization before I drowned in my own blood. The debt runs both ways. What do you want us to do, keep score?"

She leaned down and kissed me gently on the lips, and raised her head a bit to look at me searchingly, very close. In that moment I knew she was mine if I wanted to take her; but I also knew that gratitude for what she still thought she owed me, regardless of my protests, would play a large part in her decision, and who the hell wants a grateful woman? Anyway, I couldn't give her what she really wanted: the security and peace and total respectability she needed now, after all the shocking years of abuse and despair.

"Your fiancé is waiting, Mrs. E.," I said.

"Take care of yourself," she said. "Oh, here's something you'd better have back. I . . . don't think I'll be needing it anymore."

I looked down at the little penknife she'd put into my hand. I watched her go out of the room, very straight and lovely in her black mourning dress. Two weeks later I was pronounced, optimistically, fit to travel. By the time I'd made it down to Albuquerque to catch the plane east, and stumbled aboard after the usual endless wait, I wasn't so sure about that diagnosis.

I found my way to the first-class seat I'd blown myself to—or the government had blown me to, if I could manage it—since I was still taped up and needed all the fidget-room I could get. I'd picked the aisle seat for easy access and egress. I was glad to see that the occupant of the window seat was already in place with her nose buried in a magazine: a small girl in a neat beige gabardine suit and a pretty, ruffly white blouse who, judging by what could be seen of her, was hardly old enough to be traveling by herself. I got my coat stowed in the overhead locker, with an effort, and tried to shove my bag into place under the seat ahead, but bending over that far wasn't easy. The child in the window seat put down the magazine behind which she'd been hiding and leaned over to help me, making me feel quite senile.

I realized abruptly that she wasn't all that small; and she wasn't all that young, either. All dressed up in her expensive traveling suit, she was a very pretty young woman; and the cap of dark hair was very smooth, and the black eye was gone, and the freckles were subdued, and the snub nose . . . Well, there's no law saying that all girls must have perfectly straight aristocratic noses. In fact it would be a very dull world if they did.

When she straightened up to look at me, I saw that she'd grown up a lot since I'd seen her last. She was no longer a kid playing games with unrequited love. There was adult heartbreak in her gray-green eyes, behind the smile she gave me. We had something in common. We were both recent losers in the emotional crap game.

"What are you doing here, Vangie?" I asked.

"I don't know, really," Evangeline Lowery said with intriguing honesty. "But there isn't anything left for me to hang around Santa Fe for, and you're not really well enough to be traveling alone. And I kind of thought that, together, we rejects might be able to figure something out."

We did.

ABOUT THE AUTHOR

Donald Hamilton has been writing Matt Helm novels for over 20 years. An expert yachtsman, he has also written nonfiction books and articles on sailing. He and his wife live aboard their yacht, *Kathleen*, and in Santa Fe, New Mexico.